EMPIRE CITY

ALSO BY MATT GALLAGHER

Youngblood

Kaboom: Embracing the Suck in a Savage Little War

Fire and Forget: Short Stories from the Long War (Editor)

EMPIRE CITY

A NOVEL

Matt Gallagher

ATRIA BOOKS

New York   London   Toronto   Sydney   New Delhi

An Imprint of Simon & Schuster, Inc.
1230 Avenue of the Americas
New York, NY 10020

First Atria Books hardcover edition April 2020

ATRIA B O O K S and colophon are trademarks of Simon & Schuster, Inc.

For information about special discounts for bulk purchases, please contact Simon & Schuster Special Sales at 1-866-506-1949 or business@simonandschuster.com.

The Simon & Schuster Speakers Bureau can bring authors to your live event. For more information, or to book an event, contact the Simon & Schuster Speakers Bureau at 1-866-248-3049 or visit our website at www.simonspeakers.com.

Interior design by Erika Genova

Manufactured in the United States of America

1   3   5   7   9   10   8   6   4   2

Library of Congress Cataloging-in-Publication Data

Names: Gallagher, Matt, author.
Title: Empire city / Matt Gallagher.
Description: First Atria Books hardcover edition. | New York City : Atria Books, 2020.
Identifiers: LCCN 2019039694 | ISBN 9781501177798 (hardcover) | ISBN 9781501177811 (ebook)
Subjects: GSAFD: War stories
Classification: LCC PS3607.A4154415 E47 2020 | DDC 813/.6—dc23
LC record available at https://lccn.loc.gov/2019039694

ISBN 978-1-5011-7779-8
ISBN 978-1-5011-7781-1 (ebook)

For Samuel

What quality soever maketh a man beloved, or feared of many; or the reputation of such quality, is power; because it is a means to have the assistance and service of many.

—*Thomas Hobbes*

America doesn't deserve its military.

—*Emma Sky*

EMPIRE
CITY

CHAPTER 1

D^{EFY}.

Sleepy and half-drunk, Sebastian Rios tried to reason with the message carved into the wall of the subway tunnel. He'd spent the evening with friends and coworkers, celebrating the republic's birthday, and was attempting to get home. There'd been many toasts and his mouth tasted of rye. His head swam slowly, like an eel. "Defy," he sounded out to himself. "De-fy."

He ran his fingers over the word. Someone had spent time with it, he thought, given the depth of the notches that formed the letters. He appreciated that the message was both plain and mysterious, at once grounded and a bit mystical, too. Just above it lay a small, pale sticker of the American flag, its corners frayed and colors bleached by time. Sixty stars and thirteen stripes. It didn't strike Sebastian as odd, anymore, all those rings of stars in the blue canton.

It was a Friday, late, languid midsummer in Empire City. Sebastian turned around and set his back against the wall. He'd intentionally stood away from others but a man had neared. The stranger wore rags and a vacant smile and held a dull metal pole. He began waving it around like a sword, something everyone noticed while pretending not to. Sebastian adjusted his earbuds and cycled through songs on his phone.

The stranger's pole whizzed by a few feet from Sebastian, close

1

enough for him to feel a light draft. Sebastian looked up, taking in the stranger's mesh cap with the words CRETE WARFIGHTER in bright yellow on it. He was old enough to be from that war, Sebastian thought. Why wasn't he at a rehabilitation colony? Veterans with troubles lived there. But—bureaucracy. Mistakes happened. Sebastian understood that.

A bell sounded through the station. "The threat index is blue," a woman's automated voice said. "Homeland Authority reminds citizens to remain guarded."

Blue was good, Sebastian knew. No change.

The stranger in rags felt otherwise. "Defy!" he shouted, pointing to the message on the wall and hopping into the tunnel. Sebastian ignored him and so did everyone else.

"Defy!" the stranger repeated. He lifted his metal pole. Then he plunged it into the third rail, cracking the protective casing. The stranger's body lit up like an illum round. The stranger fell. Smoke rose.

Oh, Sebastian thought, looking up. This is different.

The citizens on the platform screamed while Sebastian moved into the tunnel to check on the stranger. Rigid and red, the smile had remained on the man's face.

"Masha'Allah," Sebastian said. "Be easy, dude." Then he made the sign of the cross with his phone over the stranger. He felt stares from across the platform. They didn't understand and, to his mind, never would. Then Sebastian walked home. Whatever powers he had, they didn't include resurrection.

———

Sebastian woke in his studio apartment the next morning, hungover and alone. He drank from the glass of water he'd placed on the nightstand hours earlier and checked the calendar on his phone. A commitment waited there like a blister: Mia Tucker's engagement party. Could've sworn that was next weekend, he thought. Time seemed to be speeding up to him.

A gift, he remembered. People like this notice.

It was with such a resentment that Sebastian showered. He changed into a pair of slacks and the only unwrinkled dress shirt in his closet. Deciding against a tie—he wanted to make clear he was not of Wall Street or Connecticut—he threw on a sport jacket and a pair of aviator sunglasses and stepped into the day. Monitor drones hummed from above, ever-steady, summer light beating down. Sebastian squinted into it, wondering when the absurdities of life had turned into something else.

An anxious minute passed until a cab pulled over. "Uptown," he told the driver. "Park and Sixty-Fifth." He took out his phone to avoid conversation. The cab smelled of old potato. Sebastian lowered his window. Boiled air rushed the breach.

On his phone, Sebastian read an article about Congress repealing an amendment to allow the president to run for yet another term. The parties of the governing coalition cited wartime precedent and extolled the move. The parties in the minority argued that it brought the nation closer to authoritarianism. Sebastian thought the president grimaced too much in his photos, which called attention to a protruding vein in the center of the man's bald head. He was dour enough as it was. Sebastian wanted a political leader who'd smile every now and then, even if they didn't mean it.

The cab arrived at the restaurant. Sebastian had never eaten there, but a web search yielded a year-old "Intoxicatingly Elegant" headline from the *Imperial Times*. The menu consisted mostly of foods with French-sounding names but also offered "a variety of neo-nouvelle cuisines," which Sebastian couldn't comprehend, even though he was good with words. He put away his phone and paid the driver, tipping too much because he was bad with numbers.

Sebastian looked up at a three-story building the color of melon and sighed. If he had finished reading the review online, he'd have learned he was looking at a Greek Revival town house that had once served as the headquarters for a conservationist club founded by Teddy Roosevelt, and had a garden patio in the back he might enjoy. He hadn't read that, though. Besides, his mind was else-where.

Two people with silver hair blocked the restaurant entrance, a man and a woman. They held drinks and appetizer napkins and appeared to be arguing in a restrained sort of way. Sebastian tried to part through them to get inside. The man put his arm around Sebastian's shoulders and pulled him to the discussion. Manners mattered to Sebastian, even though he pretended otherwise, so he didn't resist. The woman seemed disturbed by his sunglasses, and kept trying to peer under them.

"Here's one of Mia's military colleagues." Sebastian didn't say anything to that. The man's tongue carried conviction on it. "No other country in history could wage the Mediterranean Wars and last, let alone prosper. Don't you agree, young man?"

Sebastian nodded. The silver-haired man continued.

"A testament to our warfighters. But where's the strategy? What's the endgame? We learned this lesson in Vietnam: battles must be won before the war can be. Decisive battles."

"And your solution would be?" the woman asked. "You still haven't said."

"Wogs need to be treated like the enemy they are. Same as we treated the British. Same as we treated Nazis. How we beat back the red gooks in my day. Overwhelming force, no apologies."

"We've been at this thirty years, Bernard. When is enough enough?"

"When our way of life is secure. George Orwell said that."

Sebastian felt sure he'd spent more time in the Near East than the silver-haired man, and he didn't think George Orwell had said anything about securing a way of life, but he wasn't about to argue with a member of the Next Greatest Generation. Especially one wearing his old combat ribbons on his blazer. They'd saved the free world from communism. So he kept to listening. It seemed a heavy conversation for an engagement party, but at least they weren't talking investment portfolios.

"Isn't that the whole issue? They don't fight normal. So when we go into these countries to help, to rebuild, they blend in with the population."

The woman was right, Sebastian had seen it himself in Tripoli. But the man remained undaunted.

"They said the same about our war. Until they didn't," he said. "Locals helping enemy are enemy. Families of terrorists are terrorists. That's how the wogs fight. That's how it works. Weren't you a protestor? Flower power didn't save Saigon from the horde."

"That's not fair." To be accused of being a peacemonger was a big deal for older people, Sebastian knew. "We were doing what we thought was right. We were trying to protect our friends and classmates. Our brothers."

The silver-haired man turned to Sebastian again. "How would you feel, young man," he said, "if your friends and classmates took to the streets with picket signs while you were getting shot at for your country?"

"Hmm." The Found Generation, protesting war? An absurd thought. They'd been raised to trust the government. But Sebastian didn't say that. Instead he repeated the common wisdom used for years to resolve conversations like this. "It'd be strange. I know we're all thankful the protestors helped end the draft, though. Made the all-volunteer force possible. Which is how you all finally won Vietnam." Should he add the pat phrase you were supposed to use here? Why not. "Praise to the Victors."

The veteran and the protestor both nodded at that. Sebastian excused himself, saying he needed to find the betrothed. Eighty or so people were inside the restaurant, talking and laughing, gathered in clumps like raked leaves. Glass chandeliers hung from the ceiling and bathed the room in a yellow glow. Every man he could see wore a navy blazer with a bright summer tie. He tugged reflexively at his own collar. Waiters with trays moved around the dining room in step. Sebastian took a breath and routed for the bar, cutting through groups with apologies he didn't mean. He looked for peo ple he might've known from before but recognized no one. Maybe it's the wrong engagement party? he thought. Then he spotted the gift table with a placard on it that read, "Tucker—Stein."

A gift, Sebastian thought. Whoops.

The bar line proved long and slow-moving. Sebastian kept his head low but his ears open. He listened to a conversation in front of him. A middle-aged man was complaining about his niece going to a pricy school like Empire State to become a teacher. He listened to a conversation behind him. A pair of brokers about his age were complaining about the unreliability of their drug dealer. Getting high in Empire City used to be easier! He listened to a conversation adjacent to him. An elderly woman was complaining about the Tucker grandfather. She was descended from *Mayflower* pilgrims, too, she said. Where did he get the nerve?

This fucking place, Sebastian thought. Becoming an American city-state had only made it more of a bubble. He rubbed at his eyes under his sunglasses, wiping away beads of sweat. The line remained slow-moving. He looked up and studied the wall behind the bar. A watercolor of a broad-shouldered man wearing a Stetson and a mustache like a bandit covered it. The man stood in front of a fallen gray elephant, presumably shot by the musket the man held in the crook of his arm. He resisted an impulse to salute the painting. Serious people stood around him, and serious people took things like watercolors seriously. Still, the gun and the elephant stirred something in him. What it was felt slippery to Sebastian. He had strong feelings neither about guns nor elephants.

"Of course you'd be here," Mia Tucker said, approaching Sebastian from the side. He grabbed his whiskey and coke from the bartender—he hated drinking beer on an empty stomach—and congratulated his friend with a hug.

"Drinking away the day," Mia continued. "Tsk-tsk, See-Bee."

Sebastian smirked at the old nickname. "It's a party, you know?"

"It is," she said.

Tall and thin, Mia didn't look like the type of woman who'd

served in the army, Sebastian thought, which he knew was probably sexist of him, but he still thought it. He'd always thought of her
more as a tennis player, or the serious friend in a romantic comedy.
Her olive skin and close-cropped raven hair emphasized features
he'd once described as "hawkish" in a profile for their college
newspaper. Wearing a floral maxi dress, she may as well have been
attending a fraternity formal instead of her own engagement party.

"You look nice," he said.

"Thanks," she said. "You look like you."

Sebastian and Mia's friendship had begun as freshmen in
Philosophy 101, which felt like a long time ago to them both. The
next semester she'd convinced him to join the army ROTC program
with her, something he'd soon drop but she'd find much purpose
in, becoming the cadet commander their senior year. Just the second woman named to that position in Dupont University history,
Mia went on to commission as an active-duty officer and fly attack
helicopters in the Mediterranean Wars, fighting terror across four
combat zones (Syria, Albania, New Beirut, and the Barbary Coast).

"Biggest testes in the family," the Tucker grandfather had said
at her college graduation dinner, something only Sebastian had
laughed at. Everyone else had stared at their plates, no one harder
or deeper than Mia.

That had been six years before, though, before Tripoli. Before a
lot of other things, too.

They caught up on mutual acquaintances and gossip. Had he
heard about the volleyball girl joining the separatist cult out west?
Some people just couldn't get it together. Had she heard about
the creepy Sig Ep from sophomore year who fell off a cruise ship?
Police suspected his new bride had pushed him. Sebastian was
figuring out how to bring up the night before when a pale man
approached and put his arm around Mia. She pulled him in as if
gravity depended upon it.

"Jesse Stein," the pale man said, putting out his hand.

Sebastian did the same. Jesse squeezed hard and tilted both

palms toward him. Sebastian squeezed back and introduced himself, all the while thinking, I hate alpha power games. They're so un-alpha.

But he said, "Congratulations. Good to finally meet."

"I've heard a lot ab-about you," Jesse said, a verbal tic almost coached away dashing his words. "You're another Yankee who went south for school."

"Who says that anymore?" Mia asked. Her voice made it clear that Jesse should not be saying it anymore. "And he's not. He's not anything. He's from California."

Her attention shifted to an end of the restaurant before Sebastian could summon a response. She patted both men's forearms and walked that way. Sebastian whistled, low and without melody. Jesse tapped his foot and looked at the ground.

"So," Sebastian said. He always felt awkward around people his age who had money. He was also surprised. Mia's type in college had been different. Tall, dark, and awful, mostly. "How'd you kids meet?"

"Through, uh, work." Jesse coughed and straightened his tie— Sebastian took in his choice of a classic sack suit, deciding it was a good decision for someone with his build, round and loose, like an old balloon.

"Fantastic." Sebastian patted Jesse's shoulder and swigged more whiskey and coke. "Well done on the rock, man. That thing could blind Stevie Wonder." He tapped at his sunglasses for effect.

Jesse laughed, an honest, raw laugh, Sebastian thought, which pleased him. For a few minutes Jesse explained the complexities of diamond negotiations. Sebastian tried to care but couldn't, his mind drifting to the night before, and the man who'd defied his way into suicide.

"You were in Tripoli, too, right?" The question brought Sebastian back. Jesse stuck out his hand again. "I know it's a stupid thing to say, but America Honors the Warfighter."

"Oh." Sebastian laughed. "Not a soldier." He raised his now-empty glass to his lips to suck an ice cube. He hated nothing more than the conversation to come, and something hot burned in his chest. "I was the hostage they rescued."

"That's right." Jesse's voice turned flat. "I knew that."

The questions came as they always did, in the same order. Yes, Sebastian had been the kid who went to war on winter break. A magazine intern looking for a story and his MIA cousin. Second cousin, really. No, he hadn't embedded with an American unit. Because he'd fashioned himself rebellious back then, like a fool. No, they still hadn't found his cousin's remains and probably never would. How did he get there? By renting a car in Egypt and driving west. It'd been that easy.

Most people stopped asking questions then, either because of the subject matter or because of the strange pitch Sebastian put into his voice. Jesse pushed on, though, something that surprised Sebastian more than it bothered him. He found the memories of it all had become vague recently, like a fog he couldn't grab, so he stuck to the facts. Who? The Promised Day, a pan-Arab insurgent group. Where? Different basements around Tripoli. How long? Twenty-six days. What'd he eat? Flatbread. Sometimes dates. How'd they treat him? Well, except for one short guy with a scar like an asterisk splayed across his neck. Why didn't they kill him? Sebastian didn't know, but his family going on television and saying they'd pay a ransom probably had something to do with it. Yes, that had upset the government. What did they talk about? Soccer, sometimes. Supermodels and actresses, other times.

"Then you got saved."

Sebastian began chanting with supreme tedium. "Recognizing that I volunteered, fully knowing the hazards of my chosen profession. Never shall I fail my comrades." He was trying to sound ironic but couldn't quite pull it off. "Energetically will I meet the enemies of my country. Readily will I display the intestinal fortitude required to fight on to the objective and complete the mission, though I be the lone survivor. Rangers. Rangers lead the way."

"Well." Jesse's words were flat again. "And the helicopter pilots."

"True. I owe a lot to Mia. And the others." Sebastian took a breath and raised an eyebrow. The feeling in his chest had cooled. "That's the short of it. Empire News did a piece about it last year. If you'd like the government-approved version."

Jesse laughed again, less sincere this time. He asked if Sebastian still worked in media.

"Homeland Authority," Sebastian said. "Became a PR flack."

The two men parted ways with promises to hang out soon, the kind that only sound hollow afterward. Sebastian got another drink. He moved through the next hour in a trance, going from social circle to social circle with the stupid grin of a man over-matched. Sebastian knew little of Connecticut, and even less of Wall Street, but the Tucker family transcended even his ignorance. Mia's great-great-grandfather had made a fortune in steel, later founding the nation's seventh-largest investment bank. Though the company had long ago gone public, Mia's father still served as its asset management CEO. Despite the crash of the global economy, life for the Tuckers hadn't changed as far as Sebastian could tell. That bothered him when he bothered to think about it. He couldn't help but think about it in the restaurant.

"Eight hundred thousand just doesn't get what it used to," someone said. "Don't those people understand they're voting against their self-interest?" another asked. "Who summers in the Antilles anymore?" still another said. Class resentment raged within Sebastian, but he kept it hidden and sheathed, remembering that such a weapon never struck clean. He nodded and smiled. He also ate a lot of bacon-wrapped dates.

While Sebastian listened in on an obligatory "Where were you during the Palm Sunday attacks?" conversation, Mia's stepmom patted his arm. Sebastian had thought that Mrs. Tucker—who insisted he call her Linda—disliked him, but she pulled him away with friendliness in her grip.

"Hello, Mrs. Tucker," Sebastian said.

"Take off those sunglasses," Linda said. "You're indoors."

You know damn well why I wear these, Sebastian thought, though she probably didn't. He kept them on.

"You've been requested," Linda continued. "A new friend of Mia's. Don't . . ." Linda trailed off. "Just be normal."

Before Sebastian could ask what that meant, Linda led him to a woman in a long green chemise leaning against the back wall. A tattoo sleeve of black-and-red flames breathed down her right shoulder to the elbow. She wore no jewelry except for a dull labret piercing above her chin and little makeup, and her arms were crossed. Sebastian thought she looked bored. She had curly brown hair and big, green eyes he labeled "sad," then "defiant." Sebastian grinned wide.

"Here he is," Linda said. "Meet Britt, Sebastian. We were just talking about your, umm. Experiences."

Sebastian's grin slid away. Anything but that, he thought. Can we talk about anything else? He began chewing on his bottom lip. Linda said, "If you'll excuse me," and disappeared into the crowd. Sebastian whistled low to himself. He was about to lead with another "So" when she spoke.

"My brother," Britt said. She uncrossed her arms, a faint omega symbol on the underside of a wrist turning out against the wall. "He was one of the guys who saved you."

"Oh." Sebastian had to jam some goodwill into his voice. He knew what his rescuers' families held against him. "I'm. Well. So sorry for your loss. And grateful. Very, very grateful." He was genuinely both of those things, and did his best to convey it in his words, all the while knowing she'd find the words empty and worn. They always did. "I'd love to hear about him. Whatever you're willing to share."

"He didn't die." Britt lifted an eyebrow in amusement as Sebastian raised his in surprise. Three Rangers of forty had survived. "I'm Pete Swenson's sister."

She finally smiled, and Sebastian noticed the smallest of gaps between her front teeth.

"Oh. Wow." Sebastian stuck out his hand. "Your brother's a hero." She didn't return the gesture, so he returned his hand and kept talking. "I mean, all the Volunteers are. But especially him." She still didn't do anything, so he still kept talking. "Didn't they just finish filming a movie? They're playing themselves? It was on the news."

"Yeah." Britt couldn't hide her disdain. "Something like that."

Pete Swenson's sister doesn't regard him the same way everyone else does, Sebastian thought. That's interesting. He wanted to ask about it. But her voice suggested wariness. So did her posture. She must get questions about him all the time, he realized. So instead he asked how she knew Mia.

"I reached out a couple years ago," Britt said. "We got coffee. She was there with you all. With the cythrax bomb and everything. I wanted to know more and my brother wasn't here. We became friends."

Sebastian didn't know what Mia had told Britt, over coffee and after, but he knew what she shouldn't have told Britt, because it was the same things none of them were supposed to tell anyone. The cythrax bomb was definitely one of those things. He'd only told his mom because he figured all nondisclosure agreements had mom clauses, even federal government ones. He took a long drink from his whiskey and coke and pretended like Britt had said something normal instead.

A waiter passed with a tray. Britt snapped at him while looking the other way. It worked. The waiter stopped and lowered his tray of vegan jalapeno poppers.

There it is, Sebastian thought. A moneyed bohemian. Most bohos were, these days. The culture and the counterculture grew from the same seed of privilege. Who could afford to be genuine anymore? No one Sebastian knew, not since the new recession. He'd sold out to Homeland Authority and wasn't afraid to admit it. That's the difference between me and the boho sorts, he thought. Honesty. Britt ate the vegan jalapeno popper with a neatness that could only be taught, rigid fingers and tiny, minute chews and a paper napkin folded in half like origami, not one crumb escaping. He pushed away a joke about it and asked where home was.

"Been in Gypsy Town awhile," Britt said. "We're originally from the Federal City area, though. Little suburb called Troy."

"Right. Of course." Every war journalist on the planet had christened her brother the American Hector. Wasn't it stranger than fiction, they all asked? Something to be considered, certainly! No art in propaganda anymore, Sebastian thought. Just blunt force. He asked if the Volunteers were still in Hollywood.

"You don't know?" Britt asked. She sniffed in confusion, crossing her arms again. The omega tattoo disappeared into her body. "They're here."

"Here where?"

"*Here* here."

"Here here where?"

"Here. Empire City. The movie's over. They're on leave until they deploy back to the Mediterranean. Finally convinced the War Department to let them be soldiers again."

Something between wonder and panic dropped through Sebastian. The Volunteers were *here*, in the city *here*? And going back over there? Nothing about that made sense to him. They were supposed to be in Hollywood or touring the country, raising money for the government. That was the deal. He was figuring out how to ask particulars when a digital jingle sprang from within Britt. She pulled a phone from an unseen pocket and looked at it. "Boyfriend," she said.

Sebastian nodded and pantomimed smoking a cigarette. He headed outside for the patio, focusing on the ground as he walked. He needed to think, and wanted air and smoke for that.

A dozen or so partygoers had pushed out to the patio as well, but they all seemed the same to Sebastian. Faceless and prim, fatheaded and fake. He grabbed a seat in a corner where no stranger could sneak up, and took out a thin pipe shaped like a cigarette and packed with weed. A gray sun, masked by a grayer sky, hung on the horizon like a dreary disco ball. The sidewalks swelled with noise and angst. Where they all found the energy to do it, to do any of it anymore, Sebastian didn't know. He watched and smoked, content to be detached, detached to be content. The Volunteers were here, somewhere. Sebastian knew he should find them. He hadn't seen any of them since the hospital in Germany. They'd gone on to do brave things, incredible things. They were using their powers for good. He wanted that, too. Not just the brave or incredible parts, but the going-on. That matters, he thought. It matters a lot.

On his phone, Sebastian skimmed through fan theories on a *Utopia* message board. He hated giving any time or attention to state TV. But the show challenged the old rules. The cinematography, especially. If Bobby Kennedy had lived to become president—a genius conceit. River Phoenix mostly pulled it off, the accent notwithstanding. Sebastian never missed an episode.

Sebastian was trying to figure out how to repack his one-hitter unnoticed when Mia found him.

She sat next to him and pointed to his pipe. "Really? Here?"

Sebastian held his fingers to his throat. "It is medicinal," he said like a robotic voice box. "Please don't tell my boss. My pension isn't vested yet."

Mia laughed, a bit too easily to Sebastian's mind, which put him on alert. "How are you, See-Bee? I've missed you."

Sebastian readjusted his sunglasses and stuck the pipe into his pocket. "You're asking if I'm seeing anyone."

"Sure."

"It's your engagement party, Mia. Not the place to confess an undying love."

She sighed the sigh of someone playing a part. "You know what I mean."

"I met Britt Swenson earlier," Sebastian said. He wasn't quite ready to ask the question he'd come here for, so he asked the question he'd found here instead. "You know the Volunteers are in the city now? And going back to the war?"

Mia tilted her head. "My handler told me last week. Yours didn't?"

That made Sebastian grunt. "Mine's been busy."

"You look skinny."

Sebastian considered telling her about what had happened at the subway the previous night. Instead, he said, "I've always been skinny."

"Jesse likes you, you know. Despite my trying to convince him otherwise."

"He's cool. Good choice, senorita." Sebastian scratched his head and leaned close to Mia. "Curious," he said. "You fly anymore?"

"Of course not." Mia paused for a beat, then another. It'd been three years since Tripoli. She raised her eyes to meet his and narrowed them to splinters. "You disappear anymore?"

Sebastian laughed, quick and short. "Just teasing," he said.

"I'm not. Don't play around with what you can do, Sebastian. They'll crush you."

Sebastian clenched his jaw and felt his chest seize up. He looked back out into the maze. Mia was right, of course. But he didn't like the way she'd suggested he didn't understand the stakes. Was he being sensitive? Perhaps, he allowed. We all have our vices.

Mia patted his knee and said she needed to get back inside. He apologized for forgetting a gift and said he'd see her in there. A minute later, he decided to ghost. He walked off, concentrating on his feet moving along the sidewalk, counting each step silently until he got to twelve. Then he started back at one.

Anytime someone came up too close behind him, he stopped and let them pass before continuing. He knew he was a cliché, maybe a couple different ones, but he didn't care. All he wanted was to be by himself. A block from the restaurant, he hailed a cab by stepping into the street.

"The Village," he told the driver. "Take the expressway."

This proved the wrong choice. Traffic piled up a half mile north of the Jubilee Bridge. Cars crept along in sleepy monster fury, and Sebastian's legs began cramping, then twitching.

The driver pointed to the radio. "Crazy shit," he said.

"What now?" Sebastian asked. He hadn't noticed the radio was on.

"The consul who collapsed in Federal City yesterday. He's a deader."

"Damn." Sebastian had seen some scroll somewhere about it. "Steps of the Nixon Memorial?"

The driver nodded. "Someone hacked his pacemaker. Zap! Just like that." The driver spoke with the abrupt, flexing voice of an Empire City native, like his words had been rolled through gravel. "Technical error, they're saying. Please."

"Terrorism?" Sebastian asked.

"Not the separatists' style. They go for the big bombs, the big blood. The wogs? Had a price on his head, true enough. But the jihad don't have the tech. This was an inside job."

Conspiracies were the last vestige of the vacant-eyed, Sebastian believed, of the mediocre-minded, the not-quite-read-enough, the too-stupid-to-realize-it. Inquisitiveness was not a substitute for critical thinking, nor paranoia for reason. The American government made mistakes, sure. Because it was a government. It didn't always tell the truth but it was always true. It'd saved him, and he was a nobody, a citizen like any other. They still came for him in Tripoli. He tried to remember that any time his skeptical bone was tapped.

Still, though. An inside job made some sense. The consul had been scheduled to brief Congress on the progress of the Sinai occupation. Or lack thereof.

"Maybe it was his wife." Sebastian smiled to make sure the driver knew he was joking. "Love and war."

"Maybe." The driver snorted. "Treacherous times."

The radio trundled on. Police robots in Indiana had blown up a Sears. The body count was forthcoming. Some would always believe only radical wogs could commit such acts. Others seemed almost relieved when the far west (and very white) separatists made news for the same. Both groups of militants were largely made up of vets of the Mediterranean Wars, something Sebastian liked to sneak into conversations. A verbal pipe bomb, of sorts, meant to disrupt any pretense. The veterans came from opposing sides, sure, but that was the joke.

"Want to know what I think needs to be done?" the driver asked.

Only now did Sebastian notice the blue infantry cord dangling from the cab's rearview mirror. The driver wore a mesh cap with the words VIETNAM WARFIGHTER in bright yellow on it. Sebastian wasn't sure he wanted to be in the cab anymore. Between Mia and the silver-haired man at the restaurant, he'd had enough vet-splaining for the day.

"How's traffic?" he asked.

The driver pointed to the bridge, then to his ears. Distant sirens filled the space between.

"Could be another jumper," the driver said.

Sebastian slid a twenty-dollar bill into the driver's tray and exited, slamming the door behind him before the driver could reply. He didn't care that he'd overpaid, or that the summer heat felt like steam. He began walking home.

"Stop being emo!" Sebastian yelled at the bridge. Maybe there was a jumper up there, maybe there wasn't. Either way, he felt something loosen inside him. "Either do it or climb down! Twelve-year-old girls draw it out like this!"

The horns of angry, delayed motorists served as the sole response, twirling flashes of emergency vehicles soaking the moment in pomp. How selfish can someone be? Sebastian wondered.

Then he thought, the jumper's probably thinking the same.

He yelled at the bridge, again, this time in solidarity. "Defy!"

Again, only car horns replied.

Sebastian walked slow and south. A messy dusk loomed,

black and slate wrapping together like an ice cream swirl. He found it calming and the anxiety from earlier embered out. He thought about things long out of his control and things still in it. He thought about the dead hostages at the Indiana mall, and the terrorists, too. He thought about prayer. He thought about Tripoli, and his home, and his MIA cousin. He thought about the Volunteers, and the cythrax bomb. An hour passed. Smelling liquor in his sweat and with his throat dry, he stopped at a corner market. He bought a bottle of red wine, though he hated wine. In this America, Sebastian thought, emotion can only be expressed in regurgitation. Cultural regurgitation. Drinking wine from a brown bag is that. So drinking wine from a brown bag is the thing I will do.

He walked across a footbridge over the expressway and found a bench near the river. The dirty water flowed by with hurry. The Prince Bridge imposed itself to his left, all cables and pillars and might. In the twilight, Sebastian couldn't figure out if it was blue-gray or gray-blue. He decided it didn't really matter. Across the river in Gypsy Town, defunct smokestacks and the sugar plant sign stood proud. Shiny high-rise condos surrounded the stacks on all sides, reminding Sebastian of the man and the elephant in the watercolor for some reason.

There's nothing gypsy about Gypsy Town, Sebastian thought. He smirked, finding that clever. It should be called Trying-Too-Hard Ville.

He texted some friends to see if they wanted to join him on the bench. No one responded. Then he tried his handler. He didn't respond, either. Typical, Sebastian thought. Passing joggers rustled a scrawny wild turkey from nearby foliage. Sebastian finally had company.

"Simon the Zealot!" he said, as the turkey emerged. "A past from the blast."

When Sebastian had first moved to Empire City, Simon had been a favorite find on walks along the river. Named after a long-dead painter who'd lived in the district, Simon had landed from parts unknown years prior and become a local legend. Empire City did not house many wild turkeys.

Sebastian poured a splash of wine on the ground. He'd decided he and the zealot were kindred spirits. This resulted in an annoyed cluck from Simon, who was scrounging the shrubs for food. After a day of drinking on an empty stomach, the wine was hitting Sebastian harder than expected. "Stupid turkey," he muttered. His eyes began to ache, which gave him the motivation necessary to tip back the wine bottle and finish it.

"I need to get my shit together," Sebastian told the turkey, which was true.

He lingered with Simon and the inanity of personal tragedy a bit longer, then returned to the city for a slice of pizza. Sebastian felt invisible for much of the walk, but when he woke the next morning, hungover and alone, he didn't know if it'd been his imagination or his power.

Hello, young citizens, I'm Justice of the Volunteers. Protecting the homeland is a sacred duty, and it's one we're all in—together.

Did you know that upwards of 75 percent of America's youth today can't qualify for military enlistment? It's true! Between physical requirements and mental health screenings, only three out of ten young Americans are eligible to even try to become a warfighter.

That needs to change. No fatties or nutters in our ranks! Exercise regularly. Put down that fast-food snack and grab an apple, instead. Be open with your parents, religious leaders, and school counselors if you ever start to feel overwhelmed by life. And make sure your friends are doing the same. We're going to need you on the front someday!

Because protecting the homeland starts at home.

CHAPTER 2

Mia couldn't help it: failure brought the shakes. Not anything too obvious, just little trembles, her hands mostly, the kind warmth didn't cure, the kind that needed to be waited out. Failure had always affected her like that, which was one of the reasons why she'd committed herself to experiencing it as seldom as possible. It wasn't that she feared it. Only cowards feared failing, she thought. But the idea of her disappointment being seen and conceptualized by others drove her to achieve more than any goal ever could. Her brothers mocked it as obsession, her father admired it as drive, her grandfather called it the Tucker blood. Whatever it was, wherever it came from, Mia didn't fail often. Most everything she'd ever wanted, she did, and did very well.

Was the little plastic stick she held in the bathroom failure? She wasn't sure yet. It didn't seem like success.

I can't be, she thought, staring at the two vertical lines like they were hieroglyphics. This doesn't make sense. But of course she could be. She was.

Between the waves of nausea and sore breasts, she'd suspected for days, but there'd been the possibility of confusion, of a mistake. In Germany they'd said this wouldn't even be possible. But they'd said a lot of things in Germany, some of which had proven true. Some of which hadn't.

Mia took a deep breath, ignoring her shaking hands. This hadn't been part of the plan—she and Jesse weren't to even talk children for another four years—but she could adjust. She didn't like adjusting, but *Semper Gumby*. Always flexible. She'd learned that in flight school and still adhered to it when she needed to.

You have time, Mia told herself. Focus on today.

Today was Sunday, the day after the engagement party, and well wishes and small talk still clouded her mind. Unopened envelopes and gifts covered their kitchen table in mounds, and her good leg ached from standing for too many hours. The envelopes and gifts could remain unopened for the time being, though, and the feet were going back into wedges. Wall Street paused for no one, even on Sundays.

Focus, Mia told herself again.

She bent over and removed her shrinker. She didn't need it anymore but preferred sleeping with it to keep her stump warm. She grabbed her regular prosthetic from a shelf and brought it to her right knee socket. It felt cold and familiar in her palm, like an old metal spear. It popped into place, and when she set it down on the floor, the muscles in her good leg loosened with relief. Then came the skin cover and a pair of black leggings, ubiquitous to her life now, and a new sheath dress she'd been saving for today's luncheon. She brushed her teeth, combed her hair, and left the bathroom.

The living room was empty and dim. She'd purchased the two-bedroom condo two years before with deployment savings. Her father and grandfather had wanted to contribute, and also wanted her to live uptown. "You *work* in the Finance District," they said. "You don't live there. That's how it's done."

They also considered uptown safer and less likely to be attacked, but neither would ever say that out loud. They were persistent men unused to being told thank you, but no. Turning them away hadn't been easy, but it'd been worth it. Both to maintain her independence and to be able to walk to work.

Besides, there were worse kitchen views than Vietnam Victory Square.

Through the kitchen window the square sparkled like a church, a white spire shooting above the crowns of the trees. Mia wasn't one for daydreaming, or for maudlin patriotic symbols, but she did enjoy early morning coffees thinking about what that long marble wall meant to the soldiers and marines who'd come before. She'd find them in the park, sometimes, on her way to work. Sitting on a bench, looking at the wall or at the Legionnaires statue. In suits, in ragged combat jackets, in dad jeans and fanny packs, trying to reckon with their war, with the costs of victory, with themselves, too. She found it oddly serene, watching strangers sift through the arcane past for something like clarity.

The government had done well. It was a good monument. The Council of Victors had done well, too—it'd been their first project after taking over for the old Veterans Administration. She doubted her war would ever get anything like it.

Mia walked through the living room and into the open bedroom. "Up," she said to Jesse, who still lay facedown in bed. She turned the blinds. Lady Liberty and the blue waters of the harbor came into view, slices of late morning filling the room. This earned a deep groan into the pillows.

"Hungover," Jesse said. "No más."

"Hah," Mia said. Jesse didn't drink, something he'd never explained and she felt didn't matter to their life together. He'd gone undercover for years for the Bureau, sent to be her handler after, as a reprieve. He had a history. So did she. Persons of consequence usually did.

She turned and took in her groom-to-be. His wide, pale frame had moved to the center of the bed, and he'd buried his head into his arms to try to ward off the window light. Her family had handled his Jewishness better than expected, but their New England conceits emerged when it came to his size and stutter. Pilgrims tended to cling to sanctimony, Mia had learned, even with their own kin.

"How's my girl?"

"Her?" Mia looked out the window toward Lady Liberty. Still green, still corroding. Still sinking. "You can do better, I think."

"Funny."

Mia leaned over and kissed Jesse on the tip of the nose. "Up," she repeated. What she couldn't explain to her family and never would was how he'd cared for her after she came home. She'd been a wreck, and alone. First he'd done it as a job, then as a friend, then, later, as something more. Mia came from a family who valued success, stoicism, and means, not always in that order. Those things did matter to her. But the military had taught Mia that nothing mattered more in a human being than competence. And fat, pale, stuttering Jesse Stein was the most competent man she'd ever known.

Even if he didn't look it at the moment.

"Do I have to come?" He moved his head under a pillow. Mia recognized it as progress. "It's a lunch for Wall Street vets. I'm not Wall Street. I'm not a veteran. And I don't want lunch."

"What else."

"There's a fantasy football draft to prep for. Work league. Very important."

"Too bad. You promised last week."

"The last one of these you dragged me to was about inev-inevitably nuking China. Over trade. Depressing."

"You weren't paying attention then. Not inevitable. Just possible. And not over trade. Over Vietnam's potential statehood, and competing mining contracts in Africa."

"Let me sleep, woman!"

Mia smiled, thinking about the stick in the bathroom. He'd be so happy to know. But. There were biological concerns to consider. Super-biological concerns. The type of concerns a handler would need to know. The type of concerns a fiancé didn't need to. At least for now.

"It's two hours," Mia continued, reaching her hand under the covers to scratch between Jesse's shoulder blades. "There's a guest speaker. Famous general. Bit of a role model of mine. All you have to do is sit there."

That earned another groan into the pillows. "The only thing worse than a self-important vet," he said, "is a self-important vet giving a speech."

Mia smacked him on the back of the head. "I'm a self-important vet," she said. "And this is my speech: get up, we're going to be late."

Jesse laughed, flipped over, and pulled Mia into the covers. "Let's stay here," he said, smelling of sleep and last night's toothpaste. "Like Tupac says on his morning show. Fuck the world today."

This is why I love him, Mia thought, turning away from his attempt to steal a kiss but settling into the crook of his shoulder. He makes me feel safe, even while driving me crazy. She wondered if he could feel her hands still trembling, but if so, he didn't say anything. She let herself listen to his heartbeat through his chest for a few minutes. It reminded her, ever faintly, of the rotor wash from an attack helicopter.

Later, after she cajoled Jesse into the shower, Mia checked her phone. There was a text from Britt Swenson, asking for Sebastian Rios's email. Oh Lord, Mia thought. This can't end well. Then she texted Britt with the email and finished getting ready for the luncheon.

———————

The guest speaker for the Wall Street Veterans' annual summer luncheon was Major General (retired) Jaclyn "Jackie" Gaile Collins, sometimes referred to as Jackpot by her warfighters (affectionately and otherwise), former head of the U.S. homeland intelligence command, current deputy director for science and technology at the Agency, decorated combat hero, West Point class of 1977, wearer of an oversize West Point class of 1977 ring, noted military gender pioneer, proud political moderate, and prouder mother of two.

"Impressive," Jesse said, reading over the general's bio on

his phone in the cab to the luncheon. "The minefield stuff in Vietnam—she's legit. How'd you get her?"

"Her daughter's at Lehman Brothers," Mia said. "Easy ask."

"What's with the nickname, though. Seems—sexual?"

"Nothing like that. When a ground raid finds the enemy target they're looking for. Jackpot. As a colonel, she transformed the process for commando missions. Figured out how to work networks bottom-up instead of top-down. Went from a hundred raids per year to three thousand. Turned spec ops evergreen."

Jesse nodded, then flared his nostrils. "Agency spooks, though."

Mia rolled her eyes. Tribal fights in the army, tribal fights on Wall Street, tribal fights between government agencies, they were all the same. Before she'd gone back-office and moved to corporate compliance, she'd earned her stripes in investment banking, the front lines of money. Seventy-, eighty-hour workweeks, where careers could be made in minutes, and broken in half that. Same with entire accounts and capital portfolios that she'd tried desperately to remember were people's livelihoods, people's dreams. College educations. Retirement funds. Small businesses. It was hard, though. The game was the game. And the game left little space for contemplation. Contemplation meant time, and time meant money, and money meant everything—not just everything to the banks, or to the slick-suited creeps trying to sleep with a Tucker granddaughter, or to the bull statue tourists took pictures with because, hah hah, it had testicles. Money meant everything to those dreams she'd been charged with seeing through. That meant something, Mia knew. Even if it usually felt like nothing at all.

She'd never expected to end up in the family trade. She'd gone away to Dupont in the alien south to do something different. She'd found it with ROTC, and then the army. Then she'd volunteered for the wrong mission and it'd all been taken from her. *C'est la guerre*, she told herself anytime she felt the spider legs of regret crawling into her thoughts. *C'est la guerre*.

The dark thrills of combat could never be replicated, Mia believed that, but the military had its similarities to finance. The firm hierarchy and structure, for one. Having to prove herself in a world of brash young men, for another. Resolve and will trumping that brashness over and over again, for yet another.

Mia did miss investment banking sometimes. But she didn't long for it.

Finance was in Mia's blood. War lay in her bones.

She'd been looking out the cab window, mind adrift. Jesse tapped against the partition to bring her back.

Mia followed Jesse's nod and grin. Someone had carved FREE ABU ABDALLAH into the partition plastic. "Jackpot should be alerted," he said.

He was trying to play with her, but Mia shook her head. The terror chieftain's trial at the World Court had become a daily spectacle. Like a lot of Americans, Mia wished the Volunteers had just killed Abu Abdallah the night of the raid and been done with it. A hell of a time for them to discover courageous restraint, she thought.

The cab moved north along the city's main park and dropped off Mia and Jesse in front of a square Victorian building with high gables. The board had asked Mia about the Yale Club for today and she'd played coy. She'd called in that favor before. But the new recession had complicated her family's relationship with some people at the club. Her father insisted it would blow over. Mia wasn't so sure. Whatever hard line separated business matters from personal, the crash had snapped it clean all over the city.

The luncheon room overlooked a small rock garden and screen doors on the sides let in a warm midsummer breeze. Mia and Jesse had arrived in time—barely, she noted—and after a quick hello to some of the other junior board members, they took their seats as near the podium as Mia felt appropriate. New paperbacks of the general's *The Soldier and the State* covered the tables like confetti. Mia guessed she was one of the few who'd already read it. People in finance loved books, and loved getting their books autographed. Reading those books, though, was something else.

A waiter took their orders. Mia made conversation with an asset manager on mimosa number three. He'd been a submarine officer in the 1980s. After the Cold War ended with the Russian Revolution but before the Palm Sunday attacks. Mia knew how to deal with men like this, when to ask a question and when to laugh, and most especially, when not to mention her own combat record. From the corner of her eye, she saw Jesse talking with a man about their age with trim dishwater blond hair and no neck. Oh God, she realized. That's Liam Noonan. Mia began to eavesdrop. They were discussing the revised Warfighters Care Act. They hadn't been seated even ten minutes.

"It's personal for me. Once a Navy SEAL, always a Navy SEAL." A bond trader for a boutique firm, Noonan never failed to mention his background when he appeared on cable television. "I've had friends sent to rehabilitation colonies who are still there. I've had friends sent to colonies who received treatment and returned to society, whole and healed."

"So you're okay with the new legislation?"

"Hell no. Big government always makes things worse."

"But there's stories about drug companies experimenting on colony vets."

"Media garbage. More bureaucracy won't do a thing. We need quick and thorough solutions. Only a free market can provide that."

"Sounds like someone has colony stock options." Mia bit her lip to keep from smiling. Jesse rarely talked politics. He didn't even vote. G-men needed to be above the fray, he thought. But the report on the colony experiments had roused something in him. Mia had heard him mumbling at the television about it. "I saw on the news that fourteen percent of new vets are sent to colonies now. That's big money."

"The tribunals have explained. It's medical."

Jesse didn't seem to hear that and kept pressing. "And what

about the International Legion? Those poor bastards only get citizenship if they pass a tribunal. Way harder than the medicals here, right? That's one way to keep the ranks full."

"It's about us! Not them!" Noonan slammed his fist on the table. The stock options dig had landed. "I've shed blood for the homeland. What have you done?"

The hair on the back of Mia's neck rose. She could almost feel Jesse considering punching out the bigger man's larynx. Men are so stupid, she thought, maintaining eye contact with the still-jabbering asset manager while patting Jesse's leg under the table. That seemed to help; his body slackened at her touch.

"Just a concerned citizen," Jesse finally said. And then with a scorn so razor-fine only Mia could hear it, "America Honors the Warfighter."

"The honor is ours," Noonan replied, automatic as a pull string.

"The SEALs, that's something," Jesse said. "Weren't you all auxiliary for the Volunteers? When they grabbed Abu Abdallah, I mean."

He was now asking for a fight, there could be no doubt about it. Mercifully, the food arrived and the general appeared in the back of the room. A hush fell over the luncheon like a shroud. Jesse kept his arms crossed and winked at Mia. Liam Noonan's face remained a hot crimson.

And Jesse wonders why 80 percent of the wedding are my invites, Mia thought.

General Collins moved to the podium with the self-possession fundamental to all flag officers, a practiced ease that both belied and sustained itself with every step. She was a stout woman, Mia observed, not big, not tall, yet a full presence. She wore a gray suit with a notched collar and no shoulder pads, and peep-toe flats that Mia admired. The general set an open manila folder upon the podium and smiled wide for the room. The West Point ring on her right hand rose and fell with her gestures like a black sun, and Mia had to blink a few times to keep from following it

"Hello, Wall Street Veterans!" General Collins said. Her voice was throaty and hoarse; Mia knew a woman couldn't make it in the military talking like velvet, no matter how capable. "To be among this group is an inspiration. I'm going to bottle some of the energy and brains here and bring it back to Langley. We sure could use it."

Polite laughter filled the room. Mia didn't dare look at Jesse.

"I want to begin by thanking each and every one of you for your service to our great nation. Particularly the younger veterans in the room who joined after Palm Sunday. Your generation is often slurred because of the supposed prosperity you were born into. 'Found at freedom's peak,' former president Rockefeller said. Yet you still went to war. You knew you'd be going. You've been sent to Lebanon, Cyprus, Syria. All over the Near East, all over the world. You've conducted air campaigns in Persia, the Balkans, God knows where else. You kept Greece and Turkey from starting World War Three, even after nuclear disaster. 'The Mediterranean Wars,' they call it. What they really mean is 'Endless Conflict.' All that takes a special kind of commitment, a special kind of courage."

She held up three fingers. "Only three percent of Americans serve in the military. Three percent that loves America enough to fight for it.

"Or, as another cranky old general once put it: 'Those who can truly be accounted brave are those who best know the meaning of what is sweet in life and what is terrible, and then go out, undeterred, to meet what is to come.' That's you. I don't say this lightly. You're my heroes."

The general led the room in applause before continuing. Mia ignored the impulse to tap at her prosthetic. An old habit from the first days, checking to make sure it was still there. She clapped along.

"Whenever we joined the military, wherever the homeland sent us, we are united in—and by—that service. Wearing the uniform for thirty years remains the honor of my life. To be a warfighter— what more could a person aspire to? The question I asked myself the morning after I retired—the question some of you may've asked, too—is 'What now?'

"I've determined that continued service is the answer. And while continued service takes different forms for different people, it always involves giving back. Paying the war tax is something we all do, of course, but it's such an intangible duty. Human beings need to see something for it to be real. We need to hold that something. For me—"

Hold that something, Mia thought. Like an infant. Why now? she thought again. They had too much going on now. She felt a tug at her elbow. She ignored it and tried to focus again on General Collins's speech. She felt another tug.

"Gotta go," Jesse mouthed, pointing to his phone and rising from his seat to a low crouch. "Work. E-mer-gen-cy."

Mia's face set like a flint. A Bureau emergency. There always was a Bureau emergency. And he had the gall to mock spooks for being secretive. At least they didn't treat every hiccup like an imminent disaster. Whatever, she thought. This would keep him from suplexing Liam Noonan into a table. She raised an eyebrow to convey acceptance, if not approval.

"Thank you," Jesse whispered as if she had a choice, and then he was gone.

Mia returned to the speech. General Collins spoke about the importance of veterans in American society, how in an era of an all-volunteer military and a fraction of the population serving, each and every vet from Wall Street to Main Street had become an envoy. She spoke about the ways young enlisted veterans could benefit any organization or business, but sometimes had difficulties communicating that in their resumes.

"We taught them how to speak military," the general said. "Now they need to learn to speak business." She spoke about the stereotypes citizens held because Mediterranean vets weren't like the Greatest Generation or the Next Greatest Generation, because they hadn't "won" their war. They weren't all unemployed or crazy or bound for a rehabilitation colony. Besides, the colonies often worked! She spoke about how it was the responsibility of privileged veterans like those in this room to help their brothers and sisters in arms, and to do so in real, meaningful ways.

Mia listened to it all, transfixed. Privilege. Responsibility. Meaning. People didn't talk about doing more on Wall Street, even at summer luncheons. People usually talked about what was already being done. She could see some of the other attendees shifting in their seats, especially the older men. A lady general was one thing, but a lady general who told them they needed to do more for others? They hadn't been spoken to like that in a long, long time.

After the luncheon, a small group gathered around the general's seat. She saw Liam Noonan, among others, beat a hasty retreat to the doors. I should've let Jesse throat-punch him, she thought, half-kidding. If only to keep him off TV for a little while.

Mia lingered to the side of the circle around General Collins, wanting to thank her and perhaps get her book signed, too. The general had other plans.

"Mia Tucker." General Collins stood, parted the circle with knife hands, and grasped Mia by the palms. Mia tried to introduce herself but the general cut her off, saying, "Of course I know who you are."

Despite being the same height, Mia found herself gazing up. A slight stoop tipped General Collins's shoulders forward, something Mia hadn't noticed during the speech. Thirty years in uniform, which meant thirty years of body armor and thirty years of ruck marches and thirty years of sleeping on cots and in the backs of humvees and cargo trucks. The wear and tear didn't much show on the general's face, though, something Mia thought remarkable. Deployments showed on everyone.

"Do you smoke, Mia?" General Collins sniffed, speaking low. "I always crave one after a speech."

"No, ma'am," she said.

"I have my assistant carry around packs," General Collins said. "My family, bless their souls, are draconian about it. Walk with me."

The two women passed through a sliding screen door and into the rock garden. The formality in the general's steps was gone, replaced with the stiff casualness of someone who sleeps like a mummy. Mia didn't know why the general had recognized her. She may know about the cythrax bomb, Mia thought, but I'm not a Volunteer. I made the choice to leave. I made the choice to come home.

General Collins took a seat on a wood bench. Mia smoothed her dress and did the same. A ribbon of a stream wrapped around the garden, nourished by a tiny waterfall dribbling down a slope in a far corner. The waterfall's soft hum gave the garden its only sound. Somehow, an elevated, outdoor garden in the heart of Empire City was as insulated as a shrine. Mia found herself taken by the calm of it all.

"Where are you now?" the general asked, cigarette between her lips. She cupped it with one hand and lit it with the other. "Job, family, future. Et cetera."

"Well." Mia organized her thoughts as quickly as she could. Generals valued brevity. "I work at a bank. Corporate compliance. Just got engaged to a Bureau man. Staying here a few more years. No hard plan after."

"Kids?"

"No, ma'am." Mia resisted the impulse to touch her stomach. "Not for a while."

"Call me Jackie. I'm not one of those generals who get off pretending they're still in." General Collins took a slow, deep drag and leaned over, twisting her body to look at Mia. "I do miss it, though. Don't you? That purpose of being. The team effort, the team focus. Langley's not like that at all. There's just—nothing like it."

"There's not," Mia said, remembering. "And I do. I do miss it."

"I'll cut to the mustard." General Collins took another long drag and then flicked the half-smoked cigarette to the stone path under them. "I'm going to announce for the Senate in two months. The fanatics have too much sway, too much influence. The new parties on the far left and far right have just made it worse. One kind of extremism just enables another. If you look at our history, the center is what has made America strong. The center needs a lot of help right now. It must hold. Ever since the jihadists got Javy in Istanbul . . ."

Mia had forgotten the general had been close with the fallen ambassador. She'd still been in high school when that had happened. He'd been a founding member of the Council of Victors. Mia waited in silence until the older woman regained her verbal stride.

"I've seen all this before. When I was your age. We're on the brink again. My generation swore we'd never let another Vietnam happen. Yet here we are. Victory, but at what cost? Extremists, militants, separatists . . . all here, in America! The jihadists have evolved, too. The things they're capable of now, in terms of destruction . . . it keeps me up at night. It really does.

"I intend to win this seat. I intend to win because this country is in dire shape and needs to be reminded of the power of service. It needs to be reminded of the power of the center, and the hope it offers us all. In order to win, I need a good campaign team. Sharp. Dynamic. High energy."

Mia nodded, waiting for the general to continue. When she didn't, Mia asked, "How can I help?"

General Collins unwound her body on the bench. A medley of cracking joints followed. "Fund-raising through your connections, for one. An independent party from the radical middle has no chance without Wall Street money. You could help with that, a lot. But it'll be an all-hands-on-deck operation. We'll need team members comfortable doing it all. You're a special young woman, Mia. Someone with many talents. And you come highly recommended."

Mia couldn't help herself. Something about the way the general had said "special" intrigued her.

Something about the way the general had said "talents" bothered her.

"By who?" she asked.

"A few folks," the general said. "Pete Swenson, especially. He couldn't stop singing your praises."

Mia tried to remain straight-faced. "Of course," she said. The garden's shadows rolled through her, and she reached for a sweater around her shoulders that wasn't there. "Pete will do that."

First his sister and now this, Mia thought. I told him to leave me alone.

The two women exchanged contact information, Mia with a business card, the general by writing her phone number on another of Mia's cards.

"My personal line," she said. "Be ready. Politics is war without bloodshed."

"Chairman Mao," Mia said, and the general smiled at the attribution.

"Be ready," General Collins said again. Then she walked into the building.

Mia sat in the rock garden alone, listening to the waterfall's dribbles. She didn't care that it was fake. She only cared that the calm it brought was true. She'd heard the rumors about why the general hadn't gotten her third star, stories swapped by national security journalists and think-tank types. Jackpot had punched a War Department superior. No, others said, she'd thrown a commemorative pistol at him, a gift from a tribal leader overseas. Because she'd been lied to about a warfighter surge. No, because she'd blacklisted a subpar private military company and they'd gone around her back. Because she'd been promised the Sinai command before the privateers took over. Because after thirty years of war, she'd just had enough.

All the stories, all the rumors, agreed on one thing: General Collins was not to be crossed.

The cinder of the general's half cigarette blinked out on the ground, thin curls of smoke waning into the air. Before leaving herself, Mia picked up the half cigarette and dropped it into a trash can. Litter on the streets was one thing. Litter in a garden was another.

Apprehension shook at Mia all afternoon, though why, she couldn't quite work out. There was the baby, or not-baby, but that wasn't it. Not entirely. More than anything, Mia wanted to rip off her prosthetic and fly through the sky for hours on end, until her lungs burned cold and her skin was coated in thick, soapy vapor. Then she'd be able to figure it out.

But she didn't do that anymore. So she wouldn't.

CHAPTER 3

WHAT WAS MEMORY and what was dream? Jean-Jacques couldn't be sure anymore. Taut, frenzied firefights in night-vision green had filled his life, so they filled his sleep, too. Midnight raids coming upon villages from the holy above, blades churning, quiet as sin, loud like virtue. Propellant, hot blood, and emptied bowels, or what passed for them in the dreamscape, slid through his mind like rainwater. A mission for someone, or something, so a mission like any other, except for the missions that were different.

A hunt's thrills, a hunt's terrors. Dark everlasting.

Boot steps and battle rattle, rifles probing, into the compound they go. Shouts like hammers, voices of command and voices of care and voices of alarm all whirling together into one singular monk chant of violence. Red lasers dancing on walls, searching, seeking, proclaiming, first in brittle English then again in sky-soaked kreyol, in power, in glory, like the voice of God itself.

A touch of smoke. The taste of dust. A rifle burst into shadow. Oh, to know the unknown. The long, dirty pause before clarity, when anything is possible, nothing ripping out into everythings, mind in chest and heart in head, ready, ever ready, always vigilant.

Of their own accord.

Where's the boy? The damn boy, Jean-Jacques. Find the boy.

The particulars turn to strands of cognizance, short broken reels from the other side. Mind spew or the entirety of the universe? Who could say. Not Jean-Jacques. He didn't try to hold to them for understanding, not anymore. He forced them away by not forcing anything at all.

Jean-Jacques knew these weren't good dreams, but they weren't bad dreams, either. They were dreams. None of it was new.

A sense that he hadn't been himself on the other side of consciousness sometimes skulked around, though, in the soft corners between sleep and awareness. Like he'd been observing there. Watching, not doing. Like the soldier had been a figment all along. Not a growth. Not a progression. Just a necessity for a fixed place and time.

Too much partying with the guys, Jean-Jacques would think when he came to. Too much comfort and indulgence in Hollywood, not enough time at the gym and the range, staying lethal. But dream, memory, idle thought: all led back to the boy. To the boy he'd lost, to the boy he'd failed. He knew that. All roads led back to the war.

Jean-Jacques Saint-Preux had come home.

He'd left Little Haiti eight years before, promising to never return. He'd abided by that until now. Jean-Jacques had missed a cousin's wedding, a nephew's graduation, an uncle's deportment. Duty, he'd tried to explain. The profession of arms, a nice, workmanlike way of saying he'd devoted his life to spilling blood and snatching souls in the name of the homeland. Twelve tours between the International Legion, the Rangers, and the Volunteers. Jean-Jacques had earned his honor in the process, and citizenship, too. At some point, though, on one of those twelve business trips, over there had become more normal than back here. Months lost to filming Hollywood propaganda for the government had only exacerbated that dislocation. Jean-Jacques wanted nothing more than to get back to combat, where life made sense.

In the meantime, home had gone on without him.

The differences reminded him of that. Renovated houses, new businesses, closed ones, too, strange streetlights and stop signs. A coffee shop had opened up next to the old boxing gym on Delmas Street. A chain coffee shop. When had—he stopped himself. He didn't want to care.

The air smelled the same, though. Like hot trash and wildflower.

Jean-Jacques turned the car onto a thoroughfare. He drove slow along the water, window open and looking left, across the bay. The night skyline of Empire City had once meant everything to him. The big, scattershot lights and dark silhouettes like castles suggested something else, something more. And the power of else and more can transform a young mind. It had for him, growing up in the outer reaches of the city, hiding from bored hoods looking for familiarity in a strange land far from the Pearl of the Antilles. And what could be more familiar, more unifying, than beating on a loner?

He'd found refuge at the skate park, where enough kids from surrounding districts showed up to bring out the occasional patrol car. They'd laugh at the fat immigrant trying ollies and grinds on a ragged board from the flower power era, but he didn't mind. Laughter was peace, even laughter at him. The black Americans could call him whatever they wanted, and so could the cops. They didn't know who he was, where he came from. They thought he was different in a normal way. He'd liked that. Besides, after they went home with their jokes, he could sit on a park bench and watch the water churn and watch the night come upon the city like a mask and he could think about else and he could think about more and he could just be alone. Most important of all, he could just be left alone.

The skate park wasn't there anymore. Jean-Jacques had driven past it earlier and found a carry-out Chinese restaurant. But the skyline remained. It had matched the traces of memory, mostly. The Global Trade skyscraper lit up the end of the island, rigid as a longsword. Its force reminded Jean-Jacques of Tripoli for some reason, which in turn reminded him of that specific blend of propellant, hot blood, and emptied bowels he'd come to associate with death. Something about nothingness being something, he decided. Instead of what it was supposed to be.

The lights from the city still washed out the stars above. That left a different type of nothingness.

What kind of place doesn't have stars? Jean-Jacques considered that in the car. It hadn't been until he traveled the globe in attack helicopters that he'd seen the night sky for all its glory. The galaxy went on for forever, something that put into perspective the elses and mores offered by one city skyline. Even home's.

Jean-Jacques turned off the thoroughfare and passed under a stoplight. It was stuck and burned yellow and burned yellow and kept burning yellow, never changing. He parked the car. Across the street, behind a chain-link fence, a pair of teen boys built like fishbones played basketball on a new hoop. They didn't look his way but he could tell they were side-eyeing him through the dim.

Maybe I should've dressed down, he thought, before correcting himself. He'd worn a polo and pressed slacks for a reason. Might as well own it.

Jean-Jacques unrolled the windows and left the doors unlocked; he'd borrowed the car from one of the bohemians they were staying with and didn't want to return it less than whole. Such an act didn't seem necessary in this Little Haiti but it had been in his. He walked past the teenagers and their side-eyes toward a cluster of tall, dull buildings made of brick.

"Welcome to General Ulysses S. Grant Houses," read a blue sign held up on wooden stilts. "A Wonderful Community."

The courtyard of the public housing complex was a gray slab of cement and cold shadows. Lampposts marked the way to metal tables in the center, forming a sort of concrete pergola. Stereos from different apartment windows blasted out dance songs, the even, pulsing beats filling the courtyard with dueling shouts and sing-along. But other than a group of girls jumping rope, Jean-Jacques didn't see anyone. Sunday night, he thought. Most people would be walking the *Mache*. The moon sat tucked behind an armada of gray clouds. Black mass had descended.

Jean-Jacques strolled through the courtyard to the metal tables, head low and hands deep in his pockets. He tried not to betray any hurry. The scent of marinated chicken and sauce piquant drifted through the night air from an open window. His stomach grumbled. It'd been a long time since he'd eaten a proper Caribbean meal. Wog food relied too much on earth flavors, he thought. It needed some fire in it. And army food, forget about it—that paste was for white people. One of the girls jumping rope turned and squared him up.

"Why you walk like a babylon?" she asked. The other girls laughed.

Jean-Jacques considered the question. He'd never been called police before. He was glad to see them jumping rope with one bought from a store, made of nylon. The girls from his youth had made do with lines of telephone cable.

He shrugged. "Just how I walk," he said in kreyol. The girls widened their eyes. They hadn't thought he was one of theirs.

He sat at one of the tables. His knees cracked for the effort while his lower back ached from an old slipped disc. Twenty-five going on fifty, he thought. Jean-Jacques was beginning to feel his own mortality.

He looked around, eyes adjusting to the lamplight. A sterile conformity rustled through the courtyard, strips of neat yellow grass and power-washed walkways glinting with forced order. There was one exception: a circle with three arrows spray-painted in blood orange raced across the face of a nearby building. The arrows pointed to the lower-left inside of the circle. Underneath, written in wavy kreyol, was a message:

"DEFY THE GUARDS. GUARD THOSE WHO DEFY."

Ooh, Jean-Jacques thought. So cryptic. He had nothing but

disdain for political statements and the type of people who made them. He'd found that the minds he wanted to emulate grounded their thought exercises in the world as it was, not in a world of ifs and perhapses. Practical: he'd loved that word since he'd first heard it as a cherry private, and had tried to steel himself to it ever since.

A man emerged from under an overhang across the courtyard. He wore faded jeans and a baggy white tee much too large for him. A flat-brimmed baseball cap tilted to the side bore a big green C on it.

"Yo," the man said. It wasn't until he got closer to the tables and smiled that Jean-Jacques recognized him. "It's true. My big cousin *is* the black superman from the news. Where did all the fat go?"

Jean-Jacques returned the smile and slapped hands with the man. "Mon ami!" he said. The kreyol felt like an old sweater on his tongue, stretched and itchy, so he kept his words tight. "Emmanuel. Surprised you ain't a priest."

When they were children, Emmanuel would spend his post-mass Sundays baptizing anyone who'd let him, from little girls coloring the sidewalks with chalk to old men in wheelchairs sipping on forties. It upset some of the adult women, who thought it was sacrilege to either Jesus or Bondye or maybe both, but it'd been Jean-Jacques's mother who intervened on her nephew's behalf. "Let the boy be a boy," she would say. "Why rush a child to grow in this world?"

Emmanuel had grown, though, and the smile dropped from his face in the courtyard. "No, homie," he said to Jean-Jacques. "Gave up that foolishness a long time ago."

Jean-Jacques sat back down. Emmanuel remained standing. The younger man held a pine box the size of a firecracker and Jean-Jacques tried not to stare at it. It was why he was here but Emmanuel already knew that. No need to remind him.

"How's the family?" he asked.

"We okay." Emmanuel paused for a moment, chewing over what to say next. "Sorry my mom won't let you come to the apartment."

He paused again. "Superstitious shit. Thinks your powers will mess with the kids' brains. Give them radiation or something."

Jean-Jacques didn't know what to say to that so he didn't say anything. He considered his aunt stupid and ignorant, but maybe she's right, he thought. Maybe I would frighten children. Maybe I should, too.

"We're all proud of you. For real. Getting all those medals, saving wog babies and stuff. You've done good, cousin."

Jean-Jacques hoped the darkness of the courtyard hid the contours of his face. He knew it must've been revealing something. He'd saved people overseas, and some of them had been wogs, and some of them had been babies. But they weren't the ones he thought about since coming home.

"Need to see the Saint-Preux name getting some shine, though. Those two *blans* you roll with, they always in the lights. What's this Dash thing all about?" Emmanuel's voice flexed with the question, and Jean-Jacques knew why. Dash was both his nickname and his code name; the latter since the cythrax bomb, the former since day zero at basic, when the drill sergeant couldn't or wouldn't say "Jean-Jacques Saint-Preux" so he said "Dash" instead, and then the moniker stuck, so Jean-Jacques became Dash, too. It made things easier, and truth be told, Jean-Jacques hadn't minded. Much of why he'd joined the army was to be shaped and molded into someone new, someone different. A new name for a new identity. Jean-Jacques Saint-Preux of Little Haiti had been fat and dopey. Through combat, through the application of armed violence, through blood and sand and kills and death, Dash of the Legion and Dash of the Rangers became hard and discerning. That mattered to Jean-Jacques more than anything else. People could call him whatever the hell they wanted. He'd been reborn.

"Just a name," he told his cousin in kreyol. "Same as any other."

"Same as any other." Emmanuel repeated the phrase, slow and dry. Jean-Jacques heard something like spite in his cousin's words. "Wasn't going to tell you this—but. Your mom was dying, she kept praying about you. Said you'd left home, you'd left your people, but she wanted you to remember where you come from. Kept calling you her little miracle. Might've been the last thing she said that made sense."

Jean-Jacques closed the gap between them in a blur. When he turned rapid for long distances he could taste water in the air but this was child's play. He grasped the top of his cousin's shirt with his fists, crossing them at the wrists into a chokehold, and hooked a leg behind the man to lean him over. Emmanuel's face, only inches from Jean-Jacques's, betrayed pure, howling fear. Loose spit gathered at the corners of his mouth and mucus dripped from his nose. Jean-Jacques had seen this before in virgin eyes confronting the mystical. Speed like his could not be rationalized by human minds, nor could it be reasoned with. It could only be experienced.

"Speaking of," Jean-Jacques said. "Give that over."

Emmanuel pressed the box into Jean-Jacques's stomach. Jean-Jacques looked into his cousin's mouth—twisted teeth crashed into one another like tiny yellow crags. He tongued the back of his own. They felt smooth as ever, straightened out and aligned by the army years before. He let go of his chokehold and took the box. He unhooked his leg from his cousin's body and took a step back.

"Suuu-perrr," Emmanuel said, sounding out both syllables in English, and only then did Jean-Jacques realize he'd been trying to goad him all along.

Neither man apologized, preferring to let silence fill the void. Jean-Jacques knew he'd gained an anger abroad but he didn't know what to make of it. From floors above, he listened to a woman sing along off-key to a hip-hop song he didn't recognize.

He looked over at Emmanuel, who was panting and trying not to show it. "Who's this?" he asked, pointing up at the woman singing.

Emmanuel loosed a short laugh and shook his head. "That's Big Daddy Pouchon, homie. You *have* been gone."

Jean-Jacques snorted. "That I have. I like it. Good . . ." He searched his mind for the right word in kreyol. "*Pouvwa.*" Power.

"I'll burn you a mix," Emmanuel said. Jean-Jacques thought he was joking until he asked for the number to his cell. Jean-Jacques gave it, more out of a sense of control than embarrassment. They weren't supposed to use their supers stateside. The handlers had been quite clear about that.

With a nod, Jean-Jacques bumped fists with Emmanuel and began walking out of the courtyard. He smelled hot trash and wild-flower in the night again.

"Let's chill," Emmanuel called after him. "Got a proposition to throw your way."

Jean-Jacques smirked at that. A proposition. The child priest had become a hustler. "Let the boy be a boy," his mother had said. And then what? Little Haiti was like the rest of the world that way. No one knew.

———

Jean-Jacques walked through a group of pigeons gathered on the sidewalk. They were pulling apart a fast-food wrapper covered in hamburger grease. Most looked dirty and overstuffed to Jean-Jacques, but a young female with an emerald-green neck and long gray wings stood off by itself, watching over it all. It looked up at him and tilted its head as if it were sizing him up, in case Jean-Jacques had come for the wrapper.

Game knows game, he thought.

His phone buzzed from a front pocket. It was a text from Flowers, asking where he was. Something about another Gypsy Town party and how Pete hadn't showed either and how they'd said they were going to be there and how the Volunteers were supposed to stick together, even back here.

Jean-Jacques put his phone back into his pocket without replying. Flowers meant well. But.

The stoplight had remained stale yellow. The basketballers across the street called out to one another in thick shouts and grunts, the ball an anvil of lead in the still. A third player had

45

joined the teens, blocking their shots and taunting at their objections, looming over them like a shadow giant. Straightaway, Jean-Jacques knew who it was. There was only one Justice.

Jean-Jacques had served with Pete Swenson for four years, yet the man's physical presence had never normalized. Tall as an orange tree with outsize shoulders and legs long as roots, Pete wore khaki cargo pants and a short-sleeve rugby shirt. Every time he posted up one of the teens or bent over to reach for the ball, it appeared like he might fold in on himself, until he burst back up with raw muscular force. Other than a five-o'clock shadow, he still looked the part of a special operator—a low fade haircut and sideburns that barely met regs, wraparound ballistic shades propped up on his head. An old Ranger cadence entered Jean-Jacques's mind: "*I ain't the killer, I'm the killer man's son. So I'll do the killing—until the killer man comes.*"

"There he is." Pete punched the basketball into the air with a fist and walked over to the chain-link fence. "Get what you needed?"

Jean-Jacques answered with his own question. "How'd you get out here?"

Pete half-smiled, half-grimaced. His dark eye blended with the night, but the other one, coral green and throbbing, pierced through it. If my family thinks I'll radiate them, Jean-Jacques thought, they should meet this freak.

"Car service," he said. Dabs of sweat had gathered on his forehead and under his ears and armpits. "Yellow cabs won't come out this way, you know that?"

"Mmm-hmm." Jean-Jacques shook his head and walked toward the car, still holding tight the box he'd secured from his cousin. Car service to Little Haiti? After hundreds of missions together and thousands of orders, he liked seeing Pete out of his element.

"Dash." Pete called after him. "What's a guy have to do around here to get a brew?"

Jean-Jacques shook his head again but turned around.

"How thirsty are you?"

"Very," Pete said.

"Okay," Jean-Jacques said. "You've been warned."

Jean-Jacques got into the car and started the engine. As he reached over to open the passenger door for Pete, one of the kids playing basketball called after them.

"Superhero," he said. Pete looked over. "Why you leave Abu Abdallah breathing?"

Pete leaned over the door frame of the car and stroked his chin. He loved answering this question for citizens more than any other. Jean-Jacques understood why. It hadn't only been a good mission. It'd been a clean one.

"Didn't have a gun in his hands," Pete said. "Just a bag of his own piss."

They drove through Little Haiti. The passenger seat belt was broken and Pete couldn't figure it out. He knotted the strap around the buckle until it held and pumped his fist in triumph. Then he asked what it was like being home.

They were passing a bus depot Jean-Jacques remembered as a construction pit.

"Got nicer."

"That's good, right?" Pete looked out the window, nodding to himself. "Home should get nicer."

"Sure." Jean-Jacques again tongued the back of his teeth. He'd liked that pit. It'd been normal. It'd been consistent. It'd been a pit. "If you say so."

Pete nodded again.

Jean-Jacques took them to the Basic Lounge. It was nearby enough, and he felt like fucking with Pete. The lounge had been founded with the first exodus of Haitians, the ones who'd fled the second dictator. The ones who'd arrived when Empire City still had its old name, before it became an American city-state over taxes. Jean-Jacques hadn't spent much time there growing up, but he had made a few of its famous karaoke nights. At one, he'd received the first blow job of his life in the bathroom from an angry Cuban wife who'd caught her husband cheating. At another, he'd given the only blow job of his life to an investment banker for three hundred dollars.

The money had gone to the hospital during his mother's initial chemo treatments. He'd told her he'd earned the money carrying groceries for white people.

Jean-Jacques didn't tell any of that to Pete, instead choosing to wait and see how long it took the other man to realize where they were. The lounge, a quarter-full and languid on a late Sunday night, smelled of air freshener and old leather. Black-and-white photographs of poets and dancers from the Harlem Renaissance and curtains of red satin hung from the walls. Soft funk played through unseen speakers. Jean-Jacques and Pete found a booth in the corner and a middle-aged waitress with pink dreadlocks and eyelash extensions asked what their poison was.

"Two beers and two well whiskeys," Pete said.

"I don't want whiskey," Jean-Jacques said. "Just a beer."

"Wasn't ordering for you. Super liver." Pete turned to grin at the waitress but she was already headed toward the bar for their drinks.

"You know," Pete continued, "I expected a bit more—well, not acknowledgment, exactly. But notice?"

"Cali's cued to celebrity," Jean-Jacques said. They'd spent a lot of late nights at Hollywood clubs basking in that recognition. "It's different here." He paused until the waitress dropped off the beers and shots and left. "Even for us."

Pete laughed, then downed his first whiskey like it was tap water. Jean-Jacques's stomach ached just watching it. "Maybe that'll change when the movie comes out."

Jean-Jacques sipped from the neck of his beer and narrowed his eyes. "Why'd you come here, man?" he asked. "I told you. I was handling family."

"Got antsy. All the bohos were watching some peacemonger fantasy about Vietnam and a dead Kennedy." Indoors, it was his black eye that emerged, smoldering like hot coal. The cythrax had left Pete with the most extreme case of heterochromia any doctor had ever seen. Not that he minded. It was always the second thing strangers commented on, after his height. Young women, in particular.

Pete continued. "Gypsy Town's got some perks, but it's not authentic. It's not the real city." He shrugged. "Also, got some intel for you."

Jean-Jacques rubbed at his bald head. They'd survived the same experimental bomb, but instead of irises that exuded primal sex magic, he'd been left naked as an earthworm. No eyebrows, no nothing. He ignored the question coming up from his chest about "the real city" and instead took the bait he was supposed to, from the squad leader he'd followed into battle too many times to remember. "Intel?"

Pete leaned his long frame forward and pushed his elbows out, slipping into his command voice, terse and jumpy. It was a flaw, a goofy one. Jean-Jacques appreciated it. Kept Justice as one of them. He'd spoken with a War Department contact. Jean-Jacques's request for a platoon in the International Legion would be denied. They wanted to keep the Volunteers united. At least for another tour. It would be important to the war effort, them fighting terror together when the movie was released. For recruitment, in particular. Which had been flagging.

"I'm sorry, dude. Know you wanted it. Don't think it's dead for good. Just for now."

Jean-Jacques didn't react. Anger would come later. He hadn't wanted to participate in the movie. He'd done it to make going back to the Legion possible, to make becoming a Legion platoon commander possible. This wasn't the first time the camo machine had lied to him, though. He'd deal.

"Can't say I'm surprised," was all he said.

Pete had other news, as well. Once their leave in Empire City ended, they weren't bound for the Mediterranean. They'd be joining a spec ops team in Sudan. The war had spread there, like a virus. Rumor had it Chinese commandos were in the region. China was making a play all over Africa. A brave new world awaited the Volunteers. A brave new front, too.

"Agency folks think it was them who zapped that consul's pacemaker," Pete said, knocking back his second whiskey. "Vacation's almost over. Duty, my dude. She beckons."

"Sergeant Swenson." Jean-Jacques sighed, hoping the official rank might help break Pete from his plotting. "We got months until all that. Leave. Then train up. Then we get our assignment. A million things will change between now and then."

Jean-Jacques held deep misgivings about the Volunteers' combat readiness. It was part of the reason he'd tried to rejoin the Legion. Hollywood had made them soft. America had made them soft. More than anything, their powers had made them soft.

"I'm connected, son!" Pete's voice cracked with excitement. "Intel community knows where we're going before the generals do."

Jean-Jacques rolled his eyes, but thought of Tripoli again, and those specific smells of death. Their few missions after the Abu Abdallah raid had been fiascos. What could the Volunteers do that the rest of special ops couldn't? Armored vehicles carried more than Pete could. The web of intel networks could be way more places at once than Flowers. Stealth drones moved about as quickly as he did, with way more vantage. The Volunteers? They were more than soldiers, sure. Just not the way the others believed.

But they'd had that argument already.

He'd barely made a dent in his beer. Pete reached for his second and looked around, as if only now taking in the environment. "Gay bar," he said. "And Flowers says you don't have a sense of humor."

"Hah." Jean-Jacques took a long drink. It slid into his bloodstream and he felt his shoulders slump, then the rest of his body ease. Pete always wore him down, one way or another. Usually he lasted longer than half a beer but he was tired. He was also missing the clarity of life lived through night-vision green.

Pete looked across at him with dark expectations.

"All right," Jean-Jacques said. "Tell me about this new enemy."

FOR IMMEDIATE RELEASE
Release No: NR-043-24

TOP-SECRET MILITARY PROGRAM YIELDS SUPER RESULTS

The War Department announced today a team of super-soldiers, melding the elite training of special operators with revolutionary technology. The Hero Project was developed by the U.S. government under the supervision of the Council of Victors. Three U.S. Army Rangers—Sergeant Peter Swenson, 25, Corporal Grady Flowers, 21, and Corporal Jean-Jacques Saint-Preux, 23—volunteered for the breakthrough program. They now possess the abilities of super-strength, teleportation, and super-speed, respectively, and will be deploying to the Mediterranean to conduct combat operations. One of their focuses will be the ongoing manhunt for Abu Abdallah, the terror chieftain and architect of the Palm Sunday attacks on Federal City.

"It's our great honor to serve America as warfighters," Sergeant Swenson said. "Continuing to do so in our new capacities is a challenge we look forward to. The three of us would like to thank all involved, from the War Department to the Council of Victors to NASA. Onwards, to victory."

While details remain top-secret, the Hero Project utilized cythrax, a strange, malleable element discovered in rocks found in outer space by NASA. The team of super-soldiers will be known as the Volunteers, a name they chose as tribute to the fighting spirit of the all-volunteer American military. They will fall under the purview of Special Operations Command. According to a Council of Victors spokesman, there are no current plans to conduct another program.

CHAPTER 4

AFTER A LATE breakfast of coffee and a cold taco, Sebastian walked down the street to the basketball courts. There was an inherent fluidity to the game he'd always been drawn to, finding solace and escape in it since childhood. Though no longer in any decent physical shape, he had maintained a silky, suburban jump shot, and sometimes worked into games as a substitute. A citywide tournament was under way, though, so after watching the second half of a game between two Asian Harlem teams, he returned home.

In front of his building, a man in rags sorted through the trash, collecting bottles. Sebastian thought he resembled the man from the subway tunnel but that wasn't possible. What is it called when you think all homeless people look alike? Sebastian asked himself. Homeless-ist? He didn't know.

"Change?" the man asked Sebastian.

"I can make you a sandwich," Sebastian said.

"From the ashes, holy redemption," the man in rags said, pointing to the bottles. Sebastian figured that a no and walked up to his apartment.

He made himself a sandwich and turned on the television. *The Great Tet Raid* was on again. He'd loved the movie as a kid and so had all his friends. What American boy hadn't wanted to grow up to be the young marine captain stranded behind enemy lines, destined to save the war and someday become president? Sebastian watched until General Giap refused to flee the coming air strike, choosing instead to die in place with his men.

"I don't know what god you worship," Sebastian said along with George Clooney's square-jawed marine captain. "But He's about to get a hell of a fighting man."

That marine captain was Chuck Robb, of course. Champion of the Third Way. His lone White House term had proven a rocky one, the old radicals on the left and the young hawks on the right revolting against Robb's tenuous centrist platform. LBJ's heroic son-in-law met the same political fate as the old man. Like many moderates of her generation, Sebastian's mom pointed to the Palm Sunday attacks for the collapse of the two-party system, for the apparent end to American bipartisanship. It hadn't always been like this, she said. Sebastian wasn't sure. He wondered if the attacks had just hastened the inevitable.

Sebastian turned off the television and went to his computer. Four emails awaited. One was spam, a chain letter imploring a return to the gold standard. He deleted that one. The second, a note from his dad. He replied to that one. The third, a newsletter from a local protest group he'd made the mistake of giving his contact info to. He supported reform in the rehabilitation colonies as much as the next liberal arts major, but these people wanted to abolish them, outright. Where would veterans with troubles go? They never answered that. The fourth email was from Britt Swenson.

> Hi. Got your email from Mia. Wanted to invite you
> to the Temple tonight, some great bands. Link below
> with directions. My brother will be there, too. And did I
> mention two free drink tickets???
>
> later,
> Britt

Sebastian had lived in Empire City for three years, but could count on one hand the number of times he'd trekked to Gypsy Town. From his perspective, that district appealed to, and consisted of, three types of people: bohemian grime in black jeans, yuppies who played at the same on weekends, and natives too poor or stubborn to leave for the far townships. Being none of the above, he saw no reason to leave the center of might for an outpost in the fringe.

Artists lived in that fringe, though, good ones and bad ones, real ones and posers. He'd wanted to be a writer once, and sometimes wanted to be one again. But living among a tribe charmed Sebastian much more in theory than it did in practice. He had a bourgeois heart deep down, he knew.

An old habit seized Sebastian, and he typed *Pete Swenson* into the web search of his computer. He'd already read the top results. *America's First Real-Life Superhero*, declared one headline. *Leader of the Volunteers Opens Up*, went another. Sebastian remembered that one, a long profile about how a son of privilege had lost his father in a sarin attack and turned himself into a rugged warrior. *Justice Saves Ten in Benghazi!* exclaimed yet another. Sebastian snorted. Justice. What a stupid code name. Some War Department clerk probably had gotten a bonus for it.

Magazine articles and PR dispatches tumbled through his computer screen with alacrity. He'd read them all. Stories of the brave Justice, the bold Sniper, steadfast Dash, serving and saving, salvaging and sacrificing. They were the best of us, but also better than any of us. Heroes for the people, but not of them. They were super. And because they were super, they were beyond.

He clicked an entry titled "Top-Secret Military Program Yields Super Results." It was the press release from two years prior that had revealed the Volunteers to the world.

The propagandist in Sebastian couldn't help but admire the falseness of it all. No mention of Tripoli. No mention of the Rangers who died in Tripoli. No mention of Mia. No mention of him.

Making it seem like the government knew how to control cythrax. Making any of it seem controlled. Even the name "Volunteers" rang hollow. Who in their right mind would choose to become a science experiment?

Sebastian's phone buzzed, shaking him from his speculations. "Come downstairs," read the text, from a number he didn't recognize. Then a second text: "ASAP."

Fucking Dorsett, he thought. So paranoid. Still, after waiting a couple of minutes to protest the ASAP, Sebastian went downstairs.

The door of the first-floor apartment was cracked open. Sebastian knocked once and walked in. "Yo, yo," he said, smelling sausage and peppers. "Long time no see."

Special Agent Theo Dorsett III stood in his kitchen holding a rubber spatula like it was a torch. He wore a pair of dad jeans and a wrinkled polo stretching to fit his broad, compact shoulders. His skin was deep black, and his back was to the door. From there Sebastian could tell the food was winning. Even Dorsett's posture looked like a question mark.

"I'm impressed." Sebastian took a seat at the kitchen table. He spotted an open cooking manual propped up against the stove. "Smells good in here."

"That it does, that it does. Hungry?" Dorsett's voice carried a breeze of Carolina coast in it, something he could turn off as needed. Sebastian figured the Bureau had weather ladies who taught agents how to do that, but the one time he'd mentioned his theory, Dorsett had just laughed at him.

"I'm good." Sebastian wasn't sure what to make of Dorsett cooking for himself, other than it being a sign that his wife wasn't soon returning. "Already ate. Thanks, though."

"Do you, hoss." Dorsett shoveled the sausage and peppers from the pan onto a plate and took a seat. Sebastian got up from the table and turned off the stove's burner. Dorsett just shrugged, rubbed at his fade, and began eating. Sebastian sat back down.

"So." Sebastian didn't know where to begin. He hadn't seen or spoken to his handler for three weeks. "How's my favorite special agent?"

"Cut the shit," Dorsett said between bites of food. Sebastian thought he was chewing longer than necessary, possibly because he hadn't seasoned the meal with anything but cooking oil, but kept that to himself. "You went invisible last night. People see that, man. They call the police. Come on. You know better."

"Oh. Damn. I'm sorry." Sebastian rubbed at his neck. Dorsett stared at him with hard, dark eyes until he continued. "Too much drink, that's all."

Dorsett kept staring at him. "Shouldn't you be at work?" Sebastian asked.

"Jesus, man. It's Sunday. You miss church?" Whatever authority Dorsett had lost at the stove had been regained. He struck Sebastian as the type of man rarely at ease. Something about the way his eyes were always studying the edges of a room. "Pull it together. You ain't gonna have me around forever."

Sebastian wasn't sure he agreed with that—the handlers had an "indefinite" assignment, as far as he knew—but he didn't feel like talking about the future, so he didn't. The best way to prove to the Bureau that he no longer needed a handler was not using his power. And he'd just reset that clock to zero.

Dorsett grunted and shook his head. "My fault for not being around." Then, after another bite of food, "Should be available more going forward."

"Cool," Sebastian said while thinking otherwise, because of what "available" probably meant. The Dorsetts had uncoupled, recoupled, and then re-uncoupled over the past eight months. Dorsett only talked about it at the bar; the few times Sebastian had mentioned Anita in the bright of day had yielded only long, seizuring pauses. In the neon of night, over beers, they could be friends. Sebastian didn't have many of those anymore. Anywhere else, at any other time, he and Dorsett were something else.

Sebastian watched Dorsett finish his meal in silence. He almost brought up the Volunteers twice, but held his tongue. Of course Dorsett knows about them being here, he thought. Even a truant special agent would be aware.

Dorsett rose to put his dish in the sink and did something with his eyebrows that made Sebastian think they were done. Sebastian had his hand on the door handle when Dorsett asked, "Bar tonight? There's a Knights game on TV."

Sebastian prided himself on never lying, or trying not to, at least, so like a lot of people like that, he was adept at the art of omission. So he just said, "Can't, got a thing."

"Another night, then," Dorsett said.

"Yeah," he said. "Another night."

———

As dusk spilled through his window blinds, Sebastian rummaged through his bedroom for an old tin box. He could've sworn he'd last seen it on his dresser, next to a stack of *The Volunteers* comics. Sebastian found the writing in the issues middling—what else to expect from the War Department–funded military-publishing complex?—but the art was dazzling. In fact, on his to-do list, he'd added "Apply for Comic Book Job" some months ago. There it remained, preserved and intact from any threat of a strikethrough.

Sebastian found the tin box behind the hamper, in a pair of jeans that didn't pass the smell test. It had the red dragon of Wales on it, a souvenir from a family trip. He opened it and transferred a few blue Valiums to his pocket, just in case. He didn't think they'd expired yet. Then Sebastian slipped on a plain green tee and a pair of skateboarding shoes he thought weren't too out of trend and left for Gypsy Town. He was feeling a bit like a crusader, socially dogged and culturally ignorant.

How different can it be? he asked himself. It's still Empire City. Sort of.

At the station, Sebastian approached a fare card machine. He missed being able to buy subway tokens from bored transit employees, but times had changed. The machine answered him in Japanese. He'd pressed the wrong button. The machine kept answering in Japanese. Through trial and error, he eventually replenished his card. The line for the body scanners was longer than he'd have preferred, but he only waited for ten minutes. No tourists to foul things up, Sebastian thought. Praise the Trinity.

The subway car was crowded and smelled of human stink and Sebastian kept his back against the door but kept getting in the way of people getting on and off and it annoyed them, and him, too. He felt his senses flaring up again, so he concentrated on breathing and focused, as much as he could, on being normal. This is democracy in motion, he told himself. Savor it. He thought of the subway bombing from the year before that'd killed eleven people and would've killed more if not for the off-duty cop, but that wasn't helping anything so he stopped. His ears popped as the subway passed under the river and a girl with bug eyes and popsicle lips bumped into him and looked up at him like it wasn't her fault, even though she'd been the one moving. Sebastian gripped his sunglasses and aimed them at the girl, making a hushed laser-beam sound. The bug eyes got buggier and the girl smiled wide. Despite himself, Sebastian smiled, too.

He got off at the fourth stop in Gypsy Town; deep enough into the district, but not that deep. The station seemed grungy to his eyes, and not in a quaint way. The walls were cracking, the concrete platforms dirty, the bums more deadbeat Beat than artful dodger. The scent of sour piss filled his nostrils and he thought whomever it belonged to needed to drink more water. The subway clattered down the tunnel like a horse on the trail, pushing farther into the city's outlands. Sebastian stood alone on the platform and fingered the pills in his pocket, considering turning back. Dorsett only drank at a couple of places. He'd be easy enough to track down.

Sebastian was nervous, and embarrassed because of it. You drove into a fucking war zone in a fucking Audi, he reminded himself. You're no pussy. He found stairs and climbed them.

Stoplights and muddy stars exposed a more volatile sort of energy than across the river, as if the streets themselves had drank too much caffeine. Bars and delis and sidewalk vendors snapped with aggressive gladness. People yelled and people moved, but with an aimlessness Sebastian couldn't reason with. He hurried past them, knowing no other way to walk. He found himself not swallowed up in a sea of fringed vests and black jeans and wallet chains, as expected, but just part of another noisy crowd, as common and loud as any other. He walked half a block, then turned around after realizing he'd been going the wrong way.

"Me Want Wonder." He passed over a philosophizing Cookie Monster stenciled into the sidewalk. "Om nom nom nom."

In front of a grocery store, a young man around high school age was trying to hand out pamphlets. People parted around him like shadows under a flashlight. He wore the uniform of a suburban prep—lightweight collared shirt with rolled-up sleeves and madras-pattern shorts—and a powder-blue baseball cap.

An ultra, Sebastian thought. They're even here now!

"Hello, sir. Have you helped the homeland today?" the high schooler said to Sebastian, holding out a pamphlet. The cap carried the standard ultra slogan FREEDOM BEAST, though there were variations.

"Last name is Rios." Sebastian drew out the last syllable and pushed past the young ultra and his pamphlet, reminding himself that even a quick punch to the gut would qualify as assaulting a minor. "You wouldn't want me."

Sebastian then blew a kiss to the kid, who recoiled. He knew he should be above messing with a teenager. And yet.

The ultras had made a lot of noise about cleaving its white supremacist wing over the past few years, but Sebastian figured that didn't matter to the disciples with the pamphlets. He knew it didn't matter to him. Whatever they were claiming to be at the moment—a service organization, a political action committee, just a good ol' fashioned group of nationalist expression—Sebastian doubted it would ever appeal to him. "Freedom Beast." That meant supporting the state no matter what (for its rule-of-law members) but also defying the state as often as possible (for its libertarian members). It was all rather mystifying.

Their loudest position centered on a return to military conscription and eliminating the International Legion. They believed that would result in two things: less foreign intervention and stricter immigration. Sebastian agreed vaguely with the first, though it was hard for him to imagine that world. Only the oldest of the old radicals talked of an America like that. He found the second racist, and not in any playful, ironic way. Say what you would about the Legion's methods, but it granted citizenship to its fighters. That was important, Sebastian thought. Kept fresh the American dream.

A block from the grocery store, Sebastian checked the map on his phone to make sure he didn't get lost again, and turned left at the next cross street. It led him to an isolated building surrounded by empty cement lots. A flickering streetlight at the corner revealed a four-story structure made of brick and sandstone trim. A pointed roof shot from the top in a rush, matched by a chimney on the side. Broken stained-glass windows covered much of the front, parallel to a slab of gray stone with the year "1876" carved into it. A decaying wood sign hung underneath the windows, bearing words written in Hebrew or Yiddish or something. Sebastian wasn't sure.

"A real temple," he said to himself. "Funny."

Dance music rumbled from somewhere beneath the building. Sebastian walked around to the far side of the temple and spotted a staircase. Following the noise of the music and lights intermittently flashing blue and yellow, he came to an open steel door. A thin woman with a long neck and scarf met him there, handing over two drink tickets without a word or eye contact.

The basement was dim, the air in it dank. Sebastian waded into the throng, some of whom were indeed wearing fringed vests and black jeans and wallet chains. It was standing room only, fifty or so people jammed into darkness under dueling strobe lights. Onstage, a lanky bearded man wrapped in a camo poncho read slam poetry, his words attempting to match the beat and rhythm of the music. Sebastian found a pillar in the back to lean against.

"Splish splash, a fascist was taking a bath," the man whispered into the microphone. "All alone on a knock knocking night." Then he began chanting. "Who's there? Life! Liberty! The pursuit of diggity! Like life without the F. Or country without the cunt." His voice lowered in timbre and pace. "The fever dream . . . indulges. The gobblers . . . wargasm and . . . the . . . chickenhawks . . . crow. So . . . we . . . they . . . I . . . fought. The rest is. Is? Is!" Now he raised his voice. "Who will survive America? Another man's morning, another son's gun!" And, again, a whisper. "My supper is maroon. My star is spoon. Forever fleeting, looms."

Sebastian was beside himself. If a sense of shame didn't keep a person from free association like this, some sort of social contract needed to. The man dropped the microphone and walked offstage, out of view. A voice in the crowd yelled "Golf clap!" and a small round of polite applause followed.

Need beer, Sebastian thought. He headed to the bar in the near corner while the thin woman from the entrance walked onstage and picked up the microphone.

"Wasn't that something," she said, somehow smiling without moving her lips. "Awesome, Pablo Joe, as always." Her long neck craned down as she unfolded a sheet of paper. "Time for the next question in *Utopia* trivia. First correct response I hear gets another drink ticket. So: in episode four, on the campaign trail in Pennsylvania, Bobby confronts McNamara and—"

The crowd booed at McNamara's name.

The woman smiled again without moving her lips. "Bobby confronts McNamara and says, 'Some men see things as they are and ask why.' What does he say next?"

"I dream of things that never were, and ask why not!" Sebastian adored that line, and knew it by heart, but couldn't bring himself to shout it. Someone else did. The crowd cheered and the woman with the mic handed down the prize.

"Now, something else. A band setting the world on fire. Scene-darella calls them 'indie's next great hope.' *The Colonel Mustard Times* wrote just last week that the single 'The Emperor Has No Fashion Sense' 'resonates with burning detachment.' And *Pitchfork—Pitchfork!*—named them a Gypsy Town must-see. Please give a warm welcome to the one and only . . . Derivative."

A faint brunette walked onto the stage, followed by a tall white guy with slick-backed hair wearing a leather jacket and a tiny white guy with slick-backed hair in a tan turtleneck. The brunette wore a maroon romper and black tights and had bathed her face in a powdery makeup. The tall man in the leather jacket took his place behind the drums while his turtlenecked comrade began tuning a guitar. The woman looked over at him, and he nodded. She burped into the microphone.

"That's a burp," she said, voice blank as a state radio host. Then the guitarist started in with a long, lurid riff. The amps snarled to life and the dance floor began moving like an octopus, arms flailing one way then the other, without discernable progress in any direction. A ripple in the crowd pushed Sebastian forward. He caught himself on the shoulders of the person in front of him. He felt the body go rigid.

"Sorry," he said over the music. "Crazy in here."

A short, freckly man with ginger wisps turned around and sized up Sebastian. He wore tight jeans and an even tighter black shirt that showed off a well-maintained physique: full delts, ball-like biceps, thick triceps, and abs flat as a coffin. Show-me muscles, Sebastian thought. Superb ones. A large wooden cross dangled in front of the man's chest, held there by a leather string that wrapped around his neck.

Sebastian studied the black shirt for signs of beer spillage, and, finding none, sighed in relief. The freckly man tilted his head and grinned, revealing a pair of dimples and blocky, gapped teeth. The hostage," he said, reaching up to grip Sebastian by the shoulder. "Been a minute since Germany."

"Oh, shit." Recognition smacked Sebastian late. "Grady Flowers. Good, uh, to see you."

Grady Flowers, better known as the Sniper. Proud American, proud member of the Volunteers, fond of boating, duck hunting, and appearing shirtless on the cover of *Bourbon & Bullet*. "The extroverted yin to Pete Swenson's reticent yang," one of the profiles declared. "Grady Flowers was a high school baseball star in Oak Ridge, Tennessee, who heeded the warfighter's call.

"Every American war since the revolution has included a Flowers man in it, to include a Medal of Honor recipient who fought in the trenches of World War I. According to Grady, 'I wasn't about to end that.' He enlisted in the fabled 75th Ranger Regiment, deploying multiple times to combat zones across the globe. 'Did what we had to do to accomplish the mission,' Flowers says when asked about his tours, before citing Deuteronomy as a book that inspires him. Flowers joined the then top-secret Hero Project, which would meld his elite training as a soldier with breakthrough technology developed by the U.S. government under the supervision of the Council of Victors . . ."

"No offense, man," Sebastian continued in the basement of the Temple. "But you're pretty much the last person I thought would be here."

Flowers laughed and ordered two cans of beer. The bartender handed them over and took his cash with zero affect. Sebastian raised his hand as a show of thanks. Flowers fist-bumped Sebastian's open palm instead.

"No one here knows who I am," Flowers said, pointing out at the crowd. His accent summoned of mist and forest. "It's weird."

Sebastian nodded. He didn't know what to say. Flowers probably hadn't been anonymous for a very long time. And if he'd ever before had a conversation with Grady Flowers, he didn't remember it. All of Germany seemed a blur. He wanted to ask about everything that had happened since, but where to begin? Hey, Flowers, what's it like being the most feared killer on the planet? What's it like being able to teleport? Sebastian was a fanboy but didn't want to come across like that. They were bonded because of the cythrax bomb, and would be forever, but he knew Flowers through the stories and press. Flowers knew him as "the hostage." That was it.

He thought of something to say.

"Britt Swenson?" he asked. "She invited me."

Flowers's face twisted, confused. Then he pointed to the stage. "Right behind you, hostage."

Sebastian turned around.

"I don't love you like I love me," the singer rasped, moving across the stage in a pair of banana-yellow Converses, "and that's all, all your fault." Sebastian realized now the glut of white powder on her face was intentional; she was going for a geisha look, complete with bright red lipstick and bunned hair. She stared out above the crowd, indifferent and faraway, or at least trying to convey that. Her voice lacked the range of a pure vocalist, but its jaggedness worked, given the half-sung, half-spoken lyrics. The rest of the time it was concealed by the guitarist, who was keeping his head down like he'd stepped into a puddle. The drummer smiled open-mouthed, a knit cap cocked back so it folded over itself.

"Whoa," Sebastian said. "Didn't realize that was—she's killing it."

"Yessir," Flowers said. "Lady like that—I'd settle down, go straight and narrow. Even deal with Pete's nonsense, since we'd be family." He paused. "Too bad she's got a fag thing."

It was Sebastian's turn to make a face, first because of the word Flowers had used, then because he didn't know what he'd meant. How to tell a Ranger, a Volunteer, that language was malleable and culturally delicate and they weren't in the Barbary Coast? Sebastian didn't know. So he asked Flowers to explain.

"Those two." Flowers pointed to the guitarist and drummer. "They're gay. Like, with each other." Then he pointed to Britt.

"Also her boyfriends. Like, with each other." He shook his head and sipped from his beer. "Would never fly in Tennessee."

Sebastian held a puritanical streak, he knew, something he'd inherited from his mom and she from her mom before her. But part of moving to Empire City as a young person meant shedding the mores of the provinces, or at least pretending to. Live and let live and the like. So he just shrugged and said, "Everyone's a little gay, right?"

Flowers blinked and blinked and eventually laughed. "You're crazy, hostage."

The two men may have been strangers, but they were strangers together. So they watched the set together, too, filling strained pauses with jokes about bohemians and vague allusions to their shared stay at the hospital. Flowers said he didn't remember much from it, either. They got another round of beers, then another. Flowers asked if Sebastian would do a Truck Bomb shot with him. Sebastian winced and told him they didn't call it that here. Flowers apologized, he'd forgotten he wasn't in the South, and ordered two Kill Shots like a proper citizen. The shot roiled Sebastian's stomach, but he managed to keep it down. Sebastian tried not to look at Britt much, even though he knew she couldn't see into the crowd because of stage lights. They were pretty good, Sebastian thought, though Derivative's style and songs were a bit, well, unoriginal. He asked about Pete Swenson. Flowers said he was supposed to be there, had been the one who told him to come, but the oversize bastard was nowhere to be seen.

"Typical Pete shit," Flowers said, his voice flexing hard to sound amused. "Do as he says, not as he does."

Time passed. Derivative kept playing. Flowers left for the bathroom and didn't come back. Sebastian got another beer. Someone bumped into him, and he felt a trickle of cold liquid on his back. He counted to twelve very slowly in his head then found another pillar to lean against. Some more time passed. Derivative kept playing.

Sebastian yawned and his right leg began twitching. He took off his sunglasses and chewed on one of the ends. Then he popped a blue Valium from his pocket and wiped beads of sweat from his forehead. It's all good, he thought. All good. Something about the noise, and the sweat, and the flashing lights, and the talking with Flowers, made him think of the night he'd been rescued. The short guy with the asterisk scar had gone home, so the other militants had unbound him and let him join the dominoes game. The one with the crooked smile and construction-worker hands knew bits of English and was asking why America could put a man on the moon but not bring electricity to the lands it invaded. It was a fine question and Sebastian hadn't known the answer. Then the helicopters came on like a tempest, and the whole building began shaking. They'd bound and blindfolded him again and hid him in a pile of loose blankets and boxes and told him not to even think about making a sound and they all grabbed their AKs and ran upstairs and gunshots rang out in mad, dizzy minutes and then there was a pause like a long echo and he smelled ice of all things so he'd sat up and pushed off the blindfold against a box corner just in time to see the whole world turn to the brightest, darkest star and—

"Hey! Hostage!"

Sebastian shot back to the now.

"Sleeping standing up. I'm impressed."

"Naw," Sebastian said to Flowers, checking his chin for drool, then readjusting his sunglasses. "Praying to the boho gods."

Britt, her face wiped clean of geisha makeup, stood next to Flowers with her head tilted. The omega symbol on her arm glinted like an X on a treasure map.

"They wouldn't listen to you." Britt frowned and looked at his feet. "Nice shoes."

Sebastian shook out his legs to make sure they hadn't fallen asleep, too. "That was really good," he said. "Thanks for inviting me."

Britt brought her hands together into prayer and bowed her head.

"See Pete yet?" she asked.

"Couldn't make it," Flowers said, cutting in. "Gonna meet up with us at the lofts."

Britt didn't respond, just turned and walked toward her boyfriends, who were waiting at a rear exit. Flowers clutched at his heart, winked at Sebastian, then trailed her steps. Sebastian stayed at his pillar until Britt called over her shoulder, "Come hang with us, Sebastian Rios."

As he moved into the midsummer night, following Flowers who followed Britt who followed her boyfriends, Sebastian caught a whiff of something different, something he'd never smelled in Empire City. Rain was coming, but that wasn't it. Wood smoke, he decided. Like new beginnings. He kept that to himself, though, not wanting to sound eager. He jogged to catch up with the group.

CHAPTER 5

MIA WOKE BEFORE the alarm. She usually did on weekdays. She was a person of routine and that's what routine did. Sleep whispered like a lullaby through the black morning but she pushed it away, sitting up in bed to put her mind in order. If she'd been dreaming, she'd already forgotten what about.

Monday, she thought. Cardio.

A storm had rolled through the city late in the night, leaving the brittle musk of rain. A coldness nipped at the top of Mia's shoulder. How do they keep getting in here? she wondered, rubbing at the mosquito bite. I shut the screen last night.

Jesse hadn't come home. He'd sent a few texts, first saying he wasn't sure when he'd be leaving work, then saying he wouldn't be. All-nighters during Bureau emergencies weren't unprecedented. Mia knew the deal. All part of marrying a special agent. Even if waking up by herself in darkness brought on a loneliness she didn't trust.

Mia ate a yogurt, then changed into light workout gear and fitted her running leg and sneakers. Downstairs, the summer air smelled of metal and moss. Dim streetlights lined the corners like sentries and the sidewalks had almost dried. A garbage truck on an adjacent block groaned through the still while monitor drones pulsed red in the sky. She stretched her left leg and then her core

71

in front of her building, looking up to watch the flag whip around atop the Global Trade. Sixty stars and thirteen stripes, pale against the dark. All those rings and stars in the blue canton struck her as cluttered, still.

Mia finished stretching and tapped at her right knee. Her running prosthetic was hard and coiled, like a spring. She appreciated the city most during these early morning runs, because it was empty enough to seem welcoming, even hopeful. It reminded her of the city from her childhood. It reminded her of the America she'd grown up in.

Daybreak always ended the spell.

Cut the crap, Mia thought. These ten miles aren't going to run themselves. Then she took a deep breath, set the digital green of her wristwatch to 00:00, hit start, and began, the joints of her leg cracking with the motion while the socket of her prosthetic did the same. She headed west, toward the harbor.

Mia had run most of her life, discovering as a girl that she was good at it and being good meant respect, and trophies, and approval. It made an object of her body, but it was a functional object, something that mattered to her even before she'd figured out why. She'd pushed herself to be very good at points in her life, competing in college for two seasons before it interfered with ROTC, and later running the city marathon her first year with the prosthetic to prove that she could. But she'd never crossed into greatness, and for that she'd come to be thankful. Mia lacked the masochism of true runners, the renegade fanatical gene to ignore and ignore all the warning blinkers thousands of years of evolution had instilled in the human brain. Bloody calluses and angry muscles were one thing. Tendons ripping from bone were another.

The baby, or not-baby, entered Mia's mind. She focused on her breathing. Then came General Collins's job offer. She focused on her breathing.

The first scratches of sun were tracing the water. Lady Liberty rose in the distance, droopy torch in her right hand. The whole

statue needed repair, though how, and when, had become a political hot potato. Decades' worth of money allotted for national
monuments had gone to the Council of Victors, toward honoring
the triumph of Vietnam. No one wanted to be the congressperson
who redirected funds from that.

A lot of citizens had come to loathe the statue, considering it an
eyesore. Mia's father thought it a sentimental leftover. She sort of
liked it, the way a person enjoys a musty childhood blanket found
in storage. She remembered climbing to the torch on a field trip as
a girl, through a staircase of graffiti and rickety metal, seeing the
city from an entirely new angle. A snapshot of old American might,
sealed in memory.

They'd closed the torch after the Palm Sunday attacks, then the
entire island. Students like her adolescent cousins wouldn't ever
see Empire City as she had. No one could now. The sad, corroding
statue was their normal. It was all they knew. In the meantime,
Lady Liberty sank slowly into the island it rested on. Turned out
it'd been set on sodden ground.

Mia adjusted her sports bra and glanced at her watch. A mile
in, which meant her warm-up was over. She lengthened out her
strides.

She turned north along a waterfront path, moving into the bike
lane to dodge fallen tree branches and loose rocks. Other than the
occasional taxi striking through the predawn and a man in rags
watching the city from a bench, she was alone. The wharf across
the river jutted out like a broken jawbone, suggesting a past when
its docks did more than shuttle around office workers and tourists.

The city changed like a photo album, slowly and slowly and
then all in a rush. Repair shops became delis. Parking garages
became art studios. In the water a flotilla of coast guard barges
that'd been restored as restaurants and pubs drifted to and fro.
Steel and glass high-rises gave way to the architecture of the last
century, rowhouses and squatty brick apartments. The streets
narrowed, a few dotted by tidy cobblestone. The waterfront path

leveled off, though Mia kept her strides long. She knew an incline awaited. She wanted to meet it in force.

Sunrise arrived somewhere between miles three and four, stained-glass clouds chipping the sky. Mia passed a vomiting young man in a sport jacket too large for him. Probably an intern for one of the banks, she thought, before turning around to make sure it wasn't one of hers.

"Call in sick!" she shouted. He raised his fist and managed a weak "Defy!" before purging again. The motto of the old radicals' caucus in Congress. Funny, Mia thought.

Another mile on, Mia ran into a short concrete tunnel. The tunnel lay underneath an abandoned railway line. Sunlight filled it with a fierce yellow shine. Around ten feet long, the sides and top of it had been covered in graffiti, dozens and dozens of circles of different colors and sizes. Just about every inch of available concrete had been tagged, leaving a sort of rainbow mosaic. Each of the circles contained three arrows pointing down and to the left. The job was fresh—Mia could tell by the tint to the spray paint. She came to a stop in the center of the tunnel, her breaths sharp but controlled. She rubbed a hand against a small purple circle. It smeared across her palm.

I know what this is, Mia thought, looking at her palm, then at the purple circle, sifting through her mind to place where. It took a few seconds, but she remembered a course in modern European history at Dupont, and this shape and question from the final exam.

The antifascist sign, she thought. From Nazi Germany.

A gust swept through the tunnel, and Mia smelled storm from the night before. She fought off the urge to shiver. It was going to be a cold summer day.

———

Most mornings Mia turned around and headed home on the same pathway, but the tunnel had spooked her. She pushed east and then south instead, running the sidewalks. The light and the city rose slow, together. A medley of urban noise was beginning to tune and it sounded mostly like construction din. There was order within the mayhem; one just needed to know the refrains. Mia did. She made it back to her apartment building on time, stopping only to remove her running leg before showering and dressing for work. She was back out her front door sixteen minutes later.

The air had turned and smelled of humid dew. Mia decided to walk through Vietnam Victory Square. Under the gaze of the Four Legionnaires sculpture, a couple of kids had waded into the fountain, laughing while splashing water at each other. Across from them, a tour group stood in front of the grand white marble wall with the simple words: "Praise to the Victors/In Honor of the Brave Men who went forth to Vietnam/1955–1981." The guide was explaining why the inscription stopped there, despite the insurgency continuing after in parts of the north. He was stumbling through the history and Mia wanted to intervene. Because wars have to end, she thought. Just tell them that.

Coffee-charged angst and white-collar id crackled along the streets, bankers and lawyers and digital communications associates hustling to be at their desks before the workday siren sounded. As she turned onto Wall Street, Mia passed the brownstone Trinity Church she attended every month or so. She'd considered herself an atheist since her tour to Albania, but she still appreciated the ceremony of church and the sense of renewal it allowed for. Her family had fled to America in 1620 for that ceremony and sense of renewal. She wouldn't give up that heritage for something as banal as not believing.

Then there was Jesse. "Jesus's heroin needle," he liked calling Trinity's Gothic steeple. The church's adjacent cemetery, where a slew of American founding fathers and Union generals from the Civil War rested? "A yard of goy bones."

And he's all mine, Mia thought. Trinity was an option for their wedding, though her family wanted it held in Connecticut. One more decision that she needed to make, and soon.

Mia's bank was located in the Westmoreland Plaza, a mass of skyscrapers bundled together at the end of the island. As she neared it, a vast, bright fire engine came into view, its lights twirling and flashing like a hallucination. A row of police barricades separated the vehicle from the street, uniformed officers turning away confused citizens trying to get to work. Mia joined the crowd.

"No one's allowed in the plaza today," a cop was saying, not for the first time. "And yes, that includes you." His eyes lingered on Mia's blouse, and she stared at him flatly until he looked away. Her grandmother had taught her how to do that on her fourteenth birthday. It worked in Empire City boardrooms just as well as it had in aircraft hangars along the far edges of the world.

"Ms. Tucker." A man shaped like a square wearing a rumpled dress shirt and overlong tie called to her from a corner of the barricades, close to a large bronze globe. It was the security director of her bank. He looked wired to Mia, even eager.

"Ms. Tucker," he repeated. "The office is closed today. Your father sent out a message to everyone—work from home, as you can."

"Hadn't checked my email yet." This didn't make any sense. The office, as far as Mia knew, had never closed. Finance didn't "work from home." That was for other people, other jobs. "What's going on?"

"I shouldn't say," he said, in a tone that suggested he very much wanted to.

"Mum's the word," Mia promised. "I'll be finding out, anyhow."

"A threat," the security director said, his voice low and hushed. "Whole plaza. Homeland marshals got it last night."

"Oh." There'd been a few lockdowns in Empire City over the years, for both real and false alarms, but Mia couldn't recall any of them shutting down a main cog of the Finance District. "Must be some kind of threat."

The security director looked out the corner of his eye to make sure no one else was listening, then pulled out his cell phone and read.

WITH FIRMNESS IN THE RIGHT AS GOD GIVES US TO SEE THE RIGHT, LET US STRIVE ON TO FINISH THE WORK WE ARE IN, TO BIND UP THE NATION'S WOUNDS, TO CARE FOR HIM WHO SHALL HAVE BORNE THE BATTLE.

MAYDAY, MAYDAY. FROM THE ASHES, HOLY REDEMPTION.

"Mean anything to you?"

Mia shook her head.

"The first part's from a speech Abraham Lincoln gave. Used to be the motto of the old Veterans Administration. The second part . . . I don't know. The distress signal or something."

Mia contemplated that. "There's a Council of Victors office down here. Some crazy's angry about the colonies again?" She tried not to laugh but couldn't help it. "It all needs to be taken seriously, of course. But shut down the plaza?"

The security director shrugged. "Federals think it means something. The Mayday thing, especially."

"I see," Mia said, wondering if this was the Bureau's emergency, and if so, why Jesse hadn't said anything to her. He worked intel analysis, not counterterrorism. Though he hadn't always been behind a desk.

Mia texted him a simple "?" as she walked home, feeling a little apprehensive and a lot aimless. She owed an IPO risk assessment to her department head by the end of the day, a transaction report to a client by the end of the week, and a regulatory review to her father by the end of the month. She'd traded in the stakes of investment banking for the tedium of compliance, a decision that had benefited her both personally and professionally. Still, she felt little remorse when she arrived home and turned on the television instead of sitting at the kitchen counter. The thing about compliance was that it was always there. It would wait. It always did.

The threat on Westmoreland Plaza had reached the news, sort of. It was being reported as a gas leak. "Empire Energy and Grid workers have identified the leak's source and shut it off," the news-caster assured the screen. "Repair is under way."

Typical media, Mia thought. Passing along spoon-fed lies instead of actual journalism.

In national news, the president had announced his run for another term at the Freedom Infinity island base in the Mediter-ranean. Surrounded by soldiers, expeditionary privateers, and le-gionnaires, he argued that the nation's war on terror took priority over the traditions of the republic. He cited FDR and World War II and Nixon and Vietnam. Mia wasn't sure about that but she also thought that the hysteria about him becoming an American tyrant was too much. Things hadn't always been this divisive, she believed that. She thought of General Collins's offer again.

At the World Court, the Abu Abdallah trial limped into its thirty first week. After the Balkan witnesses had been killed with ricin pens, the man had gone on a hunger strike, falling into dia-betic shock that led to a medically induced coma for the health of the brain. He'd been woken weeks later, claiming his name was Bjorn van der Hoedemaker from the small Dutch town of Vo-lendam. Most doctors were certain he was lying, but that hadn't stopped the wild protests of innocence during proceedings. The tribunal was openly mulling a mistrial and Arabia had requested he be extradited there.

"What a dang mess," the newscaster said, punctuating with a smack of the lips.

Something hard and solid thumped against the kitchen window. Mia muted the television and heard trilling. Outside the window, a stunned bird was regaining its feet on the back of the air conditioner Jesse had installed for the summer. She considered it a waste of money and electricity and refused to run it when she was home. Their last power bill had revealed her beloved held no such inhibitions.

The bird was small and light brown and didn't appear seriously injured. It blinked at her through the pane with jade dark eyes. Mia figured it a sparrow and was still admiring it as she remembered how much her stepmother Linda loathed sparrows for what they did to other birds in her flower garden. "Piranhas with wings," Linda had called them. Which was dramatic. Still, Mia had seen the fallout of a sparrow's presence: the pecked-out brains of a mother chickadee on their front lawn remained her most fixed memory from second grade.

Mia glimpsed the progressing nest wedged between the bottom of the air conditioner and the window ledge. Something needed to be done.

She fetched a broom from a hallway closet and was working out how to open the window and chase off the sparrow when the still-muted television screen glowed like a halo with BREAKING NEWS. That got her to stop and watch. The superhuman profile of Pete Swenson got her to find the volume.

"A railroad train crashed at the transportation hub in the Old Navy Yard district during morning rush, injuring more than sixty people and disrupting the commute for thousands more," the newscaster said.

"The train was midtown-bound, coming in from the far townships. Officials say the train rammed into a bumping block as it pulled into the Old Navy Yard terminal around eight forty-five a.m., knocking the lead four carriages off the rails.

"First responders were aided by three very unlikely bystanders— the Volunteers, home on leave from the Mediterranean. Here, in an exclusive cell phone video filmed on scene, you can watch them pry wounded citizens from gnarled train carriages, helping treat their injuries . . ."

It was them, wearing shorts and T-shirts instead of commando uniforms. But it was them. Pete, pulling apart a metal carriage window to make an opening. Flowers, disappearing in the corner of the video, reappearing a few seconds later holding an injured citizen in his arms. And Dash, so skittish when Mia had known him, racing around the platform, delivering supplies to the paramedics.

That month in Germany seemed a long time ago. Because it was a long time ago, Mia thought. From another life.

Still, she couldn't help but notice Pete. A pretty man, she remembered. Not pretty enough to make up for the rest of it, though. No one could be.

The cell phone video ended and the newscaster reappeared on the television. "The Volunteers left before our reporters could interview them," he said. "A War Department spokesman said that they are aware of the incident and the Volunteers' courageous efforts.

"The cause of the accident remains unclear. According to a railroad official speaking on the condition of anonymity . . ."

Mia turned off the television. She returned to the window, but not to sweep away the sparrow's nest. That could wait. She just wanted to look out at the morning.

She understood why the three Rangers could use their powers and why she couldn't. The reasoning was sound. Yet the urge to fly again was ferocious. It'd never gone away, but like an unreachable itch, she'd been able to ignore it. Until recently.

If I did it—then they'd know. People would see a flying lady in the sky. Well, she thought, so what? Then they'd know.

Mia was thinking again about a quick spree through the sky when the landline rang. They tended not to answer it—who used a landline, other than telemarketers and grandparents?—but it was a local number. Someone from work calling for instruction, she thought. Or to vent.

A deep voice blitzed the receiver. "Mia Tucker."

"This is she." She waited for the caller to identify himself. Nothing came. "With whom am I speaking?"

"My name's Roger Tran." The man coughed into the phone and continued. "I'm with General Collins's exploratory team."

"I see." She waited and again nothing came. "As I told the general, I'd like to help out, as I can."

"We're hoping to talk specifics. You wouldn't be free today."

Mia thought about the IPO risk assessment that was due. "I could do the early afternoon," she said.

After hanging up the phone, Mia began restructuring her day. Something else tugged at her, though. The landline number. It was unlisted, she was sure of it. And it hadn't been on the business card she'd given the general. She was sure of that, too.

She heard Jesse's voice in her head. "Agency spooks, though."

———

They met in an isolated tower made of black glass at the nub of West Street. The tower housed a global investment firm notorious for hostile takeovers that Mia's bank, among others, still blamed for bringing about the overregulatory Finance Reform Act (since overturned). Mia's grandfather had once called the firm "the Barbarians at the Gate" (first to other city power brokers, eventually on the record with the *Wall Street Journal*), so it was unsurprising that Mia had never before set foot in the building. A large, abstract interpretation of a morning sky greeted her in the lobby. Above the painting hung portraits of men and women in military uniforms, their young, lean faces a collage that spelled out V-A-L-U-E-S.

As part of its image rehabilitation, the global investment firm had hired thousands of combat veterans and opened a Warfighters Institute dedicated to medical research. Mia's prosthetics came from a design that originated there, something that even impressed her grandfather, however begrudgingly.

An assistant escorted Mia through security to a trim, narrow office on the sixth floor. "Mr. Tran will be with you in a moment," the assistant said. She was alone but couldn't shake the sense of being watched. The office's lone window didn't open to the outside but instead overlooked the inner atrium of the building. Mia peered into the bowels of the old enemy and found people in business clothes hustling to meetings with manila folders and laptops. She turned her attention to Tran's desk, still feeling that unknown watcher upon her.

Three photographs faced outward. In the first, a man in a navy suit and tie knotted in a power Windsor stood with a blank-faced woman with their hands on three smiling children, in front of a new suburban house with a green lawn. He had neat black hair and a craggy face, something that became even more pronounced in comparison to the next photograph: a skinny Vietnamese soldier cradling a long rifle in one hand and a helmet with no strap in the other. The same man with the same sense of self, Mia decided, separated by thirty years and a life. Something between fresh and worn emerged in the third photograph, Tran in military dress blues holding up his certificate of citizenship next to a beaming Lieutenant Colonel Jackie Collins.

About fifteen years back, Mia figured, doing the math in her head. Tran wore the crest of the International Legion on his shoulder and a Purple Heart on his chest. A hard path, the Legion, and a hard life. All for the chance—just the chance—to become a citizen.

"Spill blood for America." The voice behind Mia was measured and flat, startling her from the photo with the Legion's motto. "That day happened because of General Collins. I owe much to her."

Tran took a seat behind his desk, and gestured for Mia to do the same across from him. He wore a similar navy suit as the one in the family photograph and a tie again knotted in a power Windsor. She expected a bit of preliminary small talk but he launched straight into campaign matters.

"All of this is hypothetical. Exploratory," he began. "Lehman Brothers. We're looking for an introduction to the chair."

"I see."

"Can you provide that?"

Mia didn't know much about politics, but she knew this wasn't how things were done in her world. There was a grace to the ask, a decorum. "You don't have that access?" She raised her palms toward the atrium. "This is a connected place."

Tran blinked once, hard. "I'm a nobody here, Ms. Tucker. Certainly you've gathered that. My title is 'Strategic Executive Advisor for Military, Privateer, and Warfighter Partnerships.' Two years in, I still don't know what that means."

Mia did admire the candor.

He apologized for his brusqueness, saying General Collins often accused him of "letting my infantry show." Then he continued in the same manner. What other fund-raising possibilities could Mia think of? He made Mia anxious, and not just because their time together began to feel like an interview more than an initial brainstorm. Tran wanted details while she offered generalities, and sought assurances when she gave prospects. And still she felt like she was being watched, and not just by Tran.

"Where were you on Palm Sunday?" he asked, veering suddenly away from the near future. Something faraway seemed to be rolling behind his eyes, like he was hearing an old song. Mia understood her answer wasn't the point to his question.

"Driver's ed," she said. "First time on a freeway that morning."

Tran nodded, straightening his back. The old music in his eyes slowed down. "Federal City itself," he said. "Assigned to the War Department. A dream gig after battalion command in the Legion. Time to reconnect with my family, to decompress. Moved there ten days before the attacks."

"Oh my God."

Tran nodded again. "We were home, thankfully. I bring it up because I saw what happened there. After, I mean. All that fear, all that anger—it turned everything in the capital rancid. Now that's seeped out, spread across the country. If you consider—well, if you consider it in a certain way, Abu Abdallah won."

Mia didn't know what to do with that idea. She knew she didn't like it. She held to the quiet, as she'd learned to do as a Tucker and then as an army officer. It forced others to their intentions.

"General Collins can save this country from itself," Tran continued. "My job is to ensure she's granted the shot."

That was heavy talk for a small-party senatorial run, Mia thought. But that's why I'm here. To be part of something again that's grand. To be part of something bigger than myself.

"I hear you," she finally offered. "I can get it. The Lehman chair. Might only be five minutes, might be a shared taxi ride, but it'll be something."

Tran nodded and his lips thinned out into a smile. "All any of us can ask for," he said. "Opportunity."

———

Mia was walking home as the explosion rumbled through the day, soft as a prayer. Strangers told her where but she knew already, nothing else in the area made sense, so she went there, pushing against the crowd to Vietnam Victory Square, and found saws of black smoke ambling into the sky. They came from where the white spire had been cleaved from its base. The monument now bent into the square, felled over like a giant clutching at its heart.

An accident, Mia hoped. A terrible mistake.

She felt the truth, though, and forced herself to it as she rushed into the square. To help the survivors, or to at least try.

Terrorism had come to Empire City.

CHAPTER 6

Terrorism had come to Empire City.

A cloudless day had ceded to a cloudless dusk. The parade of sirens had ended hours earlier, but a pall of disquiet remained. War monuments across the city had been blown apart with pipe bombs and homemade explosive. A rostral column in midtown dedicated to the USS *Maine*. The doughboy statue at the Hell Gate. A large, gilded eagle along the river celebrating the Greatest Generation. The spire at Vietnam Victory Square. The crossed-pistols gate that arched over Broadway, built in remembrance of those who fell seizing Beirut. Even a rock with a plaque honoring a forgotten sergeant from the Boxer Rebellion had been turned to pebbles. Thirty war memorials, small and colossal, famous and otherwise, exploding within minutes of one another.

Only foreign wars, though. Jean-Jacques had noticed that. Only columns and plaques and bird statues for foreign wars had gotten the treatment. Not that it mattered to a city in shock. Terror was terror was terror.

Jean-Jacques stood on a loft rooftop deep in the district of Gypsy Town, watching and thinking. Little black monitor drones thrummed the sky. Down the block, the memorial with the forgotten sergeant's plaque had been secured with barricade tape. The parties would go on, he knew. The indy shows and poetry slams, too. Boho existence would persist with or without one long-dead soldier's rock. The tyranny of life would endure.

Smoke wisps rose from across the river, scattered and pale. Jean-Jacques thought they looked like objects glimpsed in the background of an old photograph, distant and a little vague, but impossible to unsee once found. Were there any war monuments in Little Haiti? Jean-Jacques couldn't recall one. There was the bronze of Toussaint, but that was different. The fuckers best have left it be.

"Yo! Dash."

The others were waiting. He kept his back to them.

Which wisp was the spire? Which the pistols gate? Which the mausoleum for the general who'd led the Veracruz landing way back when? He wanted a map.

Everything will return to normal soon enough, Jean-Jacques thought. If ever there was a place that could get up quick from an attack, it was Empire City. Still, he thought. This isn't right. Peace abroad wasn't our goal. Calm back here was.

"Hey, bro."

He ignored another voice. He kept watching and kept thinking, rubbing at the teardrop pendant under his shirt. After taking it from the pine box his cousin had given him, he'd pierced a small hole through its casing and affixed it to a dog-tag chain. His mother's last remnant stayed on him now.

He turned his attention to the slab under his feet. The Saint-Germain lofts were a set of opposing five-story buildings, split by a side street of the same name. They'd been living there three weeks. He'd agreed to the room for its price (free) and convenience. (Pete's sister had promised the landlord an opening set for putting them up in empty rooms.) It still felt like a walk-in petri dish to Jean-Jacques. The lack of ventilation during summer's peak was wearing on him. So too were the bedbug bites found in the mornings. And the drunk-people piss in the hallway found after that, on his way to the communal shower.

"Earth to Dash."

He'd slept in some disagreeable places over the years—a damp medieval fortress in the Caucasus pass, the animal-shit ditch outside Aleppo. A rocking skiff in the Gulf of Aden while he retched dehydrated chicken into the night ocean. But those had been on the job, part of the life. Jean-Jacques knew squalor. He had no regard for a bohemian imitation of it. Especially on leave, or whatever this was.

"Jean-Jacques."

In Hollywood, they'd lived in hotel suites. Paid for by the War Department. With room service. And those foam pillows that adjusted to the shape of your skull. We got soft, Jean-Jacques thought yet again.

"Corporal Saint-Preux. We need you."

The rank did it. He turned around.

"There he is," Flowers said, holding a metallic disc in the palm of his hand like he was cupping water. "Welcome back, bud."

Jean-Jacques pointed to the disc.

"All good. Ain't no ears up in here."

They'd been supposed to turn in their equipment, but Flowers hadn't obliged. What else did that goon smuggle back? Jean-Jacques wondered. And how?

The other Volunteers, plus Britt Swenson and Sebastian Rios, had joined Jean-Jacques on the roof, among a feral urban garden decorated with wooden signs bearing local poetry. Jean-Jacques didn't like the poetry and he didn't like having the other two with them. Meetings like this weren't for citizens. But Pete had insisted.

"They know more about home than we do," he'd said.

Pete decided it was his turn to take in the Empire City skyline, moving to the edge of the rooftop. His clothes still carried the remnants of the day's rescue work, streaked with soot and blood, the bottom of his shirt severed into flaps by an upturned metal spike. His hands, cartoonishly large even on his arms, were patchworks of red pus and torn-up skin. He hadn't worn gloves, no small lapse for a man who'd spent the morning pulling open train carriages.

He looked at the group with a hard grimace, flexing his hands into balls.

"Got lucky," he said. His eyes, one hyper-black and one hyper-green, churned. "Motherfuckers were more interested in style points than a body count."

"Latest reports have eighteen dead," Flowers said, dutifully. "Fifty or so hurt. Mostly tourists hit by debris."

Pete nodded the way military leaders did when learning something they wanted to feign already knowing. "Lucky," he said again. "Won't be so clean next time."

His command voice set in again, terse, a pitch lower than normal, sticking his bloody hands into his pockets because he never knew what to do with them during a brief. Jean-Jacques heard slivers of excitement, too. He knew why. He was, too. They were in that long, dirty pause before clarity. When anything was possible.

"No one has the experience we do at hunting down terror wogs. I've reached out to some folks in the three-letter agencies. Home-land marshals, too. They're going to need our help. They're going to need our skills." Pete stopped to wet his throat. "This could happen again."

Skills? Jean-Jacques thought. What skills of ours could possibly benefit anyone right now? Even at the Old Navy Yard he'd felt like they were getting in the way more than anything. But he kept that to himself. Maybe Pete knew something they didn't.

Maybe.

"Copycat effect." Sebastian spoke, looking surprised at the sound of his own voice. Pete raised an eyebrow and gestured for him to go on. "Well. Like with serial killers." He was talking quickly, stumbling through the words, as if he wanted to start his sentences over halfway through them. Jean-Jacques still hadn't acknowledged him. He's the hostage, he thought. Nothing more.

"Media coverage helps shape it, make it seem attractive," Sebastian continued. "Like that old jihadist manifesto. *Management of Savagery*. Some Western separatist translated it last year, remixed it. Changed Allah to Jesus, infidels to feds, that sort of thing. No one read it. No one cared. Then Empire News picked it up for a piece. The manifesto spread like wildfire. Cyber command couldn't get rid of it once it reached the dark net."

"Your point?" Britt asked. She shared her brother's face, Jean-Jacques thought, sharp and angular and green eyes like minerals that bored through the twilight. There was something more withdrawn about her, though. Jean-Jacques couldn't decide if she was shy or stuck up.

"The middle-schooler who shot up Spokane last month," Sebastian answered, "was inspired by the new *Management of Savagery*. A book written thirty years ago to oppose our military occupation of Lebanon got a loner American teenager to kill his science class. The point, I guess, is that extremism translates well. Just have to change the nouns."

Long, fraught seconds passed. No one said anything. Someone coughed.

"We never heard of that," Jean-Jacques finally said. Who was this guy? He'd never even been a soldier, let alone a Ranger. And why was he always wearing those sunglasses? Jean-Jacques wanted to snatch them from his stupid, smug face. "Hundreds of raids. Hundreds of enemies killed and captured. We'd know."

"Would we, though?" Something cold swept over Pete's face. "We bag and tag. Drop 'em at work camps or the morgue. Not much follow-up after that."

"Yeah, Dash, not everything's like the gook horde," Flowers said, using the insult the rest of the military had fastened on the International Legion. The original Legionnaires had mostly come from somewhere in Asia, promised a green card and monthly pay in return for occupying Vietnam. The nickname had stuck, even for later enlistees like Dash. "It's important to ask the locals questions, not just blow up everything. Help them help themselves."

Flowers was attempting to impress Pete's sister, Jean-Jacques could tell, and he'd cut down that effort in short order. First, though, he wanted to figure out what Pete had planned for them. So he asked, direct.

"Close with and destroy the enemy," Pete said. His words were straight, but flaring nostrils suggested irritation. He never liked being questioned in front of others. "Same as always."

Big man doesn't know anything more or anything else, Jean-Jacques realized. Just wants us to think he does. He tilted his head and frowned, trying to square this Pete with the sergeant he'd met in the Rangers. Not many ex-Legionnaires made it all the way to the Rangers, so he'd pulled Jean-Jacques aside on day one to tell him he belonged there, had earned his way there the same as anyone, and if anyone said different, to let him know and he'd handle it. That had meant something to Private First Class Saint-Preux, being told that. Pete had brimmed with the same raw energy then, but it'd been sharper, more concentrated. Always about the next business trip, the next round with the wogs, how to get better, stronger, more lethal. Which C-list actress in Hollywood changed him? Which talent agent had chirped into his ear? Though blaming someone else was cheap, Jean-Jacques thought. And too easy. Pete hadn't chosen to become a Volunteer, not exactly. But he had chosen what to do with it.

They all had.

"I was wondering." It was the hostage again, pointing to the smoke across the river. "This has got to be about the Abu Abdallah trial. Right?"

That made some sense. Jean-Jacques hadn't been following the trial closely but what he knew suggested clusterfuck. The terror cleric's group had splintered into a dozen factions since they declared jackpot on the old man with the piss bag on the little island-crag north of the Barbary Coast. All the foreign policy experts agreed: jihadism could not survive without its leader. The terror wogs needed him and so did the ideology. Jean-Jacques looked again across the river. He figured the big smoke must be coming from Vietnam Victory Square. Where they'd toppled the spire.

The fucking hostage is right on this, he decided. Goddamn it.

He looked around the group, registering what the others thought. Abu Abdallah was a name that carried meaning for them all. Flowers seemed to be glowering at something else across the river, beyond the smoke. The hostage kept twitching his leg, like a dog who couldn't find the right spot to scratch. And the Swensons? They'd both gone sullen and white-hot mute.

Oh yeah, Jean-Jacques thought. Their papa.

Abu Abdallah had evaded capture for years, but his deputies hadn't. The Swenson children realized during those trials how different they were. Pete had shared that once with the other Volunteers, along some dusty battle fringe. His sister didn't find forgiveness, precisely, but vengeance proved too much. She let go to live. Not Pete. He found himself in that vengeance, watching men who'd helped kill his father get sentenced to death themselves. It gave a boy something beyond grief. It gave a boy purpose.

That boy had become a superman, and the superman looked up again on the rooftop, one eye pulsing through the dim light, the other fading into it. He spoke yet again.

"All the more reason," he said, "to put ourselves to use."

What caused Jean-Jacques to snap wasn't what Pete said, but how. He'd said it like he was speaking with strangers, with a rapt audience of grateful citizens. He'd said it like the acting coach in Hollywood had taught him to, exaggerated and slow. When did a man's power and confidence in himself become too much? When did a man's need for more, ever more, always more, become pathetic?

"This is nonsense, Pete." Jean-Jacques spoke fast, liquid kreyol in his head, heat on his tongue. "We should be getting ready for deployment, not caring about this. Not trying to be anything more than we are.

"You think this is pretend, some adventure? Supers aren't solutions. They're not gifts. We got them because some asshole dropped a bomb on us when we was going after Abu Abdallah's wife and infant. Remember? How we had to justify it by pretending to be saving this idiot?" He pointed to Sebastian. "Tripoli was a bullshit mission. Bullshit missions get bullshit results. Thirty-seven of our brothers died there. Remember them? This Justice stuff has jammed your brain. We are not special. We are soldiers."

Jean-Jacques expected Pete to yell back. So did the others; he could tell by the way they began admiring the ground. But instead the large man sighed and looked over at the falling summer sun. Against the horizon his profile seemed to swell, and he stepped into the half-shine. This delicate change in angles and atmosphere shot out jagged shadows and arrows of light, causing everyone else to step back or lift an arm to ward off the glare. Pete noticed none of it.

"How?" he asked, just loud enough for the others to hear. "How'd it get like this?"

It was the question of their time. How had it gotten like this? Where had it all gone so wrong?

Maybe everything had gone awry after World War II, Sebastian offered, when America decided it would be responsible for protecting the free world while also deciding what counted as "free." Or maybe it'd been Vietnam, and the decision to fight a ground war over an independence movement with heavy communist flavorings. Maybe Nixon's Grand Bargain had turned it all, his secret plan with Mao that ended China's support for the north in exchange for Taiwan. Without that, things might've been okay.

"Ancient history," Britt said. She pointed to Beirut. Dawn of the Mediterranean Wars. A fatwa from that spoiled young cleric soon to self-brand as Abu Abdallah. Once American warfighters crossed that seawall and stayed, it changed the whole Near East. No Beirut—well, no Shi'a Awakening. None of the coups. No need to chase ghosts in turbans all the way into the Balkans.

"And no Palm Sunday, maybe." Britt remembered low, weary. She found the words this time. About how they couldn't get ahold of their father. They'd tried, for so long. Pete nodded. He started to say something but whatever it was got stuck. He nodded again.

Jean-Jacques gave the moment a few seconds, then cut in. The adrenaline from his rant was still juicing his veins. And there was only so much wrongness a man could take.

"The Legion won Vietnam," he said. "Don't get it twisted. It knew how to fight guerrillas. It knew what it took. Praise to the Victors, sure. But 'Spill blood for America' got it done."

No one argued with that. How could they? Jean-Jacques thought. It's the fucking truth.

"Beirut," Pete said, first to himself before repeating it to the group. He was trying to get the subject to something they could agree on. "Yeah. That's the lynchpin, I think."

"But the wars didn't ratchet up *until* Palm Sunday." Flowers sounded unbowed. "And it sort of worked! New Beirut is amazing. Only peacemongers don't like it being a state. My lesbian aunts went there last year. Had a great time. Got me a snow globe. If we did more of what we did there?" He puckered his lips and whistled. "Who knows."

"Sometimes things work. Sometimes they don't." There was nothing practical about talk like this. Jean-Jacques felt an instinctive need to crush it. "Big ideas up here."

The others looked at Jean-Jacques, faces ashen and drawn, unsure of what to say, and he realized he was being pissy for the sake of being pissy. What did he know, really? He was just a trigger puller. He was just a soldier. All that mattered to him was duty. It was up to others to figure out where and why. Jean-Jacques wanted to press the turbo button and get away from everyone to clear his head. But there was no place in the city to run like that.

"Well." As if just noticing the gory state of his hands, Pete rubbed his palms across the bottom of his shirt, trying to force a wince into a toothy smile. "At least no one said oil."

Even Jean-Jacques laughed at that.

"I ask because it's easy to forget how we got here. Even for those of us devoted to the fight." Pete stopped to look at both Jean-Jacques and Flowers. "No small thing. What you said is right. And more, too.

"It's easy to be against something these days," Pete continued. Now, he looked straight at his sister. She looked back with razors in her eyes. "Anti this. Counter that. It's much harder to be for something."

Pete Swenson, true believer, was already back. And giving a homeland version of his Do Something! Speech, heard by operators, soldiers, and Legionnaires across the globe. "The risks of inaction are greater than the risks of action." "The only thing badder than a bad guy with a gun is a good guy with one." Et cetera. He didn't hear me at all, Jean-Jacques thought. He's still convinced they want us. He's still convinced they need us.

He's still convinced we're always part of the solution.

Whatever he's conjuring, Jean-Jacques decided, I'm out. Damn out. While I still can: I'm gonna do me.

"What's hell to you, Sebastian?" Pete asked, the first Volunteer to use the hostage's name. The hostage sputtered out something about other people.

"On your last day on earth, the person you became will meet the person you could have been," Pete said. "That's hell." His coral eye moved from person to person in slow consideration, his black one remaining pinned on Sebastian. Jean-Jacques knew what came next. Words about glory and grief, an ode to heroism and service in an age when such ideas were supposed to be dust. Jean-Jacques had seen it work on cynics and fools, wild men and dreamers, too, anyone and everyone in between. Not me, though, he thought. Not anymore.

"Only three percent of Americans serve in the military. Only three percent love America enough to fight for it. Our country needs help. Here, now. Everyone knows it. Everyone feels it. We can help. We can—"

Jean-Jacques's phone buzzed. He pulled it out to find a text from his cousin asking, again, to meet up. In succession, Britt pulled out her phone, too.

"Uhh, guys," she said.

"In the middle of something," Pete said, his aggravation flashing like silver.

"Okay," Britt said. "Just thought you'd want to know who blew up the city."

The entire group turned to her, expectedly. "It's okay for me to talk now?"

"Brittany," Pete said. "Go on."

"Of course, Peter." She faked a yawn and then half-smiled at her brother. "So. Jonah Gray. Age forty-six. From Ohio."

"Be serious."

"I am, Peter. This is a state alert. He's an army vet."

Something in the air seemed to curdle. Flowers swore. Pete shook his head and closed his eyes, turning away, into the dusk.

"Jonah Gray." Jean-Jacques sounded out the name. He couldn't help himself. The vet thing was bad. But opportunities to rattle Pete like this didn't happen often. "What you think, man? Sunni or Shi'a?"

Coming next year to a movie theater near you . . .

AMERICAN LIONS. An unprecedented blend of real-life heroism and original filmmaking. **AMERICAN LIONS** stars a group of active-duty military heroes in a film like no other in history. A fictionalized account of the real-life raid by the Volunteers to capture infamous terror chieftain Abu Abdallah in the Mediterranean, **AMERICAN LIONS** features a spellbinding story that takes audiences on an adrenaline-fueled, edge-of-their-seat journey. Thanks to an extraordinary collaboration between the War Department and Hollywood, the Volunteers play themselves, bringing raw, thrilling authenticity to their roles and to the film. Abu Abdallah is played by Christian Bale. **AMERICAN LIONS** combines stunning combat sequences, state-of-the-art battlefield technology, and heart-pumping emotion for the ultimate action-adventure film, showcasing the skills, training, and tenacity of the greatest action heroes of them all: real American soldiers.

CHAPTER 7

SEBASTIAN STARED AT his plate of spring rolls and tried to make sense of what Pete had told him. They sat at a corner table along the port, watching the afternoon go by. The sky was sick with heat and a police motorboat drifted in the water behind them. Different thoughts kept coming to Sebastian but he didn't know how to express them. He'd taken days to find the courage to ask his question. Now that he had an answer, understanding was slow to come. He tried again.

"So you weren't there to get me."

"We weren't there to not get you," Pete offered. "But the primary objective was Abu Abdallah's wife. And the baby. Higher thought detaining them would draw him out."

"Huh."

Sebastian hadn't known he'd been held in the same Tripoli compound as the great terror chieftain's family. He hadn't seen a woman or a child his whole time there. But that didn't mean anything. He'd been kept in a basement.

"You don't look great. Another brew? Yo! My man here needs a refill."

It'd been six days since Jonah Gray had been announced as a suspect in the war memorial bombings. Had he acted alone? No one believed that. The security state loomed over everything, out

99

and open as it could be only after disaster. Beat cops held the corners, SWAT commandos ghosted the rooftops. The mechanized hum of police helos and large black monitor drones layered the skies. "Presence patrols," the mayor had said. Nothing else had been revealed to the public.

A waitress brought another beer. She was a teenager, pretty, maybe seventeen. Sebastian felt certain she wasn't old enough to be serving alcohol. She smiled, trying to get Pete's attention. Pete didn't notice or pretended not to, taking a large bite from his pulled pork sandwich, nodding in approval. The teenager walked away. She was the first young woman Pete had ignored in their time together, much of which had been spent partying across the city.

Restraint or fatigue? Sebastian hoped for the former.

The Volunteers had tried to help. They'd wanted to. The homeland marshals passed. So had the three-letter agencies. The War Department sent an email telling them to enjoy their leave, the war abroad needed to be their focus. They'd reacted in different ways. Jean-Jacques had "family stuff." Flowers was following around Britt, carrying her band's equipment from gig to gig. Pete drank. And drank. And then drank some more. Sebastian was in awe and enduring pain from trying to keep up. He'd taken the week off from work, something that bothered his boss but he didn't care. He owed his life to Pete. The least he could do was listen to some war stories.

A kind of coherence arrived for Sebastian. "But—why lie?"

"About the Hero Project?"

Sebastian shrugged.

"I don't know, hostage," Pete said, breaking from his sandwich to drink down one of his beers. His skin had reddened under the sun, further carving out his jawline and deepening the slope of his forehead. A perma-scruff had settled across his face, something Sebastian envied. He'd never been able to grow more than fuzz.

"No one knows how this happened to us. Not really. Just theories. Us Rangers in Tripoli, the pilots, too, we all had cythrax vaccines. Dropping the bomb wasn't even the plan. Only if things went off the rails. What they told us was, if the bomb drops, it evaporates everyone without the vaccine. Poof. Old Testament shit. But we'd be fine. Breakthrough tech, they said. No one had a fucking clue.

"People need control, though. People need belief. If it came out this was a freak accident instead of a top-secret plan? Citizens would be dying every weekend trying to create cythrax in their bathtubs. We barely made it and we got the best hospital care in the world. Order over chaos, brother."

The best hospital care in the world. Those memories from Germany had gapped from the onset for Sebastian, and with time lost much of their shape. It was why he kept to the basics. Telling the full truth would've been a certain way to end up in a Guantanamo work camp, for one, and besides, no one would've believed him. There were three ways to tell war stories to twenty-first-century America: brave, sad, violent. All needed to be clean as bone. Anything else was too much. So the Rangers had saved him in a daring raid that took a great many of their own (true), and the Volunteers' powers came from a top-secret government project (untrue).

But they hadn't come for him.

"What about—me?" It's what Sebastian had been asking about before. "Why lie about me?"

Pete forced a laugh. "Same reason, dude! Hey, America, a bunch of Rangers tried to apprehend a terror wife and terror baby but whoops, almost everyone got killed by a new bomb made from space rocks? No way. That don't play. But: hey, America, a bunch of Rangers died saving this nice young man with dimples who got lost?" Pete whistled. "That plays."

"Little lies for the greater good. Helps keep everything . . ." Pete looked around the patio, toward the river and the police boat, then up at the sky toward the monitor drones. "Comfortable."

Sebastian looked around at all those things, too, and at his spring rolls and lunch beer. He hadn't grown up thinking like this. He'd been raised to trust the government. He and Pete were part of the generation born at freedom's peak. They were Found. Rockefeller had said so. When everything seemed possible, everything and more.

"You never got the vaccine, right?" Pete asked. Sebastian hadn't. "Be glad and let the rest go, hostage. You're the luckiest man in the world."

He winked at Sebastian, and clinked his beer with his own. Sebastian forced a smirk.

"Like the kids say," Pete said. "Abide to Thrive."

Their table looked over the murky gray river, parallel to a bunch of wooden ships that doubled as museums. The Old Gothic Bridge, all postcard charm, shot straight into the marrows of the city. This part of Gypsy Town once had been an industrial wasteland, a space between empire and empire's suburbs. Nothing but abandoned plants and smokestacks and rock junkies, forbidden zones for urban explorers to venture into if they dared. Then came the settlers, piecemeal at first, then in sudden waves: the gays and musicians. The freelancers and grad students. The young professionals. The baby strollers and dog parks. Corporate overlords with a vision followed, armed with boutique retail consulting firms and luxury condominium developers. The abandoned plants were demolished or restored, any remaining junkies pushed out to other lost districts. Gypsy Town had begun as a whisper, a place where stories happened. Then it became a story itself. Sometime after came Gypsy Town the band and Gypsy Town the pejorative. Now, it just was. A space between empire and empire's suburbs, again, where youngish, modish people with shopping-center faces could order weed through a bicycle delivery service.

"Since we're walking memory lane, here"—Sebastian lowered his voice even though they had the sunny part of the patio to themselves—"what do you remember from Tripoli? Detailwise."

"Supposed to be a simple mission." Pete's eyes flared like they always did when he was thinking, green eye softening, the black one turning to ember. It was always the second thing people commented on, Sebastian had learned. They'd survived the same bomb, both had their vision altered by looking into the blast, but he'd been the one left with extreme light sensitivity instead of a divine gaze. He adjusted his sunglasses and asked Justice to continue.

"Go in, get the wife. Get the infant. Turn any wog with a weapon to pink mist." Pete shrugged. "We'd heard they might have you, too. No offense, we hoped you'd still be breathing, but over there, it's not like kidnapped journos are rare. Soon as we hit the ground, way more resistance than intel expected."

Realizing his hands were thrashing through air, Pete reached for condiments. Rangers became coasters, insurgents, mustard packets. A little ketchup bottle assumed the role of Sebastian.

"I'm here, with the front assault team. We cleared the four rooms upstairs but took some casualties. Huge difference between being shot at and being shot toward, you know? We were getting shot *at*."

Pete's words cut through the summer daze like a blade. He reached for more mustard packets. "Wogs just kept coming, pouring in from that basement. We managed to breach the door, right as a helo got clipped by an RPG. Crashed quick, like an earthquake. Had Flowers in it, on the gun. And Mia, of course. She was the pilot."

Pete's jaw and temples strained when he said Mia's name. Sebastian noticed. A pepper shaker became the downed helicopter.

"Then . . . I don't know, man. I remember radioing in the breach. Then a long, dull humming sound from outside. Then the smell of ice? Then white fire. Tried to push into a pantry door with my shoulder but it wouldn't budge. No time then but say goodbye." He blew a kiss to the sky and turned all the coasters but one, tipping over the ketchup. "Then—nothing. Germany comes next."

Sebastian shook his head. "That's what I mean, though. Who ordered the bomb dropped? And why'd we live when everyone else . . ." He was going to say "burned to ash," but stopped himself. They'd been strangers to him. They'd been brothers in arms to Pete.

Pete stared out at the river and swirled the beer in his hand. "Chance or fate," he finally said. "The soldier's great question."

Sebastian thought that was an interesting idea even if it didn't answer anything. Pete kept speaking.

"You should talk to Dash. He's the one who came to first. Found you and me on the stairs. He got us home."

"Yeah." Sebastian had tried to speak with Jean-Jacques a few times, to little avail. The other man had made it clear he wanted nothing to do with him. "I'll do that."

Sebastian looked up and let the sun warm his face. He was still trying to unravel the knots in their saga, but couldn't quite figure out how. He'd left it alone for years, thinking it for the best. And it had been, for a while. Be thankful you're alive, his mom had said, quoting Corinthians: "For who hath known the mind of the Lord?"

Sometimes that was enough. Sometimes it needed to be.

Was it still?

"I feel old," Pete said. He'd finished his beers. "Too much waiting around."

"You're . . . twenty-seven?" Sebastian knew that already but wanted to appear uncertain. "The rock star age. Jim Morrison, Hendrix, all those maniacs."

"Rupert Brooke, too." Pete's voice softened a beat. "If I should die, think only this of me: That there's some corner of a foreign field, That is for ever England."

Who thinks like that? Sebastian thought. Who quotes Rupert

freaking Brooke anymore? He found it strange and odd but also endearing. Then he listened as Pete recounted when and where he'd given his youth. Eighteen—a baby-faced private patrolling the Balkans. Nineteen—a baby-faced Ranger going on clandestine raids into Persia. Twenty-one—a not-so-baby-faced Ranger helping put down the Syrian uprising, gifted a local belly dancer by a superior to mark his entry into manhood. He'd talked with the dancer about her studies, he said. She'd reminded him of his sister too much. On and on, through his formative years and the cythrax bomb, direct-action tours and long-range reconnaissance missions, from mountain caves to desert hideouts to dense, jumbled megacities. He likened the work of counterinsurgency to that of a politician, always currying favor and seeking buy-in. The work of a counter-terrorist, though, that was the work of a monk. Autonomous, as reliant on routine as it was on belief. He liked those missions the best. They were pure.

"Squeezing the trigger on a man who deserves it?" he said. "That's victory. Or the closest thing we have these days."

Then, as if his batteries went out, Pete was done. He looked down at his lap. Sebastian just nodded and kept quiet. Any words would've spoiled it all.

Some time passed. "Excuse me," Pete said, pulling out a phone Sebastian hadn't seen before. "Need to make a call."

Pete walked to the far side of the patio, yelling out a big "Yo! It's Swenson. What you got for me?" then turning his back away from the table and speaking more subdued.

Sebastian took a bite from a now-stale spring roll. What a weirdo, he thought. Heroes! They really are just like us.

More time passed. Sebastian moved his chair into the shade. Pete's phone call with someone who knew him as "Swenson" con-tinued to absorb him. Sebastian wasn't sure what to make of his continued efforts to get involved with the manhunt for Jonah Gray. On one hand, he was Justice. Of course he should be involved. On the other—he was a walking, talking titan with a magical burning eye. It wasn't like he could go undercover.

Chance or fate, Pete had asked. Sebastian knew which had saved him. It hadn't been the government. It hadn't been God. It'd been a luck even blinder than he was. He thought about his family offering to pay his ransom. They'd tried, at least, whatever the federals had to say about it. That'd taken courage. That'd taken love.

So many others had died in Tripoli. Rangers. Soldiers. Terrorists. Insurgents. Innocents, too. Why had he lived? Others needed to be there. He'd chosen to. Sebastian pulled out his own phone. Into the web search he typed *Abu Abdallah Wife and Baby*.

He scrolled down and clicked a website written in Arabic, pressing the translate button. His phone's internal stateware issued an alert—this website had not been approved by cyber command. Whatever, he thought. I turn invisible. I'm already on every watch list there is.

It was an op-ed from the *Tripoli Post*, dated three years prior.

What are we to make of the unbelievers' attack last week on a rice farm in the city outskirts? Let's start with the bodies: at least sixty dead, to include dozens of local women and children. The invaders claim over thirty of their own were killed in the gunfire. That's ninety human souls lost in minutes. For what?

Or we could start with what you, what I, what everyone in Tripoli has been talking about since that bloody day: the bomb of fire that fell upon the farm. My mother's mother says it came from Allah. My neighbor says it came from the invaders' fighter jets. My joker son says it came from a fool American on a ship who fell asleep on the wrong button. I say all those can be true, or none. I also say I've never seen anything so bright and also so dark.

Who amongst us didn't believe in those minutes we were living the Hour of Judgment?

Or we could start with the new fact that Umm Khalid was one of the Muslims martyred at the rice farm. She was one of the wives of the jihadist cleric Abu Abdallah, and not a native of our land or city. But she came here with her new child seeking peace. She came here seeking haven.

We failed her. We failed her child. We did not protect them, as was our charge.

My readers know what I think of the jihadists. They are dogs, barbarians who pervert the Quran. But after last week's bombing, I am left wondering: What now is the right choice for Tripoli? What is the right choice to keep our families safe? Things like that did not happen until the unbelievers came here.

Bomb of fire, Sebastian thought. Huh.

He put away his phone. He looked up to find Pete looming over him, wraparound ballistic shades propped up on his head, a tower of muscle and light.

"What's so vital in that phone, hostage," Pete said.

"Nothing, really," Sebastian said, trying to sound normal. "Work stuff."

Pete stared at him without blinking for what seemed like perpetuity. Sebastian knew he'd break under scrutiny. He almost hoped for it. Anything to get those two bright eyes of fury off him. Then Pete smiled wide, breaking the spell. "Just joshing. Roll out?"

Sebastian set down cash so they didn't have to wait for a bill. Where to next? Sebastian suggested a museum, or perhaps a panel discussion at Empire State University. Pete thought he was joking. As long as he was home in time for the new *Utopia* episode, Sebastian didn't care. Bobby Kennedy survived the assassination attempt this episode, and he wanted to see how. They settled on Kiernan's, a pub in the Village that claimed to be America's oldest. Lincoln had campaigned there. Women hadn't been allowed until the Haig administration. It was a historic place. Thanksgiving wishbones from World War I doughboys who didn't make it home from France still hung from the rafters.

"Have an ancestor who fought over there," Pete said. "Trenches, man. Mustard gas, frontal charges . . . fucked-up shit! Got his tin helmet in storage, somewhere."

"Me, too," Sebastian said. He didn't think his family had a helmet memento but they could have. "Great-great-grandfather? Something like that."

Pete pulled out a flask of bourbon. They shared it, Sebastian sticking his tongue in its mouth to limit the intake.

The city wasn't crowded for the hour, but it wasn't empty, either. "Defy" had taken on new meaning in the aftermath of the bombing, and citizens nodded at one another with grim solidarity. They stared up at Pete, wonder sealed across their faces, and Sebastian could hear them asking each other if they should ask for a photo. Only a Scandinavian couple and a youth soccer team mustered the courage. Everyone else just wanted to hold him in with their eyes, from a distance.

They walked the bridge, languid and sun-kissed, sipping from the flask. They talked about the day-to-day practicalities of their powers: how Pete's coursed within him, and he could always feel it, like his bloodstream had been spiked. Sebastian likened his to a lever in the back of his brain, and explained the migraines he often got after going invisible. Pete hadn't taken a pain reliever in years so he couldn't empathize. All his organs had distended, though, and doctors weren't really sure what the long-term effects would be. Pete himself doubted he'd make it to fifty. That's why he didn't worry about credit card debt, he said. Or much else.

Pete asked about Sebastian's handler, Dorsett. Sebastian said he was a nice guy. Pete asked if Dorsett ever shared Bureau intel with him. Sebastian said no, not really. Then Pete said he'd help Sebastian develop his convalescent skills. Sebastian asked what that meant. "Hotwiring cars, field-dressing wounds, picking locks, that sort of thing," Pete said. Sebastian asked why. "I'm putting you in VASP—Volunteers Assessment and Selection Program," Pete said.

Between that and the bourbon and the sun, Sebastian's soul felt warm.

Underneath the Old Gothic Bridge's far tower, a man in rags squatted in a corner. His skin was stretched and worn and his beard was matted and he held a sign that read HOMELESS VET + PALM SUNDAY FIRST RESPONDER = PLEASE HELP IF U CAN, GOD BLESS. A few passing citizens placed coins in his jar. Most ignored him.

Sebastian wondered if the man was a fake, then chided himself for it. Still, vets with troubles got placed in rehabilitation colonies—Block Island, the Outer Banks, even Hawaii. They'd earned it. They'd been warfighters. Some returned to the citizenry, full and whole again. Others lived out their days in paradise, brain-scarred but honored. It was one of the things that made America special.

Pete approached the man in rags. "Hey, brother," he said. "Who were you with?"

The man looked up with eyes like mirrors. He had the blanched look of a maven addict. Maybe he was legit. Only veterans and mega-rich assholes had access to that drug. He wore a faded ultra cap with the slogan WE THE PEOPLE on it, as well as a yellow rubber bracelet decorated with antifascist arrows. Quite the mix, Sebastian thought.

"Twenty-Fifth Infantry," the man said. "Twice to Syria. Once to Cyprus."

Pete winced, pulling out his wallet. "Tip of the spear," he said. "Cyprus was nasty."

He handed the man six twenties, $120 in total. The man put a palm on top of Pete's fist in gratitude. Sebastian wanted to tell him he'd be better off buying the man a meal, or maybe putting the money toward those credit card bills, but didn't. *I could be wrong about the maven*, he thought, looking again at the man's vacant expression and dark bags underneath his eyes.

But I'm not.

Two city police in uniform appeared on the bridge's walk-way, moving with purpose. They wore light tactical vests fitted with ammo pouches and chemical spray holders and black Tasers sleek as ice. They ignored Pete and Sebastian and went straight to the man in rags. One reached down and grabbed him under the elbow.

"Need to clear the bridge," the other said.

"Who's he harming?" Pete's words flexed, and he set his shoulders back. He stood a full head higher than both police. Ignoring him had been a mistake. "Just checked—this ain't Abu Abdallah."

The one who'd gripped the man in rags straightened his back and turned around with contrived slowness. He was thick and broad, the type of linebacker Irish that'd made up the thin blue line in Empire City for more than a century. Sebastian put him in his mid-thirties. He looked Pete up and down, registering Sebastian with a quick flicker.

"Orders are to clear the bridge."

Both cops were lacquered in sweat, Sebastian noticed, and bore the wide-eyed shine that came from recurring early mornings and long nights. The ECPD had received much of the national blame for the attacks. There was talk the police commissioner had sub-mitted his resignation. *It's been a rough stretch for these guys*, Sebastian thought. *Maybe we should—*

"Look at the city right now," Pete said. "And you're fucking with a bum."

"I'm a citizen," the man in rags said, his voice arcing. Sebastian peered closer. It wasn't the same guy from the subway, or the guy collecting bottles. This guy was leaner. More downtrodden yet younger-seeming, somehow. "The tribunal druids will just send me back. But I don't want to go. I was a lieutenant! I had power. I had a life. The colonies are clinks."

No one responded. The other policeman, slighter than his partner but still built, moved his hands to his belt, hooking his thumbs into the loops. Intentional or not, it called attention to the pistol holstered there.

"All good, officers," Sebastian said. "We're heading out."

If Pete heard Sebastian, he made no sign of it. He and the first cop were flashing invisible feathers at each other like peacocks, the man in rags between them. Dark Irish implacability versus a soldier's ambered rage. The policeman looked tough to Sebastian, and resolute. The kind of man he'd want beside him in a dim alley, and would fear provoking. The kind of man who believed in order above all else, which, combined with physical courage and a keen moral sense, made for an ideal enforcer of democratic law. But he knew the man would look away first. And it wouldn't be his fault when he did.

The man in rags saved everyone from whatever was supposed to come next.

"Now, now," he said, stumbling to his feet with the help of a beam. "We're all warfighters here."

He promptly hocked up a stream of brown phlegm into the river.

That dispelled most of the testosterone from the bridge, but not all of it. As Sebastian stepped away and Pete moved to follow, the second cop said, "Be easy, boys."

Pete stopped, cracked his neck, and seemed to consider his options. He pulled out the flask. Then he took a drink, sloppy and full, facing the police and the city at once. Pete licked his lips, staring at the cops for long, scratchy seconds.

"Defy the guards," he finally said. "Guard those who defy."

Why he was quoting far leftist dogma, Sebastian had no idea.

The police looked at one another, their faces blank but tight. The larger one raised his hands to the top of his vest, pulling it down to relieve some of the pressure from his shoulders. The other did nothing. Without a word, they turned to the man in rags and helped collect his things.

"America Honors the Warfighter!" Sebastian called back, injecting his voice with as much earnestness as he could.

The man in rags smiled and put his hand across his heart, looking down into the river. "The honor is ours."

As they walked across the remainder of the bridge, Sebastian replayed what he'd just witnessed. He felt a bit in awe, and a lot in dismay. Maybe it was the suburbanite in him. Maybe it was the former Boy Scout. Maybe it was the blood—even half-Bolivians from the upper middle class knew they didn't have white-people latitude with police. Maybe it was something else. But he'd never seen anyone treat a cop like that.

"Goose-steppers," Pete said, mostly to himself. Then, "Some people are just dented cans, you know? Nothing to be done."

Sebastian didn't want to opine about goose-steppers or about dented cans.

"Why'd you do that?" he asked.

Pete shrugged. "Part of the social contract, I think." Then he grinned up at the afternoon sun and took yet another sip of bourbon.

Sebastian wasn't sure which social contract Pete meant. It didn't sound like something from any America that'd come before.

CHAPTER 8

"M UST SEEM SMALLER to you, being back."
Mia thought the opposite—the halls of Riverbrook felt larger, somehow—and told the dean so. He shrugged and poked his head into an ajar locker.

"Memory can be a beast," he said.

Riverbrook School ("A Fine Place to Learn") had been built on a leafy, quiet block in a northwestern corner of the city some seven decades before, molding the young minds of future states-men, financiers, and an occasional drug merchant in the duration. It was modest, as Empire City private schools went: simple uniform, demanding-but-not-draconian academics, mandatory volunteer work in the community, et cetera. Mia had attended Riverbrook from kindergarten through eighth grade, and still held it in regard, if not deep affection. It was a good school, like many others.

"How are the kids?" Mia asked. Three weeks had passed since the war memorial bombings. Public transportation across the city remained a horror show and the lack of arrests had become a na-tional punch line. The academic year beginning on time seemed a little step toward normalcy, at least. "Skittish?"

"Less than you'd think." The dean closed the locker and they continued down the hall. He'd introduced himself at the front desk as "Riverbrook's Resident Tyrant." He was a bowling ball of a man,

113

sixty or so, wearing an old suit and new tie. "Young people—easy to forget, sometimes. They're adaptable."

"A gift." Mia's thoughts drifted toward the aftermath in Vietnam Victory Square, and the tour group she'd helped reunite. The young girl finding her father again had been a high point. The Korean War vet dying from a heart attack as they pulled shrapnel from his leg had been the nadir. It'd been a long evening. The acrid tang of burnt metal had lingered in her throat for days.

"So, your cousin tell you much about the class?"

"It's a history course," Mia said. "And they're studying modern conflict."

"Innovative approach, starting now and working backward. Not how my generation did things but that's okay. They'll get to Nam in November, just in time for V-V Day and the parade."

"Are you a veteran of Vietnam?" Mia felt sure he was. The dean had the look about him. The moxie, too. "Praise to the Victors."

"Protestor."

"Oh. I—" Mia didn't know what to say. She was almost never wrong about this. "My mom was one of those. A protestor, I mean."

"A long time ago," the dean said.

"Did you—did you go to jail?"

The dean nodded. "Society's tried real hard to make us embarrassed about it. But I'm not." He sniffed. "'Peacemongers.' That's no insult."

"Proud, then?" They were nearing the classroom. Mia was curious. The dean was right. Most Vietnam protestors expressed shame now. Or had learned to fake it.

"Not exactly. We were more right than wrong. But we weren't all right, either. Now it's just something I did forty years ago. A lot's happened since. My life, for one."

"I think it's good," Mia said. "You believed in something."

"Belief can be good," the dean said. "So can doubt. Like I tell the kids, it all depends."

"Depends on what?"

The dean winked and held the door. "The billion-dollar question."

They walked into the classroom as the bell sounded. Twenty or so sixth graders sat in rows as ordered as any army formation, a muted, bantam energy crackling along the verges. Mia found her cousin Quentin in the middle of the third row. He smiled a little grin and waved. Mia introduced herself to the teacher, a man about her age built like a long, spruce Y. He thanked her for coming and set up the slide show. The dean took a desk in the back.

The lights were dimmed and Mia began, selected photographs from her tours cycling behind her.

"How many of you know a World War Two veteran?" she asked. "Like a grandfather."

A few hands went vertical. They're so young, Mia thought.

"How many of you know a Vietnam veteran?" she asked. "Father, uncle, something like that."

Many more raised hands filled the room, including the dean's.

"Now," Mia asked. "How many of you know someone who has served in the Mediterranean Wars?"

Thirty years was a lot of war, but most of the hands fell like diving birds in rhythm. She pointed at those left raised.

"My brother," a girl said. She was proud, Mia liked that. "My cousin," Quentin said, and the class laughed. "My old neighbor," another boy said. "They moved to the army base in the South," he explained.

"Does my nanny's boyfriend count?" still another boy asked. Mia looked at him. He wasn't trying to be funny.

"Have you met him?"

The boy nodded.

"Then of course."

"He got blown up bad," the boy said. "Stepped on a trash bomb."

The room shifted his way. Other boys wanted to know the gory particulars. Mia asked about the recovery.

"Don't know," the boy said, slumping back with his hands in his pockets. "They broke up."

Mia discussed her own journey from Riverbrook to the military—the meaning of service, the power and importance of it, too. She talked about her early failures at flight school, and the power and importance of overcoming those failures. She talked about missing family during deployments, and the power and importance of letters and care packages. She talked about leadership, and how good leaders were also good followers. Then she asked for questions.

They weren't shy. They were old enough to be informed but young enough to be unfamiliar with the art of guile. That mattered in these conversations. They wanted to know about the helicopters she'd flown, so they asked that. They wanted to know about the guns she'd carried, so they asked that. They wanted to know about women soldiers, so they asked that. They wanted to know if she'd killed, and how many, and how. So they asked that.

Then they wanted to know where she'd been during the Palm Sunday attacks. They hadn't been born yet. All they had were their parents' stories.

Mia looked back at a photograph of her younger self smiling in Martyrs' Square in Old Beirut Town. She was wearing a desert camo uniform with a pistol holstered on her thigh. A week after that three helos in her squadron were hit by rockets in the Morning Islands, breaking like glass figurines along the sea top.

This is their normal, Mia thought. Their entire lives, they've been seeing images like this, from people like me.

"There's time for two more questions for Ms. Tucker," the teacher said.

A boy in the front raised his hand. Mia ignored him and called on a girl in the near corner.

"What about China," she asked. "My family . . . they came from Taiwan."

"We'll cover that next month, Yijun," the teacher said. "What happened with America and China with Vietnam and Taiwan is . . . complicated."

"Everything's going to be fine," Mia said. The past hadn't been the girl's question. "The media sometimes makes things a bigger deal than they are."

The girl nodded, not entirely convinced.

"Last question," the teacher said.

The boy in the front still had his hand up. Mia pointed to him.

"Do you have a leg of metal?"

"Chad!" the teacher shouted, while Quentin's face dropped into his hands. Most of the other children's eyes widened to saucers. There must've been a discussion beforehand about this, and young Chad had violated the accord.

"I do," Mia said. She reached down and raised up her chinos and black leggings to the calf. "Titanium."

The bell sounded and the class left in small herds, some stopping to knock the metal with their fists. Mia didn't mind. They were eleven. The dean thanked her and left; Quentin apologized and thanked her and apologized again. He's a good kid, she thought. She wanted so much for him to keep that sweetness in the coming years. The teacher approached last.

"This was great. And, of course: America Honors the Warfighter."

"The honor is ours."

"You know," the teacher said, "I thought a lot about joining up myself. Then college, and jobs . . . it never worked out. But I've wondered. What I'd have done in those situations. What I'd be like now."

"Did you." Mia didn't mean anything by that. She just couldn't count how many times she'd had this very conversation with men her age. Her chat with the dean had been much more interesting.

The teacher called Mia back as she reached the doorway. "Almost forgot—one more question for you. From a student home sick. Fair warning: he's a strange one."

"Shoot," she said.

"'Dear Ms. Tucker,'" the teacher read from his laptop, mono-tone. "'Why doesn't America win at wars anymore?'"

————————

The season of camo chic had arrived. It came with the first hints of fall, part of the long weekend built around Unity Day and family trips to the beach and elephantine sales on mattresses. The Council of Victors had summoned the holiday as both tribute and testament. A tribute to American past. A testament to American future.

For much of Mia's life, the season of camo chic meant some-thing else, too. It meant a return to society, to fund-raisers and auctions, black-tie galas where the city's elite could vie and flaunt. Merlot, tender veal, the catacombs of small talk, all in the name of country. The ritual of giving back to the warfighter mattered, and it mattered a lot. The donations raised, the causes championed, also mattered, and also mattered a lot. Real soldiers' lives were im-pacted. Real soldiers' families, too. If you were of a certain class in Empire City, you weren't just expected back from summer travels for it. You were required.

Years earlier, at one of Mia's first galas, her grandfather had asked her to wear her dress greens from ROTC. Because I'm proud, he'd said. None of these other bigwig capitalists have grandchildren serving. She'd refused, though. She hadn't earned the right to wear the uniform yet, at least not in the presence of the wounded vet-erans being honored. Her grandfather had been furious, but she'd stood her ground. It might've been the first time she'd told him no. It might've been the first time anyone had told him no.

As Mia smoothed out her red sheath dress in front of the mirror—was it too tight? Too red? Did it clash with the leggings too much?—she thought about those wounded vets from years before. The one with the prosthetic hook who'd been so nice and funny before drinks. The one with the reconstructed face who tried to follow her to the bathroom. The one who told her to stay in college as long as she could, until the wars ended, back when that still seemed possible.

They must've felt so alone, Mia thought. Surrounded by strangers celebrating the worst day of their lives. All for a good cause, though. Even the one with the hook had admitted that.

Tonight's event diverged from the season's usual offerings. Speeches would be made and money raised and canapés trayed and paraded, but not for any foundation. Tonight's event announced something different, something new yet old as the republic itself. Something for the season of camo chic but also beyond it. American Service. An idea. A pledge. And now a political party.

Mia and Jesse were invited guests of General Collins, one of American Service's candidates for the Senate. But only Mia would be attending. Since the war memorial bombings, her fiancé had only been home intermittently. The hunt for Jonah Gray had become his everything.

"You must have some good leads." Mia had tried not to sound naggy, or needy. Just interested. "That mug shot is everywhere."

"We do. But—it's complicated, I guess." Mia didn't press. She just told him to make her proud.

She still hadn't told him about the pregnancy. To do so now seemed self-absorbed. Mia knew he'd make a great father; he gravitated toward kids and they reciprocated in kind. But her? The maternal warmth some women possessed had always struck her as foreign. The fact that she associated it with whatever the opposite of ambition was didn't help.

What would that look like at three in the morning when the baby was demanding milk from her breast and all she wanted was for it to stop making noise? What would that mean?

She didn't know. *Semper Gumby*, she reminded herself. Be flexible.

Mia's cell phone shook like static, breaking her from the mirror and the red dress. It was a state news alert. There'd been another mass shooting in Athens, this time in the Plaka quarter. The Greek government had imposed martial law and a curfew, and it'd held, for the night at least. No one wanted a repeat of the Acropolis riots.

She began texting a childhood friend who'd moved to Greece after college, stopping a few words in. She scrolled up. For the past two years, she and her friend had mostly texted one another after an attack. "Just checking in—you okay?" "Hey—just saw the news. All good?" "You safe, girlfriend?" And so on, terror texts across the Atlantic, back-and-forths of fear and relief and promises to catch up properly soon.

Mia set down the phone. I'm sure she's fine, she thought. I'll call tomorrow, for an actual conversation.

———

Mia took car service to the event. The party—officially billed as a "Declaration to Country"—was being held at a midtown restaurant known for its two-thousand-dollar truffled lobster risotto and where years before Secret Service shot dead a comedian with a cream pie. "Somehow," the *Imperial Times* would later write, "that tragedy made getting a table for lunch even more impossible."

Body scanners marked the entryway like rock slabs. Men and women in formal wear moved through them with sporting patience, smiles and wisecracks never quite reaching their eyes. It was delicate work, maintaining one's authority while feigning deference to the structures of modern life. Never let them see you sweat, Jesse would say. It's how Mia had been raised. She removed her shoes for the body scanner and set her jawline to stoic.

Security was pronounced, a range of city police, homeland marshals, and private contractors cutting against the crowd in drab mosaic. A squad of Home Guard had posted in a near corner, with full kits and assault rifles slung low. Mia couldn't help but notice the uniform deficiencies—the untucked bootlaces, the rolled sleeves, the private wearing a death skull patch on his helmet cover. Not my fight anymore, she reminded herself. She walked by the Guardsmen with a curt nod.

Past the entryway, Mia took a moment to soak in the air-conditioning and adjust to the ballroom's faint lighting. The restaurant had once been a bank, complete with marble columns, soaring ceilings, and a large four-faced brass clock in the center. To her right, arriving guests took photographs in front of an American Service sign board with the party's presidential candidate, a governor from out west who'd spent a tour in the Peace Corps. Mia went left, toward the appetizers.

Two crunchy sake pickles and four yogurt cheese balls did little to blunt her hunger. She'd seemed to have passed through the morning sickness phase and gone straight to cravings, a trade-off she appreciated even if she could hear her grandmother's voice as she reached for a puff pastry: "In the history of civilization, no one's ever been impressed by how much a woman ate."

Sorry, Grandma, Mia thought to herself between bites of pastry. But this isn't about impressing.

Mia grabbed a club soda from a passing waiter and began scanning faces. She recognized many in the crowd. The chief legal officer at her bank. Liam Noonan, the Navy SEAL turned bond trader, handing out business cards. The executive vice president of a pharmaceutical corporation who'd gone to Yale with her father, and was on the short list for new Sinai consul. A classmate of hers from Dupont who'd gained notoriety junior year for urinating on his RA's door after a night of heavy drinking. When the RA opened the door in her pajamas, the stream didn't stop. The college newspaper published the security footage to its website, and Dupont made national news that week for all the wrong reasons.

He'd been suspended, of course, but let back into school the next semester. Last Mia had heard, he'd left the US-Deutsche DataCorp Group to run his own equity fund. The finance world had its fair share of fools, Mia knew. But what world didn't?

A man in a white tuxedo with neat black hair and a craggy face raised a hand to her in a half wave, fingers wrapped around a drink.

She returned the gesture. Mia and Roger Tran had met again in his office to game-plan the meeting with the Lehman chair she'd secured. It had ended with him talking about his first visit to America three decades before: he'd been part of the lecture tour sponsored by the U.S. government that brought over Vietnamese refugees and soldiers to speak to the jailed American peacemongers. Her own mother had earned clemency through the program, though Mia kept that to herself.

"We were tourists most days," Tran had explained. "Imagine what the Grand Canyon looked like to an ARVN grunt from Saigon—what the big sky looked like, what the air smacked like! At night, we were driven to camps to tell the wild American youth how self-involved they were, how they'd been bad humanitarians and bad patriots. After combat? An easy job."

Tran had whistled then, low and sharp, before continuing. "Whoever put that together? Masters of messaging. Much to learn from it."

There was, Mia admitted, even if the story had bothered her more than it inspired.

"Mia!" a voice whispered in the ballroom from behind her, quick and conspiratorial. "The RA Pisser's here!"

She turned to find Sebastian grinning like a sleepy jack-o'-lantern. She gave him a quick hug and smelled bourbon. He wore his normal sunglasses and canvas sneakers and a cotton seersucker suit she hadn't seen since college. And where was his tie?

"I'm trying to make it clear I don't belong here," he explained. The bourbon dripped from his words. "Finance and politics. We're in the nexus of American church."

Mia wasn't sure what that was supposed to mean, but he seemed pleased by the phrase. She left it alone.

"Some huckster gave me this." Sebastian pulled one of Liam Noonan's cards from his jacket. "Special Operations Lessons for Corporate Synergy," he read in a voice fit for an infomercial. "Life is a war. Learn to thrive, from the battlefield to the boardroom. Join our business muster and dominate. All caps, DOMINATE, Mia. For the low, low price of five grand!"

"You're shouting," Mia told Sebastian, because he was.

"The RA Pisser's here!" Sebastian repeated, dropping the card. "Wasn't he a Sigma Chi? How high does the eagle fly! Douche-canoes."

"You need to eat," Mia said, thinking she could manage another puff pastry herself. She steered him by his elbow to the far side of the appetizers, where there were fewer bodies and, she hoped, fewer inquiring eyes. In an assembly of sleek striving and dark, serious suits, the man in the wrinkled seersucker stuck out just as much as he'd wanted to. She settled them among a cluster of red, white, and camo balloons loose on strings.

"How are you even here?" she asked.

"Look at all these thirsty jackalopes," Sebastian said, not answering her question, instead scooping up a handful of choc-olate Goldfish cracker bites. "Rich kids who didn't join up after Palm Sunday. Now they're all growed up and sloppy with guilt." He paused to burp into his fist. "Pet the vet, talk about your grandpa in World War Two. Do the army commando workout from *Men's Health* three times a week. Deep down thinking you're too precious for that life. So here's some money, here's some feelings, cleanse *me*, broken souls." He burped into his fist again. "At least I tried." He shook his head and grabbed more cracker bites.

Mia was going to push back on his rant by saying he'd chosen to drop ROTC in college. No one had made him do that. But then Jared Kushner, a real estate prince who'd gone to prep school with her brother, walked by. He waved at Mia and she waved back. He was pretty and smart-looking, in a porcelain sort of way. Sebastian wouldn't have any idea who he was but she didn't feel like disagreeing anymore. Mia repeated one of her grandmother's adages.

"Resentment is like drinking poison and waiting for the other person to die, See-Bee."

"Jesus, Mary, and Allah." Sebastian looked up at Mia and smiled. "That's dark!"

She arched an eyebrow at him while sensing a presence from behind that she couldn't see. She wanted to turn but refused. She loathed that, the unknowing, the coiling tension in her chest. But still she refused. To do so would be submission. The presence neared. It was full and looming, and Sebastian's nodded up at it. Of course, she thought. That's how Sebastian's here.

"You all know each other, right," Sebastian said. "From the hospital?"

The presence stepped beside her and Sebastian without actually moving between them, batting aside an errant camo balloon. An arm like a ladder grabbed a puff pastry. It tossed the pastry into the air, where it disappeared into a constellation of white teeth and fleshy gums.

"Hello, Mia." He spoke through bites, in a voice more mild than she remembered. More cautious, too. "Been a while."

"Pete Swenson." She hoped using his full name didn't come across as coy. She flattened out her words to make sure. "How are you?"

"Same old. Was just talking about you with Jackpot." His disparate eyes shined at his casual reference to the general, black and green roiling together. He'd fitted into a black suit too small on him, though maybe that had been intentional. He needed a haircut and a shave, and he was as drunk as Sebastian, betrayed by a soft, droopy glaze. He'd managed a skinny tie, though, and his face and shoulders had finally filled out.

That month in Germany: they'd all just survived a disaster no one could explain. Mia had lost a leg and her career, her very purpose of being. She'd gained a freak power she wasn't ever supposed to use. She was a lot aimless, and not a little manic. And then there were the lurid dreams of blackness, the ones that came on like floods and only relented to pills she feared even more than the dreams. Pass the days exploring the European countryside with a tall, handsome stranger? Why not. Pass the nights in his arms? Sure.

It'd been fun, a reminder that there was life beyond war, and a lot of it. More than a lark, less than love. That'd been it, though. For her, at least.

"Last I saw you . . ." Mia had been avoiding him, she knew. He'd known her when she hadn't been herself. When she hadn't been who she was now. Now that he was in front of her, Mia needed to reintroduce herself. "You put a hole through a wall. Right above my head."

Pete tilted his head, his green eye seeming to refract around her, like waves. She looked back, not staring, not glaring, either, holding to a five-count in her mind. Then she took a long sip from her club soda. The lights of the ballroom dimmed, the cocktail hour coming to an end. The last thing Mia saw before the room went dark was Sebastian's mouth hanging open, mid-chew.

Huh, she thought. Guess he really didn't know.

The babbling din faded out. A digital sign glowed into brightness in the shape of a silver tree, American Service's chosen symbol. General Collins appeared on a stage in the center of the ballroom clenching a microphone in her right fist. She wore a gray suit and the ubiquitous West Point ring. Her short, styled auburn hair cut against the evenness of her outfit and she turned to the crowd with the grace of a piston. Many a retired general before her had failed at politics. Too stilted. Too rough around the edges. Too many acronyms. It didn't matter what the message was if the messenger couldn't appeal. Any stirrings of concern Mia may have felt in the moment, though, washed away as the general tapped the mic and began speaking.

"Friends! Romans! Countrywomen!" General Collins paused to let polite laughter sound through the ballroom. "Thank you for being here tonight. For those of you who don't know me, my name is Jackie Collins—you may call me 'General'"—more polite laughter—"and I'm a proud American Service candidate for the Senate!"

Applause carried through the room. She totally punched a superior, Mia thought, recalling the rumor for why General Collins hadn't pinned a third star. And I love it.

"We live in a moment of much divide. Perhaps not since the Civil War has America been this polarized, this angry and upset with the so-called other side. We here at American Service believe there is no other side. Not with fellow Americans. But the tribalism of the system is strong. Strong and toxic. It's fracturing our great nation.

"Now, more than ever, the center must hold. A center of moderation. A center of compromise. A center of service.

"Yes, service. It's a word tossed around a lot these days, but what does it mean? What does it look like? For too many citizens, it's something they believe in but aren't personally acquainted with. We here at American Service believe we have the answer. An answer that will fill our young people with purpose and benefit the nation.

"Everyone here at American Service has practiced what we preach. I myself spent a few years in a military uniform, and then a couple more at the Agency. Just resigned from there, actually. To do this." The general stopped for applause and after a strained beat, some came. The military was one thing, but the Empire City elite held mixed feelings about the Agency. "Service to community. Service to country. Service to our ideals, to our better angels. That's our vision. After tonight, it'll be yours, too."

She began introducing the presidential candidate, but Mia's thoughts stayed with the general. "Our better angels," she had said. Pragmatism *and* idealism, for something bigger than self. Mia felt like she did at the summer luncheon. Transfixed. Hopeful.

I'm going to do it, she thought. I'll leave finance for this, and never look back.

"She's talking mandatory national service, right?" Sebastian was in her ear, whispering. Mostly. "Like everyone has to join the army or park service for a couple of years?"

Mia nodded, her mind beginning to plot out her transition. Was the general's offer still standing? She needed to be certain. And Pete had said he'd talked about her with General Collins. She needed to know what about.

"It's my right as an American to do whatever I want." Scorn laced Sebastian's words. He burped into his fist yet again. "Especially if it's nothing."

Mia held zero regard for that. This was America, not a blithe dreamscape. She leaned up to Sebastian and said, words drawn like a revolver, "Shut. Up."

The presidential candidate walked across the stage to shake hands and exchange an awkward hug with General Collins. Mia knew little about him other than he was Mormon, came from gambling money, and had salt-and-pepper hair that never seemed to move, even in wind. If he was going to be the bellwether of this movement, she needed to learn more. She tried to focus on his speech.

"What is patriotism?" the candidate began.

It was a question, a good question, and one Mia and others in the crowd had explored in mind and heart. The ballroom turned black before it could be answered, though, as if the plug of the world had been tripped over by a clumsy god.

Through the shadows: the kiss of gunfire into dark air. Shrieks. Shouts. Metallic fear, tinny panic, primal smells for the postmodern condition. A voice, cold and singular, telling everyone to remain still, remain still, remain still if you want to live.

Through it all, Mia watched, her eyes adjusting, the tips of her fingers prickling. The nape of her neck began to itch. She heard the hustle of bodies and guns moving their way, knowing straightaway they were coming for Pete. It was how she would've planned it.

She took a knee and waited for the enemy to reveal itself.

FREEDOMBOOK

Your state-approved source for information and factual content

The Council of Victors is a federal agency that oversees a wide variety of services, benefits, and medical care for American military veterans and discharged warfighters. The Council consists of nine members, all veterans themselves, selected for renewable ten-year appointments.[1] Historically, the Council has drawn from the government, finance, and energy sectors for its executive selections, though some more recent members have come from Hollywood and academia.

The Council of Victors replaced the Veterans Administration at the conclusion of the Vietnam War due to recurring institutional failures and allegations of government corruption.[2] "The Council will be a fusion of federal power and funding with private industry's knack for innovation," founding member Ambassador Javier Contreras said in 1983. Among its early successful projects were Vietnam Victory Square in Empire City, Heroes Hall in Chicago, and the first rehabilitation colony for veterans with troubles, in the Outer Banks.[3]

In order to broaden the Council's vision and impact upon local communities, the Council of Victors sanctioned 300 local Victor councils in 1992, located across the United States.[4] The Council of Victors is strictly a nonpartisan assembly, as stipulated in its charter. Any member of the Council (local and executive) must resign before pursuing political office.[5]

CHAPTER 9

THE SCREEN FLASHED with breaking news but it was too low to hear and Jean-Jacques found the chyron on it oddly imperceptible. The attacks, the demonstrations, the street fights, they were starting to blur together. Soldiering provided agency. Life as a citizen offered anything but. He hated feeling like a bystander but what choice did he have when something was happening elsewhere? What choice did anyone? He found the remote and pressed the off button.

The room the secretary had directed him to felt like the inside of a shoebox—blank, bland, and made of slender walls. Jean-Jacques had been waiting fifteen minutes but it seemed three times as long. His phone couldn't locate any roaming service and the office's wireless connection was locked behind a password. He had two texts he needed to respond to: the first, an offer from Flowers to come hang in Gypsy Town; the second, a plea from his cousin Emmanuel to get dinner.

He didn't want to do either, but knew he'd end up doing both. Flowers needed a spotter; he was out of his element, and not just with Britt and the two boyfriends and the whole bohemian music shit-scene. Empire City had beat down many a traveler over the decades, most of them savvier souls than Grady Flowers of Oak Ridge, Tennessee. As for his cousin, Jean-Jacques needed to be direct and let the man know he wouldn't be investing in whatever plan he had conjuring. He'd say it's because he didn't mix family and business, but that wasn't it. He'd just seen too many little Emmanuels in hoods across the globe. He knew how the schemes looked and how they sounded. He knew how they ended.

Before he could settle with Flowers or his cousin, though, he needed to get this done. They'd called it an interview, which could mean a lot of things. He'd once "interviewed" a Revolutionary Guard captain in Mashhad that ended with the young Persian dangling upside down from a twentieth-floor tower railing. The memory made Jean-Jacques smile. Good times, he thought. That tour had been real freedom. The kind only frontier soldiers and far-gone outlaws knew. The kind that bayed in the savage chambers of the heart, that smelled of dark animal piss and tasted of the same, the kind that allowed human beings to lose and find themselves all at once. Some men never came back from that freedom; it was life too full, too uncut. Those who did tended not to forget what they'd exchanged for civilization. They'd made the deal for reasons, of course. But on occasion, some of them wondered about that uncut life. What they could've been. What they almost were.

Jean-Jacques was one of those.

The door opened with a soft yawn. Three men in slacks and starched white shirts came in, moving with the vertical strain that constant posture yielded. A fourth followed, less crisp than the others and hunching, holding a yellow notepad. Jean-Jacques folded his arms across his chest, balled his fists, and silently repeated his favorite saying from the Legion: *Be Polite, Be Professional, Have a Plan to Kill Everyone You Meet.*

"Hello, Corporal Saint-Pray-ux," one man said as they settled into chairs across from him. He was middle-aged, gray at the temples, while Jean-Jacques pegged the other two in their thirties. The man with the notepad took a seat in the corner. "Did I pronounce that right?"

He had not but Jean-Jacques nodded anyhow. It wasn't the worst he'd heard.

"This is Agent Stein, this is Agent Dorsett. My name is Assistant Director Larsen. They're Bureau agents here in the city, and I'm part of a counterterrorism task force based out of Federal City." He pointed to the corner. "This is Mr. Burke, a legal representative from the War Department, here on your behalf. Appreciate you coming on such short notice."

"All good. We're on the same team." Jean-Jacques said it as deadpan as possible. Starched shirts and neckties didn't change that these guys were cops. The lawyer kept his head down, writing into his notepad.

"Can we get you a coffee?"

"I'd take a beer." Not unreasonable. It was 7 p.m.

The black agent looked at Larsen, shrugged, then left the room. Thirty seconds later, he returned with a bottle of light pilsner.

"*Mesi*," Jean-Jacques said, twisting off the cap and taking a drink. "So. The bomber. What you looking to know."

They'd called that morning, refusing to say why they wanted to speak. Just that they needed to. Good with Special Operations Command? But of course. Where at? They had offices all over the districts of Empire City, name one. (Little Haiti? Eh, name another one.) Would tonight work? Sure, if nothing sooner didn't.

Jean-Jacques considered the possibilities over the day, zeroing in on army veteran Jonah Gray. Nothing else made sense, even if he didn't understand what it had to do with him, or why they asked he come by himself. Regardless, the Bureau men's faces stayed still as stone at Jean-Jacques's prodding. Good training, he thought.

"You know him? Let's start there," the older agent said.

Jean-Jacques shook his head.

"You've seen his photograph?"

"Couldn't miss that caveman stare if I wanted to. It's every-where."

"And you're sure you've never met?"

"Sure we never talked."

"Some tips we've received claim he worked with the Volunteers," the agent who'd gotten the beer said. He had an accent like Flowers, subtler though, more creamy. Whatever the language—and Jean-Jacques knew four fluently and could converse in a handful more—mountain people sounded mountain and coastal people sounded coast. This guy was coast.

"Which missions."

"The Abu Abdallah raid, for one."

"Brother." Jean-Jacques laughed. "We had about one hundred in auxiliary. Every branch had boots there. Demanded it. SEALs. Force Recon. 82nd. Some ground zoomies. Even those crazy-ass Agency door kickers. Now every vet on the planet can say they was on that island, helping get the bad man. Use it to get laid."

The lawyer kept writing. None of the agents even smiled. Too bad, Jean-Jacques thought. It's funny.

"Got another tip saying he ran su-support for you all." The other field agent, Stein, spoke now. He had a mild stammer. Jean-Jacques distrusted it. "In the Dinaric Alps."

That was interesting. That'd been one of the first missions with their supers—a running gun battle with Balkan nationalists who had them surrounded. It hadn't been publicized, since it hadn't been a glorious victory over terror. It'd been a total mess. Four days at the top of the earth with no resupply. Pete and Flowers thought it'd proven their mettle. Jean-Jacques thought it'd revealed their limitations. Nothing but the smells of death, with some desperate calls for artillery in between. Superheroes or not, they'd have been dead ten times over without that artillery. The Alps had shown Jean-Jacques what real power was. It'd shown him where it came from, too.

He kept that to himself, though. "No such support." Every word he spoke would be parsed into fragments upon fragments by analysts who hadn't seen sunlight in years. Best to keep it brief. "Just us up there."

The agents asked about Sergeant Swenson and Corporal Flowers, if either had ever expressed knowing the bomber.

"Big negative." Jean-Jacques looked at the man in the corner, whose focus remained on his notepad like it held the mysteries of the universe. Of course they sent the worst lawyer alive, Jean-Jacques thought. "As surprised as I was. We all thought it was a wog, to be honest."

The lawyer wrote faster than usual into his notepad. Probably shouldn't have said that, Jean-Jacques thought. Oh well.

Agent Dorsett leaned back in his seat, causing it to screech against the tile floor. Then he cracked his neck like he was about to power-clean the table. Fucking babylons, Jean-Jacques thought. Everything's always a show.

"I'm going to be real with you now, brutha."

"Okay."

"We figured those tips were bullshit. Timeline doesn't match. Due diligence, though. Now I need you to be real with me."

"Okay," Jean-Jacques said again.

"Only difference between us is a boat stop. Remember that."

Jean-Jacques thought about that, then thought about why a federal agent would say that to a soldier. "Okay," he said yet again.

"Thirty bombed monuments. One for each year of the Mediterranean Wars. Each monument from a different war. This was exact. Tight. Planned, with a message. We got surveillance of Gray entering Vietnam Victory Square the morning of."

"That's good."

"It is. That's just one of thirty, though. He did this all by himself? Hell no."

"Sure." Jean-Jacques sniffed. "But what's that got to do with me?"

"Your cousin." Empty seconds passed. Jean-Jacques listened to recycled air. "Emmanuel."

"What about him?"

The field agents looked at Larsen from the task force. The older man nodded and began reading from a file.

Jonah Gray. Age forty-six. From Ohio. Army veteran of the Mediterranean Wars. Tours to Beirut, Cyprus, and Albania. First as an armored cavalry scout, later as a chaplain's assistant. Upon military discharge, a medical tribunal sent Jonah Gray to a colony on Block Island for "signs of combat stress reaction and psychological trauma." He spent ten years there and was released, having met the criteria for a return to the citizenry. The Bureau hadn't been able to get much else from that time frame. The Council of Victors held tight to colony documents.

Jonah Gray went west after the colony. He'd met some separatists on Block Island and become interested in their ideas. He earned a nickname during his western travels: the Chaplain. His time as an assistant had shown him the power of reverence. A holy man held great importance to soldiers, whether in the Mediterranean or the Great Basin. He became a roving desert prophet, going from separatist group to separatist group, calling for uprising against the American government. The separatist leaders treasured him at first, seeing how this holy man inspired their rank and file. That turned, eventually. They began to fear being usurped. Jonah Gray was turning his pulpit into a platform for questioning their tactics and strategy. Sermons about God and justice were one thing. Being told they weren't doing enough for true revolution was another. The separatist leaders had banished Jonah Gray from their camps three years before.

"He fell off our radar after that," Agent Dorsett explained. "A mistake. But our focus was on the separatists, not a wandering reverend."

After the war memorial bombings, the Bureau had been trying to piece together where Gray had gone next. There'd been a vet break from the Block Island colony he must've been involved with: twenty-four veterans escaped, including a group of his former ward mates. From those men and the strategies learned out west, Gray had formed a militia of his own. They called themselves the Mayday Front.

The Front weren't political extremists in any traditional sense.

Not far left, not far right, not devoted to toppling the federal state or tax system. Other than Gray himself, they didn't even seem all that religious. "But they're angry," Agent Stein said. "And armed. A group of radical warfighters and citizens hell-bent on humiliating those they think have humiliated them. Want to destroy the re-habilitation colonies, for example. Let veterans with troubles back into everyday society.

"They're crazy. No plan for what comes after."

Gray had learned how to lead, how to plan. Like the Western separatists, like the Muslim Brotherhood and IRA abroad, the May-day Front had both a militant wing and a social service wing. He had deputies installed in both while staying off the grid himself. No digital profile to speak of, no media presence. They'd found one lone video online, a grainy speech Gray had made in the Florida backwoods while recruiting an ultra militia.

Right-wing ultras and lefty activists working for the same cause, toward the same end? That didn't reason. Jean-Jacques said so.

"Gray's fucking nuts," Agent Dorsett said. "But he's got that madman charisma. It's an ethic of total retaliation."

The militant wing had carried out the war memorial bombings. They could pin Gray to Vietnam Victory Square the day of. Now they needed to find him. Which is why they needed Jean-Jacques.

His cousin, the agents said, belonged to the Mayday Front. Not the militant wing, but the social service one. They'd had trouble infiltrating the militants—they were wary, distrustful, made up of veterans of the Mediterranean who'd known one another for years. The social service wing, though, was more nascent, run by a deputy with Haitian roots. It's how Emmanuel had become involved.

"Your cousin brings you in," Agent Larsen said. "You're a famous Volunteer. They'll welcome your presence. Jump at getting you involved in their community projects and outreach. Especially if you let slip there's something about the wars that you resent. Something you regret. Will help earn their trust."

Could Jean-Jacques handle that?

He thought about Tripoli, and the boy he'd lost, the boy he'd failed. Yes, he could conjure up something for these Maydays. But why? He needed to be getting ready for war again, he said. Hitting the gym. Doing foot marches through hills. Zeroing his weapons at the range. Shit like that.

The lawyer cleared his throat. "One, we'd protect your cousin." Jean-Jacques just blinked. If these guys were as bad as the Bureau said, Emmanuel deserved the consequences. "Two, you help deliver Mr. Gray, the War Department will authorize your return to the International Legion. You'll get a combat platoon there. Helped draft the paperwork myself."

Empty seconds passed. Jean-Jacques took all that in. Don't think too fast, he thought. They're trying to get you to say something too fast. He considered why the War Department would change its mind. What could possibly matter more than the PR the Volunteers offered? Celebrity had replaced service. GI Joe from World War II, Mud Grunt from Vietnam, the thing that'd made them heroes was their normalcy. Boys-next-door saving democracy with rifles and heart. The Volunteers were the exact opposite. Three men in a military of five million. Their heroism lay in the extraordinary.

A military of five million, Jean-Jacques thought again. That's it. More than anything, wars need bodies.

"Recruitment," he said, amplifying the last syllable of the word. "Yeah. An army of peacemonger vets would be bad for that."

"Hypothetically," the lawyer began.

"I got you," Jean-Jacques said. "That stays here."

He said he'd do it. To get back to the Legion, he'd do pretty much anything.

"One final question for you, Corporal." It was the older agent talking again, Larsen from the task force. Jean-Jacques thought for sure he was going to make the typical remark—why hadn't they been selected for the Hero Project? Federals loved that one. Instead Larsen cocked his head and asked, "Why leave Abu Abdallah breathing?"

Getting this question from citizens was one thing. They didn't know any better. Getting it from federal cops was another. They should have. The new anger he'd come home with rose into his throat like sour phlegm, but Jean-Jacques managed to keep it there, despite himself.

He stared out at the younger agents with the fringes of his eyes while remaining fixed on Larsen. "Duty, homie. That's all."

They thanked Jean-Jacques again. He stood up and chugged the rest of his beer. He tossed the bottle into a corner trash bin, making the lawyer flinch. As he reached the doorway, he turned to ask the thing that'd been bothering him since the agents had begun their pitch: Why had his little cousin become an activist? How did a kid from Little Haiti become interested in rehabilitation colonies? Why give a fuck?

It was the stammering one, Stein, who answered. "Because of you."

———

They'd left Haiti because wants had become too impossible and needs had become too scarce. His mother paid off smugglers an aid worker recommended. She and her precious, plump toddler boarded a wooden sailboat headed northwest toward the Keys, a small pack between them to carry the entirety of their lives. America awaited, and not just regular America. Empire City was their goal. Empire City, the place of old stories and new dreams.

Empire City was also where a cluster of relatives had found refuge. One was willing to pretend to be his mother's sister so they could get the right papers. That woman was Emmanuel's mother. She'd urged them to hurry. The news said the government soon planned on making it even harder for Haitians.

Glimmers of the journey had lingered with Jean-Jacques. Nothing more than images, really, disjointed and useless to trust.

The boat, overcrowded, packed full like black sardines. A little son and his mother fighting for space with shame, then elbows and teeth. Twelve nights under a tarp fine as silly string, clinging to one another for warmth against the open Caribbean wind. Nuts and jerky and bits of fish the men caught and cooked in seawater. He hadn't wanted the fish, not at first. Fussiness soon gave way to hunger.

Then, light and fresh as young rain: a trace of a private smile on his mother's mouth, her long, lean face up and defiant against the horizon. She'd set her left hand over the teardrop hanging from her neck, a little cheap turquoise thing, too scratched and worn for any thief to take notice, and she was tapping at it, ever slightly. Through constant dredging of the memory, this moment had been placed just before land was spotted, before hope and survival were, too, that isolated beachhead on Big Mullet Key their sailboat would run aground on, sparking songs of jubilation and prayers of joy to the three Christian gods and the old vodou ones, too, to anything up there that was listening. That face. Alone with herself and her pendant. Had it been a birthday gift from her parents, left over from a childhood in sleepy Port-de-Paix? A trophy her future husband had won her in the fixed street games, disregarding the odds with all the power of a bright new love? Maybe a family heirloom that dated back to the Haitian revolution. Maybe still just something she'd found in the dirt at the port. There was no way to know now. He'd never asked about the pendant when he still could have. But it was Jean-Jacques's remembrance. That image, that moment, that distant smile had happened, and it'd happened on that sailboat, his mother's secret thoughts alone against the sky of the unknown.

———

The streetlights outside the Bureau's satellite office burned with a watcher's eye. Summer's throes meant sticky air and bug songs and a fat sort of indolence. Jean-Jacques couldn't figure the last time he'd been in Ash Valley. High school, maybe, for a water polo match? The outer district was white working class and had been for a century. Too far out for the gentrifiers to care, too raw and sunken for the suburbs to come for it. Polish, Irish, Hungarian, Albanian, Appalachia transplants—different but not, the same but not, united in a sort of tacit understanding that there were worse places in the world to live.

Jean-Jacques would've found it decent enough if it weren't so gray. It was like the entire district had been dipped in chimney smoke. There was nothing ironic about Ash Valley, especially its name.

He got into the car he'd borrowed from one of Britt's boyfriends—they'd proven to be welcoming and helpful, to him at least—and considered texting Flowers. After the Bureau's interview, or whatever it had been, he felt like alcohol, good alcohol, too. And maybe light talk with a bohemian who didn't care about the things he did and didn't care that he didn't care about the things they did.

He texted his cousin instead.

Emmanuel answered in seconds. "Need you, son . . . Xavier Station. RIOT!"

Jean-Jacques closed his eyes and held his breath, letting out air slowly through his nostrils. He felt the magnetic pull of family, supreme, inevitable, the same pull he'd resisted eight years before, knowing it was all or nothing, knowing he needed to make a break for far away or he'd be stuck forever. He'd promised himself then to never return. He'd abided by that even as his mother lay dying, she herself telling him to not come back, that she'd be fine and would be in the front row the next time they redeployed back to America, clapping along with all the other proud Ranger moms. But instead she withered away like a raisin person, eighty pounds of flesh stretched across brittle bone in a one-room apartment, alone. All because he'd believed it weakness to come back, even for her. Even as she'd believed the very same.

For duty, yes. For country, yes. But also: for pride.

He read the text again. "Need you."

Yes you do, he thought. And I need the Legion. That's what I need.

Jean-Jacques rubbed at the teardrop under his shirt, once, twice, a third time just because. Then he turned on the car and drove to the expressway, toward his cousin's appeal.

CHAPTER 10

THE BLINDFOLD BROUGHT familiarity to Sebastian. He could see just enough through the threadbare. It didn't feel quite natural, but it didn't feel totally alien, either. Like riding a bike, if you'd feared and brooded over your last ride so much that frequent, crushing nightmares resulted from it, and you'd spent the years since in a drunken daze trying to ice the memories. Yes, he'd done this hostage thing before, and he'd done it for twenty-six days. He would survive this, as he had in Tripoli. He'd survived there, from having to shit into a cardboard box to the Palestinian chair exercise the guy with the asterisk scar liked putting him through until his muscles turned to jelly and he collapsed into his own filth. He would survive this. He would because he could. One second, one minute, one conversation at a time.

First things first, Sebastian told himself. Keep your leg from twitching.

His leg did not keep from twitching. He wished he could reach the box of Valium in his pocket, but somehow doubted the Home Guard or whoever had seized the ballroom would help with that.

As he sat on his knees against a back wall, a cable tie around his wrists and black sheer cut from pantyhose around his head, Sebastian's mind drifted. He thought about the crippled vet he'd met earlier that night among all the parade soldiers, the one with the pretty wife.

Could he, well. Could he still fuck? Speaking of, Mia and Pete, in Germany . . . he'd never have guessed. Was he even her type? She tended to be really picky. But I guess Pete's everyone's type, he thought.

Sebastian had a rotten habit of picturing the bedroom scenes of his friends.

His mind returned to his first captivity. The afternoon before his rescue, day 25—he'd kept track with floss shreds in his grooming kit—the insurgents had unbound him from the metal pipe in the basement and told him to enter the password for his laptop. They didn't believe his story about being an intern with an identity crisis looking for his probably dead cousin's body. Why would they? They were convinced he was an American spy, and thought something in the laptop might prove that. Sebastian inputted the password. Objecting would only heighten their suspicions. Besides, they had guns.

They looked through everything. They found his thesis on the Spanish Civil War, hapless American volunteers dying for someone else's cause. They laughed as he tried to explain. They found old photographs from a school trip to Kurdistan, making fun of the Kurds as donkey people and wondering why he took so many shots of mountain roads. "If you're in the ocean," the one with the crooked smile asked, "do you take pictures of water?"

Then they found the video file labeled "Your_Eyes_Only."

A fellow intern had made it for him before he flew to the Near East, with the express promise that he delete it. He hadn't, of course. She'd done it because she thought it brave, his going to the war. He'd asked because he'd believed the same. Still, as he again watched his lady friend smile at the camera with a coy, light heart and then coo his name with something else, he wished more than anything that he'd listened to her. Because she'd done this for him, him alone, and sharing it with anyone was a violation beyond words, let alone sharing it with dirty, horny terrorists in a Tripoli basement who were breathing like asthmatics behind him as she reached down under her panties.

"Number one, sex," the one with the crooked smile had told Sebastian, patting him on the back. They thought it was a moment of kinship, somehow. The intern/sort-of girlfriend was naked as the sun and touching herself at this point. "Sex, so good, number one. So good." Then he made the fisting motion and said something in Arabic and the others laughed.

The venom of shame coursed through Sebastian, first in the basement and years later in the ballroom. Shame for not attacking the laughing Arabs. Shame for not being able to in the first place, not unless he wanted to turn departed by a bullet to the skull. Shame for even having the video, for being the type of person who wanted a video like that and asked for it from someone who cared about him, someone who trusted him. Shame at being impotent and virile all at once, yet not enough of either to do anything but sit there and watch others watch something that was supposed to be only for him.

The laptop was destroyed during the rescue the next day. Sebastian never mentioned it to his soon-to-be-ex sort-of girlfriend, even when they were still talking and trying to find in each other what had been lost. Superstitious as he was—though he liked to think it was more providential than that, because of God and stuff—he'd come to believe it ended because of the video. He'd failed her then by not protecting her at her most vulnerable, so he'd go on to fail her more after he returned home. If she hadn't left him when she did, he'd just continue failing her again and again, like two star-crossed travelers stuck in a loop.

Ignoring her, and her life, and her hopes, and her ideas. Refusing to leave his apartment for anything but the laundromat and bars. To Sebastian's mind, those weren't reasons for why it ended, but the means. He'd wanted to explain to her about the video, because then maybe she'd understand like he did. But he never had. Whenever he'd opened his mouth to try, all that came out was garble.

Sebastian found out Mia was kneeling next to him in the ballroom when he whispered, "Mia, you there?" and the person to his right said "No," but the person to his left said "Yeah."

"Are you okay?"

"I am." A couple seconds passed. "Are you?"

"Uh-huh."

It seemed like as soon as the ballroom went dark, even before the cell phones got confiscated, they'd been surrounded by Home Guardsmen with rifle-lasers dancing on Pete. Well, men in Home Guard uniforms. Who knows who these jokers really are, Sebastian thought. Western separatists, maybe. Greek militants still angry about Crete accidentally getting nuked. Disgruntled employees who wanted a 401(k) plan. Homegrown jihadists? That was a terrifying idea. Regardless, Pete had been marched off and everyone else ordered to remain still and silent.

Some were better at it than others.

Sebastian swallowed to wet his throat. "Mia," he whispered again.

"Yes."

It wasn't the right time for this question but he'd been wanting to ask it since learning he hadn't been the Rangers' main priority. "Did you know it was me there? In Tripoli?"

Seconds passed, then: "Why do you think I volunteered for it?"

"Thank you."

"You're welcome. Now. Sshh."

It was good advice, Sebastian knew. And he believed her. Not just cause she was a good friend—though she is, he reminded himself. But because the alternative defied the odds of chance. She'd come for him, on her helo, freely, he thought. Which meant something he knew about that day was still true.

She'd lost her leg that day. Because of that choice, because of him.

Sebastian's mind drifted some more. He again swallowed to wet his throat; the cotton mouth would not go away and a slow march to sobriety was becoming a likelihood. The cravings for Valium had passed into thirst. Five minutes later, Sebastian couldn't help himself.

"Excuse me," he said, trying his best to sound mannered. "State of emergency. With my lizard."

A gruff voice replied, somewhere to his front and out of threadbare sight, "Use your pants."

"You serious?" The bourbon wasn't yet totally out of his system. "I just need to use the bathroom."

The charging handle of a rifle was drawn, metal tonguing off against metal. Sebastian didn't say anything to that.

———

"This thing on? Empire City elite! Your attention, please.

"I'll say it only once: this is not a democracy.

"I am Veteran Zero. My men and I represent a coalition known as the Mayday Front. We are not criminals. We are not terrorists. We are patriots and humble warfighters, here for our due.

"Holy shit, Tupac's here! My man. Love your show. *Thug Life in the A.M.* Gangsta, gangsta. Who's the gangster now, 'Pac? Give here that gold chain. For the cause.

"Where was I? Something, something, honoring the social contract . . . yes. The broken, the scarred, the fucking *enlisted* will be discarded no more. Invisible no more. We killed for you. We died for you. 'To care for him who shall have borne the battle.' Lincoln's words. Smart man, that dead man. But even he could not foresee what you would do to his beloved republic.

"George fucking Clooney! You were a delight in *Imperial Dreams*. Bit weepy, though. And *The Great Tet Raid*! So righteous, you got that bitch Robb elected. My, my, those are sweet cuff links. Burberry? Just touching them gets my dick hard. Appreciate the contribution.

"You people have disrespected my people for too long. Do you know how insane it is to raise money for individual warfighters while allowing the abuse of the warfighting class to continue

147

forevermore? Have even one of you assholes bothered to consider the warped looking-glass logic of that?

"You're goddamn right that's a literary reference! I'm a man of letters.

"General Collins—an honor. If I didn't think the political system was inherently corrupt and defective, you'd have my vote. I heard you pegged the War Department secretary to get your division more funding. Amazing. Tell me, where are you on jobs? Twelve million living vets of the Mediterranean Wars, yet the only steady work my men here can find is as jailers at the colonies. Fucked up, right! Guarding other warfighters from proper society. General Jackpot, please—give mind to the hinterlands. It's a real struggle out there.

"Rich people! Listen the fuck up. We're not unreasonable. We fought for this country. We love this country. But you forgot about us. Can't do that. Not in the Home of the Brave.

"'American Service.' A fine ideal. One I champion myself. And why we'll be ransoming you off in groups. To pay tribute to the service of those left behind by your plundering.

"That's it for now. Just . . . sit tight, it'll all be over soon. The honor is ours."

————

Sebastian saw shapes like puzzle pieces approaching through the threadbare. They didn't fit together, though, one long and bent, the other bulbous and plush, like they were jigsaws from different sets. A lot of these guys acted and sounded like warfighters, he'd decided, but they must've been out for a while. Especially the fat ones.

"This him?" one said.

"Think so," another said.

"The one in the clown suit, they said."

"It's seersucker," Sebastian said.

"Right," the first voice said. "Up you go."

I shouldn't have said that thing about my lizard, Sebastian thought as he was hefted to his feet and led away from the back wall. And the irony is, now I really do have to go to the bathroom.

"See-Bee." He heard Mia's voice behind him, resolute as ever. She's made of adamantium, he thought.

"Yes, dear?"

"Do what they tell you. No stupid jokes. It'll be fine."

He didn't say anything to that. Who were these guys, really? The speech about the endless wars and veterans not getting their due had sounded crazy to Sebastian. Maybe they knew he wrote ads for Homeland Authority and meant to make him an example. Death to the propagandist.

Despair began to tug at him, so Sebastian told the truth. "I'm poor," he said. "I'm literally the worst person to kill here."

"They're not going to kill you, clown suit," the second voice said. "Like Veteran Zero said earlier. Relax."

"Well," the first voice said. "He is getting bored up there."

"Naw, brother," came the response. Sebastian wanted to believe this voice. "They ain't gonna off a nobody. Orders from the Chaplain himself. High-value targets only."

They lifted Sebastian up a platform of stairs like he was a stuffed toy and someone pulled his blindfold. The first thing he saw was the digital silver tree still glowing bright. He flinched from the closeness of the light and asked if someone would put on the sunglasses in his pocket for him.

"Son, I'm not sure where you belong, but it's not here."

Sebastian's vision took a moment to adjust. He stood on the ballroom's center stage, where two hours before, the American Service politicians had been giving their speeches. Now the politicians had been replaced by fifteen mostly white, mostly men in their thirties and forties. They wore a mishmash of military uniforms and were swaddled in shiny assault rifles and ammo belts. A few sported the death skull patch on their helmets or shoulders.

One of the militants sat in a worn plastic chair, back taut, arm and leg muscles straining like varicose veins. Veteran Zero. He'd sounded the part of a good rogue to Sebastian during his speech, all pebbly-voiced seriousness with just a dash of folly. His appearance mostly measured up: urban camo uniform with rolled-up sleeves, thin black hair, scruffy beard, and dark, puffy eyes that conveyed a very specific sort of hardness. He looked of East Asian descent and there was a classless air about him. His camo top was open and unbuttoned to show a black T-shirt with the words "Gangster 4 Capitalism" etched across it.

Ahh, Sebastian thought. That's why he was screwing with Tupac.

Behind Veteran Zero, bound and surrounded, three men rested on the backs of their heels. One of the men was Pete. He was humungous as ever, slouched a bit, staring straight ahead with lips drawn tight like a rubber band.

"Before I explain your mission," Veteran Zero said to Sebastian, "I have an important question for you."

"Okay."

"It's vital that you answer honestly. Remember. My soldiers have guns."

"I promise to be honest," Sebastian said, lying.

"You've seen the fantasy show *Utopia*. On state TV."

Sebastian considered his options. "Yes," he said. "Of course."

"Did you see the most recent episode?"

"Yeah. They're at the convention."

"Good. We've been debating all week. You'll cast the deciding vote. So: Do you think Mr. Bobby Kennedy knew he was going to fail when he brought the police chief and the protest leader to conference? Or do you think he genuinely believed they'd reach accord?"

"Huh." It was a good question, Sebastian thought, if under very strange circumstances. He hoped they wouldn't kill him over it but he knew he needed to answer. Veteran Zero was waiting intently. "I think the key to that scene, to the whole episode really, is when

Bobby says, 'We can only hope. And try.' So yeah, I think he probably knew the meeting would be unsuccessful. But he went anyway."

"But he went anyway," Veteran Zero repeated, turning over the words in his mouth like a gemstone. "Well said, well said."

The head militant plucked at his beard while one of the guards with a death skull patch smacked another's shoulder and rubbed his fingers together in the money sign. If nothing else, Sebastian had settled a bet.

"Such a shame, what happened to Bobby," Veteran Zero mused, holding a beard hair in front of him. "It all could've been different. No extended Vietnam. No Mediterranean invasion. None of this bullshit."

"Next episode should be a good one?" Sebastian offered, hoping to steer the conversation to something resembling a future. "On to the debates."

Veteran Zero's mind had already moved on, though, pinging away to the next task. "You know who these men are," he said, more declaration than question. Sebastian shook his head, not sure what he was getting at.

"In this swirl of fortunate sons and fucking *profiteers*"—Veteran Zero spat out the word like it was dirty water—"they're the cherries on top." Veteran Zero snapped into the air and a bin of cell phones appeared in front of Sebastian. "Pull yours out. You're going to make a film for us."

Sebastian rummaged through the bin. He thought about an SOS text to 911 but Maslow's hierarchy was a motherfucker. Veteran Zero explained that ransoming off the politicos and celebrities had been their plan, but they hadn't expected such prestige in the crowd. "The war chest of the cause can always use more coin," he explained.

Sebastian nodded solemnly. He was talking with a lunatic, he was sure of it, one with whims, one with the clean conscience of a serial killer, the kind of insane that turned those around him into collateral damage. There was not a doubt in Sebastian's mind that

Veteran Zero himself had been sent to a rehabilitation colony, with good reason too, and somehow gotten free.

"This is for select media. Se-lect. Understand? Remember this info." Veteran Zero waved Sebastian to him. He pulled out a jack-knife and twirled it around his fingers. Then he cut Sebastian's cable ties in one firm stroke. "We are not criminals. We are not terrorists. We are patriots."

"You are not terrorists," Sebastian said, rubbing at the marks left from the ties. "You are patriots."

"What's our mission, son?"

"Getting veterans their due. What the citizenry has failed to honor. Because of the social contract."

"Good. Don't forget the part about humiliating the elite."

"Right. Soak the rich. Eat them."

Veteran Zero nodded slowly, then tossed the cut cable ties behind him, onto the ground. He shifted in his chair to point to the three hostages onstage. "The cherries. Bernard Gault. Executive vice president at Rubicon Pharmaceuticals, proud member of the Council of Victors. A warfighter himself! An officer, of course. Decorated in Vietnam for valor under fire. And maybe, just maybe, the new Sinai consul. But: Rubicon manufactures maven, which is used at colonies to keep our kin incapacitated and drooling. Management likes its patients easily controlled.

"All that honorable service flushed down the shitter, Mr. Gault. Somewhere, your old platoon sergeant is fucking ashamed of you."

Gault, a reedy man with a long chin, angled his head toward Veteran Zero. Sebastian recognized him from Mia's engagement party. They'd talked Vietnam and Orwell. He hadn't realized then Gault was so important.

"You don't even know what you don't know," Gault said, nostrils flaring. "Maven stimulates brain cells. It's going to save more traumatized veterans than any treatment program ever could. Money isn't a panacea. But science can be."

A guard mussed his hair like he was placating a child. Gault took it. Veteran Zero said, "You're lucky we follow a holy man who believes in redemption. Otherwise I'd strangle you right now for that lie." Veteran Zero seemed to take the maven issue personally, Sebastian thought. And what holy man? One of the guards had mentioned someone named "the Chaplain." What did religion have to do with any of this? The head militant sniffed sharp and loud before continuing.

"In the middle there is Liam Noonan. You must recognize him from TV. He was a Navy SEAL, you see. Where were you for the Palm Sunday attacks?" Veteran Zero didn't wait for Sebastian to answer. "Liam was a first responder. It's always the lead sentence of his bio."

Veteran Zero laughed to himself. Sebastian smiled in appeasement. It didn't seem like a thing to joke about.

"Look how mad that made him! Opportunists. Never anything selfless about their service."

Noonan growled like a dog. "I only regret that I have but one life to lose for my country," he said.

Brave, Sebastian thought. If deeply stupid.

Veteran Zero laughed again. "As long as that country doesn't include poors or brown people, right?" He clucked his tongue in disappointment and pointed to Pete. "Last we have the real prize. Odd seeing him in a suit, I know. Justice's reputation as a fighting man precedes itself. Tried to convince him of the goodness of our cause. But. Too much order and discipline on the brain. You'll come around, someday, Mr. Swenson, and see how you're being used the same way we all were."

"Okay." Pete shrugged. "Cool."

"Your adoring masses are gonna see a whole new side of you, Mr. Swenson. A vulnerable side. A tender side." Veteran Zero removed a pistol holstered at his hip, directing it above the three hostages. The pistol was sleek and compact and plated in gold. Veteran Zero chambered a round. The dark magic of the gun slammed forward.

"A side that says, 'Three Million Dollars,' or the big hero becomes worm food."

Pete took the opportunity to look over at Sebastian, coughing to clear his throat. Then he coughed again. And again. And again. It wasn't until he arched his eyebrows and grimaced, though, that Sebastian realized what he wanted.

Oh damn, Sebastian thought. He wants me to do something. And he wants me to do something while . . . invisible. Yes. That's what he wants.

Fear rose through him like hot air.

"What's wrong, clown suit?" Veteran Zero lowered his pistol. He seemed to sense something had changed in the ether. Sebastian faced the other man's bloodshot psychosis and tried not to blink.

"Nothing." Sebastian swallowed again to wet his throat and hoped no one else could hear the sounds ricocheting around his chest. I'm just a citizen, he thought. I don't do things like this. I don't even know how to. Then he thought: well, now you need to.

"Can I go to the bathroom first? Need to drain my lizard."

CHAPTER 11

"DO WHAT THEY tell you. No stupid jokes. It'll be fine."

Mia's words sounded empty even to her as the militants took away Sebastian, but she needed to say something. She'd felt his leg shaking on the ground for the last two hours, and was worried. He'd always been an anxious type, even before Tripoli, and tended to strike authority figures for the worse.

Tripoli. What in the world had compelled him to ask her about that now? She'd told the truth. Partly. She'd known he was the kidnapped journalist. Saving an old friend from college had been a motivation. It'd served as her pitch to command for why she should be the assigned pilot. And a raid going after Abu Abdallah's family? Success could be found on an operation like that. Glory, as well.

She'd volunteered for the wrong mission. It happened. Mia refused to dwell on the whys or hows. No one in the wars volunteered for anything for pure reasons, she knew, not entirely. Of course she'd wanted to help Sebastian. And of course she'd sought something else, too, something beyond charity for an old college friend, something for herself.

It was the same now, in the ballroom. Sebastian will be fine, she told herself. And if not, he's not who you need to protect. Something inside her was twinging again, sharp and knotty.

Mia was still blindfolded. Someone to her left moaned and said they felt dizzy. A charging handle of a rifle was drawn. A voice spoke to the moaner and to the group at once. "No. Noise."

Like most pilots, the military had sent Mia to SERE school. Survival, Evasion, Resistance, Escape. She'd learned how to live off the land in any environment, from the Siberian tundra to the Amazon. She'd built smokeless fire pits from scratch. She'd killed a bunny with a trap made from sticks, gutted it with a belt clip, and turned it into kebab. She'd been waterboarded. None of that would help in an Empire City ballroom seized by a militia of disaffected war veterans.

But the school had also included a sitting session on persuasion and influence. Most of the class slept through it, delirious at the chance to be off their feet for fifty minutes. But not Mia. She'd fought off the siren song and listened, because if there was anything worse than being a prisoner of war, it was being a woman prisoner of war. She'd wanted to know it all.

Two guards began speaking to each other. They talked low, wary of the ballroom's acoustics, but not low enough. Mia bowed her head and homed in, like she was lost in benediction.

"This place is nice."

"Rich people, man."

"Yeah, I know. But still. See those chandeliers? Pure gold."

"Think of how many of our people could be helped with just one of 'em. Keep focused."

"Yeah." A minute or so passed. "Ever seen anything like it before, though?"

The other voice considered. "The Temple out west," it said. "And Assad's sun palace in Syria. Before the wogs blew it up."

"Damn, you was over there then!" The veteran laughed. "You're even older than I thought."

"We were winning when I left. Then you trigger-happy bastards came along. The Found Generation, shit. You all messed up everything."

They went back and forth like that, arguing about who had screwed up the Mediterranean Wars worse, when, and where. They'd mentioned the sun palace. Mia racked her mind. The high palace had been in the hills surrounding Aleppo. The crescent palace lay in the center of Raqqa, near restaurant row. The state palace dominated what remained of Homs. The water palace floated alongside the island of Arwad. The sun palace, though . . .

"Idlib," she said out loud, surprising herself. No turning back now, she thought. This is the right approach. For me. For them. For her.

Jesse hadn't said so, but she knew he preferred a girl.

"What was that?" The militants had heard her.

"Idlib," Mia repeated. "The sun palace. I walked through the rubble there during my tour. Must've been amazing before the truck bombs."

Through the threadbare of her blindfold, Mia saw the two men approach her. What kind of group plans out something this complex, she wondered, but skimps on blindfold costs?

"You a vet?"

She nodded. "Army. Helo pilot out of Fort Sam Damon."

"Chinooks?"

Mia sniffed. They thought she flew cargo. "Black Hawks. Mostly ripping through the Morning Islands, hunting down the last of the Greek radicals."

That impressed them enough for her blindfold to be removed. The Morning Islands campaign had a reputation. She looked up to find two men of average stature and slung rifles, bafflement splayed across their clay faces. If they shaved their face stubble, they still could've been posting guard at any American outpost across the world.

"Chaplain didn't say anything about other vets being here," the one who'd been admiring the chandeliers said. He looked like he should've been delivering Mormon pamphlets house-to-house, Mia thought, not committing terror. "Only rich people and generals."

"Jonah's not here," the other guard grunted. "So loony tune's in charge tonight." Mia's ears rose at that. For one—the name Jonah. Could this Chaplain person be the man wanted for the war memorial bombings, army veteran Jonah Gray? Her fiancé, among many others, would be interested in that. For two—"loony tune" was almost definitely the Veteran Zero who'd made the unhinged speech over the microphone. Which meant this group, this Mayday Front, had internal discord. Which was something to exploit, Mia thought.

"How do we know you're speaking truth?" the other guard asked her. He *was* older, and wore the sad, dumpy face of someone who joined the military only to find the same assholes who'd made up his small town were everywhere. A short, barbed mustache would've framed his face had it been even.

"Tap my right leg," Mia said. "Think a citizen has one of these?"

The leg clinked.

The older militant crossed his arms and nodded. He'd figured her out, finally. "Officer," he said.

Mia thought about lying, but quickly decided not to. Soldiers smelled out lies like hounds.

"Don't hold it against me," she said, offering just a hint of a smile. "You two worked for a living, I'm sure."

The old joke landed. The militants asked about her deployments and units, she asked about theirs. They asked if she knew their old officers, and she did, a couple of them. She asked about the war tattoos covering their forearms, where they got them, what they meant. They told her. She asked if they'd had a hard time since getting out. They had. She asked if they'd loosen the cable ties around her wrists. They did. The younger one asked if she had a boyfriend. She said that she did, a husband, but left out the pregnant part. Babies scared boys. The older one asked why she'd come to the American Service event.

"Because I believe our government would benefit from having more people with military experience in it," she said. "Who have skin in the game. We used to behave like a republic. I think we should get back to that."

"What do you do now, ma'am?" he asked, dumpy face creasing out into corners. He was probing, still. Probably made a good barracks lawyer, Mia thought, explaining to his fellow joes how leadership was plotting against the regular soldier.

"Finance," she said. "Middle management." If she didn't get control of the conversation again soon, they'd find her name and look her up online, and then this little gambit of hers would backfire entirely. They'd believe a Tucker daughter would fetch a fortune.

There was a short cry to her left. Someone tipped forward and landed on their shoulders and forehead, forming a body caret. The two militants looked at each other, then at Mia.

"See if she's okay," Mia said. "I think that's an older person."

They helped the woman up, taking off her blindfold and binding her wrists in her lap, so she could lean back against the wall. Mia thought she recognized her—a college professor and civil rights activist who'd written a book about ethics, citizenship, and the International Legion.

In the midst of chaos, Mia thought, there is also opportunity. Some famous dead person had said that.

"You should get her water," she said, loud enough for the two militants but also for the other hostages. The woman was aware but disoriented. "And maybe a wet towel? It's really hot."

The younger one took a step toward the bar but the older one stopped him. "Hey, officer! You're not in charge here."

Some of the other hostages were stirring and began grumbling; through their pantyhose blindfolds they could see the two armed guards looming over the professor, either feeling bad for her or feeling jealous that she was able to set her back against the wall.

"You're in charge, absolutely," Mia said, recalling from the SERE class the importance of projecting deference. "Just trying to help."

"Uh-huh."

"Given how this could look. Like, media-wise."

The older veteran's nostrils flared. "Explain."

"Well. You have been very professional. But say this turns out to be serious, heatstroke, a concussion or something. Older black woman, mostly white vets . . . you know how reporters are. They might make it racial."

"We're trying to recruit more people of color." The younger militant looked upset. "We have a few Asians and Latinos. A Haitian runs our community force."

"I'm a doctor." One of the bound hostages spoke up. "I can check on her!"

The hostage next to him said, "Stop. You're a dentist."

"Everyone calm down!" the older militant shouted, pointing his rifle into the air. "We got this." He looked back at Mia. "The Mayday Front supports people of all colors, creeds, and orientations. We work for the good of all warfighters. For anyone who's done their part."

"I know that," Mia said. "But will citizens unfamiliar with your movement?"

Choice passed through the militants like wildfire. Soldiers loved to complain about the decision making of their sergeants and officers. It was a proud tradition, one ancient as battle itself. But Mia had seen this quizzical look before, many times. They either rose to the moment or they didn't.

"We should let someone check her out," the younger one said, putting his hand on the other's shoulder. "The ma'am, she's right. This could go bad."

"We should've brought walkie-talkies," the older one said, mostly to himself. "No one ever listens to me." Then he said he was going to find their medic to treat the professor, which really meant asking someone else for guidance.

"Watch them close," he told the other militant. "Back in ten."

And just like that, Mia Tucker cut down the enemy force by half.

Mia took a shallow, measured breath and sequenced through possible next steps. She'd caught some luck, being left the green militant instead of the skeptical one. If the professor was playing at illness, or better yet wasn't, that would keep him distracted. Which would free her up to start communicating with the nearest hostages and gauging who could see, who could move their wrists, et cetera . . .

"Psst. Mia."

The whisper was soft as light and she thought she'd imagined it until it tickled at her ears a second time. "Mia. It's me."

She turned her head to the right and saw nothing. She turned her head to the left and saw nothing. She loosed a small cough, hoping, trying impossibly to convey: What do you want?

It was Sebastian, the invisible man. He'd escaped, somehow, and was creeping around the ballroom. She wanted to tell him to stop, to go away, that she was in the middle of something and that she'd had training for this something and while it hadn't been a lot of training it was still better than no training and she was making progress and that sometimes the best action was inaction especially around jumpy young men with guns and whatever it was he thought he was doing, he needed to stop, time now.

But she couldn't say that. She couldn't say anything. The militant guard was still ten feet from her, giving the professor a glass of water and two pain relievers from a cargo pocket.

"I'm going to slide a butter knife under your dress on the right side," Sebastian whispered. "Don't worry, I won't look or anything."

Mia wheezed between her teeth and tensed her back but she sensed the knife already placed and Sebastian already gone. She raised her eyes again and the young veteran was looking over at her, naked questions rolling across the flat berm of his face.

"What's going on?"

"Nothing," she said, knowing it was too late. For the should-be Mormon pamphleteer, the quiet fear of being left alone now metastasized into panic. Because of Sebastian, she would be the focus of it. He walked over in four steps and hauled her upward with a

jerk of her elbow. The butter knife lay between her feet, conspicu-
ous as a bazooka. The militant looked at it for a few seconds, blinking. Mia regretted not telling him that she was pregnant, for the
same reason she hadn't earlier. Babies scared boys.

"Ma'am," the militant said, careful and conscious, which impressed her. The type of wars America fought in the world needed
more soldiers like him. "I have to take you to the bosses."

"I understand," she said.

As he put her blindfold back on and led her to the ballroom
stage, something inside her twinged again. She knew then that
she'd be flying out of that ballroom, her child safe and settled
within. No one else here, rich or poor, perpetrator or victim, superpowered or citizen, mattered the way that did.

———

What followed coalesced even in the moment. This made sequenc-
ing the events difficult for Mia, as she was asked to the next day
by Bureau investigators. Her mind, her attention, had lain solely
on escape. She'd seen the ballroom, yes, she'd heard the ballroom,
yes, but had she known it, did she understand it? She thought no,
and said so. Disorder was disorder, and disorder was anything but
comprehension. She used her power to save her unborn. She did
that and she did that alone. Anything else that happened was extra-
neous, disruptions for her captors and disruptions she was thankful
for, but beyond her.

Still, she tried.

The young veteran walked her to the center stage, her hands
bound behind her. She could see through the pantyhose blindfold,
but not well. He'd secured it tighter than before. The governor,
General Collins, and the detained celebrities had been cobbled
together and put on their knees. Across from them, Pete Swenson
and two others were being held in the same position but with
rifles fixed on them. These men have forgotten their training, she
remembered thinking, because an American soldier never raises a

weapon unless they intend on firing it. Veteran Zero began shouting about the movie man, where was the movie man? One of the militants said they'd taken him to the bathroom but now they couldn't find him, just his pile of clothes. That'd made Veteran Zero shout even more; who loses someone in a seersucker suit, he wanted to know, his protests bouncing off the ballroom ceilings. Then he'd slapped one of the kneeling men across the face, loosing a trembling echo of flesh and teeth.

Her militant escort had cringed with the sound. Then he'd asked someone nearby what to do with Mia. "She's been acting up," he explained. "Found a knife on her."

"Put her with the politicos," came the response. Then, "Wait."

Her blindfold was removed and another veteran in urban camo with rolled-up sleeves approached, studying her features like she was a zoo animal. The scrolled words "Essayons" and "Sapper" slashed across his forearms in angry, violent ink. A bald eagle tore across the side of his neck, Old Glory draped from its mouth. His interest ceded to recognition.

"Captain Tucker," he said. "I remember you. Your blue-blood family, too. You all are rich as hell."

He turned to alert Veteran Zero. Then, in something like a string, maybe, with pieces and beads almost certainly missing: a clash. A cry. A body on the ground, a body in urban camo. That body's gun, floating, its sling free as a snake. Pete shouting, "Now, hostage! Fire fucking now," his binds breaking apart like papier-mâché. Then Pete crashing into a group of militants. Unless the binds came off before that, and unless the crashing into happened before the floating gun. Either way, after and then, then and after, a shot fired. A shot, single and alone and assured. Then shots, all at once, many and together and hysterical.

The silver tree of American Service glowing bright behind it all.

The militant, the young veteran, the chandelier-admirer, the Mormon pamphleteer, whoever he was and whoever he wasn't, a man of multitudes or a simpleton fool, falling to the ground next to her, blood spilling out of his throat and his eyes slipping up to her for—what, exactly? She didn't know. She didn't care, either. Because with him dying at her feet and the others running or standing, or fighting or figuring, she could rise and rise away, and that's what she did, a swimmer's ascent through air, finding a stained-glass windowpane cracked open at the top of the ballroom and moving through it, into the summer night. She flew and she flew and she didn't stop flying until she knew for sure it was just them, her and her unborn, gone and alone in the black sanctuary of sky. Then she took them home.

11. The Palm Sunday attacks occurred on Sunday, March 28, 1998, and were a series of coordinated terrorist attacks carried out on what American target(s) in Federal City?

    A) The National Cathedral
    B) The metro rapid transit system
    C) The Nixon Memorial
    D) <u>All of the Above</u>

12. During the New Greco-Turkish War, who/what set off the nuclear device in Crete?

    A) <u>Communists retaliating for American support of the Russian Revolution</u>
    B) Greek radicals
    C) Turkish fascist militia
    D) U.S. military system malfunction

13. Which singer turned politician served as President Haig's vice president from 1984 to 1988?

    A) Bing Crosby
    B) <u>Frank Sinatra</u>
    C) Gene Kelly
    D) Elvis Presley

14. During the Persian Coup, who made off with the deposed shah's gold bullion?

    A) Kurdish rebels
    B) Shiastan militants
    C) The Persian Popular Front
    D) <u>Unknown</u>

15. President Richard Nixon's "Grand Bargain" with Chairman Mao included what?

    A) A new trade deal between the USA and China
    B) The end of the U.S. Navy's blockade in the Taiwan Strait
    C) The end of Chinese military and economic support of North Vietnam
    D) <u>All of the Above</u>

CHAPTER 12

XAVIER STATION WAS a military processing center, one of the largest in Empire City. It had marked the beginning of Jean-Jacques's military career, where he'd gone in high school to meet recruiters about the Legion, to learn how a fat immigrant could become a citizen by Spilling Blood for America. It'd mark the end of his career, too, someday: it was where area veterans went to face their medical tribunal.

He'd seen a veteran with troubles the day he went to sign his enlistment papers. The man wore a camo boonie cap and had black pins for eyes. Both his legs were bandaged stumps and he kept sipping from a cheap plastic bottle filled with something the color of maple. A woman had been wheeling him around, a wife or sister or cousin, a plastered look of both resignation and relief across her face. They know, Jean-Jacques thought, understanding even then. They know he's gonna fail and get sent to a colony.

It was necessary, of course. America couldn't have tens of thousands of vets with troubles walking around, breaking the peace. This was better for everyone. Like President Rockefeller had once said: "The colonies aren't a great solution. But they are the best one."

Still, though, teenage Jean-Jacques had thought. Necessary things can be sad things, too.

Barricades had been set up three blocks out from Xavier Station, so Jean-Jacques turned around, parked, then slipped in like sand through backyards and an alley. He wasn't sure what he'd expected but it hadn't been what he found. Emmanuel wasn't joking, or exaggerating. There'd been a riot at the station's gates.

The night oozed police. There were dozens of them, some in uniform, others in jeans and tees, still others in cumbersome SWAT gear. Siren lights swathed the block in incandescent whites and reds. A mound of confiscated weapons had formed on the building's concrete steps; pipes, bats, some switchblades, and a single flash-bang, listless as straw. One of the pipes glinted blue under the moon, smeared with blood.

The air fizzed tangy bleach—tear gas, Jean-Jacques thought, nothing like it. A large homemade painting of a grim-faced soldier tied between two poles rested against the school gates, an act of tenderness that defied everything around it. It was in the Artibonite style, all bright impressionism and surreality. Loose cries and moans filled the dark, a serene anti-peace settling in. A handful of paramedics treated injuries, but most of the bodies scattered across the sidewalk were being helped by neighborhood people with homemade first-aid kits.

A man in rags was leaning against the gates. He was breathing hard through his nose and still clutched a trash can lid as a shield. "What happened here?" Jean-Jacques asked him.

"Holy blood. Holy redemption," the man in rags said. His voice carried the starry lilt of a mystic.

"Uh-huh." Jean-Jacques ignored that madness and kept walking.

Order had been cleaved from chaos, pockets of young men on their knees, surrounded by their less arrest-worthy friends. A collection of brown and black teenagers wearing flat-brimmed baseball caps held the most handcuffed, and the most accompanying police. Across the street were eight or nine white boys wearing new tan boots and black backpacks. Their clothes were nice, prim even, and a cold stun had sealed along their faces. They were new to this, whatever this had been. Adjacent to the weapons cache, a uniformed cop spitting fury was being held back by his precinct comrades. He wanted at one of the white boys. Another large group was too far away for Jean-Jacques to make out but seemed of particular concern to the plainclothes police. He didn't see Emmanuel's bird frame anywhere.

One of the white boys in boots made a break for it, straight at Jean-Jacques. He'd slipped the cuffs from his thin wrists like grease. The police shouted after him but didn't seem interested in a foot chase. Jean-Jacques reacted on instinct. He leveled the kid with a quick clothesline to the chest. The kid dropped to the ground, too stunned to do anything but hold at his neck and gasp.

"Thanks!" Two plainclothes cops moved to the runner, cuffing his hands behind his back with emphasis. Jean-Jacques turned to move away, wondering why he'd mechanically sided with the fucking law. One of the plainclothes looked up.

"Oh my God. It's you. The Volunteer, right? Dash."

The young, fine-boned policeman stuck out his hand. Jean-Jacques gripped it with a quick squeeze.

"You—you wouldn't remember. But I was with 2nd Battalion, 2nd Marines. In Cyprus? I briefed you on targeting packets a couple years back."

"Semper Fi," Jean-Jacques said. Of course he didn't remember this babylon who'd been a marine. "Good to see you again." But a warfighter connection could be of some use tonight. "The hell happened here, brother?"

The policeman shared what he knew. The ECPD had been alerted to the anti-colony demonstration; there'd been a recent increase in them, for reasons unknown. They tended to be loud and acrimonious, a lot of sound, a lot of excitement, but nothing more than that. Never violent. A great way to earn overtime, the policeman explained. Tonight, though—tonight had been different. He'd shown up late to the scene, just as the fists began.

"The protestors started it," the policeman said. "Definitely."

"With who?"

"Oh. You've been away. The Sheepdogs, of course."

The Sheepdogs? A group of ex-military and retired police. They considered themselves keepers of peace, guardians, in a way, men with both a history of service and plenty of free time. They followed around various protests across the city, across the country, to fill the gaps of order. Protect private property. Serve as augmentee security for local police. Citizen's arrests. That sort of thing.

"Some can be assholes," the policeman told Jean-Jacques. "Have a hard time remembering they're not still in uniform. But they mean well. And they're handy in spots. Like tonight."

Jean-Jacques hadn't come to Xavier Station to talk about wrinkled-ass babylons playing at the past. He asked if the man had heard of the Mayday Front.

The policeman shook his head. "Protest groups, especially the anti-colony ones, they're kinda all over the place. Always a new group, a new name. Always splitting into different factions. It's what the angry left does."

Jean-Jacques thanked the man for his time and kept moving. Radical war veterans attacking the homeland? Organized peace-monger militias? A gang of ex-police that called themselves fucking Sheepdogs? It was tough to keep straight. Get me back to combat, he thought. Get me back to the damn war.

Still. Some of it seemed familiar to Jean-Jacques. America, abroad, it was all the same, even as the rules varied and the players changed. One name to the game. *Pouvwa*. Power.

Anything to get it. Anything to keep it.

Away from the station steps, Jean-Jacques approached the final group. It was the only place he hadn't searched for Emmanuel. His steps were measured, his hands as clear from his pockets as he could get them. The police outnumbered the citizens two to one, but there was a force still churning here that suggested anything but aftermath. The resignation of the teens and the neutered energy of the white kids became harmless contrast. Fewer were handcuffed here, but there was shouting, throaty noise being tossed around like firecrackers. And it wasn't coming from the police.

He narrowed his eyes to adjust to the gloom. Sheepdogs. Most looked big and thick, wrapped in tactical vests and camo wear. A few had walkie-talkies on their hips. He spotted a couple of iron cross tattoos and holstered pistols. Protestors or not, there was no way the teenage scarecrows he'd walked past had started tonight's brawl.

The Sheepdogs seemed to be arguing with the police over two of their own being handcuffed. "We came here to keep order," one said, his finger in a young police's face. "You're doing this wrong."

A tall Sheepdog with a walkie-talkie turned, his face cratering as he took in Jean-Jacques. "What you looking at, milk dud?" he said. "This don't concern you."

The young police told the Sheepdog to calm down, but he persisted. Then some of the others saw Jean-Jacques, too, and began shouting themselves. Jean-Jacques started walking toward them. Milk dud, he thought. Funny. Because I'm bald. His blood turned fast as he repeated the slur in his head. Anger didn't fill him so much as the cold thrill of reckoning did. This would be fun.

"Wouldn't do that, cousin." Kreyol scratched at the air behind Jean-Jacques. He turned sideways to find Emmanuel rising up from a crouch. He'd been in the shadows. "Unless you want to end up in the back of a law rider."

"Where you been? What kind of gang shit you into here?"

"Gang?" Emmanuel winced and crossed his arms over his stomach. The accusation seemed to pain him. "I'm no thug, man. I'm one of the good guys. Like you."

"Really." Everyone thinks they're the good guys, Jean-Jacques thought. Even wogs. He tried to get Emmanuel to explain the riot.

"No time now. Follow me." Emmanuel took off at a slow trot down a dark path, away from the station and siren lights. His body turned to silhouette in seconds. Jean-Jacques held still for a moment, considering his options. Then he followed, belligerent slurs trailing his steps.

———————

Jean-Jacques didn't care for regrets, nor did he have many. Not being with his mother when she died was one. Not keeping up with his kreyol was another. But from the wars? Regrets were foolish. Regrets were weakness. Duty trumped all, and duty meant looking forward, to the next mission, to the next room, to the next pull of the trigger. It meant being ever ready and staying vigilant. Regret got in the way of all that.

Though there was the boy.

In the days before the botched Tripoli raid and the cythrax bomb, the Rangers had stopped at a nearby base to finalize their prep. A base worker found Jean-Jacques there, picking up his laundry. Despite himself, he stopped to listen. Something about her desperation. The way it pierced her reserve. The way it penetrated his skepticism.

Insurgents had taken her eleven-year-old boy. Not hostage, exactly, but not unlike it, either. They'd drafted him into jihadist school. But her child, her only precious child, was no soldier. She showed him a photograph. He had big, soft eyes and a smart angular face. He was to be a doctor, she said, or an aid worker. Someone who served others. That's why they'd come here, to Tripoli, fleeing the lawless terror along the border. For a better life.

Jean-Jacques couldn't help it. He thought of his mother doing the same for him, getting them on a boat bound for land or bound for death, but bound for something different. He said he'd look for the boy. No promises, he said. But he'd try.

After the cythrax bomb fell from the sky, Jean-Jacques had been the first survivor to find consciousness. He hadn't wanted to. He remembered that more than anything. He'd wanted to stay lost in the other side, tucked into the cocoon of forever gone. But death forced him back to life, that specific blend of propellant, hot blood, and emptied bowels splintering his nostrils and then his mind.

So he rose from severed ground and took in the end times.

Before he found an alive Pete Swenson, before he found an alive Sebastian Rios, before a still-alive Grady Flowers stumbled from the helicopter wreckage with a still-alive Mia Tucker, Jean-Jacques found the boy with big, soft eyes. He lay in a field of rice stalks, less incinerated than the other bodies but no less dead. And because of that, and because of the boy's photograph and because of the boy's mother and because of the boy's mother's desperate, desperate need and because in that minute Jean-Jacques felt certain he was the last person left on earth, he cradled the boy's body with his own and wept.

He'd lost the boy by not finding him. He'd failed the boy by not finding him. That the boy never would've survived the bomb even if he had was beside the point.

He'd been her child. Her only precious child. He'd been her everything. So Corporal Saint-Preux wept, so very alone, with sorrow, with rage, with nothing in him and everything, too.

Was the boy with big, soft eyes a regret? Did it matter? It didn't to Jean-Jacques. The boy was dead. Most of the Ranger platoon was dead. Jean-Jacques lived.

———————

They walked alleys and unlit side streets, together in their steps, alone with their thoughts. Jean-Jacques didn't ask where they were going and Emmanuel didn't say. Jean-Jacques was glad for the quiet. He had a lot to mull over.

They reached a turtle shell of an overpass. Emmanuel walked up its small concrete slope. Jean-Jacques followed. They emerged onto an elevated train platform, long ago abandoned by the city. Moonlight revealed tracks covered in urban scrub, broken bottles and plastic bags and empty spray paint containers tangled up in patches of wild pale grass. In spots Jean-Jacques felt around with his boots to make sure track was still there. The summer night yo-yoed with indolence as they walked and it was strange to Jean-Jacques, being lost in his own nowhere instead of somewhere else's.

Below them, outlines of sprawling warehouses and trucking depots dotted the nightscape. Many were retrofitted spaces, breweries a century before, the last vestiges from a far-gone wave of refugees fleeing the Ottoman Purges. Their grandchildren and great-grandchildren had scattered to the winds, Jean-Jacques thought, because once money got made, people here never stopped immigrating, even if they called it something else. To nicer districts. To suburbia. To the far West or deep South. Back to the old homeland, even, once it was safe again, for a semester of fuzzy nostalgia and partying. Carrying a name with scars but none of the memories. Your progeny get soft and stupid: that was the real American dream.

Did Jean-Jacques want that for future Saint-Preuxs? Sure, he thought. Why not. As long as they still know what duty means.

Emmanuel cleared his throat. He wanted to talk. Jean-Jacques knew he needed to play dumb about the Mayday Front. His cousin needed to be the one to bring him there.

"Well. Those Sheepdogs seem nice."

His cousin forced a laugh. Those old babylons had been hired by Wall Street, he said. By the Council of Victors. To protect their business interests. The colonies were a moneymaker. Sending broken-ass veterans to wilderness camps, isolated islands away from public scrutiny, to serve as lab rats. Did Jean-Jacques know the government paid the colonies by the head? They wanted more bodies. They needed more bodies. It was all connected, Emmanuel explained, for capitalism and profit and American comfort. It was wrong. It was immoral. Emmanuel hadn't thought much about it growing up, because no one did. The colonies seemed normal, seemed humane. They were anything but. He'd been enlightened recently. He'd become informed.

"Think about it," Emmanuel said. "That could be you someday. I mean, it won't be. You got your shit together. But still."

Jean-Jacques just nodded. Of course a kid who did strange things like baptize strangers on the street would grow up to find ideas like this. He should've known all along. Weird boys become weird men.

About a mile along the tracks, they rounded a long bend. Slivers of white light bladed the darkness. Little Haiti's Market Street, the *Mache*, came into view. Hundreds of bodies packed its walkway, more crowded than usual because of the long holiday weekend. Low-roofed storefronts snuggled in tight like children sharing a bed, painted in a rainbow array of blues, yellows, greens, and purples. Music rumbled up at them and he could almost smell the mixture of dank hash and lacquered, tangy sweat. He'd avoided the area growing up, as much as he could. Too many people, too much noise, too many opportunities for a fat kid to get fucked with by people he knew and people he didn't. But about once a month, especially during the summers, the whole family went, so he went, too. So did Emmanuel, back when he'd been a boy priest.

"Not too much's changed, looks like," Jean-Jacques said.

Emmanuel scratched at his chin with long, lean fingers. "Let's see if that's true."

They hopped a ledge and eased down a rickety metal staircase. Large holograms of the American and Haitian flags projected up into the sky from the roof of an electronics store, though it took Jean-Jacques a moment to recognize the new Bicolour. Baby Doc was dead now, killed by a car bomb, his government overthrown. When he'd heard the news in the Mediterranean, Jean-Jacques had rethought some things about terrorism. About terrorists, too.

Chain-link fencing ringed the *Mache*, a mixture of styles and heights meant to suggest security if not actually provide it—any child with an ounce of courage could find a way in, or out. That wasn't new to Jean-Jacques. The armed guards at the makeshift entrance were, though, two alpine-tall young men in black muscle tees, long shotguns slung across their backs.

Emmanuel nodded at the men, who moved to the side so they

could pass through. Mossbergs, Jean-Jacques thought. Pump-action, 500 series. Fine show guns, angry-looking and burnished, good for clearing rooms in hellholes across the developing world. He doubted they'd be much use here. Crowd weapons needed exactness.

"Welcome home, my brother," one of the guards said as he passed through the gate, his kreyol cracking with awe. Big as they were, they'd have been kids when Jean-Jacques left Little Haiti. They were his age then, now.

"*Mesi*," he replied, meaning it. He decided to try to stop being a bitch. It was good to be back, even if it was only for a little while. It didn't need to be more complicated than that.

They moved into the crowd, Emmanuel exchanging pleasant-ries every few steps. Jean-Jacques didn't know anyone, or at least he didn't think he did, but the sticky eyes of recognition turned his way nonetheless. Whispers like riptides followed, and those deep-rooted anxieties of being noticed returned. Sweat pooled into half-moons under his arms and he felt his stomach clench. His pulse thumped and thumped. Emmanuel grabbed his shoulder and held his hand there.

"Told you we're proud," his cousin said, nodding toward an ad-jacent café. Jean-Jacques saw a painting in the restaurant's window. It was in the Artibonite style, like the one brought to Xavier Sta-tion. But this was a painting of him. He was in uniform, running at the observer, gripping a rifle by the handguard. It'd been adapted from an Associated Press photograph taken a few months before, after an attack in Benghazi. The artist had taken some liberties, though—he'd never hold a rifle like that, for one. But his chest wasn't that defined, either. Nor his jawline so sharp.

Three more young men in black tees with shotguns walked by, as if on a casual stroll. Jean-Jacques nodded their way and asked, "Police?"

He'd been joking but Emmanuel didn't take it as one. "One of our girls got gang-raped last year. Outsiders coming here, thinking they can take what they want. She was twelve. Who you think pay for that abortion after? Or her therapy? Not Empire City. Not the babylons. They didn't even investigate it, not really. Now, who's gonna make sure the same thing doesn't happen to her baby sister?"

An armed neighborhood watch, Jean-Jacques thought. That's one way to do it.

A child asked for his autograph on a scrap of paper. Jean-Jacques signed. Then a group of teenagers asked for a group photo. He obliged. Then another group of teenagers asked for a group photo, too, a brazen kid with a cocky smile challenging him to a footrace.

"Time to bounce?" his cousin asked. People were beginning to gather around Jean-Jacques, calling his name, pulling at his arms, causing him to sway a bit. Even pretending at anonymity wasn't possible anymore. He moved his shoulders to the beat of the closest dance song, to the crowd's delight. He heard people talking about his smile, his teeth, his muscles. "I just wanna touch you," a woman old enough to be his mother said, and then she did, rubbing her hand down his chest.

"Read my mind," he called back to Emmanuel, enjoying the homecoming for what it was.

"Got some folks wanting to meet you." His cousin's voice sounded tart, wary even, like it hadn't only been Jean-Jacques worried about mixing family with business. "If you're game."

Mayday, Mayday, Jean-Jacques thought. Then he heard Pete Swenson's words in his head, and he smiled at them, despite it all.

Duty. She beckons.

11:35 P.M.
THURSDAY, SEPTEMBER 8
IMPERIAL TIMES ALERT

BREAKING: Mills Harrah, the former governor of Nevada and presidential candidate for the upstart party American Service, was shot and severely wounded this evening at a political fund-raiser in Empire City. Gunfire emerged from a hostage situation gone awry that's left at least three others dead and a dozen hurt. Governor Harrah has been rushed to a local hospital and remains in critical condition ...

CHAPTER 13

SWEAT SLICKED HIS palms, but Sebastian felt ready. Mind, spirit, gut, et cetera. He looked ready, too, according to the galaxy of studio cameras reflecting his own image back at him. A new corduroy jacket trimmed his shoulders and chest, the white button-up under it crisp like a tunic. He'd left open the top two buttons, as instructed. "Fratty chic," he'd told the gay salesman at Banana Republic that morning, and they'd spent the next three hours figuring out exactly what that meant. His peacemonger shag had grown out since the summer, and he went through the motions of tidying his bangs. He'd swapped his aviator sunglasses for a pair of smart-looking brow lines. You're ready, he repeated to himself. He'd shaved and everything.

"Sixty seconds out." Words from the void, obliging yet hostile.

"Ever been on television before?" The newscaster leaned toward Sebastian, away from Liam Noonan, who was going over notes scrawled on an index card. Jamie Gellhorn was properly cast as an anchor lady with wavy honey hair and shiny north-star skin, but Sebastian knew she'd just returned from four months in the Barbary Coast. She had substance. She also didn't wait for a response.

"Be natural, you'll be fine. Keep it succinct. Liam's a pro—he'll take good care of you, I'm sure."

Noonan grunted, his attention still on his cards. Sebastian swallowed to wet his throat.

"Thanks," he told Jamie Gellhorn. "For having me, I mean. You and Jake Tapper are the best."

"Tapper." Jamie Gellhorn rolled her eyes. "I don't nag at power, sweetheart. I speak truth to it."

Sebastian had forgotten they were on rival networks.

The voice from the void called, "Thirty," then "Ten," then "Five." The lights behind the cameras seemed to brighten. Sebastian straightened his back and tried to look pensive.

"Welcome back to *The Proving Ground* on Empire News. I'm your host, Jamie Gellhorn. Happening around the world tonight—the Abu Abdallah trial begins anew. Designs for a new Lady Liberty statue are out, to great debate. And the Supreme Court's recent ruling on assimilation boards—what does it mean for *your* hometown? But first, live from our studio in Empire City, I'm going to chat with two foreign policy experts. Liam Noonan is a former Navy SEAL and author of *Battlefields and Boardrooms: How You Too Can Lead at Life and Dominate*. Welcome back to the program, Liam."

"Glad to be here."

"Joining Liam is Sebastian Rios, deputy assistant secretary for digital engagement, new media, and communications at Homeland Authority, and a survivor of a harrowing crisis in Tripoli a couple years back."

"Uhh, thanks, Jamie." She'd inadvertently promoted Sebastian but he wasn't about to correct it. He tried not to squint underneath his glasses; the room still seemed too bright. And hot—when had the lights turned so hot?

"I want to begin with reports of American warfighters moving deeper into Africa, into Sudan and Chad. The War Department denies there's any meaningful military presence there, only 'advisors,' but we've heard that before. With America at war in twenty-four countries—that are publicly known about—what do these new fronts mean for the Mediterranean Wars en masse?"

"Well, Jamie, there's two prongs to this," Sebastian began, not sure why he was using the word 'prong.' He never used that word. "Can we even call them the Mediterranean Wars now? Some of these places don't come close to having ports. It's fast become the everywhere wars. There's also—"

"We are not at war with twenty-four countries!" Liam Noonan cut off Sebastian with something just below a shout. "Sorry to interrupt, hoss, but can't let that go."

"What would you call it, then?" Jamie Gellhorn shifted her posture and attention toward Noonan.

"We. Are. At. War. With. An. Ideology. One. Singular. Ideology." Noonan's talking points were pronounced and bullish. "We can't win, we won't win, until our country accepts the threat for what it is: wog fanaticism. One fight. One enemy. Then and only then will we turn our military loose to do what it's meant to do. By any means necessary."

Jamie Gellhorn leaned back, craned her head, and swiveled her chair and attention yet again. "Sebastian Rios: agree or disagree?"

The vortex of talking-head tribalism whirled around Sebastian in all its slobbering idiocy. It sought his scalp, his voice, his critical thinking, and the other sorts of thinking, too. All or nothing, it demanded. Nuance is weakness. Us. Them. You. Him. We. They. There was power in the black, there was clarity in the white. Equivocate now and be branded a moral coward, in front of millions. This wasn't the time or place for contemplation, for consideration. This was cable television.

Sebastian knew all that, already. He believed some of it, too.

"First, that's not the preferred nomenclature, my man. And it's an interesting term to use for a guy held hostage last month by . . . who again?" Sebastian asked, rhetorically. He saw Jamie Gellhorn's mouth hint at an upward twist while Noonan's jaw clenched. "Oh, I was there, too. American war veterans. Mostly white ones, if that matters. One fight, one enemy, whatever. Let's answer Jamie's questions here without any posturing. Maybe we'll educate a viewer or two in the meantime."

Such nonsense, Sebastian thought as he looked into the cameras and smirked his smirkiest smirk. Such glorious nonsense.

"I was going to ask about that night, it's so incredible," Jamie Gellhorn said, and they were off. Sebastian's fears, over his sunglasses, the bright lights, the hotness of those bright lights, they all fell away like old coins. They talked terrorism and fanaticism, and the expansion of the Freedom Infinity island base in the Mediterranean. They talked American invincibility. They talked about what should happen to the jailed vets awaiting trial and what might happen to the comatose governor awaiting surgery. Noonan barely got in a word. Sebastian had been the one who saved an Empire City ballroom, after all. He'd been the one who vanquished Veteran Zero. He'd been the one who shot the enemy.

Sebastian couldn't talk about going invisible. But he could talk about becoming a hero.

"Only thirty seconds left," Jamie Gellhorn said. "We must have you back, and soon. Before I let you go—Sebastian, care to shed any light on the rumors that you're now an honorary Volunteer? A 'Page Six' item today."

Sebastian smiled, wide and happy. He'd done well, and he knew it. You too can lead at life and dominate, he wanted to tell Noonan. But he didn't. Instead he said the one thing he could think of even more obnoxious.

"That's too much. They're friends, sure. They're the best of us. They're warfighters. Me?" he asked. "I'm just a normal citizen who cares."

———

The segment finished and Sebastian and Noonan made way for a discussion on the recent flurry of anti-colony demonstrations. A panelist compared their potential to the peacemonger movement that had marked the early Vietnam War days. Sebastian found the analogy intriguing. Divisive as they'd been, those protests had led to the all-volunteer military and the International Legion. Could these also effect positive change? Maybe they need an almost-famous propagandist to help lead the cause, he thought, casually. He wanted to stay and listen to the entire thing but he was meeting up with Pete and didn't want to be late.

Sebastian turned on his phone in the cab. It lit up like a glow bug. Text messages from friends, from family, from numbers he didn't recognize, congratulating him, letting him know they'd seen him from everywhere. "Looking good, kid," read one. "You made that meat-rocket look like a fool, yo!" went another. "Drink soon?" asked at least four. There was even a voice mail, just one, from his mom, saying he'd made her proud.

The cab stopped and Sebastian overtipped. "Share the cheer," he told the driver, who responded with a thumbs-up. An Indian summer greeted him outside, the air washed and sticky. Global warming or good fortune? Sebastian didn't care. He felt too right to care about things beyond his control. He passed through the gates of Columbia, inhaling what he imagined to be bright air. The quad green was an ocean of frisbee and idle gossip. They're all so clean and beautiful, he thought, admiring more the untouchable energy than any specific person or body. Not for the first time Sebastian thought about applying to grad school here. Which program didn't matter. He wanted to hang a framed Ivy League degree someday.

He found Pete sprawled across the library steps in jeans and a long-sleeve thermal. The other man had taken to walking the city in his combat boots, ragged and torn and caked in the dust of faraway lands. A man in repose, Sebastian thought, yet a soldier in wait. When would the Volunteers return to the war? The War Department had extended their leave indefinitely, much to Pete's chagrin. "Why?" he kept asking. No one who knew would say.

Pete's eyes opened at Sebastian's approach, dark eye blending with the twilight, the coral one piercing through it. He'd grown out a half beard and hair had reached the top of his ears. A folded envelope lay on his chest like a chevron.

Pete untangled himself and sat up, flexing his back with a wince. He handed the envelope to Sebastian.

"Can't make heads or tails of it."

Sebastian opened the envelope and looked over the enclosed letter. It was from the IRS. "You need to report your income for the past four years."

"I've been deployed."

"You still need to file. For their records."

"Fucking Christ." Pete spoke loud, an iceberg of heat beneath his words. Passing students turned to look at the large man in his anger. "Goddamn stupid."

"Should be straightforward enough. I'll help you with it." Sebastian put the letter and envelope in his back pocket. "See the segment?" he asked.

"Yeah." Pete put out his arm to be helped up and Sebastian obliged, though it didn't feel like he provided much lift. "Good work. Liked that bit about the wars being everywhere now." He rotated his neck. A sharp popping sound followed. "That last part, though. Super douchey."

"Oh." Shame chilled Sebastian, but so did defiance. How many super-douchey things has this guy said to reporters? he thought. "Good to know."

They walked the campus, free and youngish. They split a six-pack Pete had brought and talked about how much Navy SEALs sucked and how much Liam Noonan specifically sucked. The beaux-arts buildings and walls draped in ivy gave the school a sleepy quality; there was a soft and gentle quiet that Sebastian at once wanted to bathe in and shatter. They passed the famous alma mater statue, the one of Athena seated on a throne that'd been bombed in the seventies by homegrown radicals. They passed the new business school and the antique liberal arts center. Along the eastern border of campus, beneath the cliff occupied by the school on the hill, loud yellow lights roared up from Old Harlem streets.

Sebastian considered asking where the others were, but there was no need. Britt and Flowers were together, doing something. Dash was alone, doing something else. Pete slept on Sebastian's couch now. He said he found the lofts boring. Maybe that was it, maybe it wasn't. He'd fought with his sister about something. Sebastian had steered clear of knowing much about it, or anything at all. It seemed personal.

In front of the dining hall girls too young for them asked if they wanted to party. Pete said no but Sebastian asked where, just in case. Near the bookstore an international affairs professor asked Pete if he'd come visit his class to talk policy. Pete said sure, maybe, but then again, probably not. Only policy I care about is right here, he said, holding up his trigger finger. Near the school pond a group of young Republicans in polos recognized Pete and thanked him for his service. He thanked them for not serving. Someone's grumpy, Sebastian realized, later than he should have. Pete had been deep in his own head for much of their walk.

"Let's get out of here," Sebastian said. The insulted youths were slinking away. "Do something different."

"Different, huh," Pete said. "Got just the thing." As always, he had a plan. This one involved going west, to the river, past the large Gothic church with a social justice bent, then north along muddy banks to a tomb of white granite a bit out of the way with a cupola and a façade of two angels and the epitaph "Let Us Have Peace." West to the river, then north, to the resting place of the man who wrote in his memoirs, "Nations, like individuals, are punished for their transgressions."

It was a quiet place. Tranquil too, Sebastian thought. A fine place to spend infinity. The river churned and crickets trilled and the two free and youngish men sat along the tomb's front, leaning against marble columns under an arcade of pine trees.

"Best spot in the city." Pete took a long drink from a bottle and held it against the moonlight as tribute. His plan had also involved buying chicken sandwiches and a fifth of Old Crow bourbon on the way there. The bourbon tasted like castor oil to Sebastian but it'd been General Grant's favorite. "No bullshit, no hysteria. Just . . ." He paused to take another sip. "Hard-earned grace."

Pete nodded to himself again, pleased, and handed over the bottle.

"Glad the bomber left this alone," Sebastian said. Pete raised an eyebrow. "Jonah Gray. Such a stupid fucking name."

"Even terrorists bow down to the savior of the Union."

Sebastian laughed. He took a short drink and passed back the bottle. Pete seemed to relax over his sandwich and bourbon. Sebastian wanted to ask what'd been bothering him but didn't. That wasn't how Pete worked.

"California," Pete said. "Good part or other part?"

"Miss the pinecones." Sebastian thought about that some. "About it."

"I'm never going back to Troy. Nice place to grow up. But."

"Hector, leaving home is one of our primary duties in life."

"You pirate bitch." Pete laughed at himself. He was drunk, or close to it. They both were. "Still, though. What if you stayed? A funhouse mirror for the brain."

"What you see in yours?"

"Someone wishing he'd had the testicular fortitude to try something else. What is hell again, Sebastian?"

"Something about meeting your other loser self but him being a better loser than you? And you being like, fuck, I wish I was that loser."

"Close enough." Sebastian lay across the ground, wrapping his hands behind his head. Pete braced himself against the column and eased up his body. He didn't look old but he moved it. "Hang cleans. Merciless."

"Where you going?"

"Leak." He took five steps and unbuttoned himself under a pine, singing a cadence about bayoneting wogs.

Through the dim Sebastian glimpsed the top of Pete's ass. It had a strange, gnarled shape on it. A flesh tattoo, Sebastian thought, like he'd been branded. He narrowed his vision, trying to focus. It was the Volunteers' "V," banshee blue and stout and enclosed in a circle. The one from the comic books. Sebastian had read an interview with the artist who'd designed it. The government bought it from him and he'd become rich. And now his emblem was on the ass of Justice. Was this life imitating art imitating life? Or the other way around? Sebastian couldn't figure. Pete pulled up his pants. Sebastian lowered his eyes and pulled out his phone.

"What's new in the world," Pete asked, sitting back down.

"Well. Chuck Robb died."

Pete shook his head. "That guy," he said. "Didn't agree with him on much. But at least he was true. He was a true person."

"Probably our last president who went to Vietnam," Sebastian said, repeating an idea he'd read somewhere. "Whatever that means."

"I doubt that. I doubt it very much. There'll be one more." Pete sounded certain. "What was that slogan from his campaign?"

"A Third Way?"

"No. The other one."

"Ahh. The Man in the Arena."

"That's it." Pete picked up the bottle and raised it against the moonlight once more. "To the old lions. Robb. Grant. Sherman and Teddy. To hard-earned grace."

"Yes. I like that."

"Me, too." Pete returned to the ground, lying out on his back. Then, some minutes later, "Heroism feels and never reasons, and therefore is always right."

"You pirate bitch." There was something liberating in calling the great Pete Swenson that, but also something reckless. Pete whistled, low and without melody. Then he laughed.

"Let's play a game," he said.

"No cards or marbles. I travel light."

"Twenty Questions, then."

"Sure. You start."

"Okay. It's . . . a thing."

"An action figure of the brave Justice."

"Hah. No. Nineteen left."

"Have I seen it?"

"Doubt it. I have."

"Something from abroad? From the wars?"

"That's two questions."

"I'll use both."

"Yes. Yes."

"Is it specific to a culture or society?"

"No."

"A weapon?"

"Hmm. Not in the obvious sense. But definitely."

That answer was interesting to Sebastian. He considered it.

"You asleep?" Pete asked.

"Just thinking. Those little blue pills you all give sheiks for information. The ones for their wangs."

"Good guess. No. Twelve left?"

"Can you drink it?"

"I wish."

"Snort it?"

"Sure."

"Smoke it?"

"Why not?"

"Is it tangible? Like can be held?"

"In the palm of your hand. Well, mine. Not your baby hands."

"Do you miss it?"

"Can't miss something you've hidden away for yourself. Down to five."

Sebastian had mostly been screwing around but now he wanted to win. He stayed silent for a minute. "Is it something of value? Like more than sentimental."

"Hell yeah. Four."

"How much would it cost if I wanted it?"

"Best question yet. Would need to get it appraised, but a few thousand bucks per."

"I got no idea." Sebastian narrowed his eyes into the dark sky. "The cythrax vaccine."

"Oh man." Pete loosed a contrived laugh, the kind that came from the top of the throat. "That goddamn thing. What a sham."

Sebastian didn't understand. He asked Pete to explain.

"Maybe dud is a better word? They thought it'd work. It didn't. Obviously. Why'd you live when the rest of our platoon became deaders? We asked in Germany. They said the vaccine had worked in trials. They said they'd been certain. Cost thirty-seven good men, good Rangers, to show otherwise."

Sebastian tried to reason with Pete's newest Tripoli scrap. The cythrax vaccine being worthless did explain the dead Rangers. It didn't explain the survivors. He felt his skeptical bone being tapped at again. He was still coming to terms with his own expendability to the American government. Would a Ranger platoon be treated likewise? No way, he thought. He knew from his time at Homeland Authority that bureaucratic incompetence explained the unknown more than conspiracy ever did.

Still, though. It was all very weird. He pushed Pete for more.

"If I knew, I'd share." Pete's words were bored, not defensive. He paused to burp into the night. "Should've said it earlier. We're just like you. No one knows why we lived. No one knows why they died.

"Chance or fate," he said again.

Sebastian didn't say anything to that. Through his drunkenness, he felt a searing need for clarity. Ever since Tripoli, he'd gotten by to get by, glad to be alive, certain with his uncertainty. For some reason—for whatever reason—that didn't feel good enough anymore. Not even close.

"One last guess." Pete wanted to finish the game. Sebastian went with it.

"Your mom?" he offered.

Pete made a buzzer sound. His green eye shined through the black, triumphant. "Time's up, friend. The answer you were looking for? The shah's missing gold."

They played again, switching roles. Sebastian's answer was a pint of Guinness. Pete guessed it in twelve questions. A flock of geese passed overhead in an irregular V. Church bells sounded midnight through the space between. Today was now tomorrow and tomorrow promised more of today. Sebastian found the bottle and took a long swig.

"You asleep?"

"No," Pete said. "Just thinking."

"Say," Sebastian said, "what about this Mia thing?"

"What about it?"

"You ever in love with her?"

"Not really. Maybe for a bit."

"I'm sorry, dude. I've known her a long time. She can be, I don't know. Selfish."

"All good. I don't care."

"You know, uhh, she's pregnant, right."

"Yes."

"All these young lasses around the city. Poor things. Communicating their feelings to you must be like trying to negotiate with a vending machine."

"Funny. Let's talk about something else."

"Like what?" Sebastian steadied his words. "Tripoli?"

"No, like . . ." Pete pointed to the church and laughed. "Like God."

"Big fan," Sebastian said. He tried to focus on what Pete wanted to talk about instead of what he did. "Just wish He'd show up a bit more."

"So you're a believer."

"Hell. Why not."

"I used to be. Trying again."

"What happened?"

"Life. War. Books. The usual."

Sebastian knew he was one of those people for whom things just tended to work out. He always had been. Life wasn't fair, but what could you do? It could all go awry any instant. Pete and Britt's father had taken the wrong metro one morning and been exposed to sarin. A life of joy, a life of success, all gone in seconds.

"I barely remember pulling the trigger," Sebastian said. "In the ballroom, I mean. I was hammered, you know? I'm just glad I didn't hurt someone else. People died in there, man."

"Mmm." Pete was near sleep. Sebastian closed his eyes and breathed in night air. I'm going to figure out what happened to us, he thought before he drifted away, too. Somehow. In life, it's important to understand why.

CHAPTER 14

GENERAL JACKIE COLLINS had devoted her life to country. She deployed to war zones ten times over the span of her career, for surges, for counterinsurgencies, for occupations and invasions, too. She'd spent the entirety of her adult life thinking through the intricacies and human terrains of those war zones. She possessed a gift for strategy, and through successes and failures, had honed that gift into a mental blade. She knew how the enemy would think before the enemy thought it. Jackpot had turned American special operations into the world's greatest killing machine by demanding it be the world's smartest killing machine, the world's most precise killing machine. In ways known and others not, she was one of the finest generals to ever serve the republic. She was tough, and resilient, and thorough. More than anything, she planned. Nothing was done without knowing possible effects, and the possible effects of those effects. Jackpot didn't react. She anticipated.

The American citizenry didn't care about any of that, though. War, peace, generals, privates, army, legion, it was all the same, obscure and faraway, foggy and notional. Service. Sacrifice. Et cetera. They paid the war tax, mostly. They knew kids who went to battle and came back, sometimes. They remembered kids who went to battle and didn't return, sometimes. They watched the news to learn Something Had Happened Again, less than they should have.

General Jackie Collins: credentialed, yes, impressive, yes, knowable, not really. And, in star-spangled truth, lady generals threatened some who'd never gone and borne the battle themselves. What did she know that they couldn't intuit from the stories, from their being, from the testicles hanging between their legs? Through many decades of foreign war, the citizenry had been told not to concern themselves, not to scrutinize, not to engage or peer too deeply. Clap, yes, believe, yes, care to question, no. The people were good patriots. They met that duty.

How to bridge the divide, then? How could someone of Jackie Collins's exacting background and worldview earn the everyman vote? It mattered in a democracy. It mattered a lot.

———

Knights Stadium was either half-full or half-empty, Mia thought, a full-scale Rorschach test. The afternoon sun halved the stadium into shadows and light, remnant heat sludging the fall air. Fans ambled through the bleachers with the vigor of sloths. They'd been lucky to get the general this ceremonial first pitch. The Yankees hadn't returned any calls, and neither had the Knights until someone on the Council of Victors contacted the owner. The Council wasn't supposed to get involved in political races—it was in their charter—but Roger Tran had told the staff not to worry about it.

"Worry about everything else," he'd advised. "Especially money."

Twenty games out of the pennant race and in their season's final home stand, the Knights players lined up for the anthem, mirroring the fans' torpor. From the owner's secondary box, they looked to Mia like outsize children—cartoon uniform colors, big heads and long arms that didn't fit the rest of their bodies, a strange inability to remain still for even ninety seconds. That many of the players were younger than her only occurred to Mia as she watched them fidget.

She'd always found professional sports bizarre. It was tribalism without purpose, expression for the sake of nothing but itself. Both the soldier and athlete in Mia felt separate from those standing beside her in the box, and beneath her in the bleachers. It was more distance than disapproval. Why devote so much to something you couldn't impact?

Her hand lay across her heart as the anthem droned. Mia looked down at the clean green field and tried to understand. Was it the guise of fairness? That's what Jesse said. That sports provided equal opportunity, or at least the possibility of it, in ways that life never would. But of course that was false. The Yankees' payroll was three times that of the Knights. The Knights' star was a brawny Cuban outfielder. He'd quintuple his current salary in the off-season, either moving uptown to the Yankees or far beyond to one of the California squads.

And he'll deserve it, Mia thought. Because that's how the game works.

Knights Stadium sat in a soft basin in Ash Valley, built in the sixties on land Mia's grandfather remembered as dumps and mechanic shops. The franchise had served as a redheaded stepchild for the community since; it belonged to the outer districts and lower denizens, to anyone who objected to the empire in Empire City or scoffed at the City in the same. It'd made the World Series three times, won it zero times, and missed the playoffs twelve years running. Mia's family were Yankees fans, of course. She could recall visiting that baseball cathedral many times growing up. Had they ever trekked out here? We must have, she thought. At least for a concert. But she couldn't place one memory. It was like it'd never happened at all.

The anthem ended to subdued applause and a few lost shouts. Mia exchanged looks with the other staffers in the box and focused on the bottom of the diamond, where General Collins was walking out to the mound, back straight, hand aloft. She looked settled on the jumbotron, not too detached, not too friendly, either—she'd spent the morning finding that balance with a consultant. She wore a navy-and-gray Knights windbreaker with suit pants, and white high-tops the consultant had suggested.

"Please give a big Knights welcome to retired major general Jackie 'Jackpot' Collins!" The PA announcer sounded like he was calling a kid's birthday party. "General Collins served thirty-five years in the army and the Agency, deploying multiple times across the globe for America. She's been decorated for valor under enemy fire in Vietnam and Beirut! Praise to the Victors!" Scattered applause emerged from the bleachers. "She's now running for Senate with the American Sacrifice Party."

I can't even, Mia thought. Service. Not sacrifice. How do you get that wrong?

"Go General Jackpot! Go Knights!"

Mia joined the other staffers in the box and clapped. More scattered applause emerged from the bleachers. She watched a woman below yawn into her pretzel. Three rows beyond, an overweight man struggled with a divider so he could get into his seat. Across the way, a pair of early twentysomethings kissed like the other had a lemon drop wedged in the throat.

The military called people like this citizens. Politics knew them as voters.

General Collins reached the mound and began kicking at the dirt, like the consultant had showed her. A large, milk-brown mitt enveloped her left hand and wrist. The general was a rightie with little physical grace. Mia had spent the previous two afternoons in a parking lot near campaign headquarters, helping the general practice. The throws had improved, in fits and starts, though not before a dented car and an upset feral cat. They'd considered tabling the pitch until the spring but couldn't be certain the chance would still be there. Odd as it was, a militia of disaffected veterans seizing their inaugural had helped American Service's reputation.

Or American Sacrifice. As the people prefer, Mia thought.

A round, smiley young Knight trotted out to shake the general's hand, then took his position behind home plate. General Collins stared into his mitt like it had violated a direct order. She rocked her body back then forward, and slingshotted her arm out and away. It was more push shot than throw, but it's what had worked in the parking lot.

It did not work on the field.

Mia held her breath as the ball dropped ten feet in front of home plate, dribbling to a leaky halt. Someone behind her cursed. Anyone in the crowd bothering to pay attention shrugged, as did the round, smiley Knight, who began jogging toward the general with the ball in tow.

General Collins raised her mitt. No self-conscious smile dared speckle her now. She remained unmoved and pounded into the mitt with her free hand. She said something to the player, who asked her to repeat it.

She wanted the baseball again.

This wasn't supposed to happen. This didn't happen, as far as Mia or anyone else in the box knew. But with the general refusing to move, ironic encouragement rose up from the crowd. They'd seen plenty of poor first pitches before, but they'd never seen any-one demand a second try. They loved it, or were at least amused by it, and when the Knight threw back the baseball, genuine cheers broke out at Knights Stadium for the first time in months.

General Collins stared deep into the catcher's mitt. She rocked her body back. She rocked her body forward. She slingshotted her arm out and away.

This throw was a rocket, though an errant one, sailing well be-yond the outstretched glove of the young Knight.

The general raised her mitt again, pounding her hand into it. The player rose from his crouch, no longer grinning, and looked to the edges of the field, hoping for intervention. Then the crowd started up.

"Jack-Pot." The refrain began somewhere behind first base, where a group of day-drinking frat boys had taken nest. "Jack-Pot!" It moved through the crowd like an electric current. General Collins remained on the mound, unmoved, mitt raised, calling yet again for the ball.

She got it again. The crowd stood en masse now, shouting, whistling, chanting. "Jack-Pot! Jack-Pot! Jack-Pot!"

General Collins stared into the player's mitt once more. She rocked her body back. She rocked her body forward. She slingshotted her arm, out and away.

The ball fired into the Knight's mitt like a bullet. A perfect throw. A perfect strike. As the fans reached fever pitch and the players trotted out to shake her hand, General Collins raised a fist to the sky.

It'd all gone as planned. Someday Mia hoped to anticipate this precisely. To form stakes from nothingness. That more than anything impressed her. The act of creation from a void. The triumph of will over expectation.

———

Mia left after the second inning for midtown, citing a meeting. In the subway station, just beyond the body scanners, she passed a cluster of wanted posters. Veteran Zero had been hospitalized and arrested after being shot in the ballroom—by Sebastian, of all people—but he was only a lieutenant. The true leader of the Mayday Front remained at large. Jonah Gray's mug shot leered at her, long, sloped chin and cloudy eyes seeming to rise from the grainy black-and-white photograph. He looked like someone Mia had once known. From her youth? From the army? It pricked at her, like a hangnail, but try as she might, she couldn't place him.

"Should be considered armed and extremely dangerous," the posters read in big red print. "If you have any information concerning Jonah Gray, please call 911 or your local Bureau office."

Her fiancé still spent most of his waking hours at a local Bureau office, the hunt for Jonah Gray his everything. They'd been able to sneak away for dinner the week before, their first date in weeks. In a taxi home, he'd pulled her over to him, wrapping his arms around her body, an open smile and a distant, starry look gobbling up his face.

"Can't promise I'll be much more than mediocre," Jesse had said. "But you're going to be an incredible mother."

Her tell? She'd poured herself a small glass of wine but hadn't touched it.

He hadn't asked, he hadn't prodded. He'd just figured it out, and was overjoyed. Jesse's reaction contrasted so sharply with her own that she'd almost resented him for it. Then he started talking names and Mia let herself get lost in his enthusiasm. By the time they fell asleep that night, Mia had decided she'd be one of those moms who loved her own child fiercely while remaining indifferent to children as a whole. That seemed doable. An incredible mother? She doubted that. Would an incredible mother have needed to super-fly her child from a ballroom to get away from gunfire? No. An incredible parent wouldn't have put them in that position to begin with.

Semper Gumby, she'd reminded herself. I can do this. I will do this.

The general's campaign headquarters lay in the northern reaches of midtown, a prewar walk-up shaped like a loaf of bread, close enough to Asian Harlem that they used it as a media talking point. They'd occupied the third floor, above an agency that represented professional animals and below a comedy website geared toward college students. It was a long way from Wall Street. On her first day, Mia had shared an elevator with a golden retriever in a cardigan and a degenerate Santa.

A man in rags sat in front of the building, head between his knees. Mia first took him for a maven addict but as she neared the entrance he looked up, his eyes both clear and probing.

"With the campaign?" he asked. His voice was lucid, too.

Mia nodded.

"Where's the general on the colonies?"

Mia considered the question, and why this man would be asking it. They'd discussed the rehabilitation colonies a lot, of course. How could they not after what had happened in the ballroom? It seemed an opportunity to lead, to separate General Collins from the pack. But the national party had advised caution. Vets' issues didn't play with voters.

"We're seeking out a few subject-matter experts," Mia said. "Internal reform seems necessary. But what those reforms look like, we're figuring out."

The man in rags stared at her. And stared at her. And stared at her. He didn't respond but Mia seemed to have disappointed him. She asked if he needed money. He didn't respond to that, either, so she walked into the building.

She rode the elevator by herself. The golden retrievers and drunken Santas were already gone for the day. Their floor was humming: news of the general's success at Knights Stadium had already reached cable sports. It'd make the news channels by hour's end. She high-fived a couple of volunteers and assured them that yes, it had been even more impressive in person.

Mia pushed close her office door, the din falling away with it. She'd been with the campaign for just over a month, and still found the tempo unsettling. Finance moved as a river, a constant force that could swallow up the careless and excitable alike. Politics seemed more like traveling with family. A lot of sound, a lot of fury, bursts of weary idleness in between.

At her desk Mia took off her flats, rubbing the sole of her left foot. She wasn't quite showing yet, but one of her favorite blouses hadn't fit that morning, something she knew shouldn't have frustrated her but still had. Her skin kept breaking out, too. It wasn't all bad, though. The prenatal vitamins had turned her fingernails into wonders. They were long and thick and while she'd never been a nail woman, it seemed a waste not to be now.

Her phone rumbled on the desk: a voice mail from Linda. Her stepmother kept calling, wanting to pregnant-talk. Mia did not share in that desire, at all. How would her real mom be handling it? She wasn't sure. Leaving her alone, at least. Her mom had been different, always marching to the beat of her own drum. Not many scions of Old Greenwich had spent five months in a peacemonger camp, refusing her family's legal connections out of principle. If ovarian cancer hadn't taken her when Mia was six, her only daughter joining the military might have.

She'd had courage, Mia knew. A lot of it. That's where her own came from. It had little to do with the Tucker blood. It was pure Roosevelt.

Mia pulled out her to-do list, the additions outpacing the strike-throughs. Purchase the train tickets to Babylon—done. Confirm the rally venue there—not done. Register the radiation detectors with the homeland marshals—done. Look over the press release about drug companies' testimony to Congress on maven treatments—not done. Red-pen the speechwriters' latest attempt at the Service-for-All platform—not done. They hated the "New America" line and were trying to quash it. They weren't wrong, Mia thought, but it didn't matter. The general liked it.

Mia had joined the campaign as a fund-raising coordinator. By the end of her first week, she was running the finance team. By the end of week three, she'd been made a deputy campaign manager. Turnover had proven a constant; General Collins demanded a lot from her staff. Small as it was, Mia had remained in the same office throughout the staff shakeups. It had everything she needed (a door, four walls, a little window that provided slivers of gray light) and none of what she didn't (a whiteboard for feedback loops, word clouds and doodles from feedback loops, people who used terms like "feedback loop").

A knock came, then a voice, then the sound of the door opening and closing: Mia looked up to find Roger Tran stepping into her office.

"You're here," he said. Tran wore his customary navy slacks and power Windsor. "Superb."

"Just got in," Mia said. "Was at the first pitch."

"She's a genius."

Mia nodded. It had struck her as cynical, at first, but she'd warmed to the idea over time. "We could unveil a new Marshall Plan for the entire Near East and get a tenth of media play this will. Crazy world."

"Three kids. I think that every day." Roger Tran's voice never rose and it never fell. He carried the vague title of senior strategist, which meant he was involved in everything. The staff called him "Mr. Fix-It" behind his back. Sometimes as a compliment. Sometimes not.

Mia's predecessor had left partly because of Tran. He was as demanding as the general, but twice as meticulous, and uninterested in the rah-rah talk frequented on the trail. This wasn't another job for him. It was the only one.

"Wanted to follow up with you." Tran shook off Mia's gesture to take a seat. "Yesterday's meeting."

"Which part?"

"The security plan. You disagree."

"I do, but it's not my call." Mia smiled while keeping her lips pressed together. She had no interest in suggesting she wasn't still bothered. "That's your lane."

The morning after the inaugural, the security team had been fired in entirety. The question of who to replace them with became an issue. An upstart senatorial campaign didn't have the coffers for elite contractors. Tran's solution was fiscally sound, if nothing else: the Sheepdogs would do it. They were cheap, they were loyal, ex-military and retired police who had lived American Service themselves. No ragtag vets from the outlands would get through them.

There was one problem, though. The Sheepdogs were ragtag themselves, and being even loosely affiliated with fringe ultra politics made zero sense for a new party with centrist ideals and ambitions. Mia and some of the junior staff had pushed back on the proposal. The general heard their concerns, she said, but still, they'd be going forward with the Sheepdogs. There was just no getting around the money it'd save.

"No one's going to care who's providing security."

Mia wasn't so sure about that and had said so in the meeting. But rather than repeat herself she said, "They'll need background checks. And look the part. Shaved, in suits. Polished shoes."

"Of course, Ms. Tucker. No scrubs in the ranks." Tran rubbed at his chin. His fingers were long and sleek, like darts, his face a map of wrinkles and sunspots. A career in the infantry that could be traced from mark to mark, each one a distinct story and trial. Just as effective as reading a soldier's ribbons from their uniform while twice as true.

"They consider themselves devotees to the Bill of Rights," Tran continued. "That's all. I'm sure you had soldiers like them. Even the Legion had some. And we weren't citizens yet."

"I did." Mia filled her voice with false cheer. "Why do you think I'm worried?"

"Spill blood for America," Tran said, wistfully. The International Legion's motto.

His lips eased out into a smile. He did have a sense of humor, albeit a very dry one. He'd shared his journey once, at a staff gathering over drinks. How a reticent boy from Saigon had grown up to lead a Legionnaire battalion in combat. How a son of a bar girl raised by his grandparents now owned a house in the suburbs. Two floors, in a cul-de-sac. How America, for all her failures, for all her hypocrisies, had made such a life possible. How it was his duty now to pay it forward.

He almost never talked it, he almost never revealed it. But Roger Tran was a believer.

"They'll do their job well," Tran said. He meant the Sheepdogs. "Make the general feel safe. And feeling safe is an essential part of being secure."

That's my line, Mia thought. From the general's planned foreign policy speech on bringing home the warfighters, slowly, methodically. Not end the wars, exactly, but give public responsibility for them to host nations, which really meant more contracts for the privateer military companies and more operational freedom for the Legion. It was a decades-old idea pulled from the President Robb era. Who would accuse General Collins of being a peacemonger? Not even the young hawks caucus would dare.

"Your partner. The Bureau man." Tran pointed to a framed photograph on Mia's desk. It was from their trip to Hawaii, her looking straight at the camera, Jesse mid-laugh, leis around their necks, a tide of silver battleships in a quiet teal cove behind them. She missed what the humidity did to Jesse's hair when he let it grow. "He knows about compromising for the greater good. We could all learn from him."

"You don't need to worry, Roger. I don't agree but that's fine." What did he want from her? She noticed he kept looking at her from the sides of his eyes, like he was trying to find the right light. General Collins sometimes visited here, to talk. Maybe that bothered him. "I'm sure there's plenty of moments like this in politics. On to the next one."

"Indeed." Tran swiped away a loose wisp of hair from his forehead, quick and clean. "You'll get that next one, too, if I had to bet."

He seemed in a decent-enough mood. Mia decided to take advantage of it. "There's a rumor going around the office."

"Joy upon joys."

"About the report on the war spreading through Africa. That it leaked to Empire News from the War Department. From an angry American Service supporter there."

"And?" Roger Tran arched an eyebrow, conveying either amusement or disappointment. She couldn't tell.

"Is it true? The timing seems ideal."

"You actually want to know?"

"I do."

"Okay. Yes. It is."

That pleased Mia. It meant she was working for professionals. It meant working in a midtown closet surrounded by Santas and strange men in rags would be temporary.

Tran turned back at the doorway, clearing his throat. "Almost forgot," he said. "The press release. For the drug companies."

"My fault. They got it to me this morning. I'll look it over and have it to you within the hour."

"No need." Tran tapped at the door frame once, twice. "We're going to reevaluate our position."

"Huh?" This was why he'd come to her office, Mia now knew, but that still didn't explain the policy shift. "This is a slam dunk. Retired general calls for closer scrutiny of treatments for troubled veterans. It's easy. Straightforward."

"New poll." Tran's voice became even more neutral, removed entirely from the words it carried. "Twenty-nine percent of voters believe it's a major national issue. Sixty percent do not."

Mia clung to the silence to keep from saying anything.

"Democracy in action, Ms. Tucker. We're moderates. Important to stick with the center."

"This . . . " Mia closed her eyes and sighed. This was why they'd dropped broader colony reform, too. "It matters, Roger. Beyond the politics of the moment. It's a chance for us to lead. Show we're different."

"Yes." Tran formed his hand into a finger gun. He moved it down along his cheek, then held it in front of his lips. He blew air on it. "There'll be others." He left open the door behind him.

———

Mia's phone rumbled again. It was a text from Britt Swenson. "need to c u. Free for dinner?"

It was Thursday, and Jesse had the late shift, again. He'd taken it so they could go to a Saturday jazz festival along the seaport. She was looking forward to it, and he said he was, too. She almost believed him.

Mia felt a headache coming on, the kind a couple of pain relievers wouldn't quite dispel. She needed a quiet night at home, she knew, but she wanted noodles, and to talk about something inane and faraway, something that had nothing to do with polls, or voters, or Sheepdogs. And while she didn't like thinking about it, sound sleep had proven tricky since the ballroom.

An occasional nightmare, maybe not all that occasional: She's in a hospital delivery bed, alone. No Jesse, no doctor, no nurse. No one else is there. She's alone and all the desperate pleas in the world for otherwise don't change that. Mia begins to scream, not so much feeling the baby coming as she senses it, and then it's there, free and clear from the space between her legs. It's not the pristine baby girl that Jesse seeks, though. It's not even a child. Her baby's born dead as the young Mayday veteran, the chandelier admirer whom the loose bullets came for with mad, raw chance in the ballroom, whose eyes slipped up to Mia in his final moments, howling for clean hope, or dirty understanding, or maybe eternity. She didn't know because she'd flown away. To save herself. To save her unborn. In the dream, the born-dead man raises a hand to his throat to quell spurting blood, looking upon his new mother. He tries to speak. A high whistling sound like an incoming mortar comes out instead.

That Mia always jolted awake then was of small comfort.

In the confines of her office, Mia texted back the other woman. "Sure. Noodles?"

Britt suggested a place in the Village. She couldn't make it until 10 p.m., though. Was that too late? Mia tended to be on the couch at that hour, or at her dresser, picking out clothes for the following day. She couldn't remember the last time she'd been out that late on a weekday.

"Perfect," Mia texted. "See u then/there."

———

Mia worked late, moving through her to-do list with automation. The Babylon rally got confirmed. The Service-for-All speech was red-penned. She tracked down the names and contact info of three local (and untroubled) veterans who might fit for a campaign ad.

She connected with the McNamara Institute in Federal City about a potential contribution. They had billionaire money behind them, and loved the idea of American Service. They loved the idea of Senator Collins even more.

Was she disillusioned with her new job? Sure. But so what. Part of the messy business of democracy. Silent, arcane Roger Tran had a point there. Besides, she knew how to work while disillusioned. She'd been an American military officer in the Mediterranean Wars. Embrace the Suck.

Mia took the downtown subway to Kissinger Square, walking up the stairs behind a group of Empire State students who looked far younger than she recalled being in college. Something began twinging inside her again. Life was speeding up. The night was pale as an egg and smelled like aloe. Fall just wouldn't come. The north end of the square was dominated by the arch, tall and tusked, a drab outline against a chrome sky. The arch itself was seamed in historic bullet holes and fresh graffiti. Mia saw death skulls and antifascist arrows and extremist messages like "Freedom Beast" and counter-extremist messages like "Defy."

Not for the first time, Mia longed for the America of her childhood. Things hadn't always been like this. She thought it important to remember that.

Mia cut through the square both to save time and to people-watch. A small crowd had massed around the central fountain. Mia approached, honing her ears to the strident chants coming from its core.

"Our veterans are under attack! What do we do? Stand up, fight back!"

"From the Isles of Greece to the Near East, we demand justice, we demand peace!"

"Save our warfighters! Mayday! Mayday!"

It was an anti-colony demonstration. Parents, professors, even a few students stood with arms linked, chanting, singing, calling to passersby to join them. They were only a couple dozen, easily outnumbered by the observers, but the energy felt crisp, even potent. They wore suit jackets, blouses, collared plaid. A television crew filmed a couple of the older demonstrators showing a student how to draw a dove with chalk. Two large American flags billowed behind the group, enclosing the scene for the cameras in frame.

Mayday. That's what they were chanting. That's what their cardboard signs said. Mia considered the word and its possible meanings. Not the Mayday Front. Just Mayday. Nor did the protestors look anything like the militants from the ballroom. But still. Mayday.

"Fuck the president! Fuck the Council of Victors!" someone yelled. "Free our brothers, free our sisters, burn the colonies to the ground!"

The crowd cheered.

Mia had trouble determining what she felt exactly as she watched the protestors chant, and sing, and laugh, and rage. She believed the colonies needed changes, meaningful ones. They needed more oversight and transparency. It pained her to think that some veterans with troubles weren't receiving the care promised to them. It seemed beyond decency that the medical treatments being conducted in the colonies weren't always first-class. The media reports about "experiments" seemed exaggerated but she wasn't a fool. There was probably something there, a few cases of overzealousness. She'd fought for the campaign to pursue this issue because it mattered to her. Mia believed in incremental reform.

She did not believe the colonies should be burned to the ground.

Squint hard enough and you could pretend this mob was participatory democracy, she thought. Like what her mother had devoted herself to with the peacemonger protests. They'd been arrested and sent to jail, sent to camps. That was real. And it had worked, in a way: the government ended the draft. The military won in Vietnam.

In contrast, Mia found the protest in Kissinger Square a farce, absurd in concept and execution. Didn't these people have something better to do? she thought. If they cared about the foreign wars, if they cared about the use of American military force, if they truly cared about veterans with troubles and the colonies, they'd had decades to express themselves, to push back. To "defy." But there hadn't been a whiff of any of that in America for years. Yet now, here, was a blanched imitation.

Why?

And to align themselves with domestic terrorists. Mayday—how dare they, Mia thought. Grow up. She felt proud that she was seeking to effect change the right way.

Mia looked for the dean from Riverbrook. He wasn't there. "Just something I did forty years ago," he'd said about his days as a protestor. Only now, a month later, did she hear his understatement.

This is why there's a warfighting class, Mia thought. General Collins's three percent. To keep *this*—what this was felt slippery to Mia, in her anger—removed from actual decision making. The purpose of the military was to maintain the American Way of Life. That superseded all. Volunteers or conscripts, that was the truth of the past. That was the truth of the present. That would be the truth of the future, too. Mia hadn't known that when she joined, but she knew it now, knew it as intimately as the shiny naked knob at the bottom of her stump.

And had I known? she thought in the square, the chants of protest nipping her ears. If I knew then what I know now, I wouldn't change a thing.

———

The restaurant was tucked away on a side street off the square, across from a gray-brick hotel Hemingway had stayed in on his way to France. It was filled with steam from an open kitchen and half-full, mostly students loitering over closed books and drinks. Britt was already seated at a corner table and greeted Mia with a big smile and hug. Above the bar a television blared with the day's news. Mia looked only to make sure the protest in Kissinger Square wasn't on it.

"You seem . . . happy?" Mia said. "And tan. Very tan."

Britt rolled her eyes, but remained smiling. "Jamaica," she said. "We snuck away last weekend. On the down-low. Grady could get in trouble with the War Department."

"So." Mia smiled, despite herself. Her friend was in love. "Things going well?"

They were. Britt told her about Kingston, and the beaches, and how Grady Flowers was nothing like she'd expected him to be. He was kind, and generous, and funny, and was interesting, and said interesting things, was interested in what she had to say. There was the sex, too, of course. He wasn't a musician. He had shoulders.

She'd never thought she'd ever date a soldier. Jocks with guns, she said. Gross. But here they were.

Mia wanted to ask what came next—what happened when the Volunteers deployed again? But she didn't. Let them have this, she thought. Sometimes it's more special when you know it's going to end.

"My brother's not happy about it." Britt shrugged. "Who cares what he thinks, though. How's all that?" She pointed to Mia's stomach.

Outside a little back pain, Mia said, she was okay. That was mostly true. The waitress came. Mia ordered a sliced beef and broccoli entrée, Britt, the pork dumplings. She also tried to get Mia to split a bottle of wine with her.

"Some doctors, like, recommend it." Britt shrugged. "Don't worry, I'll drink most of it."

Mia abstained, unsure if the other woman was kidding. Britt asked about the campaign, whether it was for real or just more politics. "Both," Mia told her, which was odd to say out loud, because she'd barely admitted it to herself.

"That's why I texted you, actually." Britt scrunched her face, slight sun streaks from Jamaica overlapping. Mia heard and recognized the slight tonal change. She was about to be asked a favor. "Thought maybe you could help."

Britt had a friend, a bouncer who worked freelance security for various Gypsy Town music venues. He was a good guy, Britt explained. Nicest three-hundred-pound man she'd ever known. After years of just getting by, he'd found good, steady work with a big security firm. It came with a 401(k) and everything.

"The firm who worked the American Service inaugural?" Mia knew where this was going. Britt looked surprised. "Lucky guess."

It had been that firm, in fact. They'd fired everyone who'd worked the inaugural because of what happened, to include Britt Swenson's bouncer friend. And it wasn't his fault, she said. Did Mia—could she maybe ask around, explain the situation, help get this guy a second chance?

Mia sighed, trying not to show any irritation. "We're not working with the firm ourselves anymore, so I doubt they'd care what we have to say." Britt meant well, she thought, but didn't always think things through. "We just decided on their replacements. Sorry."

"Oh." Britt took a long sip of wine and hummed her lips. "That's too bad. It really wasn't his fault. One of your campaign people let in those Mayday freaks."

Mia tilted her head. "Did your friend say that?"

He had. He'd told Britt that he'd been standing near the back entrance when the veterans dressed as Home Guard rolled up through the kitchen. Their credentials checked out but his supervisor had seemed perturbed by something. They'd begun a deeper verification when a campaign staffer intervened, saying he'd vouch for the Home Guard.

Mia was going to let it go—twisted gossip, almost certainly, from someone with a grudge—but the old army officer in her wanted confirmation. She asked Britt to clarify with her friend.

"I'll text him." He responded within the minute. "Older dude in a tuxedo, he says. Had a bunch of military medals on his lapel. Didn't get his name. But he acted important? I don't know."

And the supervisor? One of the people killed in the gunfire. "It's a sad thing. He had kids."

There'd been plenty of important older men in tuxedos with military medals in the ballroom that evening, Mia remembered. And this information, if she could call it that, was at best round-about. Still, though. Something felt off. It seemed too weird to dismiss outright. Her leg that wasn't there began to ache with phantom pain.

The waitress came with their meals. Mia tried to hold off a yawn. It'd been a long day; coming out tonight was a mistake, she thought. Four bites in to her sliced beef and broccoli her phone started buzzing from her purse. "Jesus, Linda," she said out loud. She explained for Britt. "My stepmom. She won't leave it alone. I don't want to talk about being pregnant with her. I wish she'd just get that."

Whatever Britt responded with, Mia didn't hear it. Her eyes had taken her focus to the television screen above the bar.

The chyron was loud, clear, decisive. No room for misinterpretation.

"Governor Mills Harrah Succumbs in Surgery," the chyron read. "American Service Presidential Candidate Dead at 57."

FREEDOMBOOK

Your state-approved source for information and factual content

The Sheepdogs are a constitutional militia made up of former military and retired police officers, firefighters, and first responders. Founded in the aftermath of the Palm Sunday attacks to serve as volunteer civil guard, the Sheepdogs organized from various ultra ideological movements.[1] The organization encourages its members to take direction from state security authorities, unless in conflict with U.S. constitutional law. Occasional armed disputes have arisen due to the inexactness of that guidance, such as the 2004 Democratic National Convention, the Redoubt Siege, and the Valdosta marches.[2]

The Sheepdogs claim a national membership of 250,000, though that number has been disputed by researchers at the McNamara Institute.[3] Detractors of the Sheepdogs have alleged it is an organization that "borders on [being a] paramilitary, incapable or unwilling to know the line between keeping order and political violence."[4]

Various media reports have drawn a connection between the organization and Western separatism [5] In response, the organization's national leadership began requiring its members to reaffirm their oath to the U.S. Constitution to maintain affiliation.[citation needed]

CHAPTER 15

D UTY HAD HUMBLED Jean-Jacques many times. His first day in the Legion, he'd been ordered to sweep sunshine off the sidewalks. He'd been kept awake long past the point of sanity on combat patrols, all his weaknesses and failures exposed in the aftermath. His decision making in the Balkans had gotten two junior Rangers shot through their chest plates, only the miracles of modern medicine keeping them alive. Duty took many forms and faces, but it always led to humility.

Today's looked like canned fruit and a church lady.

"Labels out, please." The pantry manager of the food bank was steadfast in her politeness while unwavering in her exactness. "The cans in the back, too. They'll be pushed to the front soon enough."

Jean-Jacques was on day twenty of volunteering for Mayday. Each morning he was assigned to a different community program across the city, from soup kitchens to public libraries. Each evening he returned home and awaited instruction for the next morning. He didn't get to ask questions in Mayday and he hadn't gotten one whiff of its mysterious underground leader. Mayday was structured on tiers, not unlike ranks in the military. He was Tier 1, and had an orange-stickered lanyard to prove it.

"Good, Mr. Saint-Preux. Only thirty more racks of diced pears. Then we'll get to the grains."

The pantry manager ran the Ash Valley Food Bank for the underserved, and she ran it with disturbing attention to detail. She was seventy or so, ninety pounds dripping wet, a smiling pixie in a gardening hat with the heart of a tyrant. Jean-Jacques's old slipped disc in his back had been aching all afternoon from stocking the pantry but he wouldn't say a thing. The food bank mostly served wog refugees from the Mediterranean. That seemed worthwhile. And the pantry manager held sway in Mayday. He needed her support for Tier 2 and a green-stickered lanyard, which might, perhaps, bring him closer to Jonah Gray.

For the Legion, he thought. For a platoon command. Then he picked up three more racks of diced pears and carried them to the pantry.

The food bank lay across gun-metal-gray concrete that absorbed window light rather than reflecting it. Ten rows across, ten rows deep, the shelves were all marked with laminated signs naming their goods. A dull hum of industrial refrigerators and an ice machine in an adjacent room gave the space its only sound. Jean-Jacques had asked earlier about a radio for music and been told there was no time for an indulgence like that.

The pantry manager watched as he stocked from a stepladder. She'd proven to be anything but a talker but Jean-Jacques decided to try. He couldn't work his way up Mayday the diligent way. He needed access to its leadership ASAP.

"Ma'am. Gotta say. Your pantry. As clean and organized as anything I've seen. Even in the army."

The right play. "Navy daughter," the pantry manager said. "And marine mom." She bowed her head. A thin silver cross hung from her neck.

Her father had been a retired navy petty officer, supply, a veteran of the Pacific campaign in World War II; her mother, a devout farm girl for whom "cleanliness as godliness" was no mere phrase. She herself protested Vietnam as a young woman, something she still felt great shame for. She'd earned clemency through a peacemonger camp, she said, but it'd been the lectures by Vietnamese refugees at the camp that remained with her all these years later.

"They taught me that force can have purpose. That it can protect the weak," she said. "As the Bible teaches, too."

Her son had joined the marines on his eighteenth birthday. Because of his grandfather. Because of his mother, too.

"He still in or did he get out?" Jean-Jacques asked. Something like a shadow bladed across the woman's face, and as quickly as it went away, Jean-Jacques knew he'd misread her and her commitment to her post. "Oh, ma'am. I'm sorry. I didn't know."

Her son had been sent to the Mediterranean three times. Syria. Greece. Cyprus. Upon his discharge, he was assigned to a rehabilitation colony. She couldn't visit, only write letters and call once a week, but he'd sounded like he was getting better with the mental therapy sessions there. He was released after three years, having met the criteria for a return to the citizenry.

He killed himself five weeks later, running the car engine in her garage while she weeded the backyard vegetable garden.

Jean-Jacques didn't like touching strangers, but he put his arm around the woman's shoulder. She didn't move into his hold but she didn't move from it, either. He looked again at the thin silver cross around her neck. He felt her agony. He sensed his opportunity.

"He's in a better place," he said. "You must take comfort in that."

"I do," the pantry manager said. Her resolve lingered, but was softer. Jean-Jacques pulled out the teardrop pendant under his shirt and told the story of his mother, and his mother's courage, and his mother's death.

That he welled up during it was not part of the plan but it still happened.

"She's with the Lord now," the pantry manager said.

"Do you believe that? Like—for real?"

Jean-Jacques didn't feel good about exploiting this woman's faith. It waon't a good thing to do. It waon't an ethical thing to do.

But he'd killed. He'd destroyed. What was one more little sin in the name of duty?

She told him that yes, yes, she did believe and he needed to, as well. It didn't take much more to get her to the Chaplain. Jean-Jacques needed a holy man to find holiness, after all. Did she know of anyone like that?

"He's . . . it's tough to explain. I was raised Presbyterian. We show our belief and love through deed. We don't talk. We don't share. We live in the quiet, and consider. Then we act. The Chaplain, though, it's different."

As she talked about him, her face took on a look similar to those Jean-Jacques remembered from the isolated beachhead on Big Mullet Key, where all the Haitian adults on the sailboat sang and prayed for their safe deliverance.

"It's—well, it's divine. I don't know what else to call it."

Jean-Jacques nodded and asked if there was any way he could hear this man preach. The pantry manager didn't seem to hear him, though. She'd slipped into the free association of people on the cusp of oldness.

"It's not true what they say about him, you know. None of it is. The news. The government. They're all liars. They're all atheists. They made up that story about kidnapping the politicians in the ballroom. To make him look bad. To make us look crazy.

"The federals?" The woman sniffed with a righteousness so pure it could've pierced glass. "They killed my son."

With that she told Jean-Jacques they needed to get back to work.

———

Jean-Jacques was already in line for the subway body scanners when Emmanuel texted. "Meet at the bus stop on Myrtle Road." So Jean-Jacques walked up the stairs to the street and met him at the bus stop on Myrtle Road.

They took seats in the rear of the bus, the only other riders a wild-eyed boho girl high on something and an old man in a collared linen shirt and straw hat who reeked of cigar smoke. Jean-Jacques had figured they'd be Little Haiti–bound, but the bus sliced southeast instead.

He turned to his cousin. "Can I ask?"

"Sure." Emmanuel shrugged, taking off his crimson-stickered lanyard and sticking it in a pocket. He was Tier 4. "I can't tell, though." Jean-Jacques stared hard until the younger man coughed out more. "Lamar Pierre asked for us. I don't know."

Jean-Jacques nodded, and settled into the window seat, sliding down and tucking his legs against the seat in front of him so his knees were horizontal to his eyes. The city passed in flashes of iron and cement. Lamar Pierre, huh. It wasn't the Chaplain. But it was leadership.

Maybe he'd spooked the pantry manager over his inquiries during their holy talk. She could've called Lamar Pierre as soon as he left. He hadn't seen Pierre since the first night Emmanuel brought him into Mayday. The older Haitian man had greeted him with a full hug and a solemn "Be home, brother."

Pierre had mapped a similar journey as Jean-Jacques, with one major distinction: after Haiti, after Empire City, after tours of combat duty with the International Legion and the U.S. Army, he'd been sent to a rehabilitation colony. Block Island, to be exact, which must've been where he met Jonah Gray. Jean-Jacques hadn't mentioned that, though, during their time together over asosi tea. Instead he'd listened to the older man hold forth on the importance of service, about how too many warfighters got lost in the margins of America because they forgot that true power came from working for others. Too many warfighters, Pierre opined, wanted to be celebrated. Too many warfighters wanted to be served themselves. It had had a corrosive effect. On souls and society alike.

"Selfless service is one of the army values," he'd said that night, deep in his speech. "When's the last time you heard anyone say that out loud?"

Despite himself, despite his mission, too, Jean-Jacques liked Pierre. He even admired him, in those long, dark minutes he'd listened to the Mayday pitch. The way he talked about duty was pure Legion, and Jean-Jacques agreed with much of it. The group before the individual. The mission before the group. Quiet professionalism, no matter what. But there was something off about the man, and it wasn't just the way his face always twitched when he shifted from kreyol to English and back again. The singularity in his vision smacked of fanaticism, and Jean-Jacques reminded himself that Pierre had failed the medical tribunal for a reason. They had a lot in common, true enough. But he was an active warfighter. Pierre was a veteran with troubles. That difference mattered.

The bus continued through the far districts of the city, miniatures of street life and human rumpus at every corner. The neon glam of a boho district somewhere between up-and-coming and trendy. The punk grime and graffiti of the district just beyond it. The tidy bedlam of the market in a Taiwanese district, an old lady holding a dead rooster by its neck in one hand and a designer purse in another. Wide avenues, overpasses, chrome and mortar. Then thin arteries of bumpy road among a haze of concrete. People got on the bus, people got off. Emmanuel listened to music through a phone while Jean-Jacques kept to the window. They crossed into a district made up of wogs, the kind that went to food banks. Did Jean-Jacques hear a faint prayer chant of a muezzin or was he imagining it? He couldn't tell. They passed a landfill set along a row of sunken houses raised above ground level, old dirt backfilled around the buildings. To Jean-Jacques, it looked like a row of urban igloos. Antennas spotted the houses' roofs while droopy power lines connected them.

He thought about Little Haiti, and it being nicer now than it had been during his boyhood. Maybe Pete was right about that, he thought. Maybe home should get nicer.

They crossed brown water over a high bridge. On the other side was a big green park with big green trees framed by a big empty sky. The road widened out into avenue size again. Pylon dividers became strips of grass. Wood houses with front yards and mailboxes sprang forth. Jean-Jacques cracked the bus window. He smelled wind and sea.

He turned to his cousin. "Where are we?"

Emmanuel took out his earbuds. "Cape Hope," he said. "Never came here for a beach day or crazy Irish girls?" When Jean-Jacques didn't respond his cousin just laughed. "Need to get out more, homie."

They got off at the next stop and their fellow travelers headed toward the ocean. He and Emmanuel walked the other way. Gulls drifted through the sky like monitor drones and Jean-Jacques inhaled deep from his chest, sea air rushing his nostrils. If he didn't know better he'd have sworn he was somewhere in the Mediterranean— one of the Greek isles, maybe along the Turquoise Coast—not his home city-state. They walked a gravel path to a field of thistles and turned left. At the end of this path was an old brick building with a fading red sign: CAPE HOPE FIRE DEPARTMENT.

"We really are everywhere," Emmanuel said, impressed. "Mayday, Mayday."

Emmanuel believed in the cause. He was earnest, eager to move up tiers and not just because of the stipend increases. That the Bureau had promised to protect his cousin once all this was over mattered some to Jean-Jacques now. He wasn't one for mercy, not usually. An exception could be made for blood.

The firehouse proved abandoned, smelling of rot and mildew. Pierre waited for them in a conference room. A loud lime paint from disco times chipped from the walls and a dull metal pole plunged through the center of the room. He was alone, feet up on a long metal table, eating a deli sandwich and listening to what sounded like state radio.

"Podcast on nonprofit management," he explained through a mouthful of roast beef and lettuce. "Tax deductions, my brethren. We gonna get legit."

Pierre was shaped like a bull walrus, all paunch and gullet with short, stubby arms that belonged on a man half his size. He wore a denim jacket over a white tee, black pants folded over wide construction boots. A small pin with three antifascists arrows glinted from his jacket lapel. His beard was thick and snarled, so much so that Jean-Jacques almost felt grateful for the cythrax killing off his own body's hair follicles. Pierre took one more bite of sandwich, then motioned for the cousins to join him at the table.

"That story you told of the child in Tripoli." Pierre was talking to Jean-Jacques. "Checked out. Sounds like a fucked-up scene you woke up to over there, boy."

Jean-Jacques nodded but said nothing. Of course the story checked out, he thought. It happened. He'd used it as justification for why a dedicated soldier of the state might be interested in helping out a ragtag band of social-service homeland guerrillas. That Pierre had sought to verify it meant some things. One, he didn't yet trust Jean-Jacques. Two, Mayday had people in the War Department who could pull up files, even top-secret files, which meant these fuckers weren't necessarily as ragtag as they presented.

And three, Jean-Jacques thought. He wants me to know all that.

Pierre asked about their weeks. Emmanuel spoke of the work going into another anti-colony protest, the permits collected from the parks department, the meeting with other protest groups and the inroads made therein, the official and unofficial security measures being put in place to counter any Sheepdog presence. They weren't going to be caught unprepared again. They had former police in the ranks, too.

Pierre shifted to Jean-Jacques. No more devoted follower, he told himself. He was here to stop these peacemongers. Not become one.

"I moved some boxes," he said, voice coiling. "Made some soup. Got spit on breaking up a fight over a cot." Jean-Jacques stopped a beat to let that settle in. "Yessir, all my best skills being put to use.

Who knows when the War Department sends me back overseas. In the meantime, I serve my community."

His cousin made a sucking sound with his teeth and turned his attention toward the ground. Jean-Jacques hadn't meant to embarrass him, but he needed to get moving. A man with super speed didn't like being patient. Hell, a man with super speed wasn't supposed to be patient.

Pierre didn't look angry, though. He didn't even look surprised. All he did was fold his arms across his chest and sigh.

"You ever visit a colony, Saint-Preux?" he asked.

Jean-Jacques had not.

"I have. Six years of my life I'll never get back. All 'cause I said the wrong thing at my tribunal. All 'cause I dared to tell the truth about my 'good kills.' Don't get me wrong—it ain't all bad. Clean living, prepared meals. No bills. Gyms and trees and hand-job nurses. But there's no change. No freedom. It's lockdown, sanitized. You know that warfighters sent to colonies are disproportionately veterans of color? Fourteen percent of new vets go to colonies now. That number's closer to twenty-five if you're brown or black.

"Our brethren who don't make the jump from the Legion? Forget about it. They fail their tribunal, it's back to where they came from. No cush colony for them. Just a shiny piece of tin and a certificate of achievement. That's how America really Honors the Warfighter."

Jean-Jacques leaned forward to break in—he'd known some Legionnaires who experienced that, true enough, but they'd almost all been scumbags who hadn't put in the work for citizenship. Pierre left no space for it.

"Then there's how this impacts us out here. This shit's all by design, brother. America can stay at war as long as it doesn't have to confront the consequences. A warfighter with a face of brain is that. Send him to a colony. A warfighter raped by her commander is that. Send her to a colony. An immigrant grunt who'll speak

MATT GALLAGHER

truth about the rules of engagement?" He meant himself, of course. "Send him to a colony.

"We're fighting history here. Institutional power. It's not just the money behind the colonies. It's the idea of them. I've read the colony plans drafted by the original Council of Victors, way back when. As cynical as it was genius. 'Americans value comfort above all else,' it said. Our job now—no matter fucking what—is to tear into that. Whatever it takes. Shock and awe."

Speeches, Jean-Jacques thought. Always more speeches, everywhere I go. Pierre was good at them, at least. The fact that he looked normal and sounded reasonable made him all the more dangerous. Jean-Jacques was practical, though. He didn't argue theory. He didn't argue history. He just asked what any of that had to do with him doing chores the past three weeks when he could be sent back to the Mediterranean at a moment's notice.

"Not trying to be special," he said, eyes fixed on the dark rings in Pierre's eyes. "But I am."

Again, Pierre didn't get angry. He seemed a reservoir of understanding. His face twitched as he briefly slipped into kreyol.

"Yes, mon ami," Pierre said. "Committed egalitarian here. But you speak truth."

Pierre had received orders: the Saint-Preux cousins were to be assigned a new mission. V-V Day was fast approaching, which meant the V-V Day Parade was, too. The one event for which the entire star-spangled nation turned its eyes toward the Victors. To praise them, to hail them. The parade was run by the Council of Victors, though, which meant only a certain type of Victor marched. The clean kind. The quiet kind. The kind that came home from Vietnam and got a nice job, a nice family, the kind that put the business of killing red gooks behind them for the business of contributing to society. No veterans with troubles, essentially, because they remembered what they did, what they saw, how America had triumphed in Vietnam and the messy slaughter it entailed. It'd been thirty years since the Liberation of Hanoi, which

226

meant this year's parade fell on the pearl anniversary, which meant the Council would be pulling out all the stops. Praise, praise, praise: Praise to the Victors. Which also meant: Praise to Themselves.

Mayday intended on crashing the party. To show America the real faces of the great victory in Vietnam. To remind America what war really looked like. A group of Vietnam warfighters, the broken, the scarred, the fucking *enlisted*, would be massed to infiltrate the parade and march up Fifth Avenue. Jean-Jacques and Emmanuel were to figure out how. And where. And when.

"And the veterans?" Emmanuel asked.

"We'll get the bodies there," Pierre said.

"Cool." Emmanuel's voice turned rapt. "Another vet-break from a colony."

Pierre just winked.

The parade was always a tightly run affair, covered by state television and the major networks, police and private security smothering the route like whale blubber. Mayday needed the cousins to find a soft opening along that route. If Emmanuel used his conceptual brain for that, great. If Jean-Jacques used his star power for the same, that'd also be great.

How many?

"'Bout a hundred," Pierre said. "No small thing, I know. But one hundred angry, dirty warfighters on Fifth Avenue? Can't ignore that."

It was a hell of an idea. The kind that could open minds. The kind that could mainline the ambitions of Mayday into the veins of the general population. There might be a renegade speech by the Chaplain involved, too. Pierre wasn't sure.

"Big pressure on you two," the large man continued. "Tell me now if you're up for it."

Emmanuel nodded straightaway, but Jean-Jacques stroked at his chin and tightened his eyes into little raisins. He'd been ordered to leave the war to make a propaganda film about the Abu Abdallah raid for the government. Now he needed to help hijack a national parade for the antigovernment to get back to the war. It all seemed a cruel irony. He just wanted to soldier again.

"If I agree, you mean," he finally said. "I ain't hearing an ask here."

"I don't want this." Pierre leaned forward and clasped his hands, his voice unmoved as ever. "We have tiers for a reason. I'd have you hammering nails for a year. That's the process. Lot of war widows and soldier moms out there doing good work. People who need help. But orders are orders." Jean-Jacques held off from asking who'd given those orders. He knew. "You don't want this, go with God. Mayday marches on. The fight is bigger than us all."

Jean-Jacques sorted through the possibilities, each choice a tripwire certain to set off new, myriad choices he couldn't see from the here and now. Infil a parade with veterans with troubles? No way that was all they had planned. Something else was going on. He wanted no part of Mayday. The government had used him, too, but at least it'd been stylish about it. A Hollywood suite had been involved. But walking away meant no chance at finding Jonah Gray. Walking away meant no chance at the Legion. The Legion was his only way out. And sometimes, he remembered, a lot of times: the only way out is through.

"What the hell," he said, louder than necessary. His voice shot through the firehouse. "For my fellow warfighters."

CHAPTER 16

MONTHS AFTER SEBASTIAN had first moved to Empire City, his grandfather passed away. Sebastian flew home to California to help his family with dead people things. He'd found the visitation and the funeral the easy parts. Just nod and smile at the old people still alive, maybe help guide them to the platters of free food. One kept making jokes about the Found Generation being the beginning of the end. Sebastian laughed to be polite.

Born in Cardiff, his grandfather had crossed the Atlantic as a baby and lived the much-vaunted, ever-elusive American dream. A shipbuilder's son turned admiral. A war veteran, part of the Greatest Generation that rescued the world from fascism, he became the CEO of a regional steak house chain after leaving the military. Self-made money accumulated through diligent, prudent investments over the course of fifty years. He only drank socially, limiting himself to two drinks per occasion. He rarely missed church and never missed his early morning walk.

He also distrusted Japanese people, but that was beside the point. We all have our faults, Sebastian thought, and at least he had justification for his. The rest of us just kind of make up reasons as we go along.

His grandfather's heart had given out on mile two at the age of ninety-three. The old ladies who found him in the backwoods of the retirement community swore they discovered him laid out across the path, chin raised and back straight as ever.

He looked like an angel, one said.

He looked like a popsicle, the other said.

He'd maintained his posture, either way.

Sebastian stayed in California for a month. When he wasn't packing up boxes or reading paperwork he couldn't make sense of, he was drinking at bars with old friends from high school. They told stories, the same stories they'd been telling each other for a decade. It was fun for a bit, but after that, even the beer tasted stale.

The money was split between Sebastian's mom and her sister, but Sebastian inherited his grandfather's military memorabilia. In the boxes Sebastian found a long naval sword, issued for ceremonial purposes sometime during his grandfather's thirty-year career. One of the family's favorite stories involved their patriarch grabbing the sword during an earthquake. After ensuring his wife was safe beneath a door frame, the story went, Sebastian's grandfather raised his head skyward, toward the Lord Almighty. He then directed up the sword in salute.

Before Sebastian left for the Near East, he'd asked his grandfather about that. He would've felt ridiculous, but didn't say that part out loud.

His grandfather had thought over the matter. "Well," he eventually said. "What else could I do?"

Sebastian thought about shipping the sword to Empire City and mounting it above his bed, but he ended up putting it in storage instead. Maybe I'll need it someday for something, he thought. Even if just in pretend.

———————

Sebastian was hungover again. The world slipped and slid as he found verticality. Organs throbbed from somewhere between his ribs and heart. A thousand little drills bored into his brain, the construction project of sobriety under way. A bruise shaped like

Missouri splattered across a thigh, its origins mysterious. His mouth seemed full of cotton balls and his thoughts began grappling for regrets it couldn't quite identify. They were there, though, lost and drifting.

He was working from home today, which meant an afternoon conference call in his boxers. Pete wasn't on the couch, which surprised. It was nice to be alone again, even like this. Aspirin, bacon-egg-and-cheese, shower, he put together. In that order. He found his way to the bathroom, then to the couch. Beer only next time, he told himself. No more liquor. You're not indestructible like he is. He turned on the television. General Collins blinked to life, grave and severe against a backdrop of droopy flags and muffin-faced onlookers. A placard with a silver tree hung in front of her podium. Despite himself, Sebastian raised the volume.

"My fellow citizens: I stand before you today with grief in my heart and resolve in my blood. The evil of terrorism has taken one of our great civil servants. Governor Harrah was a leader, a father, a friend. He was a champion of service, a living embodiment of the ideals that make America special. He loved his family and he loved the West. He spoke of both often in our conversations. He was also a man of profound faith. I've no doubt he's now with God above."

No doubt? Sebastian thought. Not even a little pinch? As a burnt-out idealist, belief without scrutiny struck him as juvenile.

"Who are these Mayday extremists? Why did they target Governor Harrah? How did they gain access to the campaign event? These questions must be answered. And they will be. Right now, America's best and brightest are working tirelessly to find those responsible. Justice will be served. I'm as certain of that as I am of the sound of freedom's ring in the American dawn."

Now that, Sebastian thought, is terrible speechwriting.

"Terrorism can feel very far away and vague, something that happens somewhere else, to other people, until it's right in front of us. For nearly two decades now, more and more Americans have been forced to reckon with this brutal truth. It's not the way life

231

should be. It's not the life we dream of for our children. But still—it's the way life is, here, now.

"Does it have to be? I'm here to say that it does not."

Better, Sebastian thought. Truth and reckoning and kids always land.

"It's not American Service the political party or American Service the campaign that threatens these wicked fanatics so much, though. It's something much more important. It's American Service the idea. They hate it. It's the promise, it's the dream of American Service they loathe. It's democracy itself they attack.

"They fear American Service because we will transform this country for the better. We will have a safer America. A more free America. A new America."

Here it comes, Sebastian thought. The big enchilada.

"Governor Harrah believed in this dream. He should be the one standing before you, ready to see it through. He's been taken from us too soon. By cowards who seek to defy and destroy rather than build and sustain. In his stead, I believe it's my sacred duty to serve for him. It's what he would've done had our roles been reversed.

"This is why today I'm announcing my candidacy for president of the United States.

"The center can hold. The center will hold. Because it must. While the political left whines, while the political right raves, American Service stands in the breach of the radical middle. We stand in the breach ready to lead, ready to sift through the dirty work of governance.

"My name is General Jackie Collins. And I can't wait to get to work for your vote."

Sebastian vomited in the shower. He'd been thinking about the general's speech and trying to figure out why it bothered him, so he blamed the purge on that. He wished he'd paid more attention to history assignments in college and read more closely; he'd received a first-rate education and not retained enough from it. If I had, he thought, before trailing off. His mind was unable to cohere. Something something, he finished. Rome and Athens and the colonialism.

Mandatory national service? What would people like him do? Write dispatches about forest fires from Montana? It sure is hot here, citizens. Hot and burning. Be glad you served out your time singing at retirement homes!

As he toweled off, he heard someone knocking. "Come in!" he shouted. He figured it was Pete, returned from whatever sex den he'd spent the night in, but instead he found Dorsett on his couch, watching a replay of General Collins's speech.

"She's got a real chance," Dorsett said, pointing at the television. "Early, I know. But people seem tired of the same ol' same ol'."

Sebastian didn't say anything to that.

"A lady general centrist who talks openly about drawdowns and bringing home warfighters. This is quite a country, Rios."

Sebastian just grunted. He'd already given the general and American Service too much thought this morning.

They watched the rest of the replay together, then a segment about the growing colony protests happening across the nation. There were clips from Berkeley, Chicago, Seattle, even Texas. Unlike General Collins's call for gradual change abroad, the protestors demanded an immediate closure of all rehabilitation colonies. Sebastian admired their spirit. Takes stones to do that, he thought. They have to know it's futile. Dorsett turned off the television.

"Enough politics. Rots the brain."

"What's new?" Sebastian hadn't seen much of his handler recently. The war memorial bombings, he figured, though Dorsett hadn't said. Terrorism took precedence over much, to include superpowered bureaucrats living upstairs.

"Nothing for me." Dorsett leaned back into the couch. "You, though? You famous now. What you pulled with those militants. Even my boss thought it was cool."

233

Sebastian liked that, and smiled through his hangover. "It was kind of a blur, honestly."

"Hey, man." Dorsett's voice turned, the Carolina gust falling from his words. This was his serious-business tone, Sebastian knew. He usually heard it when he forgot to not go invisible. "I need to talk to you about Justice. Know you been spending some time together."

"You mean Pete."

"Same guy."

Sebastian didn't like the way Dorsett was looking at him from the tops of his eyes, like he was staring down a weapon sight.

"Okay," he said.

"What's he like. What he wants from you. That sort of thing."

"We're just . . ." Sebastian wasn't sure what to say. "Drinking buddies. He's crashed here a few times. What's he like? I don't know. Tall."

Dorsett leaned forward on the couch and crossed his arms, the same position Sebastian was in. This made Sebastian self-conscious, so he leaned back into the couch, copying the relaxed position Dorsett had just abandoned.

"The Chaplain. That mean anything to you?"

"'Course," Sebastian said. "Jonah Gray. Leader of the Maydays you all are hot and frothy over. Same assholes who took over the ballroom."

"Has Swenson ever said anything weird about them? To you? Around you?"

"No. Definitely not. Other than being pissed about them putting guns on him."

"He ever say anything weird in general?"

"Huh? You're freaking me out." Sebastian rubbed underneath his sunglasses. Weird in general? Like saying the cythrax vaccine was a dud? Or suggesting he'd hidden away some of the shah's missing gold? What about that cryptic phone call at the port? Dorsett had been good to him, always. Probably should answer his question, Sebastian thought. But he didn't. Pete had enough to deal with. He didn't need overzealous Bureau agents bugging him, too.

"Nothing like that. We wander around and he talks war stories. He's killed more people than cancer, sure. But here? Here he's just bored and confused. Can't figure out the rhythm of anything."

Dorsett nodded and cracked his knuckles. Sebastian wanted his apartment back to himself again. "We're getting a bunch of crazy-ass tips. Be careful with him, that's all I'm saying. He has a reputation for using people."

Sebastian wasn't sure what to make of that. He thought again about the vaccine conversation and his drunken pledge to himself to figure out what happened in Tripoli. He'd thought of one way to pursue some truth. He told Dorsett he wanted to see a government doctor for a checkup.

"'Bout time. You've been putting it off long enough."

"Like the kids say," Sebastian said with a shrug. "Abide to Thrive."

Dorsett didn't respond, rising from the couch with a groan. Only now did Sebastian realize how tired the agent looked, his face wan and his eyes bloodshot, stubble splaying across his face. He asked his handler if he was doing okay.

"Long week," Dorsett said. "Longer month. Now I get to crash." Then he was gone, forgetting to close the door behind him.

———

Sebastian's conference call went well, which meant he made his presence known by using terms like "omni-channel" and "granular" and "messaging optics." He'd never get promoted but he'd never get fired, either, especially now that he'd been on TV. That had capital at Homeland Authority. Sebastian intended on using it for more working from home.

"You're famous now!" his colleagues said to him. It wasn't totally true, he knew. But it wasn't totally untrue, either. He played the ironic aw-shucks routine, which conveyed to them, as intended, he was anything but.

Sebastian felt accomplished, so he put on the new episode of *Utopia*. The first debate with Nixon had gone poorly for Bobby. He'd been caught off guard by the older man's stagecraft; the Nixon who'd failed to play to the television audience in 1960 had adapted. The line about Bobby not serving abroad in World War II had been cheap. Contrasting it with Nixon's own service and dead John's too had been even cheaper.

LBJ called Bobby in the episode. "Son," he drawled through the receiver, confounding Bobby and Sebastian alike, "I hate you and you hate me. But we both hate Nixon more. It's time to take off the gloves. It's time to do what needs to be done. For the sake of the republic."

And then, in the alternate world of *Utopia*, LBJ told Bobby Kennedy about Nixon's secret plan with China.

Sebastian was riveted. He didn't care that the show's isolationist undertones were starting to become isolationist overtones. Ultras aren't wrong about *everything*, he thought.

The rest of the day was his. He considered his options. Scheduling a doctor's appointment through Dorsett had been a step forward. Both because of Tripoli and because he'd read an article about brain aneurysms and he had questions. Sebastian decided to chase more clarity. He picked up his phone and texted the missing Volunteer.

They met at a dive bar in the eastern reaches of the Village, where punk nostalgia met bohemian chic. The bar was mostly empty and dark as a cave. It smelled of mop water and bleach. Britt Swenson and her bandmates were onstage, tuning guitars and going through lyrics of a new song. "Hello, Sebastian Rios," she half-sung into the microphone. "We see you."

Grady Flowers brought over two bottles of beer. Sebastian tried to demur but the other man insisted. "Hair of the dog," he explained. "It's the only way back."

They clinked bottles and Sebastian said it looked like Flowers had been spending some time in the sun. Flowers smiled wide with blocky, gapped teeth.

"Vacay, hostage," he said. "Had more sex last week than my entire life. Combined."

"Ahh. Well. Good for you." Sebastian felt more than a little envious. He too aspired to have sex again, whether with an attractive bohemian singer with a raspy voice or otherwise. But he hadn't come here for another man's carnal tales.

"There's no way to bring this up naturally," he said, "so I'm just gonna say it. Tripoli, man. It's been bugging me. I'm trying to figure out why."

Flowers blinked once and sipped from the neck of his beer.

"Pete told me the cythrax vaccine was a dud. I never understood why I survived but the vaccine explained why you all did. Now? Nothing adds up."

Sebastian left out how he'd gotten that information. It seemed superfluous.

"Did he now." Flowers swished around the mouthful of beer before swallowing it down. "Well. That's his opinion." Flowers set down his bottle and cracked his neck.

Sebastian stuck his hands in his pockets and leaned back in his chair, trying to appear as unprying as possible. "You disagree?"

"I didn't say that." Pulling out the small notepad in his pocket where he'd scrawled some questions seemed a bad idea to Sebastian. He tried again.

"Not trying to be a pain. Whatever you're willing to share, I'd be grateful. I'm just trying to piece together my life. That's all."

That relaxed Flowers some, putting the burden of focus elsewhere. He returned to his beer.

"Vaccine wasn't a dud," he said. "Not for me. Not for Dash. Not for that female pilot. Not for Pete, neither. I wish he'd stop saying that."

"Did anyone ever tell you—anyone ever say why? Why it worked for you all, but not for anyone else?"

Flowers shook his head. "We've asked. Trust me, we've fucking asked."

"You were in the same helicopter as Mia, right? On the gun?" Flowers nodded. "What happened there?"

"RPG clipped the tail." Flowers whacked the table with his palm. "Boom. We're all tangled up, trying to figure out what is up, what is down, who's bleeding from where. My gut feels like I've been punched by Cassius Clay or some shit. Still got my headset on, listening to Higher scream for a sitrep. That's when the bomb hit."

Sebastian looked up. Flowers had been on the radio. "Who ordered it?" he asked. "Who called for the cythrax bomb?"

The contours of Flowers's face seemed swallowed up by the void of the bar.

"No one." Words from the dim while loose guitar strums echoed around them. "I was on both nets, platoon and command. No one on the ground called for the fucking thing."

Sebastian silently counted to twelve before exhaling through his nose. "You're sure?"

"Sure as eggs. Not something you miss."

Just that morning, Sebastian had stood in his shower and chided himself for not retaining enough from college. He searched there, starting with the history courses, but nothing in history offered guidance for superpowered warfighters. Then he tried literature, but neither highbrow epic poems nor grand Victorian novels dealt with the dark, messy labyrinth of the Mediterranean Wars. What the hell else did I take? Sebastian thought, trying to remember.

Bio hadn't covered cythrax vaccines, whether they worked, whether they didn't. He never took chemistry. He had taken philosophy. Freshman year, with Mia. He could almost hear her in the Dupont library, quick and dismissive, like she couldn't believe he didn't know the answer to such a basic study question.

"Occam's razor, See-Bee. Come on, now."

Occam's razor. The simplest solution tended to be the correct one. Which would mean what here?

He looked up at Flowers, finding him through the darkness. His eyes were opaque, and a little distrusting, too. Sebastian felt something snap together inside him as he formed a cohesive idea from disorder and uncertainty.

"They dropped it on purpose, dude."

"Shut the fuck up, hostage."

"Think about it. Five survivors: three Rangers, one pilot, and me. One hundred killed, between the Americans, insurgents, and locals. One hundred people dead to turn five super."

"Shut the fuck up, hostage."

"For superpowered warfighters. Ones beholden to the state. No matter how many others died."

"I said shut the fuck up!" Flowers's hand shot across the table, grabbing Sebastian by the collar.

"They wouldn't do that. Not to us."

Sebastian put up his hands in submission. "Maybe not."

"We weren't nobody grunts. We weren't native security forces. We were American Rangers. You know how much money they put into just one Ranger's training?"

"You're probably right."

"No chance. No fucking chance."

Flowers rolled his knuckles into Sebastian's throat, an act of suggestion more than anything, then let go. Sebastian tried not to exhale too loudly.

They were of the Found Generation. They'd been raised to trust the government. They'd been raised to believe the government. And Flowers was a loyal soldier. A Ranger. A Volunteer. Sebastian got all that.

He, though, was none of those things.

"You useless shit," Flowers muttered. He wasn't yet done. "We weren't even there for you. You shouldn't have even been there. Why do you get to live when our brothers got snuffed out? That's what I hate. That's what I think about. I'd trade you for any of them. Even the shitbags. Even the officers. I want you to know that."

239

Sebastian nodded, reflexively rubbing at his throat. He thanked Flowers for his time, praying it didn't come across as sarcastic. Then he told Britt he'd try to make their show later, not meaning it. He needed to be alone, and needed to be someplace he could think, so he could reason with what he'd just conjured.

In front of the Sniper, no less, he thought, an insolent smirk finding him. In front of the goddamn Sniper.

He moved north, and east, across a footbridge over an express-way to a bench near the river. The bench was just as he'd left it, as were the river and its dirty water, and the bridge, too, with all its cables and pillars and might. Across the water, the defunct smokestacks and the sugar plant sign of Gypsy Town stood proud, surrounded by shiny condos made from every color of glass. Sebastian sat down on the bench and brought his hands together, half-bowing his head.

So, he began. Let's say this is true. That would mean someone in the military, someone in big government, had set them all up. His presence in Tripoli had been, at best, an alibi. More likely just happenstance. Fine, Sebastian decided. So be it. I'm still here.

Who would risk an elite Ranger platoon, though? Flowers had a point there. It still felt like blasphemy to Sebastian to think like this, but also freeing. His mind erupted with possibilities. The president. The Council of Victors. The generals, the consuls, the business titans, anyone and everyone who stood to profit from the wars going on and on into infinity, the lifeless bodies of homeland soldiers and foreign legionnaires and brown wogs all but marks and tallies to keep the days with.

Slow down, he told himself. This is how conspiracy theorists talk. Conspiracies are for the vacant-eyed, the mediocre-minded, the not-quite-read-enough. Be better than that, he thought. Focus.

Loose, barbaric shouts came up the river path, a pack of teen-age boys laughing loudly and kicking at the bushes. A couple were holding long, pointy sticks like spears and they passed around a bottle filled with some sort of clear liquid. Sebastian found himself envying their sense of verve until he realized what they were after.

"It's somewhere in there!"

"Can't fly away? What kind of bird can't fly?"

"Come out, come out, it's time to end the hunt!"

Ahh, man, Sebastian thought. They're fucking with Simon.

There were five of them, fourteen, maybe fifteen years old, Sebastian thought. A passing jogger told them to stop. One kid with slicked-back hair and neon sneakers told her to come closer and he'd start doing something else.

Not our best and brightest here, Sebastian decided. He needed to do something.

The wild turkey emerged from the foliage, clucking hysterically. It darted across open dirt to Sebastian's rear. The boys spotted it and began whooping in chase.

Why hell, Sebastian thought. Let's give the people a conspiracy worthy of the times.

He stood up, adjusted his sunglasses, and moved the lever in the back of his brain to invisible. A warmth like bathwater filled his body. As the teens neared his bench in a wild sprint, he channeled his best morning show Tupac impression. "Greetings, young players," he said. "Better back the fuck up before you get smacked the fuck up."

All five stopped on a dime, their faces awash in confusion.

"Who's—who's there?" one boy asked, voice squeaking like a rubber toy.

The one in neon sneakers spat on the ground. "Faggot wind," he said. "That's all."

Sebastian took two steps forward and smacked the boy on the nose, harder than intended. It felt good, he thought, hurting someone who intended to hurt others.

"Defy, my dudes," Sebastian said, before they fled down the path the other way. He tried again, louder. "Defy!"

CHAPTER 17

T HEY WERE A year from the election, to the day. The presidential announcement had come as a surprise to much of the staff. But it made sense. For the general, for the party, for the country. Mia believed that. The stakes now, though—nothing mattered more. The dream of American Service would be reality.

There were different pathways from dream to reality, different approaches, different strategies. All required the green of capital.

"That's why united service is the answer to what ails us." General Collins was finishing her fund-raising pitch in the summit auditorium. It was technically sponsored by Lehman Brothers but financiers from all over Wall Street were in attendance. And ready for the cocktail reception, Mia noticed. "That's why united service for our young people will bolster and reinvigorate the republic."

They'd learned to avoid words like "mandatory" and "national" in speeches—it made their centerpiece idea sound like a chore. "United service for all," though, was soft and inclusive. Something that both intrigued and inspired, vague enough that people could see themselves doing a variety of different jobs between high school and college. Teach. Build homes. Join the parks department. It had worked in other countries. Why not here?

The general had improved her delivery, too. She was smoother on the pitch now, less stiff and mechanical. She got up at five in the

morning to practice, before practicing again on the gym treadmill during lunch.

"That's it from me," the general said. "Any questions out there?" Someone in the auditorium groaned. She still needed to improve at reading an audience. Young suits in finance were not as disciplined as the soldiers Jackpot had commanded for three-plus decades.

A hand in the front row shot up. More groans followed.

"General Collins, very interesting idea. And I do think it'd have some of the net civic gains you mention." Mia knew that voice. It was Liam Noonan. We should've made this invite-only, she thought. Noonan continued. "But given the state of foreign affairs—the Mediterranean Wars keep expanding despite operational victories, and the very real possibility of conventional ground conflict with China in Africa—isn't this just a dressed-up way of bringing back the draft?"

Wow, Mia thought, annoyed at the lucidity of the question. I didn't think Noonan had it in him.

"Absolutely not." The general had rehearsed answering this for media, Mia knew. "United service, service of all kinds, will return the military to the people. Just as the military has sworn to defend the people, the people will remember it's their duty to defend the military. It'll bring to everyone else the pride and devotion we warfighters of the three percent know."

Nailed it, Mia thought. A perfect straddling of the line. They'd have to get more specific the closer they got to the election. But the longer they didn't have to, the wider they could make the center. And the wider the center, the stronger it would be when the attacks from the margins came.

General Collins answered two more questions, one regarding her views of the trade deficit with the Latin American League, the other concerning the new Lady Liberty statue design. ("A concern but one I'll handle with diplomacy and force," and "A sword and shield look right on her, don't you think?")

Mia had helped set up the event and used her connections

to bring people to it, so her reception was spent making rounds, glad-handing like she was the candidate herself. The chief risk officer from her old bank who couldn't quit his cocaine habit. The global head of geothermal trading at Lehman who had a reputation for sleeping with interns, gender indiscriminate. The vice president of industrials investment at US-Deutsche DataCorp Group who seemed to have no vices, which made him the sketchiest of all.

Through it all, large, suited men with radios and faces blank as tin watched from the corners of the room. The Sheepdogs were now fully in charge of campaign security, and they'd done a good job. She'd only had to remind them twice to shave before public events.

Bernard Gault, the executive vice president at Rubicon Pharmaceuticals and something like a friend of her father's, waved from a standing table. He'd been up for Sinai consul but the president had selected someone else. She was relieved to see he'd come—a number of donors who'd attended the ballroom inaugural had declined. His silver hair flashed as ever, and he bent down to greet Mia with a kiss on the cheek.

"Thank you for being here."

"Wouldn't miss it," Gault said. "No fanatic militia this time. A shame."

Mia smiled after he did.

"Hit the water this weekend," he continued, rotating his shoulders. "Felt good. Tell your father it's past time he get back out there with us."

"I will." Bernard Gault had rowed for the national team back in the seventies. Mia's father hated doing anything more than wading into water. He'd never rowed with anyone, she was sure of it. "He sends his best, of course."

Gault made a neutral sound with his throat. He asked how the change from finance was going. Mia said she liked politics. She asked about the new CEO at Rubicon. Gault said he stayed out of the way, which was ideal. The shareholders seemed happy, and the advances being made with maven were just incredible. That's what really matters, Gault said. Helping our vets.

Mia thought about the campaign's sudden policy change on the colonies and drug companies. Whatever had summoned the change, it hadn't been any poll.

She thanked him for General Collins's speaking invitation to the V-V Day Parade, and asked how planning was going. Gault sighed and said there were a lot of opinions and ideas to manage. It was the pearl anniversary, after all. The Council of Victors wanted to make sure the Vietnam triumph was given its proper due.

"Three more weeks and it'll be over," he said. "Then the Council will turn our attention to the next thing."

From a corner, Mia saw Liam Noonan lurking, drink in hand, watching her and Gault converse. As soon as the older man excused himself, the younger man approached, joining her at the standing table. Noonan tried to hand Mia a business card. She waved him off.

"That question in there," she said. "Come on, Liam. It's a fund-raiser."

"I don't see why that matters." Noonan cracked his no-neck. "Just trying to figure out your angle. Your agenda."

"Angle? We don't have an angle. And our agenda is right there in the name. American Service."

"Of course you have an angle. You're a political party, Mia." Noonan scrunched his brow. "You know General Collins was forced to retire before her third star, right?"

Mia rolled her eyes. "Many colorful tales out there."

"You can't tell the Joint Chiefs to kiss your ass. There's a chain of command." Noonan looked sincere, and Mia wasn't sure what to make of it. "Anyhow. My condolences to you all for Governor Harrah. I gather he and the general were close."

"Thank you. It's been difficult." Mia left it at that. The truth was the two had barely known one another, brought together by the vague idea of future citizenship at a think-tank panel two years before. But that truth had been wiped clean with the antiseptic of narrative. What mattered now was what came next, not what'd come before.

"How goes the hunt?" Noonan asked.

"You know what we know," she said. "The investigation remains ongoing." An *Imperial Times* story the week before said that the jailed Mayday Front members were proving uncooperative, the gored Veteran Zero, in particular. "Just a matter of time until his lawyers claim insanity," one anonymous official had said. Meanwhile, the infamous Jonah Gray persisted across the nation as a name and mug shot, but nothing more. Had he fled to Canada? To the separatist camps out west? To the moon? That someone could simply disappear in this era of technology and mass surveillance seemed impossible, yet here they were.

"Mia. Be honest." She couldn't quite believe it, but now she heard uncertainty in Noonan's voice, even as his face remained rigid and pink. "What's going on here? General Collins would be the second woman president ever. The first elected woman president ever. But that's never mentioned. Instead we're getting a recruiting pitch for the country. Three different Council Victors are here. Three. They're supposed to be apolitical. Gault turned down that Sinai gig, I heard. Who does that? The chairman of the rehab colonies is here, too. So is the head of a big privateer outfit. Very important people for a candidate most of America never even heard of three months ago."

"Your point, Liam?"

"What's broken in America—it's connected to how we wage war. We surge somewhere, withdraw somewhere else, shoot and kill everything we can in one place while trying counterinsurgency and diplomacy in another. Something works for a bit, maybe, something else works for a bit, maybe, but nothing works for good. Rinse and repeat."

"Speak plain."

"Okay. I think it's time we stop pretending that civilians are up to the task of running the military. Which, let's be honest, is the only part of this country left that is actually functional."

"Why are you here, then?"

Noonan lowered his voice, his eyes shining like wax. "I know we differ on some issues, but we're both patriots. We both shed blood for the homeland. Warfighter to warfighter, Mia: all this? It's a military oligarchy trying to get one of its own elected commander in chief. I'm on board, is what I'm saying. I want in."

Mia wasn't one for conspiracy theories, and she told Liam Noonan so. "You sound like an ultra," she said. "You're better than that."

He walked away with a shrug. Oligarchy, she thought. Heck of a word.

———

The reception finished and Mia stayed to collect donor information and attendance sheets. The married bankers went home to the far townships or to uptown co-ops, the single bankers out to dinner and drinks. She was boxing up a stack of remaining campaign brochures, mentally sorting through her takeout options, when Roger Tran approached to ask if she wanted a ride home.

"I'm fine, thank you. Short subway trip."

"General's orders. Town car's out front."

Mia nodded and touched the top of her belly. It was still slight, but she'd been showing for a couple of weeks. Nothing wrong with taking a break from subway steps, she thought.

Two Sheepdogs stood near the town car, fingers looped around their belts, as if to suggest they were armed. They weren't, Mia knew, at least not here. Lehman Brothers had insisted. One opened the rear door for Mia and inside she found General Collins on a call. She signaled to Mia with a raised index finger that she'd be done in a minute. Mia took a seat in the middle row, facing the other woman.

"Wonderful," the general was saying. "So glad he's coming along. More to follow."

She closed her cell. "Apologies," she said. "Some good news for the campaign."

"Donor related?"

"Could be. Down the line." General Collins wore a black suit with a notched collar, and against the black leather interior and the tint of the windows, Mia could only make out her body's outline. It protruded from the seat in a right angle. The general rubbed at her temple, her West Point class ring glinting like a dark star. "Numbers from tonight?"

"A hundred and forty K, maybe one fifty. Securities and Investments manager verbaled another fifteen. We'll see, though."

General Collins sighed and rubbed at her temple again. They'd been hoping to clear two hundred. "Nothing's ever easy," she said. "Reminds me of the time in the Barbary Coast with the Salafists. Remember them? Desert rebels with the crossed-Kalashnikovs flag? Bunch of pests. We had all the intel in the world saying eight council princes would be meeting at a rice farm. First time in years they'd come together. Special Forces hit the farm like lightning. But they could only find six."

"Then what?" The general didn't tell war stories just to pass the time.

"Told them to search again. Nothing. And again. Nothing. Then again. Even the best need prodding, sometimes. They found one hiding in the well. Then the last one dressed as Grandma. Got all eight. Effectively snuffed out fanaticism in that pocket of the Coast with one raid."

Mia thought about what she was being told. She needed to get better at direct asks with donors. She was a Tucker. People wouldn't tell her no. "I'll follow up tomorrow with some folks," she said. "We'll make it happen."

"That's my girl." The general leaned out of the shadows to light a cigarette. The flame from the lighter snapped the spell of darkness, then blinked out just as quickly.

"Sorry for that draft question. We ll start screening Q-and-A's."

"Not a problem." General Collins took a long drag and waved away Mia's concern with her free hand. "Goose-steppers are everywhere. Might as well get used to them. And hey—they vote."

Deep, muffled voices approached the car and the door opened again, slivers of incandescent light rushing in. Roger Tran climbed in, sitting next to Mia and diagonal from the general. In the dim, the bones in his face cut even more precise.

After considering it some, she hadn't mentioned Britt Swenson's bouncer to anyone on the campaign, nor his claim about the mystery man in a tuxedo who let in the Mayday Front to the ballroom. Mia had decided the chances of him being mistaken were much, much higher than anything else. Besides. What was done was done. They had a White House to win.

"We'll drop off the general first since she's got an early TV spot," Tran said. "Then you, Ms. Tucker."

The engine started and the car began moving. Mia sensed a strain she didn't recognize. She wasn't sure where it was coming from, or who from.

"How's everything?" General Collins asked, cracking a window to let out the cigarette smoke. "Health-wise."

"So far so good," Mia said. "If the kid remains this well behaved through life, it'll be a dream."

She'd been seeing a government OB the Bureau had recommended. "Healthy and normal," the OB had said earlier in the week. Which meant no sign of superpowered complications. Mia was still trying not to get attached to the life, or almost-life, growing inside her. She knew she might have to do the right thing by it if those superpowered complications came to be. Women without them lost babies often enough—some of her friends had, at seemingly all stages of pregnancy. But "healthy and normal" was affecting her inner calculus. She'd spent that morning looking at cribs online.

General Collins and her husband had adopted their daughters, one from Vietnam, one from Lebanon, relatively late in the children's lives. Which means nothing, Mia thought. She's been a mother in ways you can't even comprehend. You're being reticent because Roger is here. No other reason.

Still, Mia felt that strain again through the black of the car, rolling through the silent night of Empire City. She didn't think it had anything to do with pregnancy or birth, or motherhood or adoption. She held to the quiet. It always forced others to their intentions.

"Where are you now, Mia?" General Collins asked. She took one last drag and tossed the butt out the car window. "You're doing excellent work. No need to be humble. You know it, I know it, Roger knows it. You've proven indispensable."

"Thank you," she said. "I appreciate that."

"Do you like the campaign?" Tran interjected. "Politics? Know it's been a change."

Mia considered her options. She wasn't sure where this was coming from—perhaps they'd noticed her annoyances at the frenzied pace, something that had not abated with the jump to the presidential race. No, she thought. They're asking because they need me.

Mia liked being needed.

"The campaigning, no," she said. "I've never been one for spectacle. Politics, though—yes. Absolutely." Then she repeated a line from the first time she'd met the general, crossing her legs and squaring her shoulders to better face the other woman. "War without bloodshed."

That brought a smile to General Collins's face. "One of my favorites. You're good at this. Once we get to the White House, you'll have options. I want you to start thinking about it. And I'm not just talking staff positions. You'll make a fine candidate yourself, someday. Sooner than later, if I had to bet."

Mia tried to look surprised. But she'd already thought about it. Congress needed more bold centrists in its ranks. To lead from the front. To bring the country back from the brink.

The car came to a stop. A Sheepdog got out of the front passenger seat and opened the door for General Collins.

"Good night to you both," she said. "I have a bubble bath and a martini in my near future."

"Six a.m., ma'am."

"Yes, Roger. I've been getting up before the sun for forty years. I'll remember." She unfurled her body from the car with the toil of old bones, turning back to nod at Mia. Then the door was shut and darkness returned.

Mia moved to the general's seat. It was still warm and she fit into the folds of the leather like a child in her father's shirt. Tran was now diagonal from her and cleared his throat as the car began moving again.

"What's in that?" They passed under a stoplight and Mia saw through the faint green shine that he was pointing toward her leg.

"Titanium, mostly." Mia ignored the old impulse to tap at it. "The rest is carbon fiber and aluminum finish."

"I wasn't sure about you at first, Ms. Tucker. Failure of my background. But I'll be honest. In my experience, female soldiers weren't worth the headaches that followed. Female officers, especially. General Collins being an exception."

"Thank you for that honesty."

"You don't get rattled. I admire that. An important skill. Took me years to learn. What the general just said. She's right about you."

"I appreciate that, Roger." This wasn't natural for him, Mia could tell. She could also tell he'd rehearsed.

"Do you know why General Collins didn't get a third star?"

"I've heard rumors." Mia was trying to sound as neutral as he did. This could be dangerous territory. "Just talk."

"It involves you," Tran said. "And what happened in Tripoli."

"Oh." That made sense. More sense than anything else she'd heard. It also explained why General Collins had pulled her aside at the luncheon those months before. Mia clung to the quiet once more.

"She's a woman of principle. She . . . it's not my story to tell, but you should know she stood up for you, for all the survivors. Others wanted more control. More oversight. More everything. She went to war with them. It cost her her career. You should know she gave you a choice. It was her."

Mia started to say something, but she couldn't formulate anything. Her throat was dry and she swallowed but it didn't help. The ask was coming next, she knew. Whatever they'd been sizing her up for.

"She's got something for you. Something a bit outside your wheelhouse."

"Anything for the mission."

The town car stopped under a light. Cinder red seeped through the tinted windows. Tran leaned forward into it, clasping his hands. Mia tried to suppress a strange fright rising in her chest and reminded herself it was just silent, arcane Roger Tran across from her.

"Glad to hear it," he said.

The campaign had been contacted by Jamie Gellhorn at Empire News. Her investigative team possessed (alleged) documents from General Collins's time at homeland intelligence command that revealed (alleged) improprieties. Underground interrogation centers on American soil. Unlawful tapping of citizens' phone calls and emails. Secret courts that rubber-stamped warrants and fudged evidence. It was all nonsense, of course, though Tran couldn't speak to the particulars. It would be disproven soon. He was certain about that.

Then there was the Hero Project. Empire News had learned that it hadn't just been the three Volunteers involved. They'd also talked to witnesses about a flying woman and an invisible man at the American Service inaugural. They were looking into a connection.

"Well, yeah, obviously," Mia said. "But the Hero Project wasn't a real thing. Just public cover for the accident in Tripoli."

Tran nodded. "But they have 'documents.'" The folds in his face deepened into a sneer. "Means a lot in media. We think it's just paperwork generated to keep Tripoli off the books. So fake paperwork. But still. Problematic, perhaps, for the general. Since she was in the chain of command."

How to disprove a fabrication? After talking with her inner circle, the general decided that confronting this particular mistruth with the company line was the best solution. Which brought them to Mia.

"We'll need you to talk to Empire News. They've agreed to go off the record. Just background. Keep your identity private. I know that's important to you."

Mia considered all that. "Okay," she said. "Sure."

"One last thing."

"But of course."

"We'll need you to hold to that company line, too. For the country's sake. That you all volunteered for the Hero Project. That you volunteered for it."

Mia waited for Tran to explain why. That had never been a mandate. If she'd wanted to be a Volunteer, she could've been. She chose otherwise. The government had asked her to keep the cythrax bomb quiet, for national security. She'd done so. But staying silent and stating falsehoods weren't the same.

"It's better, you see," Tran continued. "That's where the Volunteers came together. But you got hurt. Shuts down a stupid line of questioning. Simplifies it for everyone. But the media—if they could, they'll spin it into something else. We've talked with the intel community. They agree this is the best approach."

A little white lie, Mia thought. But why?

Who would she hurt here, lying to a journalist? Who would she be protecting? She thought about Noonan's wild-eyed oligarchy. He'd seemed so out there saying it. She thought about the mystery military man from the ballroom. It seemed so ridiculous, still.

The town car pulled up to her building. Mia said she'd think about it. Roger Tran didn't like that, she could tell. She opened the door and stepped into the night. It was dark and dim and cold harbor gusts swirled through the air. She shivered into it, hand still on the door of the car. She turned back to say good night.

"Cling to that center, Captain Tucker." It was the first time Tran had used her rank. He'd retired a lieutenant colonel. "But moderation in the pursuit of justice is no virtue. Centrism for the sake of centrism isn't centrism at all. Remember what we're trying to do here. Remember what we're up against. As a party. As an idea."

———————

Mia called the journalist the next afternoon. Jamie Gellhorn sounded warm over the phone, even cheery, and Mia remained guarded. She'd never trusted people happy to meet strangers.

You're the flying lady people saw in the ballroom? Yes. Why'd you fly away? To save my baby. You're a member of General Collins's staff? Yes. You say that you volunteered for the Hero Project? Yes. And then lost your leg in a training accident? Yes.

"We have evidence that suggests the general was rather . . . involved in the Project," Gellhorn said. "Can you speak to any of that?"

"I can't," Mia said. "We met the first time a few months ago."

"And you happened to end up on her campaign staff?" Gellhorn asked. "Neat."

"She asked me to be on the team because I'm rich and connected," Mia said. "That's much more important than flying."

Gellhorn laughed. Then she asked if Mia knew of any other superpowered, beyond the three Volunteers. Like the supposed invisible man.

"No," Mia said. Then, unable to help herself, she asked, "Why?"

"Sweetheart." Gellhorn's cheer refused to waver, even when condescending. "The Hero Project. It's two decades old, at the least. They've wanted people like you for a long time."

THE FEDERAL CITY POST—BOOKS

Review of *My Brothers' Keeper*

by Mark Daily

If Americans cared about the war policies being carried out abroad in our name, *My Brothers' Keeper* would be atop every bestseller list there is. We don't, though, which is why last week's lists were headed by another book on Sinatra's extramarital affairs as vice president, alien werewolves that live beneath the ocean, and yes, somehow, three more personal testimonies to the grand American victory in Vietnam.

As an army veteran of the Mediterranean, I want to be clear: I Praise the Victors. I Honor my fellow Warfighters. But someday, as a culture and society, we're going to have to stop indulging in past glories to reckon with the present.

Which returns me to *My Brothers' Keeper*, a debut memoir by marine veteran and former Pelican Island colony guard Edwin Rodriguez. With searing clarity and brave truth-telling, Rodriguez chronicles his journey from artillery missions in Sinai back to the homeland.

"Everyone wanted to shake my hand and say the good, pretty words about country and patriotism," he writes. "Only Pelican Island offered a job with health insurance."

Seventy percent of guards at rehabilitation colonies are military vets themselves, according to the McNamara Institute. This results in daily encounters like those outlined by Rodriguez, where "A fellow warfighter I would've trusted with my life three years before was now asking my permission to get another Jell-O helping." Last year's infamous Pelican Island riot is detailed in full here, with a direct view of the president's controversial decision to send in federal force.

What kind of country does this to those who gave their youths to our republic and empire? What kind of country maintains such a status quo and shrugs at any attempt to remedy it? *My Brothers' Keeper* asks those hard questions. It also provides a possible way forward.

"Some of the veterans with troubles had developed hard politics," Rodriguez writes. "They'd say that maxim: 'Defy the Guards. Guard Those Who Defy.' It was a joke that bridged the divide between them and us.

"Now, after the riot, after everything, I don't think it's a joke. I was a guard. My colony brothers defied us, and some got killed for it. Now it's my turn to defy. I don't know what the right answer is. But it's not this."

CHAPTER 18

THE POWER OF bone splitting bone shot up Jean-Jacques's arm, knuckle to shoulder, like a cold marble. He punched again. Beneath him, the man's nose cracked open while the back of his throat gurgled with animal dread. He lashed around trying to buck off Jean-Jacques. Jean-Jacques kept his hooks in and threw down more punches and hammer fists until the man stopped lashing. Then he found another and did the same to him.

The men were Sheepdogs.

One of the Sheepdogs got on his back and dragged him to the ground with a metal chain. Jean-Jacques dug in his neck to protect it, arched his back for leverage, and threw back three elbows. The last one connected, snapping the man's head into the cement. A sound like dead radio fizzed out into the darkness.

Jean-Jacques untangled himself and took the chain as his own. Adrenaline was juicing his veins. Bloodlust smothered his mind. He reminded himself to breathe through the pain in his ribs.

The young men in the social service wing called these Mayday hunts. They weren't supposed to do them. Lamar Pierre disapproved and had ordered them ended. But Lamar Pierre couldn't control everything. Social service Maydays looked up to the Mayday soldiers. They wanted to be like them. To fight for the cause, with force. And besides—now they had a war hero of their own.

Deeper in the park, Emmanuel was exchanging knife slashes with a tower of a man. Jean-Jacques used his speed and came upon the Sheepdog with an open palm, keeping the strike at elbow level. The man dropped like a razed building. Anything harder would've killed him and Jean-Jacques was proud of himself for the restraint.

"Motherfucker," Emmanuel said, his mouth gored, face already swelling with welts. Jean-Jacques noticed not-so-shallow cuts across both of his arms. "This is mad fun."

They'd followed the group from a beer hall in the Bowery to a district across the bridge, past the rusting lady statue with her torch to a quiet place with wide, curbed streets and matching square houses and big porch flags. Emmanuel had set the bait, one lone immigrant lost, far from home. The Sheepdogs took it, following him into the black of a park on a hill. They smelled like whiskey and cigarette smoke and a couple had firefighter tattoos. That might've bothered Jean-Jacques a few weeks before, attacking public servants.

He knew better now.

They finished the fight, not too quick, not too slow. Then the ritual commenced. The Mayday version of bagging and tagging. Gather the bodies together, masking tape across mouths for silence, shirts over heads for impotence. Sprinkle around their coins, their lighters, their teeth, like faerie dust. Take the boots, toss away the shoes. Break the phones. Steal the weapons. Take out the can of black spray paint, shake the can of black spray paint. A black circle with three black arrows across each face, each stomach, each groin.

"Freedom Beast, my niggas," Emmanuel said, both for them and for the others, too.

Mayday hunts, not so different than midnight raids abroad. Of their own accord, for one. Quiet as sin, loud like virtue, for another. A mission for someone, or something, a mission like any other. Voices of command and voices of care and voices of alarm all whirling together into one singular monk chant of violence.

A hunt's thrills, a hunt's terrors. Dark everlasting. Jean-Jacques was home, again.

———————

"Wake up, brother."

Jean-Jacques opened his eyes to find his cousin looming over his bed. It was still ink-dark outside. His body called out for Vicodin and coffee and ached in a general way that would become very specific as soon as he moved. They were supposed to have the day off. That was why they'd gone on a hunt the night before. He looked toward the floor, past a heap of dirty clothes. The digital green of an alarm clock read 4:04 a.m.

"Get dressed," Emmanuel said. "We've been chosen for rite."

Jean-Jacques tried to form an objection but all that came out was incomprehension. Emmanuel took it as a question.

"Mayday ceremony. Gotta be there by sunrise. The Chaplain runs it."

That got Jean-Jacques moving. He found the light switch. Finally, he thought through his predawn stupor. Finally this fucking guy appears.

He put on jeans, boots, a hoodie and reached for his wallet and phone.

"Leave them," Emmanuel said. "No IDs, no electronics. Rules of rite."

Jean-Jacques nodded and waited for his cousin to turn around. He needed his phone to text the Bureau agents. But Emmanuel kept looking at him, severe as an owl.

"I'm serious, man. We can't screw this up."

With no recourse, Jean-Jacques left the wallet and phone untouched. It wasn't until they were already on the subway that he decided he'd erred. He should have insisted, or found an excuse to turn back to his room. Now I'll have to put hands on this clown and bring him in myself, he thought. Like a citizen's arrest. Not that he minded. It felt good to have his knuckles raw again, stinging with the work of violence.

The entrance to Revolution Park was marked by granite columns adorned with carved faces of bygone men. Bronze eagles perched atop the column tops, one with wings tucked, the other's outstretched. The Front had left this place alone during the war memorial bombings because it didn't venerate a foreign war. It still seemed a stupid distinction to Jean-Jacques. There was no such thing as clean war, wherever it got fought. They were all dirty. Why did Mayday want to pretend otherwise?

"Some battle during the American Revolution was here," Emmanuel said. "Killed a lot of British with cannons. Goddamn cannons."

"Says on that plaque the Americans still lost."

"So." Emmanuel shrugged. "Won the war."

Traces of almost-light had begun to speck the horizon. They crossed an open field to a dirt path through trees. A half mile or so down, the road diverged into two forks. Emmanuel and Jean-Jacques went left. Forest dark snuffed out the almost-light and midges buzzed at their faces. A bird warble filled the air. Then down a muddy slope, up another muddy slope, across a running trail. Gathered around a small barrel fire were a group of people in rags who didn't bother to look over as the cousins approached. Homeless enclaves deep in the bigger parks were nothing new but Jean-Jacques hadn't ever seen one before.

"Is rite always back here?" he asked.

"We ain't there yet, homie," Emmanuel said. "And no. Always changes. My first one was in a high school gym."

Jean-Jacques was considering a quick leak to super-speed his way back to the running trails to borrow a jogger's phone when the sound of engines rose from the surrounding park forest. Three all-terrain vehicles rumbled up to the firelight, all hitched with long utility trailers.

"Get in," a voice shouted, all drill sergeant force and conviction. "Hoods on."

Burlap sacks lay across the seats of the trailers. Jean-Jacques followed Emmanuel's lead and put a sack over his head so he couldn't see where they were being transported to.

Bureau's wrong about these fools, Jean-Jacques thought. They're nutters, sure enough. But there's nothing amateur about their operation.

They drove about fifteen minutes, hard east, best as Jean-Jacques could tell. The all-terrain vehicles never got above ten miles per hour, but the autumn wind still bit in the half dark. The dank smell of a person in rags next to him drifted into his nostrils and Jean-Jacques swallowed away a swig of throat bile. Not for the first time he thought he was getting too old to mix late nights with young mornings.

The vehicles stopped and they were told to remove their hoods. Jean-Jacques blinked back to clear vision. They sat in a low meadow, raw sun spilling over a hillside. A set of chewed-up plastic chairs had been placed in front of a small pond. A stream hissed with rushing water while midges continued to buzz at his face. Jean-Jacques smacked one from his neck and hopped off the trailer side.

There were about three dozen people in the meadow beginning to greet one another with hugs and blessings. Big, round Lamar Pierre emerged from the crowd and slapped Jean-Jacques across the back.

"Welcome, Saint-Preux. Peace be with you."

"And also with you." Jean-Jacques hadn't been to Mass in well over a decade but still the refrain came out. He shook his head. "Huh. That's still in there."

Pierre laughed. "They beat me in the name of Jesus," he said, citing a vodou song from slave times. "They burn me in the name of Jesus."

Jean-Jacques nodded at the reference. "Seventy percent Catholic, thirty percent Protestant, one hundred percent vodou." Before Pierre could take the old joke as a sign of comradeship he added, "Don't leave much room for the church of Mayday."

The other man crossed his stubby arms, the omnipresent three-arrowed lapel pin rising up his jacket. Through the murky dawn he looked older than his fifty years. Jean-Jacques felt certain he'd finally rattled him. But then Pierre smiled and raised a hand to Jean-Jacques's shoulder.

"Nothing better than converting a skeptic."

Jean-Jacques raised a non-eyebrow and asked if Pierre wanted an update on the plan for the V-V Day Parade. Jean-Jacques hadn't done shit, but Emmanuel had taken the mission to heart—he'd tapped into the Haitian community and found a disgruntled bouncer who'd worked parade security in past years. They had three years' worth of parade security plans because of it, and were going to walk Fifth Avenue themselves to identify any soft spots.

Pierre shook him off, though. "No business here," he said. "Rule of rite."

The lack of specifics and group paranoia were beginning to wear on Jean-Jacques. That both were serving their intended purpose made it even worse. He was about to instruct the Mayday lieutenant to trust him when a soft chime sounded through the meadow, then another, and another. Bodies began massing toward the pond. The rite was upon them.

———

Jean-Jacques remained standing, following his cousin's lead and facing the pond. Some older people took the plastic chairs in the front. With the arriving light, Jean-Jacques saw that not everyone at the gathering was homeless; some were deadbeat bohemian types who belonged in Gypsy Town, some were students with loose khakis and backpacks, a few others were middle-aged business folks in crisp blazers and slacks. A thin, wizened man wore a motorcycle jacket with a bunch of different military unit patches Jean-Jacques figured from Vietnam. He even counted four other black people there, not including Pierre and Emmanuel. Whatever Mayday rite was, it had attracted something like a cross section of Empire City.

The ceremony began with a blond-haired girl in an Empire State track sweatshirt singing "My Country, 'Tis of Thee." Her voice drifted through the meadow like a scratchy requiem. She changed the line "Land where my fathers died" to "Land for which my brother died," which made another girl with blond hair and an older woman with blond hair clasp one another's shoulders. Many of the people around Jean-Jacques grabbed hands and hummed along but he kept his hands and his silence, too.

The song ended. Jean-Jacques smacked a midge on his neck. Bug guts stained his fingers. The man with the motorcycle jacket switched places with the girl. A large burn the tint of old copper covered much of the man's jaw and upper neck.

"This is a poem," the man said. "Some of you here helped me write it. It's for the boys, the ones who didn't come down from Hill 937. I call it 'Praise to the Victors.' "

It was not a good poem, as far as Jean-Jacques could tell. It didn't rhyme, it didn't use big words, it didn't use imagery in interesting ways. But it had power, the kind that came from telling something straight and telling it true. Hill 937 sounded savage, like hell on earth. Jean-Jacques started picturing the faces of the fallen he'd known through his twelve tours. Good men, mostly. Good soldiers, mostly. Then he stopped. I'm here for the Legion, he thought. Duty looks forward, not back.

The man with the burned face finished his poem and sat down. One of the homeless rose from a plastic chair and hobbled toward the pond, barefoot. He was a hunchback and wore a flimsy woodland camo jacket and took slow, measured steps into the pond water until it reached his calves. He turned around, palms outstretched, and straightened his back. A long chin jutted from the man's face, but it wasn't until Jean-Jacques saw his eyes, cloudy and hypnotic pale, that he knew he'd found the man he'd come for.

A man in rags, Jean-Jacques thought. But of course.

Jonah Gray stood a scrap over six feet, a black watch cap folded over his forehead. Tufts of dark gray hair stuck out from the bottom of it. His face was shaved clean. He carried a body of loose angles, like a scarecrow, and moved with the affected presence of someone used to being watched. He began his sermon, turning his hands outward, toward the congregation. Thick, gnarled crosses were seared into both palms.

"Mayday, Mayday.

"Fellow believers. Fellow citizens. Welcome to rite. From the ashes, holy redemption." He spoke like a metronome, each word, each syllable, a chant. The softest of lisps hung from his voice, measuring his diction more than it feminized it. The agents had warned about his charisma, Jean-Jacques remembered. I should just slap him out and be done with it.

He listened, instead.

"They call us revolutionaries. They call us fanatics. I posit: What is revolutionary about peace? What is fanatic about wanting the bounties of American life to come from honest work? To protect those in need rather than exploit them? What is crazy about wanting our homeland to fight fascist encroach, to stay true to the ideals it was founded upon?

"No, we are not revolutionaries. We are egalitarians. We are patriots. We don't seek chaos. We seek reckoning.

"Everyone here is either warfighter or warfighter family. Everyone here knows what has been demanded of our caste, our tribe, for thirty years. We've lost friends, siblings, parents. To everyone here, words like Honor and Duty and Sacrifice are much more than hollow phrases. They have been ways of life. We did not expect reward, but we do deserve care. We deserve dignity, not humiliation. We deserve answers.

"Everyone here has arrived at this understanding: no more. As Americans, as children of God: no more. If we are to Honor the Warfighter, we must free the Warfighter. Yes—free the Warfighter! At home and abroad.

"'Care for those who have borne the battle.' America believed that, once. We're making it believe again. Through resolve, through force. That is my charge to you today. Bring them to your days going forward, and Honor your Warfighter in the process. Through holy blood, holy redemption."

Jean-Jacques snapped from the trance of church. Holy blood, holy redemption. Another man in rags had said that to him weeks before, the night of the riot at Xavier Station. He hadn't looked anything like Jonah Gray. Had he? He couldn't recall what that man looked like—just that he'd been decrepit. Dismissed in a single moment with a curt nod and brush-by.

He thought of something an old sheik in the Near East had said during a manhunt for a bomb maker. He couldn't place which tour it'd been, or even which country, but the sheik's words came back to him in the meadow.

"The best place to get lost isn't somewhere. It's everywhere."

They never had found that fucking bomb maker. Gone and disappeared into the infinite shadows of the wars. Just one more name for the rolling list of targets across the Mediterranean. But now, Jean-Jacques thought, I've got this target right here. Jonah Gray may have been everywhere this whole time. But now? Now he was somewhere very specific.

Jean-Jacques tried to keep from grinning and began prepping his assault. A quick choke hold would be easy enough. Getting the man out of the park would be trickier. If he could get the keys to one of the all-terrain vehicles, though . . .

"Do not think that I have come to bring peace on earth. I have not come to bring peace, but the sword." Jonah Gray had reached the apex of his sermon. Catholic, Protestant, vodou, Mayday, it was all the same. Jesus quotes came at the end. "Now, communion.

Please bow your heads. Think of someone you love who's departed this world for the next. Someone who gave themselves for someone else."

Now, Jean-Jacques thought. Now's the time to move. Everyone was looking toward the ground with eyes closed, including Jonah Gray. He wet his lips and took a slow breath, ready to go turbo and come upon the man with an open palm. He felt something biting at his chest. He reached under his hoodie and pulled out the teardrop pendant affixed to a dog-tag chain. It was glowing warm through the dawn.

Jean-Jacques was back on the sailboat, with his mother. A trace of a private smile across her mouth, her long, lean face up and defiant against the horizon. Just the two of them, together against the sky of the unknown. He'd been here before, with her, but not like this. Not exactly this alone. Not exactly this together.

"Mom?" he whispered.

Jean-Jacques's mother turned on the boat, showing neither fear nor worry. She placed her hand on his. He felt life in it. Human touch, channeling from her hand to his.

The Chaplain's voice came from above the sea, repeating in melody: Honor. Sacrifice. Love. Honor. Sacrifice. Love. Honor. Sacrifice. Love.

Honor. Sacrifice. Love.

Then, quick as Jean-Jacques had left, he was back. Back in the meadow, in the park, in the city. The morning smelled of wet dew. Midges hovered and buzzed through the air. He was still alive. His mother was still dead.

What in the . . . He couldn't even finish the thought. He bit the inside of his mouth to feel, to ground himself through pain. What the hell had just happened? Jean-Jacques tried to focus on his bewilderment. If nothing else, that was real.

"Remember them," Jonah Gray told the congregation. "They remember you. Holy blood. Holy redemption."

He'd been transported somewhere else, Jean-Jacques was certain of it. He'd stood on the boat. He'd smelled fish. He'd felt ocean sun. He'd touched his mother.

But he hadn't. Of course he hadn't.

The ceremony ended. Jonah Gray moved through the crowd, kissing hands and cheeks. Then, suddenly, he halted, tilting his head. He spun on the balls of his feet and beelined for Emmanuel.

"My friend. You're hurt."

Emmanuel lifted his sleeves and showed the knife wounds he'd sustained the night before, during the Mayday hunt. They were dark red and crusting with yellow pus and Jean-Jacques thought at least one would need stiches. Still, he became angry at his cousin. The hunts were supposed to be kept from leadership. A real soldier would've known better.

"See Daven," Jonah Gray said, pointing to the man with the burned face who'd read the poem. "He'll tend your wounds."

Emmanuel did as told. Jonah Gray shifted to Jean-Jacques, who looked up to meet the taller man's gaze. Pale clouds peered down, seeming to both study and pity him. Jean-Jacques forced himself to not look away, despite wanting to, despite something in his mind begging to.

You're the badass killer, he reminded himself. You're the Volunteer.

"Good to see you again, Corporal." It must've been him at Xavier Station, after all. "Come. We have much to learn from each another."

Jean-Jacques followed the other man around the pond. The Chaplain's back remained vertical, but a slight hitch in his steps slowed their pace. I should end this now, Jean-Jacques thought. And he intended to. Just as soon as he learned how his mother had been conjured.

They reached the slope of a stream. They could speak alone here, the Chaplain said. They could speak true. The sound of the stream would keep their words from prying ears.

"What did you think of rite?" The chanting in Jonah Gray's voice from the ceremony had been replaced with a more floaty delivery, his words fine, even placid.

"What you preach. How you reconcile it with what's been going on?" Jean-Jacques meant the bombings, though any number of the Front's recent actions could work.

"Well." Little waves seemed to run through Jonah Gray's eyes. He stooped his thin frame over Jean-Jacques and pulled tight his camo jacket. "Dirty for dirty."

"What does that mean."

Jonah Gray didn't answer. Instead he said, "I've watched you, you know. All of you. For weeks. All you fortunate, all you heroes. All those chosen by the cythrax. I learned Dash is the most dangerous. You don't trust. You don't believe. Yet you still do. A man like that can't be managed. But he knows others need to be."

Jean-Jacques swallowed to wet his throat. The Chaplain had been following *them*?

"That's why you'll join us. Your country needs you, Corporal Saint-Preux. No greater duty than that. We're saving America from itself. In doing so—it's not peace versus violence. It's peace *and* violence."

There was a hard vagueness to the Mayday vision. Jean-Jacques thought listening to its leader would've helped with that but instead the Chaplain had only exacerbated it. Jean-Jacques realized now that that was part of the genius, part of the appeal. Mayday was a cipher, a catch-all for the furious and disenfranchised. Be against the powerful and elite. Be for equality. Be against those who benefited while you suffered. Be for the arrows of antifascism. Mayday radicalism meant everything. It meant nothing, too.

But after opening Pandora's box, did they have a plan? If they were right, and America was barreling toward a clash between corrupt order and upheaval—well, Jean-Jacques knew where he stood. He'd walked the war rubble of too many aftermaths to make any other choice.

"What you preach," he repeated, deciding to be more specific this time. "Egalitarians, you said. They kill governors?"

Jonah Gray's face tightened like a sling. "That wasn't us." Jean-Jacques shrugged but the other man persisted. "I'm serious. My men carried AR-15 rifles that night. A couple had Ruger pistols they got from God knows where. Those fire .45 caliber, though. Governor Harrah was killed with 9-mil rounds. Said so on the news."

He paused for a few seconds.

"9-mil. The preferred round of police and military."

That's interesting, Jean-Jacques thought. If true, that's very interesting. Jonah Gray was still talking like a grim prophet, and Jean-Jacques didn't think everything he was saying made sense, but some did.

"We were promised no drama that night. A campaign mole let us into the ballroom. Said they wanted to make headlines. We sought to make an impression, and accrue some capital, too. Win-win. We were used, for ends I can only guess at."

"That's fucked up."

"They'll get theirs, Corporal. I swear that to you. No one plays Mayday twice."

Something else tickled at Jean-Jacques. "Chosen by the cythrax, you said." What did that mean?

Jonah Gray exhaled through drawn lips. This close to one another, he smelled of clean sweat and shaving cream to Jean-Jacques. He may look like a man in rags, he thought, but he ain't living it. The Bureau would want to know that part.

"To believe, Corporal, sometimes we must see. Do you think that you all were the first? That you all were the only?"

The Chaplain seized Jean-Jacques by the wrist and squeezed.

Jean-Jacques found himself in a yard of grass and pavement. A worn sky carried the plastered hint of sea in it, though he felt it more than smelled it. A low wire fence ringed the yard, and clumps of hunched men milled about in groups, talking soft, kicking at the dirt beneath them. They all wore matching yellow slickers, and so did Jean-Jacques. One man tossed a frisbee at another, who watched it land at his feet, face barren as drought.

He'd been transported, again.

"Gray!" A voice like an anvil sounded through the yard. "Gray, Jonah, last four: 6380. You're due at medical in ten."

"Shit." A voice behind Jean-Jacques spoke, flat and even. He recognized it as Lamar Pierre's. "Now they got you doing procedures back-to-back. Be strong, my brother. Be strong."

Some sharp, primal brew of emotions filled Jean-Jacques's chest, fear and rage and despair all swirling together in a maelstrom of the soul. He willed himself to words.

"Just flesh and bone," Jean-Jacques found himself saying. "Just scalpels and needles."

"Be strong," Pierre repeated.

Quick as he'd left, Jean-Jacques was back. Back in the meadow, in the park, in the city.

"Yours?" He could only whisper to Jonah Gray about the memory. "From Block Island?"

The Chaplain didn't answer. Instead he walked back around the pond, toward the others. Jean-Jacques followed. Fascination had overtaken any other feeling he had, short-circuited any other motivation. He didn't know what he wanted to do but he knew it wasn't what he'd planned. The holy man began speaking of the Hero Project, a real Hero Project, one undertaken at rehabilitation colonies against the will of its subjects. Maven was one drug used on veterans with troubles at the colonies. To subdue them, for control. Cythrax had been another, an experimental substance distilled from rocks found deep in space. He pointed to the man with the burned face. "Not Vietnam. A colony." He pointed to another man with a slope where a shoulder should have been. "Also a colony." He pointed to a woman about Jean-Jacques's age who had the saggy, vacant countenance of a blind person.

"War? The colonies?" Jonah Gray asked. "What's the difference, in the end?"

Before he'd been released, Jonah Gray had been selected for cythrax treatments, too.

"It's how I summon memories," he said. "They didn't know, of course. Otherwise they'd never have let me out."

Jean-Jacques had been clocked at 460 miles per hour. He had a friend who could lift a bus and another who could teleport the length of a football field. It took a lot to impress him. The Chaplain's power did. A man who could conjure dead people, even only for a few moments—a man like that was different. A man like that was a threat.

"It comes from my God, but also from my enemy." Jonah Gray seemed to know exactly what he was thinking about. "The duality of man: all things through Him.

"This power? My own duality, I suppose."

The Chaplain continued his oration. Sometimes the cythrax killed at the colonies. Sometimes it scarred. Sometimes—sometimes, it did work. The man with the burned face had a small ability for healing. Another of the Mayday tribe could distort faces for short periods of time—a handy thing for a group of domestic militants. Jonah Gray had even met an escaped veteran out west who could turn objects into explosives with his hands.

"Parlor tricks compared to you," he said, the reverence from his sermon returning to his voice. "Compared to the Volunteers. You are us, but realized. Man beyond."

"But." Jean-Jacques didn't know what to ask so he asked for everything. "Why?"

"Come now." The Chaplain smiled. "I know you were infantry, young man, but must I explain everything?"

A joke. To lighten the mood. Jean-Jacques offered a courtesy laugh. Then he asked the other man to continue. Well—as any scientist knew, subjects responded differently to experiments in captivity versus in the wild. Whatever happened in Tripoli, whoever ordered it, had listened to a scientist. Veterans with troubles with minor cythrax gifts offered those in power little. Special operations soldiers with major gifts? They offered much more.

Jean-Jacques's head was spinning. They'd dropped the bomb on them on purpose? There was no way. It was impossible. Command never would've allowed it. The military did fucked-up things, sure. But to other people. To the enemy. Not to its own. And yet . . . officers could be sketchy bastards. And what was the government if not a collection of officers in suits? Flowers always swore he'd never heard anyone radio Higher for the bomb.

He was about to ask the question no one would ever answer—why did they live when so many others died?—when Emmanuel approached in a bit of a daze, holding up his forearms. The wounds were gone, mostly, dark red pus and yellow crust replaced by long pink scars that looked years old.

"Daven's no miracle worker," Jonah Gray said, rubbing his fingers over Emmanuel's scars. "But for an old warfighter, he can still impress."

I came here to take this man, Jean-Jacques reminded himself, one last time. He couldn't even muster pretending anymore. He hadn't been turned, he felt. But he had been baffled.

Which was maybe worse.

Jonah Gray took Jean-Jacques by both shoulders and kissed his cheek with dry lips.

"I don't know how long you're with us, young hero, but I do hope it's longer than first planned." He patted Jean-Jacques's chest where the teardrop hung from its chain. "We'll meet again." His voice turned to a hot whisper so no one else could hear. "My best to our government friends, of course."

Then the holy man was gone, disappearing through the crowd and into the new morning, just another homeless man wearing a combat jacket too thin and ragged for the coming winter.

"So," Emmanuel said, still rubbing his arms. "What you think of rite?"

CHAPTER 19

FOLLOWING THE GOVERNMENT doctor home proved simple enough for Sebastian. He'd scheduled the last appointment of the day, so after it, he slipped into a bathroom, went invisible, and found a seat in the employee waiting room. Eleven minutes later, just as Sebastian began to wonder how long he could stay unseen without bringing on a migraine, the doctor passed through, signing out with a wink for the administrative nurse.

The hospital sat on a ridgeline along the river, farther uptown than Sebastian could remember ever going. It was a district for old people and rich people, which explained why the hospital was there. The government doctor lived five blocks northwest of it. He stopped for groceries then again for a glass of wine, which allowed Sebastian to switch off his power and wait outside.

The appointment had been as bland as Sebastian expected. Nurses took his measurements, noting he'd gained four pounds and remained the same height. His blood pressure was a bit high for a man his age, but nothing extraordinary. They asked about his drinking and he modulated it as much as he thought believable. They said it was still too much. Then they drew some blood and told him to wait for the doctor.

The doctor had come in ten minutes later, apologizing for the wait. He was youngish, about a decade older than Sebastian, a trim man with floppy hair who'd just returned from the Burning Man festival out west.

"Third time to the playa," the doctor said. "Changes my life every time."

Sebastian nodded and asked if it was true that the big California tech firms had paid off separatist militias to keep them from attacking the festival camp.

The doctor just shrugged. "I go for the spiritual transformation," he said. "And the tits."

Sebastian found it odd the government entrusted this man with big federal secrets like the health of a citizen with the superpower of invisibility, but—well, bureaucracy. Mistakes happened.

After he finished his evening wine, the doctor walked home. Sebastian trailed a half block behind, keeping his head down, pretending to read his phone while watching the other man from the tops of his eyes. The doctor lived in an old brick high-rise with a doorman and Sebastian went invisible again before reaching the revolving door. In the elevator, the doctor looked at the space he stood in, seeming to sense a presence next to him. Seeing nothing, he snorted to himself and began picking his teeth in the reflection of the elevator door.

It's a good thing I'm not a creep, Sebastian thought in the elevator. I could really abuse this if I wanted to.

At the appointment, the doctor had asked Sebastian how often he used his power. Sebastian said not often, only when he got bored and wanted to see if he still could. And in the ballroom with the Mayday Front. Because he'd needed to. Then the doctor asked how long he'd stay invisible. Sebastian thought about that. "Five minutes," he said. "Maybe ten minutes a few times."

The doctor had been holding a chart in his lap. He peered into it.

"Says here you once went twenty-one minutes and twelve seconds."

"Under medical observation. Killer headache for a week. So I lay off."

The doctor nodded. "You're not supposed to use it at all, as I understand it."

Sebastian began to sputter, which made the doctor laugh.

"Don't let the Man get you down," he'd said. "The playa taught me that. Power to the people!"

Sebastian had just nodded at that, keeping his disbelief to himself. He'd spotted the camera with the blinking red dot in the ceiling corner of the examination room minutes earlier.

The doctor's apartment proved austere the way only a space kept by a career bachelor with obsessive compulsions could be. The doctor took off his shoes while Sebastian drifted in behind him, like air. A large, state-of-the-art entertainment center dominated the living room, the plush carpet beneath it soft and unstained. An open floor plan gave way to a shiny marble kitchen, the stove and oven in it virgin-clean. Not a cook, Sebastian observed from the couch, feet up on a glass coffee table. The doctor opened the refrigerator to put in groceries. Sebastian glimpsed nothing in it but white wine bottles and takeout leftovers in styrofoam boxes.

Hours earlier in the hospital, the doctor had said Sebastian looked fit as a fiddle, and wrote a special prescription for migraine medication "just in case." He assured Sebastian that he wasn't any more susceptible to brain aneurysms than a regular citizen was. "Live your best life," he'd said, remnants of Burning Man philosophy splashing his words. "Any last questions?"

Sebastian said yes, he did have one more.

"Does anyone know why I lived yet? In Tripoli. The others . . . they all got the vaccine. For the bomb. But I never got a cythrax vaccine. It's . . . well, it's weird, you know? My handler thinks it's a dumb question. But he's just a field agent. Maybe someone like you might have an answer? I don't want to bother the wrong people with this."

At that, the doctor had set down his chart. He'd cleared his throat and said he'd be right back. Then he'd left the room.

279

As he'd waited for the doctor to return, feeling the blinking red dot of the camera in the ceiling and trying not to look at it, Sebastian decided to follow the other man home. Maybe the doctor would know, maybe he wouldn't. But anything like a straight answer would require privacy.

The doctor had applied some sort of feng shui theory to the back rooms of his apartment—art prints with Chinese characters adorning the walls, his dresser full of crisply folded blue dress shirts and dark jeans, the bookshelves in his bedroom empty minus some nature photography books. This is the most boring motherfucker alive, Sebastian thought, walking around free and visible while the doctor showered. He'd come here hoping to find . . . he wasn't sure what, but something more than a grown man's pristine loneliness. Secret files? Listen in on a phone call about the top-secret medical examination he'd just conducted? Something like that. Instead he was snooping through a stranger's apartment like a goddamn thief.

Sebastian opened a small closet door off the doctor's bedroom and decided he'd wait for the other man to finish showering, after all.

During the appointment, after the Burning Man conversation but before the vaccine one, the doctor had posed his own question to Sebastian. "What's that Justice guy like?"

"Tall," he'd said, his normal response meant to both deflect and get a quick laugh. He'd learned that people always wanted a piece of the brave, noble Justice, and when they couldn't have that, they wanted a piece of someone who did. Somehow, he'd become that someone.

That hadn't been enough for the doctor, though. He'd wanted more. So Sebastian had balked. "Media's overplayed it," he'd said. "We don't know each other all that well." Which was true, Sebastian thought, in its way. Despite all their time together, there had remained something deeply unknowable about Pete Swenson.

Hours later in the doctor's apartment, he understood why the other man had asked about Justice. The small closet off the bedroom proved to be a shrine to America's greatest combat hero. A framed black-and-white photograph hung on the back wall, Pete's outsize side silhouette overlooking some cityscape in the Mediterranean night. Unopened action figures filled a shoe rack under the photo, the bold Sniper, steadfast Dash, and nefarious Abu Abdallah all represented on the second row. The top row had been reserved for three distinct versions of Pete—raid commander Justice, mountain warfare Justice, and jungle stealth Justice. A garment rack held an adult medium costume of the Justice soldiering uniform, complete with combat boots, a hard-shell helmet, and a plastic assault rifle. Two cardboard boxes stacked upon each other contained every published issue of *The Volunteers* comic, even some variant covers Sebastian had never seen.

I bet this guy even has Justice bedsheets, he thought.

The sound of running shower water ended, and Sebastian heard the doctor whistling to himself in his bathroom. He needed to make a decision and make it now.

He went to the kitchen, poured two glasses of wine, and waited on the doctor's couch, visible to the world and smiling his smiliest smile. A few minutes later, the doctor walked in wearing a thermal shirt and pajama bottoms and promptly screamed.

"Easy now. Swenson sent me," Sebastian said, holding out a wineglass. "He needs you."

A total lie, of course. But what was one little fib in the pursuit of grand truth?

"Justice?" The government doctor still seemed wary, but he accepted the wine. "Why? How?"

Sebastian laid it out: he'd been asked by Pete to go to the doctor's appointment. *They* would be watching the great Justice closely, of course, but him? The hostage kid? What did he matter? Pete wanted to know about the cythrax vaccine, and he'd looked into the doctor. "He knows you're someone we can trust," Sebastian said. "That you're not like the others."

The doctor nodded. "I'm not," he said. "But—even having this conversation . . . I could lose my clearance."

"We understand," Sebastian said. "It's why we've been so cloak-and-dagger." That he'd been anything but seemed beside the point. "To protect you, and your job. But we still need your help."

The doctor sighed, took a swig from his wine, and rolled his lips. Sebastian saw doubt cross his face once, then pass, then again. He tilted his head.

"You said you and Justice weren't close."

"Had to say that. I saw the camera in the ceiling. I knew we weren't alone."

Sebastian could feel himself having a bit of fun with it all. Not a game, he tried to remember. This is beyond for real.

The doctor took another drink of wine, then sat on his couch next to Sebastian.

"They told me to stick to the basics. Draw your blood so the lab can see if it's altered at all since we saw you last. They said if you asked any tough questions, to say no change. But your vaccine question—it was so specific. I panicked. That's why I left the exam room. Wanted to make you think I was looking into it."

"You looked up the answer?"

"I mean, already kind of knew it." The doctor rubbed at the back of his head, finished his wine, then reached for Sebastian's. "It's just a theory. An idea. Please stress that to Justice."

"'Course."

"Not my area of expertise, but a friend in NASA lives and breathes this stuff. He's obsessed with what happened over there. My understanding is they thought they'd figured it out. They gave everyone that shot as something designed to spark powers. It didn't work, obviously, but what was especially weird was that you lived. You hadn't received anything. Decades of studying this, and your survival taught everybody how little we know."

"Okay." The government hadn't sacrificed a platoon of Rangers. It'd sought to create a platoon of super-Rangers. Much more reasonable. Much more in line with the America Sebastian thought he knew.

"My friend thinks it has something to do with World War One. Turns out, you survivors all have an ancestor who fought in the trenches. In the Argonne, to be exact. Immunity to cythrax must be tied to mustard gas, somehow, and the way it remains in DNA. The Haitian kid, they're less sure about, but—"

"Mustard gas." Sebastian wasn't so much confused now as he was deeply, wildly frustrated. Why all the lies? Why all the obfuscation? "Our great-great-grandfathers got gassed like roaches a century ago. That's what saved us."

"Just a theory! I can't stress that enough!"

It did explain why no locals or insurgents in Tripoli had survived, Sebastian thought. It made more sense than any dud vaccine ever had.

No god above had chosen them. No training had saved them. It wasn't probability, nor combat skill, that had delivered them from the bomb. It had been in them all along, where they'd come from, who they'd been born as.

"You'll tell him, right?" The doctor's hand holding the wine was shaking, and the pitch in his voice had turned wafer-thin—it had dawned on him what he'd just shared. "Justice needs to know I'm like him. One of the good guys."

Sebastian got up, grabbed the wine bottle from the kitchen, and returned to the couch. He poured the doctor another glass, then started drinking straight from the bottle.

I really do fucking hate how wine tastes, he thought.

"So where'd you go when you left the exam room?" he asked.

"There's a POC listed on your file—all your files. I tried to call him but that office said he's not in the military anymore. Then I called my supervisor and he told me to stick with the script. That's why I came back and told you there'd been no change."

"That no one really knows for sure. That no one might ever know."

"Yeah. Listen—" The doctor reached to grab Sebastian's shoulder, but the younger man recoiled. "I'm sorry. Telling you that was just part of the job. I hope you get it. I'm just a doctor. Just a person trying to serve our country and live his best life at the same time."

Despite himself, Sebastian did get it. "No judgment," he managed. "I'm a propagandist." They sat together on the couch for a few minutes more, Sebastian drinking slowly from the bottle, the doctor asking if a meal or drinks with Justice might be a possibility. Sebastian interrupted on a whim to ask if the doctor remembered the POC name from his file.

"It was a lieutenant colonel," he said. "Asian name. Tong? Tran? Trang? Something like that. Mean anything to you?"

It didn't.

———

Sebastian hadn't seen Pete in a couple of days but when he returned to his apartment and found him on his couch watching TV alone in the dark, he wasn't surprised. Chance or fate? he wondered. They'd melded together a long time ago for the superman.

For anyone caught in his wake, too.

Sebastian took a seat next to him to watch the final minutes of a documentary on the Battle of Ha Long Bay. "Vietnam's Midway," Admiral McCain called it in his memoir. "Where we salvaged victory from the jaws of defeat and ensured the northern advance would be justified." It was the first major battle where American generals used the International Legion, who proved themselves worthy with great ferocity. "Napoleon said that a soldier will fight long and hard for a bit of colored ribbon," a retired army major who'd fought at Ha Long Bay said. "I'm here to say that no one in the history of warfare fought longer or harder than my brothers in the gook horde did that day."

As the credits rolled over still images of mangled bodies, blown-up tanks, and other war gore, Pete turned to Sebastian.

"Wish we still had battles like that."

He sounded drunk. He smelled drunk, too. Sebastian stood up and found the light switch.

"You need to hear this," he said. Then he told the great national hero what he'd learned, what he suspected, about Tripoli, about what Flowers had said, about what the government doctor had said, too, about their World War I ancestors and what he thought it meant and why he thought it mattered and how he thought there was more to the story, much more, and how they could find out that much more by working together and figuring out a plan.

"Someone did this to us, and intended it," he said, feeling the buzz of resolve in his declaration. "Just a matter of moving up the government chain until we find out who."

Pete had crossed his arms and was leaning back into the couch, still in TV-watching mode. His voice slurred with boredom, like he'd only been half paying attention.

"Why?"

"Why?" The question caught Sebastian off guard. He'd prepared for all sorts of reactions but not this. "Well. Why not? For the truth."

"Truth?" Pete's eyes crystallized, one hyper-black, one hyper-green, and he sat up. A new hostility blitzed his words. "I don't fucking get you, hostage. You could be the world's greatest spy if you wanted to. Someone who helps. Someone who protects. A bomb fell from the sky and turned us super. Turned us beyond. That's truth. That's the only truth that matters."

Pete rose and took four long steps into the kitchen. He threw a light jab through the top of the metal refrigerator. A sucking vacuum sound rushed from it and the lightbulb inside zapped out. Pete raised his fist in admiration and laughed, more to himself than anything, the fridge now framed by a hole the size of a children's basketball.

"This power." Pete turned back around. "I owe it to my fallen brothers to make something of this. Soldiers die in war all the time. That's what we're here for. To die so that America could build the greatest army ever? An entire army with powers like ours? How is that not defending the homeland?" Pete stepped toward Sebastian like he was going to grab and shake him but stopped halfway with a sneer.

"You're just like the rest of them." He finished by spitting out one last word like it was a pox. "*Citizens*."

They stood apart from one another in strained silence, one man standing tall and straight, the other hunching a bit. So, Sebastian thought. Pete had figured out Tripoli, too. Maybe had known a long time. He didn't understand where the other man's anger came from, but it didn't matter. He knew he'd replay the speech in his head over and over again for days on end, and he'd do that because there'd been some legitimacy to it. People needed help, everywhere. He could help them, somewhere. He hadn't. It's not that he'd thought about it and chosen not to. It was worse than that, he realized.

He'd never even considered it in the first place.

"I don't deserve my powers. I know that."

"You don't."

The intensity in Pete's voice had lessened in pitch. He cleared his throat. "Apologies if any of that—I don't know." Sebastian gave a half nod. "What happened to us? It happened. I didn't sign up for it specifically but I signed up. That's how it works. So I look forward. I believe you want to help people. You have it in you. It's what brought you to the Near East in the first place." Sebastian half-nodded again. He believed that, too. "Only three percent of Americans serve in the military these days. Only three percent loves America enough to fight for it. Our country needs help. Here, now. Everyone knows it. Everyone feels it. And I'm here to tell you that there are public servants, combat veterans, in government just like us. People willing to do what's necessary."

"I'm not following," Sebastian said, because he wasn't.

"You can do incredible things, Sebastian. I want you to be a Volunteer. But not overseas. Here, in the homeland."

Sebastian's head was swimming and his conversation with the government doctor seemed months old, not hours. He took a chair across from the couch because he thought Pete had more to share but instead the other man grabbed an envelope from the kitchen table and handed it to him.

"It'd be a big change, I know, but a good one. Give you purpose. There are people—things are going to change, man. They'll need you. We're going back to war soon. Real soon."

"What people?"

"Think all this over. It's a lot to digest. If you're in, we can talk details. In the meantime, read that over. It's what people think of you, now. It's my gift to you. It's my charge to you, too. To do something."

Then Pete was gone, out and away from the apartment, and Sebastian was by himself again, alone and adrift in a world that never had made much sense to him and, he knew, probably never would, no matter what he did, no matter how hard he tried. Was that clarity?

He opened the envelope.

COMMENTS BY SPECIAL AGENT THEODORE P. DORSETT III

Re: Subject Sebastian Gareth Rios

I. Subject is a survivor of a botched War Department mission whose details remain classified Top Secret. Falls under the umbrella of the "Hero Project" though Bureau analysts have filed reports expressing doubts about this (see: "Black October" files, 149-774, 149-780). Subject was a nonmilitary citizen who sought return to American soil. His request was granted under the provision of a five-year observation tasked to the Bureau. Subject works communications at Homeland Authority, a position the Bureau helped him obtain. Agency reps familiar with the "Hero Project" agreed that keeping subject employed at a government agency would be ideal, as subject is impressionable and does not understand the threat he poses to others and/or the United States government.

II. Subject possesses ability to turn invisible for iterations of time: the longest on record for twenty-one minutes and twelve seconds (under medical observation). Subject complains of severe headaches after utilizing this ability, which serves as an active deterrent for utilization. Subject has a minor problem with alcohol that sometimes leads to inadvertent utilization. Subject has been warned repeatedly about this.

III. Subject's medical reports reveal unstable molecules that "swell" when subject goes invisible (full medical report attached—Annex #4C). In layman's terms, it remains possible that subject could fully disappear from common sight if he continues to utilize this ability.

IV. Subject's minor problem with alcohol shows signs of developing into a chronic issue. Subject might grow out of it—subject is in his mid-twenties—but subject does match the psychological profile of someone with addiction issues. Utilization of the invisible ability increases with subject's incidents of alcohol abuse. Subject has shown recurring signs of depression, post-traumatic stress, and social anxiety.

V. Subject believes the "Hero Project" is a deception put out by the War Department. Subject believes he was the rescue target of a spec ops mission gone awry in the Barbary Coast that left thirty-plus American operators dead. Subject does not seem aware the "Hero Project" has existed in government files since 1985. Subject expressed much regret that so many operators lost their lives while rescuing him from captivity. Subject erroneously believes his rescue was the purpose of the operators' mission (see: "Black October" files, 302-307). Subject has not been advised otherwise.

The pages went on like that, agents writing about his life in the cold detachment of administrative-speak. Sebastian read them all, drinking it in through his eyes like elixir: how the government had chronicled his passive liberal politics, about the anti-colony newsletter he'd signed up for, about how Sebastian had been overheard at work gatherings describing what he did for Homeland Authority as "minor acts of neocolonial propaganda." He probably had said that, he thought, but over beers or something. Not at actual work. They'd even written a page about his family's immigration from Bolivia, trying to figure out if there was any connection to the Communist Party. There was also a section on his personal life, his occasional successes, his many failures. "Seems likely to marry the next serious partner," the document stated. "Which should further moderate the subject."

None of the information was wrong, though much of it seemed unnecessary and histrionic. Were they that worried a kid from the California suburbs would become radicalized? It all felt a tremendous violation to Sebastian. This is my life, he thought. And they make me sound like a fucking dope.

He thought about why Pete had given him this file, and how he'd gotten it in the first place. He understood that the other man had come here to break him. Break him to build him back up. It's what people like Pete did. Sebastian knew that.

"I want you to be a Volunteer," he'd said. "Here, in the homeland."

For who, though? It hadn't sounded like Pete meant the government. But who else could it be, if not the state?

As he knew he would, Sebastian spent many hours of the late night and early dark replaying in his head over and over again what Pete had said.

"A bomb fell from the sky."

Yes. And.

"Turned us super."

Yes. And.

"Turned us beyond."

Yes. And.

"That's truth."

Yes. And.

"That's the only truth that matters."

No.

Volunteer #1: *Hello, young citizens, I'm Justice of the Volunteers. Protecting the homeland is a sacred duty, and it's one we're all in—together.*

Volunteer #2: *There may be an "I" in Sniper, but there's no "I" in team!*

Volunteer #3: *Or in "Volunteers."*

Volunteer #1: *Good point, Dash. The three of us learned a long time ago the importance of teamwork and the group. Only together have we reached our goals. Only together have we tracked down and brought vengeance to America's enemies abroad.*

Volunteer #2: *Only together did we get that clown-scum, Abu Abdallah!*

Volunteer #3: *That's true.*

Volunteer #1: *To be in concert with friends and teammates, working toward the same goal? It's the best. Whether for a school project or the big game, make sure you're doing the same. Be a part of something bigger than yourself—you'll learn who you really are in the process.*

Volunteer #2: *See you on the high ground, team!*

All Volunteers, together: *Because protecting the homeland starts at home.*

CHAPTER 20

HURRY UP AND wait. An old military axiom that applied to parts of life in the homeland, too. TV shoots, for one, Mia was learning. They'd been told the general needed to be on set at 7 a.m., not a minute late. But the way the light was reflecting off Lady Liberty in the background hadn't been to the director's liking. So they waited. And waited. And remained waiting. The now late-morning sun cast the statue in its best possible light, Mia thought, clear enough for a full profile but with enough of a gray autumn tint to shade its rust. Nothing computer graphics couldn't clean up, at least, given the episode of *Utopia* they were filming was set in 1969. But the director was god here. So they waited.

The Heights district perched high on a bluff, hard east from the harbor and statue. Mia was facing north, peering straight into the stony labyrinths of the Finance District. The Global Trade rose across the river through the sky, low clouds wrapped around it like a garter. It was strange for Mia to see the tower from such an angle. She knew it up close, the thick steel knots of its foundation, the way the glass panels seemed to turn to Spanish moss the higher one looked. The flag thrashing atop the roof, sixty stars and thirteen stripes, pale against the horizon. From here, the skyscraper seemed larger yet somehow less imposing. I can reckon with it now, she thought, and contain it. That only happens with distance.

"You must miss that life." Roger Tran walked up beside her, his crisp slacks and Windsor protruding from the sea of baggy plaid worn by the production crew. "A lot happens in those buildings every day."

Tran was skeptical toward Wall Street and its role in American life, even while he implored the staff to keep raising funds from it.

"I miss having weekends off," Mia said. "I'll admit to that."

Tran laughed. "Are you a person of faith, Ms. Tucker?" he asked.

Mia considered the question, and why Mr. Fix-It would be asking it. He hadn't mentioned church before but that didn't mean anything. "I believe in the importance of belief," she said. "Why do you ask?"

"In case a countryman of yours becomes poor and his means with regard to you falter, then you are to sustain him, like a stranger, that he may live with you."

"Hmm. Not a creed you'll find etched in any of those buildings. Old Testament or New?"

"You'd think New, wouldn't you? That's where much of the direction on wealth exists. But it's from the Old. The book of Leviticus. From Yahweh Himself."

"I dislike riddles, Roger. I thought you knew that by now."

Tran laughed again. "No masked intent here, Ms. Tucker," he said. "Just making conversation while the general goes over her lines."

General Collins was playing a small but vital role in the episode: that of a Gold Star mother who lost her son in Vietnam. President-elect Bobby Kennedy, weeks from assuming office, is strolling through the harbor park with his wife, staring out at the statue beyond, contemplating the challenges ahead. General Collins's character approaches and asks, without preamble: "How do you ask a young man to be the last to die in Vietnam? How do you ask a young man to be the last to die for a mistake?"

It seemed a strange role for a retired general and decorated Vietnam War hero. But that's what makes it so good, Mia thought.

No one loved *Utopia* like left-leaning bohemians in their twenties and thirties. If they could convince even a slice of that voting bloc that General Collins shared their values and worldview, the center would grow. Their ranks would grow along with it. The radical middle could begin to represent both stability and progress.

That General Collins believed peacemongers were fools more interested in moral purity than pragmatic realities was beside the point. Same with the fact that the guest spot came through an executive producer who sat on the Council of Victors. A platform like this couldn't be assigned a price, not one that'd do it justice. By Yahweh, Mia thought, or anyone else.

She asked Tran if he'd heard anything about Empire News. The report hadn't yet aired but staff had been briefed it was only a matter of time.

"Not much," Tran said. "Seems like they're focusing more on the homeland intel command. Not the Hero Project. Which is good."

Mia nodded. She'd asked the general point-blank about the journalist's allegation of other superpowered citizens. She'd expected Jackpot to deny. Instead the older woman had just shrugged. "I don't know, Mia," she'd said. "I'd say it's unlikely but here I am talking with a Roosevelt heir who can fly through the sky. Even at my highest command, there were files and programs I didn't have access to."

Mia believed her, or at least didn't disbelieve her. Still, the possibility of what had been raised lingered. It suggested that what'd happened in Tripoli hadn't been a freak accident. It suggested something Mia loathed deep in her bones. It suggested conspiracy.

Mia left the view of the Finance District to check in with the security team; it bothered the Sheepdogs that a deputy campaign manager talked perimeter details and sectors of fire with them, which made her do it all the more. Across a park trail, outside his trailer, River Phoenix worked with a voice coach on his Kennedy accent. All these episodes later, it still didn't sound quite right.

She returned to the set. General Collins sat in a folding chair under a tree conversing with the executive producer, a silver-haired man with a salt-and-pepper beard. The general waved Mia over to them.

"America Honors the Warfighter." Mia greeted the man, adding, "And Praise to the Victors."

"Right back at you, young lady!" The man talked with his hands, and more quickly than his business equivalents on the Council. He had thick, black eyebrows that seemed glued to his face. He formed finger guns and aimed them at Mia's slight bump, a way of congratulating her. She nodded and in turn congratulated him on *Utopia*'s success. It was everywhere.

"My baby, in a way." The man spoke with exclamation marks in his voice. "Twelve Emmy nominations is nothing to sneeze at, nothing to sneeze at. And the ratings! Up to 7.4 million last episode."

"Crane was just telling me about the struggle to get *Utopia* on air," General Collins said. The slight stoop in her shoulders tipped the older woman forward in her chair. Mia noticed that the makeup team had used concealer on the dark circles under her eyes; the late nights and early mornings of the campaign were affecting them all. Mia herself was spending far too much money on a caffeine-free protein energy drink designed specifically for pregnant women. "Now look at it. The talk of the country."

The man launched into the particulars of that struggle: how network after network told them an uplifting alternate history would never work. Viewers wanted dystopian escape, they were told, to make the real world more tolerable. Who'd watch a show about an America that valued diplomacy? Who'd watch a show about an America that attempted restraint? The politics seemed muddled, too—using liberal Bobby to push what seemed an anti-intervention message? Framing the grand victory in Vietnam like it could've been otherwise? They didn't understand, and especially didn't understand why the Council of Victors was championing it.

State TV couldn't say no, though, the producer explained. They'd been desperate.

"In a way, it was the perfect place for *Utopia*," he continued. "The revolution will be televised!"

The man laughed and laughed at his own joke, the general managing a grin for the same. Mia wondered, not for the first time, just how long ago this campaign had been planned out.

————

The producer excused himself to check on River Phoenix and River Phoenix's accent. Mia pulled out her phone and found an hour-old text waiting there like a stale crumb. It was from Britt Swenson.

"Remember my bouncer friend I told u about? He saw the guy from the ballroom on TV—promo for Victory Parade. Bernard Galt (sp.?) Old white guy."

Then a second text: "Yes he's sure, in case you ask."

Mia put away her phone and took a deep, measured breath of city air, a bladed darkness entering her mind. She walked away from the set to find some space. Was it betrayal she felt? Something like it, she thought. That son of a bitch, she continued, meaning Bernard Gault, meaning the Council of Victors, too, meaning Roger Tran and the whole lot of them. Anyone involved in this stupid little oligarchy. They could shove it. They could keep it. She didn't need them. They must've thought her a fool, a dupe. She could've lost her child in the ballroom that night. One errant gunshot would have ended it all.

Mia wasn't one for rash decisions. But something gave way within her as she remembered the ballroom, because of their recklessness, because of their self-regard. These people didn't deserve her. As Mia returned to the set in full, furious strides, she was still putting order and structure to her thoughts. Her intent felt plain as light, though. She was going to quit the campaign.

"General Collins. A word, please." Mia stripped her words of any question or deference.

The older woman heard that edge. She stood and sent away the campaign aides.

"Go ahead, Mia."

"I have it on good authority that the Mayday extremists were let into the ballroom the night of the inaugural." Mia didn't hesitate or falter. "By your friend, Bernard Gault."

The general didn't object; she didn't dispute. She didn't even blink. She just took Mia by the elbow and told her to walk with her.

"We're winning, Mia." Her voice was low, wary. "We're winning."

"I'm sorry?" Mia didn't understand what that had to do with anything.

"It'll be public tomorrow morning. New Harris/Tugwell poll has us up two percentage points. One poll, but: we're not a dark horse anymore."

"That's . . ." It was great news, amazing news, but Mia could not reason with it right now. "Did you hear me, ma'am? I said Bernard Gault aided the militants who took us hostage. The ones who shot Governor Harrah. The ones who killed him."

"Lima Charlie." Military-speak for loud and clear. "I hear you Lima Charlie, Mia." The general squeezed Mia's elbow, hard. They stopped walking and faced one another, the view of the Finance District on their periphery. General Collins's slight stoop tipped her shoulders forward, and Mia looked up at the other woman, finding a taut aggression she'd never seen directed her way before. "Now I need you to hear me."

Mia pursed her lips but nodded.

"As a pilot up there in the sky, you didn't see all the work on the ground that goes into successful counterinsurgency. Not that the Mediterranean's offered many successes, of course. But there have been some. Crete. New Beirut. Those victories didn't happen by accident. They didn't happen through nice intentions, either. Deals were struck. Bargains made. I broke bread once with a cleric in Syria married to his own twelve-year-old cousin. He raped that girl. He hit that girl. He took whatever he wanted from his tribespeople, because he could. A little tyrant of dirt. Everything about him disgusted me, ran in violation of my beliefs. We awarded him a road paving contract over chai. I swallowed my pride for the mission. For peace."

"That's over there."

"That's over here, too. I thought you knew that already. You think America is so different than those places? Than anywhere else? America, it's made up of people. And people will always disappoint, Mia. They lie to their spouses. They cheat on their taxes. They con their neighbors. Why do you think we need to bring united service to them, instead of them clamoring for it?"

Mia attempted to speak but the general held up a finger.

"Citizens are like soldiers: they're only as good as their leadership. And good leadership, real leadership, sometimes means grabbing your biggest, dumbest grunt by the scruff of his neck and ordering him to post guard. Because someone has to."

General Collins pulled out a cigarette and put it between her lips, letting it dangle there as she finished.

"Come down from the sky, pilot. Come get your hands dirty. Victory requires it."

Mia exhaled through her nose, keeping her lips pursed and her back straight. The only response she could form in her head—"Wrong is wrong"—felt childish and paltry. Layers of gray were one thing, but people had died in that ballroom. Lives altered, forever altered, American lives, because of Machiavellian scheming.

"Did you know?" she finally managed. "Before."

The general shook her head no.

"You're smart enough to know that's by design," she said. "But as I understand, it wasn't supposed to be like that, at all. It was supposed to be small, contained. Nonviolent. The governor was a good man. He'd have made a fine president." She shook her head again. "Like war, though. Adapt and overcome. Or be overrun by the horde."

Mia felt an overwhelming need to fly into the deep of sky but didn't dare move an inch now. She held to the precious quiet yet again.

"Take off a couple days, think things through," General Collins said between long, contemplative drags. "The parade next week, though—from there, it's all systems go. No time for doubts. No space for regret."

Her eyes fell upon Mia's stomach.

"You and I want the same thing: a new America. For your beautiful child. For all our children. They deserve hope. They deserve a promising nation, a rising one, like we knew. Tomorrow—tomorrow is what matters."

General Collins took a final drag, then flicked the half-smoked cigarette to the ground. Mia wrapped her arms around her stomach and kept them there for many minutes, trying to make sense of everything that'd been said, and everything not, watching the cinder of the half cigarette blink out.

———

Acceptable harbor light arrived just after noon. General Collins and River Phoenix finished their scene twenty minutes later. The general, Tran, and a group of Sheepdogs headed to the train station—an evening talk at the McNamara Institute in Federal City awaited. Defying the general's order, Mia headed uptown and into the office for a couple of hours. She needed to work to calm herself. After verifying the order for American Service banners and signboards to hand out at the upcoming V-V Day Parade and a conference call with campaign deputies in the western states, she texted Jesse.

"Horrible day. Home for dinner tonight?"

She didn't know yet if she wanted advice or a sounding board, but either way, she needed to talk things through with her fiancé.

That he was also a special agent for the Bureau—well, they'd figure it out, together.

Her phone buzzed thirty seconds later. She grabbed it with alacrity.

"Need to see you ASAP!" It was a text from Sebastian Rios. "Free this afternoon?"

Mia rolled her lips. I suppose I am, she thought.

They met at a coffee shop in Old Harlem. Amid a scattershot of antifascist arrows, someone had spray painted "Die Boho Scum" on the building's side. Sebastian had already arrived, sitting at a corner table, wearing a long-sleeve pajama top and faded jeans. His face was pallid and drawn, his hair holding a greasy tint to it. He got up and pulled out Mia's seat for her.

She ordered ice water and a panini, Sebastian a vanilla latte and scone. He pointed to her stomach and asked how she was feeling.

"Oh, fine," she said. Did he actually want to know? She figured not. Sebastian didn't seem like the kind of person who'd given much thought to the rigors of pregnancy. "Small complaints, of course. But worth it."

The urge, the desire, the craving to share—Mia rarely felt it, but she did now. The morning conversation with General Collins had spooked her. It already felt like a mad daydream, but it had happened and she needed help working her way through it. Had she been threatened there at the end? It'd felt that way in the moment, even if the words hadn't matched. An old friend like Sebastian might be able to remind her of who she'd been long ago, when she'd been certain about the world and her role in it.

I'll tell him, Mia decided. He and Jesse will make for good advice foils.

Before she could, Sebastian opened a spiral notebook on the table and turned it toward her. She saw a collection of lists and scribbles and dark strikethroughs in it.

"I wrote it out so I could keep it straight." Sebastian put his elbows on the table and leaned forward, close enough to Mia that she could see insomnia in his eyes. This was why he wanted to get coffee, she realized. "Bear with me, please." Then he launched into a tale about Tripoli, and what he thought had happened there, and why, his words darting about like bats in the dark. He spoke low, hushed, and kept itching at the stubble around his chin. Ancestors from World War I and the cythrax vaccine were mentioned. Mia let him ramble, choosing to keep silent.

"Look." He pointed into the notebook. Mia saw the word GERMANY circled with a line connecting to TRIPOLI and another to EMPIRE CITY. The phrase "Volunteers, Stateside" had a variety of scribbles beneath it she couldn't decipher. "It all connects."

Mia sipped her water and clasped her hands in front of her. The morning's revelation of the Council's plotting had upset and frightened her. This was the opposite. She found Sebastian's paranoid conspiracy sad, even repellent. Tripoli? Why did he care so much about Tripoli?

Mia no longer felt compelled to share her discussion with the general.

"For what end?" she asked.

"For . . . it's like Occam's razor. From philosophy class? For this end. For super-soldiers."

"Why go through the big charade? If 'they' "—Mia couldn't help herself, she paused to put air quotes around the word—"wanted to do something like that, why not do it in secret? In an underground bunker? An empty desert out west?"

Sebastian rubbed under his sunglasses. He believed what he was saying, she thought. There was no doubt about it. "Listen, I know how this sounds. But you know me, Mia. I'm no nutter. I like America. I like being American.

"I don't know what the truth is. We haven't been told it, though. I'm asking—I'm asking for your help. You know people, in finance, on the Council of Victors. You work for a retired general. What really happened to us?"

Mia took that in, considering both the vagueness and specificity of what Sebastian was suggesting. She moved her hands from the table to the top of her stomach and tapped at it. There was no response this time, but there had been the morning before. Life grew within Mia, and grew more so with every new day.

Could the nation she'd sworn to defend be capable of this thing Sebastian was suggesting? She'd given her youth to America. She'd given her leg for America. She'd almost given much more. So of course. Of course America was capable of such a thing. Capability was one of the things about her country she admired the most.

"I swallowed my pride for the mission," General Collins had said. Mia knew now she needed to do the same. The alternative sat across from her, wildly lost. A regular citizen, not a warfighter, doing his best, trying his best, but overcome by the forces of order. Mia was one of those forces of order. She always had been.

"You know, See-Bee," she said, clearing her throat. "My baby began kicking last week."

"What?" His voice was scratchy, irritated. He corrected himself. "That's great. Really."

"It is." She knew she was going to come across harsher than she wanted, but they were too old for this type of talk. Sebastian was a friend, yes. But whether he knew it or not, he was also a threat. "I'm going to be a mother. I'm going to be a wife. I'm going to be an aide for the next commander in chief."

"I—"

"You're going to let me finish. General Collins likes to remind the staff that it's not about yesterday. It's about tomorrow. Our aim is not small. It's to transform the country. To ensure my child knows an America like we grew up in. Something hopeful. Something safe."

Sebastian stared back at her, openmouthed. He looked more crestfallen than angry. Maybe a bit surprised, too.

"War changes us," Mia continued. "I get that. We went over-

303

seas for different reasons, I think, but we had this in common: we wanted to prove that we could. It changed you, See-Bee, and that's okay. It changed me, too. But don't let it define you. Don't let one month of your life shape everything that remains. Please. As someone who knew you when you were just a goofy college kid without a care in the world: tomorrow. Tomorrow is what matters."

Sebastian sighed, opening his mouth to say something but then stopping himself. He chewed his bottom lip a couple of times before trying again.

"You sound like Pete," he said. "He thinks like that, too."

And then he was done, closing his notebook and packing up his things. He slid over a five-dollar bill for his latte and scone. It wasn't enough but Mia didn't object. She'd cover the rest. She almost asked him to stay to smooth things over but instead she patted his forearm and told him to text if he needed anything.

Tough love, she thought. We all need it, sometimes.

Jesse called later that afternoon. She told him she was feeling better about things and not to worry. He's busy enough, she decided. He's focused on bettering tomorrow. So am I.

———

"Welcome to *The Proving Ground*. I'm your host, Jamie Gellhorn. We begin with an exclusive investigation into the background of retired major general Jackie 'Jackpot' Collins, a presidential candidate who's gone from a virtual unknown to serious political player in a few short months.

"Our investigative team has obtained documents from General Collins's time at homeland intelligence that suggest, at best, a fuzzy regard for the rule of law. The documents are redacted of top-secret material but still reveal the general oversaw implementation of underground interrogation centers in ally nations such as Malta—a loophole meant to work around current military law. She also helped lay the groundwork for a covert military court system that has, at times, declared American citizens suspected of ties to fanatic groups as enemy combatants.

"Empire News has uploaded all supporting material to our website. We invite viewers to scrutinize the documents themselves. They may serve as keyholes into the ethics and decision making of a contender for the highest office in the land."

CHAPTER 21

THE AUTUMN WIND carried a mean, frosty air to it that hinted of more. Hands deep in his jacket and chin tucked, Jean-Jacques walked through Kissinger Square, the tusked arch clashing against the dark of sky. Old bullet holes from the Vietnam arrests slabbed the base of the arch, and Jean-Jacques paused to run his fingers through them. The smaller dents meant rubber slugs, he figured, but the deep cavities meant lethal rounds. Bolt action, looked like, .30 caliber.

Dirt farmers in the Mediterranean carried better weapons than that. The riot here had marked the peak of the antiwar movement and been put down by Home Guard. Poor bastards, Jean-Jacques thought. Enemy was one thing. Citizen mobs were something else altogether.

Mayday, Mayday.

He met the agents in a neon diner a block north of the square. It was just the two younger ones, Dorsett and Stein, alone at a table in the rear. They could not have looked more cop if they'd tried, all rigid backs and jolty energy, wearing department store sweaters. Jean-Jacques took a seat across from them, facing the kitchen.

"City diner, late night," he said. "Real original, gentlemen."

Neither seemed in the mood for pleasantries. "You had him."

The larger one, Dorsett, put his elbows on the table and leaned across it. There was venom in his words. "And let him walk."

"Watch your tone, G-man." Jean-Jacques kept his hands in his jacket and his eyes fixed on the other man. Then he repeated the agent's own words back at him, imbuing them with a soldier's irony. "Remember now—only difference between us is a boat stop."

The agent with the stammer asked him to go through what happened at Revolution Park. Jean-Jacques talked about the vague instructions, the comms ban, and the all-terrain vehicles. He talked about Lamar Pierre being there. He told them how the people at rite hadn't been homeless at all, but from all over the city, all colors, all classes, citizens who'd lost a soldier somewhere along the way. He explained the girl in the track sweatshirt who sang, the veteran and his poem, the whole secular church vibe for burgeoning revolutionaries.

"The Chaplain." It was Dorsett again. "What about him."

"He was—" Jean-Jacques knew what he was supposed to say, what career federals wanted to hear. Jonah Gray was a threat. Jonah Gray was a danger. Jonah Gray was mad, deranged, a warfighter who'd slipped through the cracks of ordered society and was desperate to bring down others with him. And he was, he was all those things. But he was also something else.

"He's a believer himself." Jean-Jacques let that settle in for a few seconds before continuing. "Whatever he's doing with this group—it's not for play. It's not pretend, it's not just to blow up some statues to get some media shine. It ain't even rationalized in his head, the way I thought it would be. He really believes in giving power to the powerless. In antifascist creeds, in equality. He really believes America's failed the warfighter class by glorifying us. He intends to change all that. Whatever it takes."

The sounds of the diner filled the space between. The sizzle of coffeepots brewed ready, the bubbling of eggs in a skillet, the ping of bells and timers in the kitchen. Jean-Jacques tipped back his chair and continued in a lowered voice, saying that he'd wanted to detain Jonah Gray, but hadn't been able to figure out an exit strategy, which was true. Besides, he said, Lamar Pierre had been packing a street pistol, which was not true, but could've been.

"We'll see each other again," he finished, for the agents and for himself, too. "Gray said so."

A waiter came over. Dorsett and Stein had coffees in front of them. Jean-Jacques stuck with tap water and ordered an omelet. The waiter left. Dorsett asked about the social service Maydays. What they'd had him doing, where, and for who. Jean-Jacques wasn't about to narc on a dead soldier's mom who ran a food pantry for refugees, so he started talking about the special project they'd been assigned.

"They want to invade the Nam parade next week," he said. "Fill it with dirty vets, angry ones. Got us figuring out where to do it. Me and my cousin, we're walking Fifth Avenue tomorrow. ID the soft spots."

Something about the way neither agent responded to that suggested to Jean-Jacques they didn't care or already knew. He guessed the latter. "I'm thinking there's more to it, though." Still neither agent responded. "What your big cop bosses saying?"

That, finally, drew an answer. Not because of any trust, Jean-Jacques thought, but because they resented being called cops. "Anuth-another source reported similar," Stein said. "Think Gray will show?"

"Yeah. Pierre said something about the man giving a speech."

"Good. Make it happen then, Corporal. Get those broken warfighters into the parade."

A long silence followed, Jean-Jacques feeling the agents' wariness from across the table and him conveying the same. His omelet arrived. The waiter refilled Dorsett's coffee. He wondered who their other source in Mayday could be. They'd not mentioned that before. Fucking babylons, he thought. They'd made it seem like he was the only one who could access the militants. They'd made it seem like it was him or nobody.

"You don't like us, I get it. But we need you, you need us. So I'm going to be real with you, again. Boat stops and shit." It was Dorsett, of course. He tried his coffee before continuing, finding it too hot. "You're right about the parade-crashin'. It is for something else. We're hearing it's to go after some VIPs."

"Go after?"

"Shoot. Blow up. Gas. Guillotine. Something. The vice president's gonna be there. Most of the Council of Victors. Bunch of senators and consuls and bank CEOs, too. That lady general running for president, she's giving the keynote. Target could be any of them. Maybe all. These Mayday fucks don't seem to discriminate. But we gotta draw out this Chaplain. Orders are to end this, now. So you do your part, Dash of the Volunteers. Best believe we'll do ours."

Jean-Jacques considered all that. It took sack to use all those VIPs as bait. He admired it, in its way. He shared the last thing he'd been holding on to.

"He knows about you all," he said. "Told me to say hello to 'our government friends.'"

"Screwing with you. A test."

Jean-Jacques shook his head. "Not the type. I'm telling you, guy's an earnest. He's not like the jihadists or the separatists. He's not like the homegrown radicals you spend your usual days tracking down. What he wants—he can do it. He can get it. And he knows it. It's the idea that needs killing, not the man."

They didn't hear him, he could tell. They began asking about Mayday the organization, its structure, its logistics. They wanted to know about its finances. They needed to be asking about Mayday the message, Jean-Jacques thought, Mayday the rage, Mayday the hope. They needed to be asking about the girl who sang the song, not about who the lieutenants were. They needed to know the way the woman at the food bank talked about federals being enemy. They needed to know about the force in the veteran's voice when he read his poem about Hill 937. They needed to know more about everything they weren't asking about and nothing about what they were.

There was a saying in the army, though: Stay in Your Lane. Jean-Jacques had learned long ago as a cherry private not to do others' work for them. Made things messy. Made things harder. So he stayed in his lane and kept those images and moments to himself.

All for the better, he thought. The truth was, Jean-Jacques hadn't yet figured out what to do with them, either.

———

Jean-Jacques left the diner intent on the gym. A midnight workout to clear the mind and soul, help get the body ready for the Suck. He'd been slacking, he knew, could feel it in his shoulders and legs, and playing at community activist hadn't helped with his regimen. Monitor drones pulsed red in the well of sky and he looked up at them wondering, again, what kind of place didn't have stars.

Homecoming's luster had dulled for Jean-Jacques. The want for life beyond had returned. For the Legion, he told himself. For duty. More than even that, though, was something else. A ferocious need to keep going, to keep moving, no matter what.

His phone buzzed near the subway steps. It was a text, from Pete: "BROTHER," it read. "Need you! ASAP." An address followed, a few blocks north and a lot of blocks west, along the river.

Pete needed him, now? They hadn't seen one another in weeks. The big freak must be seething that we're still over here, Jean-Jacques thought, smirking to himself. And I'm the reason why. Still, he heeded his sergeant's call. It was nice, running super on the streets of Empire City, leaving bedlam in his wake. Screams of panic, shouts of confusion, an overturned hot dog stand or two, all in the span of thirty seconds. Speed like his could not be rationalized by human minds, nor could it be reasoned with. It could only be experienced.

Sure, someone might call the police, he thought. And say what? The texted address led to a low roofed, stand alone building made from slate. To the south, the Global Trade tower shot into the above, illuminating the night's licorice tint with white celestial light. To the hard west, across a bleak strip of highway, the river toiled away in its infinite work. The air here was wetter, Jean-Jacques noticed, but not colder. His heart was still battering from the short use of his power so he took a moment to collect himself. A large tiki mask carved from wood covered much of the building's door, some sort of spiked rainbow crown shooting from its head. He knocked twice on the mask's brow. When no reply came, he pushed open the door.

The wide bay of a space designed for packing in throngs of young bodies raced up at Jean-Jacques. Christmas lights covered the ceiling like kudzu and the smells of clean sweat and spilled beer stuck to tile swamped the air. A glowing fish tank in the near corner guided him to a coatrack. A couple of booths were filled with the hunched silhouettes of drinkers still clinging to their plans but most of the bar had gathered in the back, cheering in sloppy rhythm. Jean-Jacques found Pete there, the epicenter of it all.

He was chugging a full pitcher of beer, donned in a thick white headband and shirtless. An oversize American flag framed the wall immediately behind him, a large death skull in the blue canton instead of stars. Most every onlooker held a phone in front of them, filming the scene. Thick veins and full muscles twitched as Pete gulped along to their cadence, a medley of old battle scars dancing under the Christmas lights. But it was the mismatched tattoos that demanded the most notice: an M-4 carbine, barrel down, sprayed itself across his rib cage. The North Star with blue flames shooting from it rested above his left pec. The words "*Sua Sponte*" wrapped around the top of his chest in a scroll, from shoulder to shoulder, an homage to their simpler days in the Rangers. A long, silver Roman numeral I cleaved his sternum from the bottom of the neck to the navel. At first glance it looked like the length of a sword blade but Jean-Jacques knew it represented something else, an old quote Pete revered: "*Out of every one hundred men, ten shouldn't even be there. Eighty are just targets. Nine are the real fighters, and we are lucky to have them, for they make the battle. Ah, but the one, one is a warrior. He will bring the others back."*

Pete had been that one, once upon a time. Before the cythrax bomb, before they became Volunteers, before they become celebrity super-soldiers, Pete had been that one. The warrior. The man who brought others back. He'd lost it, though, somehow, somewhere along the way. He didn't think he had but Jean-Jacques knew so.

His power had diminished him.

Pete finished the pitcher and threw it against a wall, shattering it to bits, much to the crowd's delight. Two white girls with little waists and large chests emerged from the mass and settled under his arms.

"What is this?" Jean-Jacques asked the person next to him, a skinny white kid who was dressed like most everyone else in the bar, in a pastel button-down and khakis.

"That's Justice!" the kid shouted. "Like, the famous soldier dude. From the wars. He just made a movie about capturing that terror chief, you know that? He's chugged twelve pitchers, what a fucking freak! Better than the circus."

Something about how the word "freak" inflexed off the kid's tongue caused Jean-Jacques to punch him in the gut. Not too hard, he thought, though the young man did double over. Jean-Jacques used that word for Pete out of love. It sounded different coming from a nobody citizen.

He pushed through the crowd and shouted to get the other man's attention. Pete smiled wide, his dissonant eyes blazing like candlelight, and drew Jean-Jacques into a group hug with the white girls.

Jean-Jacques also liked drinking. He also liked the pursuit of sex with large-chested females and he too liked being beloved by the masses. But this was too much. They needed to be getting ready for the Mediterranean; they needed to be getting ready for the wogs. Too much America, he thought. Way too much.

Pete unwrapped himself from his admirers and motioned Jean-Jacques to a corner booth. "Fear not!" he called out behind him, voice slurring. "Promise to return." Shouts of drunken cheer followed.

They settled into the folds of the booth across from each other. Pete's eyes churned, one hyper-black and one hyper-green, trying to focus, his face blank as a puddle.

"I like your necklace," he said, pointing at Jean-Jacques's turquoise pendant. "Where'd you get it?"

Jean-Jacques ignored him. "You texted that you need help."

"I did! I do." The superman force-chuckled and yanked at the headband around his temples, as if surprised to find it there. Jean-Jacques suddenly regretted not checking in more. Soldiers of all kinds could get lost in the homeland. Even this one. "I'm in deep with some shit, Dash. Big government stuff. Politics stuff. They . . . it's hard to explain."

Jean-Jacques asked him to try. Pete shook his head.

"I'm good. When I texted I needed to vent but now I'm good. For real."

Jean-Jacques asked if it had to do with the Mayday Front.

"Those guys are terrorists. Trash fuckers. But I'm talking, like . . ." Pete sighed and closed his eyes, raising an arm toward the ceiling. "People up high. I just miss the war. Once we get back there, everything will be fine. For sure. Need to pull the trigger on men who deserve it again."

All of Pete's schemes, all his long chats with the three-letter-agency types, all his *contacts*—it was bound to catch up to him, eventually. Power did crazy things to people. *Pouvwa.* Anything to get it. Anything to keep it. Should've kept to soldiering, Jean-Jacques thought. Should've kept to the mission. Though maybe that wasn't fair. He'd been allowed to keep to soldiering because Pete hadn't, because Pete wouldn't. And Jean-Jacques understood all too well what a man wanting to get back to combat was willing to do.

For friendship, for duty, he asked again. Pete yielded more this time.

"Those people up high. They need me a little too much, you know? 'Cause I'm Justice. 'Cause I'm super. 'Cause I'm hero." He paused again and cleared his throat. "And I've been okay with it. It's fine. For a bigger good. I don't know. I mean, it is sorta about those trash veterans. Mayday! Whiny bitches. That night in the ballroom? You weren't there."

Jean-Jacques nodded to convey he knew about the night in the ballroom.

"Hypothetical. Let's say it was done on purpose. By both sides. Wouldn't that be fucked up? They keep using you and using you and using you, holding the Mediterranean over your head like a piece of cheese. So you go along with it. That night, I mean. Play your part. Things go haywire for other reasons but you play your part. That was it, they said. Then you and your boys can deploy again. But now there's another thing they want. Stand up with them at this damn parade. Help them look good. Which, whatever. It's small. Easy. 'Course, they said the same thing about the political bash. Small. Fucking easy."

Jean-Jacques leaned back into the booth, splicing apart what Pete had just said. The Maydays had used the politicos while the politicos had used the Maydays? Yeah, that checked out. A plan involving guns and hostages had gone wrong? That also checked out. The whys and how-comes, Jean-Jacques didn't care. For power and money, that's what it always came back to. "They'll get theirs," the Chaplain had said in the park about the politicians. Sounded like they deserved to. And Pete was right, in his way. What he described was fucked up. Any more fucked up than going undercover for government cops intent on crushing peacemongers who ran food pantries and built homes for Gold Star families?

Pete was lost here. Lost and pathetic. Jean-Jacques wasn't,

though. He knew the way forward. Time for action, he thought. Time to take the lead.

"That hypothetical?" Jean-Jacques rubbed the back of his head and whistled low. Once he got Jonah Gray, he'd free them all from the homeland. He'd free his fellow Volunteers and then he'd free himself. He wouldn't get caught in this game of extended favors, either. "I'm with you, homie. That is fucked up. Let's get back over there. Late-night raids, night-vision focus, squeezing that trigger. All of it. We'll be good, then. We'll get life back, then."

"Regret is weak, I know." Pete began rubbing at his North Star tattoo, sounding like he was talking to himself more than responding. "We signed up. We signed the dotted line. That's how it works."

Jean-Jacques thought he understood what his squad leader was getting at now. It wasn't the hero thing, but the service thing. Smaller, in its way. Much bigger at the same time.

"Naw. We didn't sign up for everything," he said. "We volunteered to be soldiers. Not all this other nonsense. That just happened. Way beyond us. Okay to remember that. Okay to live accordingly."

That made the brave and certain Pete Swenson blink in thought. Something in his face seemed to loosen. Then he cracked his neck and grinned, too. "Yeah. You right. You know, man, these citizens here were asking for a good war story. The real shit, they said. What you think? Should I tell them about the sniper nest in Cyprus? Maybe the torture basement in, fuck, Damascus? Homs? Somewhere. Smelled like guts. A goddamn sewer of guts."

Jean-Jacques leaned back into the booth and shrugged. He didn't have the heart to tell his friend it didn't matter. The people just wanted him to tell anything. Then they could make it something different, something all their own, something they could pretend to have a little claim to but no responsibility for.

FREEDOMBOOK

Your state-approved source for information and factual content

The Liberation of Hanoi was the capture of Hanoi, the capital of North Vietnam, by the International Legion and the Army of the Republic of Vietnam (ARVN) on or about 27 November 1981. The event marked the formal end of the Vietnam War and the start of a transition period to the formal reunification of Vietnam into an American territory.

According to one of the few American ground advisors present for the Liberation, Vietnamese General Duong Van Minh's forces blockaded the city in August, aided by U.S. Navy ships in control of the Red River.[1] A protracted siege ensued, resulting in the deaths of tens of thousands of Vietnamese civilians. Legionnaire Commander David Hackworth arrived with his 13th Legion (predominantly Korean and Filipino war veterans) five weeks after. Plans to take the city began in earnest with Hackworth's arrival.[2]

Some historians dispute the Liberation of Hanoi as an official marker of the war's end. Much of North Vietnam's political and military leadership fled the city before the Legion began its entry, and the People's Army continued to wage guerrilla war from the mountains in the northwestern provinces of Vietnam. [3] The insurgency continues to this day, though related acts of violence have declined steadily since the Accord of Dien Bien in 1993.[4]

CHAPTER 22

THE GREAT CITY of the conquering people held a parade for the Victors every year, though victory as both a concept and construct had been left in the last century. Sebastian thought this was why the parade had become such a sacred affair. It harkened back to a place that wasn't anymore, that couldn't be, anymore. A good enemy had kept America true. A known enemy had kept America united. Even casual study of Vietnam showed a long, dirty war, of course, one with manifold cases of human suffering and loss. But it had been necessary to end the communist threat. It had been necessary for democratic ideals to persist. It had been necessary to prove that America was different than those that'd come before. That's what the V-V Day Parade honored. That's what it paid tribute to.

Thirty years later: Praise to the Victors.

It felt right to Sebastian to be attending the parade on its pearl anniversary. The Next Greatest Generation wouldn't be around forever, after all. Though, with a little prodding, one of its number might still be able to shape the future for the better.

Sebastian had spent days and nights wandering the city, thinking everything through. The hidden truths about Tripoli still bothered him. It was hard for him to know where to go next when he wasn't sure he knew where he'd been. But he'd still decided Pete and Mia were right. He needed to look forward. He needed to work toward making things better. He needed to help others. More important, he wanted to be the type of person who did things like that. He'd called Pete three nights before and said he was in. He'd do it. He'd be a homeland Volunteer for the people who needed him to be.

Sebastian still held concerns about American Service. But he'd come around to General Collins. At Pete's suggestion, he'd watched more of her speeches. They suggested she could do for the real America what Bobby Kennedy was doing in a pretend TV one. That mattered, Sebastian thought. It mattered a lot.

He sat on a picnic table in a corner of Battle Hymn Park among a leafy canopy, arms draped over his knees. The morning smelled of grilled meat. Loud men with bullhorns directed vague orders through the air. Britt Swenson and Grady Flowers sat next to him, pawing at each other like teenagers about to be separated for a long weekend. Sebastian was trying his best not to gawk. The flashes of skin from the gaps in Britt's overalls made it difficult. A nearby group of JROTC cadets fidgeting in olive drab uniforms that fit their bodies like papier-mâché held no such qualms.

"You're gonna give those boys a physical situation," Flowers said. "Right before they march up Fifth Avenue, too. Whole city's gonna see their little peckers standing at attention."

"Stop," Britt said, in a way that suggested she didn't care one way or another if he did. She settled into the crook of his shoulder. "I'm just worried about you."

"Hell, woman! Today ain't no thing." The pitch Flowers put into his voice struck a perfect balance between recklessness and confidence. "Now, the time we got stuck in the Alps without resupply, that was worthy of your concern. There we were, no shit, and your damn brother . . ."

Britt may not have heard about the Dinaric Alps, but Sebastian had. He tuned out the Sniper and instead focused on the surrounding revelry: the massing vets in charcoal-gray blazers under the banner "Vietnam Vets for Liberty"; a man on stilts dressed as Uncle Sam handing out sofa discounts; the tent of young financiers from Lehman Brothers distributing pamphlets about the firm's warfighters hiring initiative.

Today was to be Sebastian's first mission as a homeland Volunteer. There'd been threats made on the parade VIPs, threats the Council of Victors deemed serious and legitimate. The Council would never cancel the event, but it had requested the War Department loan out its super-soldiers to help with security. Be a show of force, if nothing else. Pete hadn't been able to suppress his joy at finally—fucking *finally*—being utilized.

Sebastian had prayed the night before, really prayed rather than talking to a vague entity in his head, bowing his head and clasping his hands at the foot of his bed and everything. His prayer had been simple, half-ironic, but half-earnest, too, and he figured God understood why.

"Please give me the strength to do what You intend of me. Gracias and Amen."

Sebastian still didn't understand why he'd been gifted his power, why he'd been chosen, and why he'd survived when so many others hadn't. Maybe it was the ancestor gassed in the trenches a century back. Maybe not. He'd developed a rough idea that helping General Collins get elected might allow him to gain access to some answers, full answers, as long as he proved himself worthy to her and her people. Thinking about it all again was making his leg twitch, though, so he took out his one-hitter.

"Curbing the edge," he told Britt and Flowers, who laughed and called him a crazy hostage, again.

They found Pete striding through the milling crowd, a head-length taller than anyone else, exchanging handshakes and hellos. He was wearing his dress blues, rows of ribbons stacked on his chest like fruit salad, his combat infantry badge shining under the dreary sun. He'd gotten a haircut, trimmed his sideburns, and even shaved, he looked like he did in government commercials, the mask of the great Justice slipped over hard-partying Pete Swenson. People bunched around him in clumps, taking photos and video with their phones. Only the silver-haired veterans in blazers kept their distance. Even on their own day, Victors couldn't compete with young celebrity.

"Such a dork," Britt said. The Swenson siblings weren't fighting at the moment, as far as anyone else could tell. "Pretending to be shy."

"That's nothing," Flowers said. "If I'd gotten dolled up today, I'd have a crowd three times that. Citizens don't want bashful. They want style! They want flair. Come on, Pete, kiss some babies, flex for the people!" Flowers shook his head and whistled through his teeth. "Man gets to be a superhero and doesn't even do it right."

Sebastian did admire Flowers's ability to live free. He took a deep breath and let the weed steady his being. Be good and do good, he thought. That's it.

With the help of some Council security guards, Pete eventually made it to their table. He didn't bother with a greeting. "No Jean-Jacques, then," he said. Disappointment filled his voice. "Thought he'd be here."

It seemed out of character for Dash not to show when it mattered, but Sebastian didn't pry. It's not like he minded. He knew how poorly the Haitian man thought of him.

Pete turned his attention to Flowers, frowning. "Jeans and sneakers." Sebastian wore similar but he had the excuse of needing lightweight clothes to turn invisible. "We're on a job."

Flowers shrugged. "You said business casual, brother." Britt laughed, which only deepened her brother's scowl.

In oblique language, Pete briefed the day's mission. They were augmentee security: Flowers and Britt held front-row seats on the steps of the library, where the parade's dignitaries would gather and the general would deliver the keynote.

"You see a bright blue light flash onstage, or you see something wrong, anything, you grab the nearest VIPs and 'port out of there," Pete said. "Grab and go."

Sebastian had been tasked a rover. "Do what you do best," Pete said. "Go hidden, check out the reaches of the crowd. Go up to rooftops and the upper floors of surrounding buildings. See anything off, anything odd, find security."

Sebastian said he understood. He didn't know how long he could stay unseen, but he was ready to push through the headaches to find out. He felt through his pocket to make sure the one-hitter was still there.

"Anyone specific we looking for?" Flowers asked. "Or just mystery bad guys?"

"Be alert for anything. There's a rumor the Mayday leader's gonna show. Jonah Gray. So careful attention to any vet with troubles. You know the look—camo jacket, old boots, maven-addict stare."

"Scraggly. Beaten up by the world."

Pete nodded. He went on to explain that he'd be onstage with the general, bodying her wherever she stepped. "Hence the monkey outfit."

"Will play great on TV, too." Britt tried to ice her words with a smile, but even Flowers winced. "Oh, come on. Like you don't know. You're a big deal to people, Peter. They'll see you up there and take it as open support. Won't the War Department be upset? Something about keeping the military away from politics?"

"Screw them," Flowers said. "They been playing politics with us since the day we joined up."

A thin wind blew through the park, and the four young people clung to the moment before going their separate ways.

"Thanks for being brave," Britt finally said. "Really. I love all of you for it."

Pete winked his coral eye through the daylight. He patted Sebastian's shoulder, then lightly tapped at Flowers's cheek. He put his arm around his sister and squeezed her close. Sebastian thought the big, famous leader of men was going to say something about the Volunteers, or the Rangers, or maybe something about America. Instead he said something much better.

"We're pretty fucking awesome, aren't we?"

———

The invisible man moved through the city like haze, watching, searching. He eased himself into his power; three minutes on, six minutes off, then doubling that ratio. Then he cleared eight minutes, taking off thirty for good measure. He still had two hours until the general's speech; he saw no need to burn out before it.

Thousands had begun to line the avenue sidewalks. Bankers and clerks and tourists and digital communications associates, all gathering for their warfighters, for their Victors. Sebastian pushed out and probed deeper, to the edges.

He found strange people and strange groups along those edges. A small number of gray-haired black men had assembled under the Flatiron Building, wearing mesh caps and long-sleeve navy shirts bearing the words LITTLE HAITI VICTORS. He walked up to one of the men, sixty or so, short and ropy, with deep folds like trenches along his face. Through the man's mirrored sunglasses, Sebastian saw absolutely nothing. He coughed. The man looked up, bushy eyebrows turning to question marks.

"Who's there?" he asked.

Sebastian walked away, smiling to himself, leaving the man to ask if anyone else had heard what he had.

Sebastian blinked into visibility, he blinked out of visibility. He ambled north and then west, taking a break with his one-hitter and a bottled water. He paused across the crossed pistols gate arching over Broadway, built in remembrance of those who fell seizing Beirut. It remained under reconstruction. The Mayday Front had blown apart one of the pistol's barrels, and scaffolding enveloped that side of the monument like wood lace. Up the block, a woman with wavy honey hair and shiny north-star skin talked to a man in a charcoal-gray blazer on a raised platform. They were facing a knob of television cameras. Sebastian stopped to listen, recognizing Jamie Gellhorn first, then her guest.

"Welcome back to *The Proving Ground*! We're live from Fifth Avenue in the one and only Empire City, for the one and only V-V Day Parade. Praise to the Victors!

"It's my privilege to welcome Bernard Gault, executive vice president at Rubicon Pharmaceuticals. As a younger man, he served a distinguished tour in Vietnam. He sits on the Council of Victors and in that capacity, will be today's grand marshal. Well-deserved recognition for a true patriot."

A true patriot who misquotes Orwell, Sebastian thought. Tell the people that, lady!

"Thank you, Jamie. Though 'grand marshal' is a ceremonial title. Nothing more."

"What does today mean to you? To your generation of war-fighters?"

"More than anything it's hard to believe it's been thirty years. Where did the time go? I swear it was just yesterday we were in those rice paddies. As for what it means for our generation—we had a lot to live up to. Our fathers saved democracy. There was a lot of doubt in the middle years of our war whether we'd be able to do the same."

"Do you remember where you were when Hanoi was liberated?"

The tritest question. Sebastian rolled his eyes. Most every Victor on the planet had cut their answer into a diamond years before.

"Of course," Gault said. "By the time the Legion took Hanoi, I was back in the States, attending business school. A group of us got together and watched on a small TV and just celebrated. Lot of cheers, lot of hugs, a few beers may've been involved. And many tears."

"What a memory. Thank you for sharing it. Switching gears some—today's keynote speaker is a controversial choice."

"Only because of some faulty media reporting on this network, Jamie."

"Well—I'm not sure I can agree. Regardless, the parade's keynote will be delivered by presidential candidate Jackie Collins, who—"

"Is an American hero. I'd be happy to read aloud her Silver Star citation."

Now that, Sebastian thought, is a hell of a flex.

"Everyone here is aware of the general's valor and devotion to our nation." Gellhorn sounded flustered. "Still, her poll numbers have dipped since our report revealed some of her national security . . . excesses."

Gault was ready. "The Council of Victors is strictly a nonpartisan assembly. It's in our charter. It's something we take very seriously. General Collins will be speaking in that capacity today. As a citizen who volunteered to serve America in battle, time and again. She's not interested in politics today. She'll be transcending all that."

Sebastian didn't know where masters of the universe learned how to control a conversation, but he was impressed. He knew firsthand how quick and professional Gellhorn was, and Gault had her backpedaling like a student who'd read the wrong assignment.

"We look forward to it, and will be carrying it live, across the country, across the globe. One last thing before I let you go: you wanted to talk about some developments at Rubicon."

"Yes. The progress we're seeing with new treatments at the colonies is just amazing—our research teams and clinicians are top-notch, as you know, and are ensuring that our vets with troubles get the care they deserve. It's my honor to announce today that thanks to some of these medical advancements, the federal government has green-lit a second Hero Project . . ."

At that, Sebastian left the knob of television cameras. He had a mission to tend to. Thinking about the Hero Project, particularly a second Hero Project, would hamper that. The long game, he told himself. The long game is your only way to actual truth. For once in your life, you're going to be patient and strategic about something.

He made a mental note to watch the Gault interview later, in its entirety. More superpowered would make Sebastian either more important to those masters of the universe, or less. He'd figure out which. Patiently and strategically.

The sidewalks became more congested the farther north Sebastian went. A mass of human traffic at Thirtieth Street began snarling out, causing a standstill. A large, smelly man in sweats pushed through it with a fever of expletives. Sebastian fell against a metal railing securing the street as a parade route. He cried out more from surprise than pain, though he did feel a hot sting on his knee underneath his pants, followed by the chilled ribbon of blood. He rubbed at his knee and got out of the way of the many shoes and boots who didn't know he was there.

A block later, someone bumped into his back and he bristled and clenched his fists and felt sweat puddling under his arms. He closed his eyes and counted to twelve, listening to his heart slow. He took yoga breaths. Once he made it to twelve he opened his eyes, pushing his tongue against the roof of his mouth to help find focus. Hands now deep in his pockets, he turned into an empty alley and returned to visibility. Ten minutes and fourteen seconds. He was working his way up, with only a distant gleam of a headache coming on.

So that's good, he thought.

Fifty minutes from the general's speech, Sebastian entered Haig Common. He hadn't meant to go this far west, but the side streets that would bring him back to the parade route had been filled with staging floats. Haig Common proved just as active. In addition to the schools of shoppers gliding through the sidewalks, and the human statues and dance troupes hustling for dollars, a group of a few dozen had gathered at the southern fringe of the common, under a large bronze cast of the former president. They wore a mishmash of camo tops and overgrown beards, and most were hinterland lean. About half were gray hairs, Victor age, the others younger but no less grungy.

It looks like a pirate ship crashed here, Sebastian thought.

He walked through the common and its new arrivals, still visible. The gnarled traveler stare took in Sebastian. A few bristled at the sound of a nearby taxi horn. Whoever they were, they didn't like being here any more than anyone else liked having them. His eyes found their cardboard signs, limp on the cement.

THE COLONIES ARE PRISONS!
THE HONOR IS OURS. WHY NOT THE SPOILS?
FREE VETERAN ZERO!!!

Jesus, Mary, and Allah, Sebastian thought. The Mayday Front.

He remembered most intensely these men and women, and what they were capable of. Free Veteran Zero? That man was enemy. His bloodshot psychosis had returned to Sebastian more than a few times since the ballroom. So had his loud, ragged screams after being shot in the face. Sebastian had never hurt anyone like that before and it had made him feel powerful, which in turn made him feel bad about feeling that way. He'd been glad he hadn't killed Veteran Zero. Now, confronted with the idea of a free Veteran Zero, he was less certain.

America needed sanity. Veteran Zero represented madness. So too did the Mayday followers, warfighters or not. Sebastian felt very sure all of a sudden that whatever threat the parade VIPs were under, these people were involved. He took slow, measured steps into a department store bathroom and soon returned to the common, gone from the world.

He followed the complaints to find the leaders. He didn't recognize anyone specific from the ballroom—they were all still in jail awaiting trial, he reasoned—but many still carried a vague look of familiarity. The same dusty hair from motel shampoos, the same sun-brown skin. The same untucked laces and the same crooked sleeve-rolls. More than anything, he saw the same hollow-eyed rage born from defeat.

How many of them are out there? he asked himself. How many are still to come?

He settled outside the circle of arguing leaders, close enough to hear, far enough away to not get bumped into. A tall Hispanic man wearing a boonie cap was speaking, sounding very much like a person tired of repeating himself.

"There's fifty of us. Maybe another hundred downtown. That's a drop in the bucket compared to the tens of thousands marching. We need to be smart, cool. Jonah said to wait until we get orders. So we wait. Can't just go rushing Fifth Avenue 'cause we're antsy."

"Orders?" A man with long, salty hair in a ponytail and scratches in his voice laughed. "Orders got my friends killed all over the Delta. I'm too old for 'em. All I want, all we want, is what we are due."

"We're going to have to take it, though. We're going to have to crash through barriers to remind folks: we are here."

The dispute went on like that, the moderate radicals championing waiting and restraint, the extreme radicals advocating for moving their ranks into the parade in force. No one would shoot them for it, they said. But if the police did—well, that'd actually be good. The media would be all over it.

No one mentioned the vice president or General Collins or any VIPs. No one mentioned the library steps or a speech. Still, Sebastian stayed and listened.

The argument grew louder and more riven, until a woman's voice cut through: "Got word from Pierre. Wants us at Twenty-Third Street in twenty. They found an entry point."

"Here we go." The man with the ponytail began clapping and hooting. "Here we go! Whatever it takes."

"What about the vice president?" Sebastian spoke low and into his fist. Only a woman in a hoodie near him turned around, wondering where the voice had come from. "What about the general?"

"Who cares?" Everyone nodded at that, even the moderates. "Fucking brass. What they're doing has nothing to do with what we are."

Not the first time my instincts were wrong, Sebastian thought, moving away from the common. He found himself somehow wishing the Mayday Front well. Hijacking the Victors parade would make for spectacle, if nothing else. He could even picture the red-faced anger on the face of Bernard Gault. That alone would make it worth it.

He checked the time to see how long he had until the speech began. Fifteen minutes. Which meant he'd been invisible for a half hour. A good stretch longer than he'd ever been before. He knelt beside a parked car to switch off his mental lever. Nothing happened. He closed his eyes and tried again. Nothing. He squeezed his temples tight. A bolt of pain shot from the top of his spine through the reaches of his neck, but nothing changed. He remained unseen and apart. He'd never before thought about his power like this, and thinking about it made it seem much more impossible. Raw, wild fear tore through him. He was finding breathing difficult so he curled into a ball against the car and began exhaling into the top of his shirt, like it was a paper bag.

Change, damn it, change! He couldn't be stuck like this. He just couldn't be. Sebastian bit down on his lip and threw a fist into the side of the parked car. Then he felt his brain lurch. He turned dizzy, then blind for a long, few seconds. He collapsed to his side. The lever set into place. It came on like a fastball to the ribs, a force unto itself, too quick to hurt, too brutal not to. Sebastian became unstuck, though. He became seen again.

This wasn't how today was supposed to go, he thought, tears streaking his face as he sat up against the car, clinging to his knees. This wasn't how it was supposed to go at all.

"Son. You okay?"

Sebastian was still curled against the side of the car. Now a tall, trim man in army dress blues and a maroon beret bent over him, his face wrinkled with concern. A long, sloped chin jutted from the man's face and toward the ground.

"Yes." Sebastian stood up. He couldn't stop trembling but knew he couldn't stay beside the car forever. "Appreciate you noticing. Really."

The army man laughed. "It's my job to notice strangers," he said. Simple silver crosses marked the man's jacket lapels and his shoulder boards carried eagle insignias on them—he was a colonel. Not general high, but way higher than Pete and the Volunteers. A colonel who's an army minister, Sebastian thought. Cool.

The man put his hand on Sebastian's shoulder. "May I?" he asked. Sebastian nodded, noticing another cross seared into the man's palm. That weirded him out a bit. Holy was one thing. Too holy was another.

"Life can be difficult, sometimes, young man," he said. He had pale, cloudy eyes and spoke like a metronome, each word, each syllable, a chant. He seemed familiar to Sebastian, like a forgotten friend found in an old yearbook. "Think of someone you love, someone who's departed this world but worked toward giving you a better life."

Sebastian did. He became transported. He felt himself with his grandfather again, but as a boy, standing beneath a door frame as his grandfather pointed a long naval sword toward the sky, toward the Almighty, telling Sebastian everything was fine, that everything would be okay, as long as he was a good boy and remembered to listen and do as he was told, always.

A voice sounded from above, where his grandfather had directed the sword: "Love. Hope. Love. Hope. Holy blood, holy redemption."

Sebastian opened his eyes, feeling a warm glow throughout his body, from the center of his gut to the very tips of his fingers. He didn't feel alone anymore. He didn't feel overwhelmed. He felt part of something great and massive, a small part, to be sure, but still part of it.

"How?" was all he could manage.

The army minister bowed his head. "Enjoy the day, son. Praise to the Victors."

Sebastian watched the other man walk away, the warm glow still saturating his body. He wanted to feel sunlight. He wanted to look at grass. He wanted to sit and think and maybe read a book over a beer. He wanted to call everyone in his family and talk about how good a man his grandfather had been, how blessed they were to have had him in their lives.

He did not want to play at being anything more than he was anymore.

The mere act of movement helped with the trembles. His heart slowed and he felt the cool of sweat on his brow. He knew he'd wake up the next morning with a ferocious migraine but he'd manage. He found an isolated bench near a playground. He watched kids on a merry-go-round and smiled at their small joys. He pulled out his one-hitter. It felt sweet in his throat, and he breathed out into pale sky.

That minister was great, he thought, still lost in serenity. Though they're not called ministers in the army. They're called . . .

It was the cloudy eyes that did it. Slowly at first and then all at once, Sebastian realized why the colonel had seemed familiar. He'd been the man in rags he'd talked with in front of his apartment building months before. The one sorting through trash and collecting bottles. The nutter talking ashes and redemption.

Sebastian knew he'd just spoken with the Chaplain. The wanted man, the holy militant, Jonah Gray. He'd found him, chanced upon him, really. Then he'd let him walk off free into the parade, because—well, because he had.

The hell is wrong with me, he thought. I should've done something.

Then he thought: I still can.

CHAPTER 23

T HE CITY PASSED in flashes of bright steel. The sidewalks were bare and vacant, citizens either in midtown for the parade or gone entirely for the long weekend. A pall was settling across the lower part of the island, hard grayness edging in from the harbor. Mia cracked open her window and let some of it into the town car. She needed to hear the city to think. She needed to smell it.

"We're eleven months out," she said. She didn't know how to convince them that the speech today was a bad idea, but she was trying to, yet again. They needed to hear her this time. "Plenty of opportunities between now and then. It's just not worth the risk, ma'am." She almost mentioned Governor Harrah but held off. That would only encourage the general. "If this threat report is true, no amount of security can protect you on that stage. You'll be too out in the open. Too many surrounding vantage points. No one will blame you for bowing out. How could they?"

Mia sat next to Roger Tran and across from the general in the back of the town car. They reached the West Side Highway. The tires beneath them stopped fighting the pavement and began rolling smooth, like they were moving on carpet. Lady Liberty emerged in the distance, still green, still rusting. Her torch was bound for a city park, the rest of the statue, still to be determined.

333

Mia had heard rumblings that Lehman Brothers had offered. They wanted it for their courtyard.

"How comfortable are you, Roger?" General Collins wore a gray striped suit with a notched collar, a "V for Victor" pin gleaming on her left lapel. Her speech lay in her lap, marked up with strike-throughs and last-minute edits. She brought her hands together in a prayer clasp and tapped at the black stone on her West Point ring. "Give me a percentage."

"Zero percent." Tran made no attempt to hide the concern in his voice. "Ms. Tucker is right. This is a risk. An undue one. The Bureau can be overly cautious sometimes, yes. But they have sources in this group. All say something's planned. At least one says, definitively, you are the target. And if it is this Jonah Gray—or some other colony vet who received cythrax treatments—well, they'd have their reasons for being upset with us."

Tran looked hard at Mia. They'd been saying more and more things like that in front of her. As a test, she knew. She also knew how to pass it. She held to the quiet.

Poor Sebastian, she thought. Looking for the truth when he needed to be listening for it. Mia knew she had him to thank for her recommitment to the campaign. She'd told the general she was all in and meant it. Her old friend had shown her the limits an individual had when confronting entrenched power. People, serious people at least, who wanted to change systems and institutions? They didn't do it from beyond or afar. They did it from within.

On instinct, Mia moved her hands to her stomach and held them there. The sonogram the day before had confirmed what Jesse had been saying all along: it was a girl.

A healthy baby girl, Mia thought in the town car. Who will know a good America.

"Roger." The general reached across the car and patted his knee. "Your infantry is showing. I don't doubt the Bureau's sources. Nor do I doubt their seriousness. But think this through, strategically: If these Maydays want me and me alone, why strike today? Why not wait for an actual campaign event, when there's no other VIPs and extra security around?"

Tran didn't respond. The general continued.

"Today could be a breakthrough for American Service. Think it's possible someone connected to the administration exaggerated all this to rattle us, to get us to back down? I do. Think it's possible the good, hard-earned information gathered by rank-and-file Bureau agents gets shaped into political missives by clerks in Federal City? I do. Think it's possible this is a hoax for ends and purposes we can only begin to guess at? I do.

"Besides, even if it is this Jonah Gray and his band of dis-enfranchised, they're just zealots. Broken ones, at that. Not rocket scientists, not servants of the state. What could they know, really?"

Mia didn't know anything about that. As the general had pointed out on the *Utopia* set, she'd only been a pilot. But her time in the cockpit had given her a topographical view of the wars and, perhaps, of how human beings behaved during conflict. "With re-spect, ma'am," she said, "broken zealots have little to lose. It's not so much what they know or what they can access. It's more what they're capable of, in spite of those things."

Tran pointed at Mia to show his agreement. General Collins considered this possibility, then reached for a cigarette. They waited while she took a drag and then another, staring out the window at the passing river.

"I think everyone here served in the military for a similar reason," she finally said. "To become the person we aspired to be. As tribute to the families and homes that produced us. But also to escape them."

That idea coalesced with her cigarette smoke for a few seconds before she continued.

"You and your grandparents in Saigon, Roger. Your family, Mia, such an American success story. You owe them everything. And yet. You both set out to be as different as possible. An odd compliment, don't you think? I'm the same, of course. Very much so.

"The day after I turned sixteen, my father killed himself. He was a sad man. Pathetic, really. Alcoholic. Angry to be angry. Not particularly smart, not particularly handy. Not kind. The army wouldn't take him during the war, so he got a job at a weapons plant and never left. Heck, I don't think he ever left western Pennsylvania. He did love us, though. He loved us fiercely. He just didn't know what to do with it. He didn't know what to do with himself.

"Our mother found him in the basement. Hung himself after too many drinks down there. No note, wasn't his style. But we knew why. Life just took and took and took from him.

"And I remember realizing that day—there was sadness, yes, I was going to miss him. He was my father. But more than anything, I remember relief. It was overpowering. For the first time, for the only time, as far as I knew, I could do anything I wanted. I was totally free.

"I wrote about him in my application to West Point. Because I wanted to honor him. But also because I knew it would get me in. Through his death, my father opened to me a world of possibilities, a world so far beyond western Pennsylvania neither of us could've even imagined it. He gave me this life."

The cigarette was only half-smoked but General Collins was done with it. She tossed it out the window. None of this was in the general's book, Mia thought. None of this has ever been shared.

"I didn't come this far to be afraid. I didn't come this far to be cautious. I decided the day I graduated West Point I was willing to die for the idea of America. Same as you. Why should that change? I'm an old lady on the backside of life. I can't become a coward now. That's not how it works.

"If this fucker wants me, he'll get me. Today or tomorrow, it's all the same. Here's the thing, though." The general smiled wide and rapped her fingers against the window, toward the river. "He best not miss."

Mia found her reserved seat in the third row, facing the library steps. The speaker before General Collins, a retired admiral who'd participated in the naval siege of Hanoi, was twelve minutes past his allotted time and still going. Mia spotted Britt Swenson and Grady Flowers at the end of the first row—from the side, Britt's profile looked like a long-haired replica of her brother's, all sharp-jawed symmetry and hyperalertness. Flowers, meanwhile, had slumped low in his chair, making no attempt to hide his boredom, wraparound sunglasses perched upon his head like a crown of ballistic.

Should I be nervous? Mia wasn't sure, considering the question as she smoothed out her blouse and fixed her attention upon the stage. The seated audience sprawled across the open pavement of Fifth Avenue, hundreds more on their feet packed in behind them. She hadn't attended the ballroom inaugural knowing it was under threat. Yet she'd come here today, knowing the parade was. Was that something a good mother-to-be did? Was it something she needed to try to justify to herself?

She decided no. She wasn't nervous, and that was that. If Mia felt anything, it was the long, taut calm she associated with helo missions abroad.

Semper Gumby, she reminded herself. After all, I can always just fly away.

Loose applause shook Mia from her ruminations. The admiral had concluded, and General Collins was striding across the stage, back rigid and shoulders cocked, West Point ring on her hand glinting like a black sun. She seized the podium with a smile and cleared her throat. The microphone carried the noise with a fist of an echo.

"My fellow Americans: It's a great honor to be speaking with you today. Praise to the Victors! The American triumph in Vietnam is everyone's to remember, and everyone's to take solace in. It took a special people to push back the onslaught of communism.

"My message today is simple. We are still those people."

Mia treasured that line. In the draft she'd read, she'd underlined it and placed an exclamation mark along its side.

"I come to you with a message of consideration, and of renewal, and to share a few thoughts with my countrymen. Thirty years ago, Hanoi fell and put to end a seemingly endless war that engulfed a generation. Thirty years ago, American resolve saved the world for democracy. A force of goodness did that, yes. So too did dirty work and messy labor.

"Much blood was spilled along that strip of land in Southeast Asia. American and Vietnamese. Lives lost, families destroyed. Every Victor here saw a brother or sister in arms fall, someone who deserved to come home and live a full life, but didn't. Unlike us standing here today, with our old, wizened faces and fading scars, they remain frozen in time. Still impossibly brave. Impossibly young. Still impossibly fierce and a bit silly, too. They remain as they were, forever, filled with the hopes of a future they'll never have.

"I'd like to tell a story about one of those fallen. My friend Javy. I met him in school. He was one of those young men seemingly born for the life—he . . ."

As the general entered the personal anecdote section of the speech, Mia allowed herself to study the crowd. They were engaged, interested. Even Flowers had sat up. Unlike the admiral, General Collins knew how to inflex her voice. She knew when to pause and she knew when to push, her voice steady in both rhythm and variance. When Mia had first met her, the general spoke her message at audiences. Now she was bringing the audience to that message. It was a small, crucial difference, felt more than anything else. She's gotten good at this, Mia thought. All the work, all the practice, was revealing itself today. She sounded— well. She sounded presidential.

"When his wife called with the news, I broke down." She has them now, Mia thought. Even those fringe citizens who distrusted warfighters would connect with this part. "Years of combat had numbed me some to loss, to death. But Javy felt different. I found solace that evening in ancient words, words I'll share with you today, as we look back, together.

"'And even in our sleep, pain which cannot forget falls drop by drop upon the heart, until in our own despair, against our will, comes wisdom through the awful grace of God.'

"The Greek poet Aeschylus wrote that. The father of tragedy. An Athenian. A man who knew democracy's strengths. A man who knew its weaknesses, too."

Mia looked around again. Every face was awash, every pair of eyes intent and full. This is it now, she thought. Bring us home, Jackpot.

"Some of you may have seen my name in the news recently. Now's not the time to discuss that, but I will say this: I won't apologize for protecting this country. I love this nation. When I swore an oath to protect it, I knew that meant going abroad in search of monsters. We weren't perfect. I'd be the first to admit that. We weren't pure. War never is.

"My name is General Jackie Collins. I'm a veteran. I'm a Victor. Not that long ago, I was one hell of a warfighter. America's the greatest nation this world has ever known. And I'm here to say: let's make it even better."

Mia saw a blue light flash behind the general as the speech ended. It was a signal to get her off the stage. Mia rushed for the stairs, making it to the rail before she heard the shout, strident and clear: "Thus Ever to Tyrants!"

Then came the sound of the first bullet snapping air. She looked to the stage, searching for the general. She could only find bodies massing, then bodies falling.

CHAPTER 24

I N THE END, his cousin got it all done. The paramedic uniforms, the fake permit, even a fresh paint job for the old ambulance they'd found in a salvage yard. Four cops had come by and checked on them. From the driver's seat, Emmanuel had yakked with them with a silver tongue Jean-Jacques never knew he had, agreeing with the older babylons that the Victors deserved the parade and more, then matching the younger ones' disdain for having to yet again celebrate this ancient triumph.

"You're an artist," Jean-Jacques told him, both proud of his cousin and wary, too. "Where you learn this?"

Emmanuel shrugged. "For the cause," he said.

The ambulance was parked directly over a manhole at the corner of Fifth Avenue and Thirty-Seventh Street, a few blocks shy of the library, the stage of dignitaries, and a whole slew of television cameras. The manhole connected to a short sewer tunnel used by subway maintenance. A gaping hole in the floorboard of the ambulance would allow the Mayday veterans to funnel from the tunnel straight into the parade, three or four at a time. What came after, Jean-Jacques didn't know. He'd done his part. He'd done as ordered.

In the meantime, they waited.

Signs of early parade pomp were beginning to stir. Young sol-

341

diers carried flags past the ambulance, headed toward the library steps. Private security teams were seizing their assigned corners, not looking twice at the ambulance because it was already there. Jean-Jacques even watched Pete walk by, laughing with three old men in suits and a navy admiral. Pete had donned his dress blues for the day, clean and pristine as a new morning.

The true believer up on that stage, for all the homeland to see, Jean-Jacques thought, recalling how confused and lost Pete had sounded at the tiki bar. The perfect image for citizens across the empire: generals, senators, and Justice, together and united.

Our sergeant has become their show pony, he thought. If the boys at Regiment could see him now.

Rolling tanks in Paris, marching battalions in Nicosia, Cold War helos and artillery guns in Cairo and Beirut. Jean-Jacques had attended military parades the world over. He didn't so much dislike the cocktail of pageantry and show of force as dismiss it. Nothing about the parades was for the actual soldier or veteran. It happened for everyone else, to make them feel whatever it was they felt like feeling, or felt like they needed to try for. All the real warfighters, they just wanted to be left alone, he thought. To sleep. To fuck. To eat. To breathe. To live free, whatever that meant, however it looked.

"Where these scrubs at?" he asked Emmanuel. "Can't sit here forever."

"Pierre said as soon as the parade reaches us. Then we roll."

Jean-Jacques grunted in response. Duty, he told himself. She beckons.

———

They were still waiting and watching twenty minutes later when Jean-Jacques looked across the avenue and saw the hostage kid who'd been following Pete around like a bootlicker arguing with a uniformed police. He tried to ignore them but found himself captivated by what was happening: the hostage red-faced, gesturing wildly with his hands, while the babylon listened with absolute indifference, arms folded across his chest. Passersby began to stop, interested in whatever the hostage was going on about, and then the babylon shook his head, telling them no.

"Back in a minute," he told Emmanuel, shutting the ambulance door behind him before his cousin could object. He reached the group just as the front of the parade appeared down the avenue, the marine band in the lead with big, brassy horns. To the north, toward the library, he heard the grumble of a microphone. The general was beginning her speech.

"Dash!" the hostage said before Jean-Jacques could make the shush sign. "Thank Christ you're here."

"Take a breath, hostage. Speak clear."

"I was trying to tell this goon"—Sebastian closed his eyes and exhaled through his nose—"Jonah Gray. He's here." Then he started talking about a tall, trim man in dress blues with a maroon beret who made Sebastian feel a memory that hadn't even happened, but he'd been transported, into his own head and away from it, too, and before he'd figured out how, the man was gone, walking toward the library and the parade stage.

Jean-Jacques's chest seized up. The policeman was laughing, shaking his head. Jean-Jacques bowed his head and tried to think. The Mayday veterans were indeed just a distraction. But why? The Chaplain was smart; everyone thought he'd be with the dirty warfighters when he'd gone clean as could be. What would Pete do? he asked himself. He'd stop this, he knew, or at least try. Jean-Jacques looked around the maze of rooftops surrounding them. It was a sniper's dream, a fantasyland for any professional with a rifle.

The marine band was now steps away, playing "Rally 'Round the Flag." The hostage asked Jean-Jacques something but the horns drowned it out. Then the hostage pointed across the street. He looked over. Bodies had begun swarming from the ambulance like ants.

They were ragged, lean and hollow-eyed, mostly men but some women, too, all swathed in a jumble of urban and desert camo jackets. One began whooping like a hostile and the others answered him with the same cry. In five seconds there were a dozen in their rank; ten seconds later, three times that. And they kept coming. The police radioed in their presence but made no move toward them. He seemed to know a losing fight when he saw one.

Whether they were all real Vietnam Victors seemed beside the point to Jean-Jacques. They looked the part. A deep horn sounded. Jean-Jacques first thought it came from the marine band but instead he found a five-ton truck moving onto Fifth Avenue, cutting straight through the band. Big, round Lamar Pierre sat in the driver's seat, wearing a faded army cap, the truck's open bed bunched full with colony Victors too broken to walk. A collection of crutches lay in the truck's corner, stacked like firewood. A long white banner hung from the truck's side, carrying the message THE HONOR IS OURS. These veterans were jeering obscenities, screaming and shaking their fists at the dismayed citizens. Jean-Jacques waved up to the five-ton, toward a man in a boonie cap with black pins for eyes. The man smiled and promptly flipped off Jean-Jacques with both hands. The five-ton began moving up the avenue, toward the library, ambling like a war elephant. The Mayday veterans on the ground whooped even louder.

Through the mess of noise and chaos came the soft droning of speakers still projecting a speech. "Get those VIPs off the stage," he said, pointing to the police's radio. "Now."

"Maroon beret?" he asked Sebastian, who nodded. That meant paratrooper, which would at least narrow a desperate search through a crowd. "You've done your part," he told the hostage. Then he ran north, toward the library, as fast as any human being had ever moved upon earth.

Hundreds of grateful American citizens packed the street and library steps, facing the stage, forcing Jean-Jacques to throttle down. There were too many people for him to maneuver freely. This is fucked, he thought, knowing that finding the Chaplain in this mass of humanity would be like finding one particular grain of sand in a desert. Still, he hopped up onto the base of a traffic signal for higher vantage.

He scanned and scanned while General Collins talked and talked. He had no idea why she was still up there, why the VIPs hadn't yet been evacuated. The audio from the speech began to clash in the air against the hard chants marching up the avenue. "May-day! May-day! MAY-DAY!" The horn of the five-ton blared over and over and people in the crowd started turning that way, to see what the bother was.

Then he caught it, just a glimpse of paratrooper maroon but enough: on the stage itself, rows behind Pete Swenson and the dignitaries. He hopped off the traffic signal and began moving through the messy, faceless horde of citizens. The general kept speaking and speaking.

Precious seconds dripped away under a gray sun. Jean-Jacques zoomed through the bodies with as much exactness and precision as he could. He spun around a child, hurdled a person in a wheelchair. The general kept speaking. Then, from a deep, hidden cave of the mind, the Chaplain's voice found him: "They'll get theirs." He stopped running.

This lady general and her Council of Victors? They'd played Pete for a chump. They'd used him and probably used us all, Jean-Jacques thought, somewhere along the way. They used the broken fucknuts in Mayday, too, who, despite everything, were still warfighters. Lamar Pierre was a good person. The pantry manager was a good person. They deserved better than this. They've used us, Jean-Jacques decided. They've used us all, now and always. Sending us to kill and conquer over there so they can control here.

Fuck them. Fuck the power.

Jean-Jacques knew the way forward. Detaining Jonah Gray for the federals meant the Legion, meant freedom for himself and the Volunteers, too. And I'll do that, he thought. Just as soon as my man up there finishes his blood crusade.

Jean-Jacques began moving again, but not at super-speed. He

didn't run, he didn't even hurry. He walked like any regular person would through a crowd, navigating his way to the front with empty apologies and sharp elbows. He'd almost reached the library steps as General Collins finished her speech: "America's the greatest nation this world has ever known. And I'm here to say: let's make it even better."

A fat beat of silence was swallowed up by the day as those words echoed through speakers and into the crowd. Then, behind him, in the thin sliver of time before applause, came a shout, strident and clear: "Thus Ever to Tyrants!"

Everyone but Jean-Jacques turned to that voice. Everyone but Jean-Jacques turned to the Victor with long, salty hair in a ponytail who belonged to that voice. Everyone but Jean-Jacques saw that man holding his hands out and above him, making it clear he held no weapon but walking like he was, perhaps, strapped to one. Everyone but Jean-Jacques didn't see that man for what he was: one last misdirection.

You're on, holy man, he thought.

It all seemed to happen at once, as best as Jean-Jacques could ever recall. Gray's uniformed arm appearing from the back of the stage holding a small revolver, neat and elegant like a good weapon should be. The ponytailed man still shrieking away, to the singular interest of everyone else. Pete, big, brave Pete, recognizing what he wasn't supposed to, lunging across the stage to tackle the general.

The sound of the first bullet snapping air. The sound of a second. The sound of a third.

He didn't remember using his power, not in the moment or after, but Jean-Jacques must have. It was the only way he could've gotten to the man. Jean-Jacques rushed him. The fight was over before it began. He snapped the man's arm at the elbow and kicked away the gun. He pinned the Chaplain to the ground, holding his forearm tight across the neck.

He wanted to ask about sacrifice. Why give yourself up when your cause still needed you? When your people still needed you?

Was killing a politician worth all that? Was killing one retired general really worth the electric chair? But Jonah Gray acted first, pale eyes brittle like the sky blinking up at Jean-Jacques with recognition, then acceptance.

"Quick, Corporal. You're quick." He bore his teeth, straight and white, to show a little capsule between them. No human being was fast enough to stop him from biting down on it. No superhuman was, either. As poison entered Gray's bloodstream, shutting off the oxygen supply to his brain and turning his heart to vacant muscle, he leaned up to whisper in Jean-Jacques's ear.

"I suppose," he said, "every cause needs a martyr."

"What you mean?"

The other man tried to respond but all that came out was garble. His body slumped to the side and Jean-Jacques felt it tremor.

"What does that mean?" Jean-Jacques was screaming now, shaking the void of a man beneath him like he was made of straw. Deep, severe voices were gathering around them and arms began pulling at Jean-Jacques. "The hell does that mean?"

Every cause needs a martyr. For many years, through a long career in the Legion and after, Jean-Jacques Saint-Preux thought about those words, wondering which cause the man had meant, and which martyr. Jonah Gray could've meant himself, and the cause of freeing veterans with troubles. Or he could've meant something else entirely, for which Pete Swenson of the Volunteers took three hollow-point bullets to the chest and throat.

CHAPTER 25

"HELLO, I'M JAMIE Gellhorn. We begin with today's ceremony in Empire City, where the new Lady Liberty statue was unveiled to the public for the first time. Four times larger than the original, the statue is made from Montana limestone with a shield strapped across her back, and holds aloft a longsword in her right hand. According to the project's civil engineer and sculptor, 'The shield shows vigilance, a readiness to defend democratic principles across the globe.' The sword is made from quartz mined in the Ozarks and can be seen from fifty miles away. 'A message of hope for those who seek it,' it was described today. 'A forewarning to others.'

"President-elect Collins was on hand for the ceremony, and gave a speech that made the case for the statue representing 'a new dawn' in America. Responding to an earlier remark that likened the statue to her own election, President-elect Collins joked that both she and Lady Liberty have seen too much to be considered beautiful anymore, so they'd have to make do with strength and might.

"The president-elect dedicated the statue to the late Peter Swenson, better known as Justice of the Volunteers, who famously saved her from an assassination attempt during last year's V-V Day Parade. 'May his memory and commitment to united service be our guiding light,' she said at the close of her speech. 'Now and always.'

"And now breaking news.

"We are following reports of a prison break at Triangle Island Penitentiary, north of Empire City. Gunfire and explosions have been heard from the island, and police helicopters have been spotted flying over the surrounding bay with searchlights.

"We've learned that the prison escape involves members of the Mayday Front. They claim to be an organization of military veterans from the Mediterranean Wars, though government officials dispute that. Last month, the War Department secretary confronted members gathered in Federal City, calling them 'frauds and undesirables,' instructing any real veterans in their ranks to go home and make something of themselves.

"This was on the eve of the Union Garden riots, of course.

"And—okay, we just received a communication from the Mayday Front. We've decided to read it on-air in the interest of public notice. This is an Empire News exclusive. Of course we do not endorse this message in any way. It's from a man calling himself Veteran Zero, an alleged leader in the organization. He claims to be one of the fugitives who escaped tonight.

"These are his words, not mine:

"'We had been told on leaving our native soil that we were going to defend the sacred rights conferred on us by our fellow citizens, and to aid populations abroad in need of our assistance. Make haste, America, and tell me that our fellow citizens understand us, support us, and will protect us, as we ourselves protected the glory of our great nation. If it should be otherwise—if we should have left our brothers' and sisters' bleached bones in those distant sands in vain—then beware. We will get our due. We will take our due. For those who have borne the battle. Beware the anger of the warfighter, America. Our time has come. Beware the wrath of our legion!'"

ACKNOWLEDGMENTS

My gratitude to:

Annie, Sam, Mom, Dad, Luke and the Gallagher, Boisselle, Scott and Steinle families; Nick Allen, Brian Castner, Philippe Dume, Eric Fair, Ted Janis, Phil Klay, and Sanaë Lemoine; Molly Atlas, who believed in this book, through it all; Daniella Wexler and Loan Le, for their support and guidance; and Ernie.

A breakthrough in this novel's development occurred in Rion Amilcar Scott's worldbuilding class at the 2017 Bread Loaf Writers' Conference.

Early drafts were completed at The Writers Room in New York.

Many books helped out with research, to include: Andrew Bacevich's *America's War for the Greater Middle East*, Võ Nguyên Giáp's *How We Won the War*, John Hersey's *A Bell for Adano*, Leslie Gelb's *Power Rules*, Franz Kafka's *Amerika*, Lou Michel and Dan Herbeck's *American Terrorist*, Alan Moore's *Watchmen*, Katherine Anne Porter's *Pale Horse, Pale Rider*, Joseph Roth's *The Radetzky March*, and Emma Sky's *The Unraveling*.

To those I mentioned, and to the many others I didn't—*Sláinte*.

ABOUT THE AUTHOR

MATT GALLAGHER is a Wake Forest graduate and U.S. Army veteran. He's the author of the novel *Youngblood* and memoir *Kaboom: Embracing the Suck in a Savage Little War*. He holds an MFA in fiction from Columbia and has written for the *New York Times*, the *Atlantic*, *Esquire*, and the *Paris Review*. He lives with his wife and son in Brooklyn.